THE FIG TREE

LEAH RICE

CONTENTS

PLAY LIST

Vivaldi, Four Seasons, L'inferno
Kalinka
Liszt La Campanella
Beethoven - Concerto No. 5
Tchaikovsky - Swan Lake, Op. 20, TH.12 / Act 2 - No. 10
Vittorio Monti - Czardas
Ludovico Einaudi - Experience
Prokofiev - Dance of the Knights
Rachmaninoff - Concerto No. 2
Beethoven - Moonlight Sonata

PART TWO:
Chopin - Fantaisie-Impromptu Mozart - Symphony No. 40
Tchaikovsky - Sleeping Beauty Op. 66
Mozart: Symphony No. 40 in G Minor
Shostakovich - Waltz No. 2
Mozart - Rondo Alla Turca
Rachmaninoff - Liebesleid
Beethoven - Rage Over a Lost Penny.
Prokofiev - Peter and the Wolf
Tchaikovsky's Concerto No. 1
Ralph Vaughan Williams - Fantasia on Greensleeves
Chopin 12 Etudes, Op. 25: No. 12 in C Minor
Dvořák - Symphony No.9 in E Minor, Op.95, B.178
Ilya Shatrov - On the Hills of Manchuria
Sir Henry J. Wood - Fantasia on British Sea Songs
Mendelssohn - Violin Concerto
Beethoven, Piano Concerto No. 5 in E-Flat Major
Schubert - Trout Quintet 3rd movement
Beethoven - Für Elise
Dvořák - Symphony No. 9 4th Movement
Dvořák - Romance in F minor, Op. 11

Lizst - La Campanella

Beethoven - Appassionata (3rd Movement)

Tchaikovsky - Concerto No. 1

Chopin - Nocturne op.9 No. 2

Tartini - Devil's Trill

Franz Liszt- Love Dream (Liebestraum), S. 541 No. 3

Dvořák - Romance in F minor, Op. 11

Chopin - Nocturne No. 20

Tchaikovsky - Concerto No. 1.

PROLOGUE

In my many lives, I've collected scars—battle wounds etched deep within me. Some might toss around fancy labels such as depression, disassociation, acute anxiety, the list goes on. But these wounds run deeper. They are far superior to silly little disorders. I wear each wound as a badge of honor, imprints of a life I once commanded. A life where success was the only currency, and failure simply did not exist. These scars are the signs of an era when I reigned supreme, when I possessed everything I have ever wanted—a life where every piano note I played was a masterpiece, and the world bowed to my talent. The connection between me and my music was unbreakable, a love affair beyond worldly boundaries.

The deepest scar I bear traces back to that unforgettable night when Ivan first entered my life. I surrendered to the irresistible call of freedom, guided by Ivan's influence. He revealed to me the idea of serenity amidst motion, grounding me firmly in the present. As our paths separated, I was left with only the echoing melody of what was and what might have been.

I'm haunted by that final, triumphant performance—the night when everything crumbled, my dreams fracturing into irreparable shards before my eyes. I agonize over the choices I could have made, each one carrying the burden of an alternative fate.

But I also consider the sacrifices, the parts of my soul I would have surrendered to reach those towering heights. How much more of myself could I have given, and how many dear souls would I have left behind?

My time as a pianist has shaped who I am today, for better or worse. It's a paradox I've become accustomed to, a mysterious dance of fate and destiny woven into my existence.

A life without my piano is a life not worth living. A life without my time in Russia, well… I often ponder the darker shadows my visit to Russia has cast upon me. It's a haunting thought that lingers like a ghost, a constant reminder that every choice, every twist of fate, can bring both growth and downfall. For better or worse.

One cannot ascend to such heights and emerge unscathed on the other side. The aftermath is inevitable, a life of mending wounds, burying the past, and forging ahead.

Now I am required to navigate the complexities of my mind. I glide through the stages of cognitive behavioral skills, tirelessly in pursuit of that elusive "here and now," a place where the past no longer haunts, and the future's shadows do not intrude. I proceed through life concealed by my many masks. I have mastered the art of transformation and adapt seamlessly into each role: a healed being, a devoted mother, a passionate and attentive wife—each veils the fractures beneath.

And now I have emerged from the wreckage more resilient than ever. I'm not just healed; I'm unstoppable! My past is behind me, my future a blank canvas, and I—

There's a whisper on the winds, a foreboding shadow that dances at the periphery of my vision. It murmurs of troubles unseen, of the unknown gathering on the horizon, and I can't shake the eerie feeling that this healing may be but a moment in time—a fleeting calm before the storm.

As my mind sinks into the depths of these racing thoughts, I frantically reach for my lifeline—my phone.

With precision, my hand finds my phone; my fingers move across the screen in a well-rehearsed choreography.

Deep diving into the playlists displayed, each swipe and tap becomes a deliberate effort to free myself from the memories of the past. I scroll through the music, seeking an escape route to different melodies, a departure from my usual preference for Chopin's graceful compositions.

"Have you ever go into a room, lock the door, and dance, dance so crazy?" Ivan, in his broken English, once posed this question long ago, in another world, within the confines of a different paradigm.

I wait, poised in anticipation of a song, a singular composition that holds the power to puncture through the layers of my mundane existence and extract raw, unfiltered emotion.

And then, it arrives.

Perfect!

Michael Sembello's "Maniac" erupts into the atmosphere, the guitar, synthesizer bass, and keyboard coalescing into a mesmerizing storm of sound, electrifying the air. The pulsating energy feels almost supernatural.

Yes!

I surrender myself to the music's control, permitting it to dictate the rhythm of my body. It's a moment of liberation, as the world dissolves into nothingness. The music guides me toward a new existence, free from the constraints of my daily fears and doubts.

As I dance, I sense a transformation unfurling within me. I cast off the mundane and clothe myself in something extraordinary, something celebratory and carefree. An old gown beckons me, one I have never had the opportunity to wear—yards of acid lime tulle.

Excellent!

I zip up my dress and release my hair, letting it flow freely. I look at my reflection in the mirror and steal a brief look at the girl who exchanged her youth for a life of triumph. I apply a bold, crimson hue to my lips, and they contort into a twisted smile. It's all me—the culmination of every sacrifice, every grueling struggle, every bone break, and twisted wrist. I am that same person, molded by my relentless pursuit of greatness.

My smile remains fixed as I sense a breeze calling from the veranda, inviting me to step outside. It gently cools my feverish body as I venture into the open air.

In this moment, I'm more than just Cleo; I've become a whimsical concoction, a figment of my imagination. My limbs respond as I dance with newfound liberty and audacity. The music's intoxicating melodies envelop me. The instruments communicate with me, their impassioned voices dictating wild, erratic movements of my body. As I merge with the music, my surroundings dissolve into obscurity. I sway on the veranda, immersed in my private realm, oblivious to the watchful eyes of the night.

"Cleo?" My husband, Conor's voice breaks the enchanting spell of music and movement, and I am abruptly confronted by reality. I twirl around, almost losing balance. Before me stand Conor and our three children, their eyes wide with surprise. I'm not sure how long they've been standing there, but seeing me in this ethereal gown, lost in my dance, must be a startling and perplexing sight, especially considering the tumultuous year we've all endured.

But I can't stop now. Allowing the music to course through me as if it were the elixir of life itself, I continue to sway to the rhythm. "Yay, Mommy!" Olivia and Sebastian, our bundles of joy, clap their tiny hands and bounce along to the beat.

"Mommy, you look like a princess!" Olivia shouts over the music, her innocent admiration reflecting in her sparkling eyes.

"Come join me, guys!" My heart aching to share this moment with them, I extend the invitation.

Ciara, our thoughtful and reserved eldest, hesitates, her eyes reflecting clear resistance to this display of exuberance. But Olivia and Sebastian, not burdened by such reservations, eagerly join me outside.

Cherishing their existence, feeling the warmth of their rosy cheeks, watching their bright blond hair bounce as they jump, and savoring the essence of their innocence and purity, I hold their chubby, petite hands in mine.

"Oh, come on, Ciara!" I call out, a plea to draw her into our spontaneous celebration.

"Oh. No-no-no-no-no!" Her hands dramatically wave in response, but there's a glimmer of curiosity in her eyes.

Conor embraces me, his love a palpable force that weaves our family together. It's a love that's true, undeniable, messy, uncomfortable, and complicated. I feel Conor's arms wrapped securely around my waist, as he plants a gentle kiss on the back of my neck.

"Oh, come on, Ciara!" Conor urges her once more.

She rolls her eyes and concedes, a reluctant smile creeping across her face. We all cheer.

I feel Conor's arms tighten around me, and his head rests gently on my shoulder. We both smile as we watch our three children dance freely, a reminder of the beauty that life has to offer.

Moments like these, I know, will eventually be replaced by the relentless march of nightly rituals, the chorus of crying kids, and Conor's unfaltering reassurances that "It's okay."

Tomorrow, the weight of my fears might return, but in this fleeting moment, all is calm. For now, those concealed wounds remain buried, any ounce of transformation is locked away, locked in an enigmatic silence. Its secret intentions shrouded in darkness, waiting to emerge from the depths of the distant horizon.

PART ONE

1

MOTHER RUSSIA

Moscow, Ten Years Ago

A haunting melody of fate surrounded me as I walked the dimly lit corridors of the Moscow Conservatory. In front of me stood two narrow mahogany entry doors. There's a future behind these closed doors, one shrouded in uncertainty and full of possibilities. Beyond these closed doors, an esteemed jury of judges awaited, ready to scrutinize my every note and expression.

The usher's hand gently covered the handle, waiting for the signal. The weight of my heels shifted impatiently from side to side, mirroring the restlessness in my heart. The sound of my palpitating heart grew increasingly louder, drowning out the world around me, and the distant voice of tonight's host became a mere murmur in the background.

"Number five: Cleo Wilson, United Kingdom," I believe he announced, followed by a storm of applause, yet all I could hear was the ringing vibrations of white noise in my head —the sound of silence.

"Tchaikovsky - Piano Concerto No. 1, *Kontsert Nomer Odin*," the announcer continued in Russian. I waited for my conductor's facial cues to know when it was time to go ahead.

I surveyed my surroundings as I stepped onto the stage. I take a deep breath, trying to calm the racing of my heart. The spotlight shines brightly, and the hushed anticipation of the audience sends a shiver down my spine.

The Moscow Conservatory's Great Hall.

I had finally made it.

The seating capacity was one thousand, seven hundred and thirty-seven; I looked it up online the night before. The lack of empty seats was now quite apparent, not to mention intimidating. You would think such a hall, with its grandeur and prominence, would have set up a better lighting system, one where the performers could avoid the audience's unwavering intrusion.

I gradually got closer to the shiny black grand piano in the orchestra's center. It was the only vessel that projected my expressions, my emotions.

The strict pre-performance etiquette commenced on autopilot: a dance of tradition and formality. I bowed, shook the conductor's hand, shook the concertmaster's hand, sat on the bench from the left side to right, placed my hands in my lap, and gave that rehearsed, slight nod to the conductor. I positioned my bare fingers on the chosen notes, took a much-needed deep inhale, and when I exhaled, the power of Tchaikovsky filled the room.

I'd contemplated **Tchaikovsky - Piano Concerto No. 1, Op. 23**, as my opening act. It was the obvious choice from Tchaikovsky's symphony. Despite its emotional charge, the pianist must display virtuosity to bring it to life.

I ultimately went with a piece that reflected me, moved me. It took me back to age ten, playing this concerto at home, seemingly in a different, more petite body—holding the same vulnerabilities and melancholy.

I listened to the music as it played, as I played. It almost felt like I was an outsider, a member of the audience. An out-of-body experience, some might say. I could almost forget I was playing, and if I concentrated on the tempo or the pressure of my fingers, I might mess it all up.

This moment… Oh, it's everything I've ever dreamed of. From the time I was a small child in London, my heart yearned for this very opportunity—to compete in the Moscow Classical Music Competition. The weight of its grandeur, the prestige, it became the pinnacle of my existence.

Like the Olympics, every four years, I would find myself captivated in front of the telly, eyes wide, invested in the process of who would move on to the next round. It was my sport, my soap opera, my reality TV. I knew I would find myself on that stage one day, in that conservatory in Moscow.

The looming age limit of thirty-two casts a shadow on my heart. The chance of playing after the age limit never occurred to me, yet there were rumors of musicians who participated in various competitions regardless of their age. Regulations and rules were in place for a reason, and I always complied. This year, this competition, it's my chance, my destiny, and I cannot let it slip away. Time waits for no one, and I refuse to be a spectator to my own life. Every note I play, every ounce of emotion I pour into this music, it's a testament to my lifelong dedication and passion.

I feel it in every fiber of my being—the weight of the years of practice, the sacrifices, the tears, and the triumphs. The intensity of the moment is overwhelming, and I can feel the weight of every decision I've made leading up to this point. The sleepless nights of practice, the endless rehearsals, the sacrifices of a social life—it all culminates here. This competition is not just about showcasing my talent; it's about proving to myself that I can achieve greatness.

There's no room for missteps or second-guessing. Every move is calculated, every note deliberate. I have rehearsed this piece a thousand times, dissecting each phrase, each nuance, until it became ingrained in my very being.

The moment I arrived in Moscow, I had no choice but to succeed. I demanded control of every aspect of my performance, obsessing over every detail. From the way I sat on the bench, to the angle of my head during the bow, nothing was left to chance. My red gown, carefully chosen from Ulyana Sergeenko's couture collection, to exhibit the best of Russian fashion, the red symbolizes honor and beauty in Russian culture and history—or does it represent communism? I'm not sure.

Liam, my coach, mentor, and teacher—the real triple threat—should have been concerned about the intensity of my obsession with these details rather than my repertoire. The sheer energy I poured into every aspect of my performance might have been alarming to him. Yet, I couldn't let him see the depth of my fixation; it was better that he remained unaware. My every move was calculated with precision; my every decision meticulously weighed. The focus I placed on those details was more than just an obsession; it was a sacred ritual, a way to ensure that every element of my performance aligned with my vision. So, masking my fervor with an air of nonchalance, I feigned indifference while knowing that my passion burned hotter than anyone could imagine.

As my fingers touch the keys, my mind drifts into a trance-like state. I lose myself in the music, letting it carry me to places I've never been before. The notes flow from my heart, each one infused with the raw emotions of my journey. This is not just a performance; it's a revelation of my soul.

Time seems to blur as I pour my very essence into the music. The world around me fades away, and it's just me and the piano, locked in an intimate dance of passion and expression. The doubts and fears are silenced, replaced by a sense of purpose and determination.

When the last note resonates through the hall, I am left breathless, my heart pounding with exhilaration and exhaustion. The silence that follows is deafening, and for a moment, I wonder if I have failed to move the audience. But then, a thunderous applause erupts, and tears fill my eyes.

I had completed my first round.

* * *

I waited outside the conservatory as Liam located the car. I took a deep inhalation of the crisp air and focused on the snow covering the trees like white linen. I stood with pride in front of the magnificent statue of Tchaikovsky. A sense of satisfaction washed over me. Now I was in the best company, among the greats. This was where I belonged.

That feeling of traveling alone was both exhilarating and daunting. It was a moment of liberation, a chance to test my independence and see just how far I could go on my own.

Growing up an only child for the first six years of my life fostered that sense of independence. I was capable and determined; I was unstoppable. After my sister Annie was born, it only exacerbated my need for freedom, and I would revel in my alone time. When the adults occupied her, it meant less noise and more uninterrupted piano time for me.

I held on to my early memories with Annie, as she was often settled beside me on her baby rocker while I practiced. She'd wail until the music pacified her to sleep. I would start playing with annoyance. Why is she in my space? Why is she adding to the noise? Then, once the room went silent and all I could detect were the sounds of Mozart coming through the piano, a sense of accomplishment overwhelmed me. A sense of control.

Everyday noises punctuated my life. They disturbed me, and I had to conceal them with my piano. When it was too quiet, it would cause a hypervigilant response, a hint at something not being right. Music became my refuge, my way of concealing the noises that plagued me. Silence could be deafening, telling too much about what lay beneath. I felt the burden of responsibility to maintain peace at home, to hide the tensions that I couldn't fully comprehend. I couldn't express these feelings to anyone; I didn't even have the words to describe what I was experiencing.

I started playing the piano at the age of three. I vividly remember the day I discovered the grand piano in the middle of our house. Initially, I believed that my mother bought this grandiose instrument as a way for us to connect with music. But the older I got, the more I realized that my mother held no attachment to these melodies; rather, she formed a notion that the power of my sonatas could uplift the ambiance at home. Like the music would somehow wipe away any other noises that were lingering inside our walls or, at the very least, quiet them.

Was I projecting my sensitivities to the sounds, or lack thereof? I wasn't sure. Either way, it was a responsibility I held on to throughout my childhood, and it only grew with time. It was my obligation to maintain peace at home. It wasn't always chaotic, but sometimes silence can be worse than chaos. Sometimes silence tells too much.

The burden of this responsibility flooded me every day. I couldn't share this feeling since I had no reason to believe that something was going on. I didn't have the words to express the eeriness I felt at home and the need to play music to conceal these emotions.

So instead, I would savor my alone time—a way to block out my thoughts and control the sounds around me.

The therapeutic effect of traveling alone became apparent.

Although, technically, I didn't travel alone. Liam always traveled alongside me, like a guardian would for an unaccompanied minor.

Liam's presence in my life was both comforting and unsettling. He believed in my talent and saw something in me that others didn't. I yearned for his approval, for him to recognize my potential and guide me to greatness. He became the vessel through which I could channel my musical power.

I was introduced to Liam when I was a student at the London Music Conservatory. I remember how I found his looks to be somewhat distracting. He was tall, with blue eyes and dark hair, and only ten years my senior, but the years he had on me academically were monumental. He was a virtuoso teacher in the world of classical music, and he enjoyed the process of teaching more than the need to perform. I never understood that. When you hold such talent, why not share it with the world? Why find another vessel to convey that power?

The wind passed straight through me as I shivered desperately, trying to keep my body warm. The street had become increasingly crowded, making it more difficult to locate my car in front of the conservatory. Where was Liam? I hugged my oversized fur coat shut, struggling to gather the excess tulle that was now contracting wet patches from the ground. It became a juggling act, between the tulle, my tedious red heels (now switched out for a more responsible white trainer), and my tote bag full of belongings.

"*Privet*," a prominent voice called out from behind me.

I jumped. I turned around and saw a tall, assuming Russian boy standing behind me, cigarette in mouth, unlit.

His hair was undeniably familiar, that almost white, icy blond you don't come across often. Mine was borderline platinum, but it took hours of fidgety salon visits for me to get there. His, for some reason, seemed natural, flawless.

His crooked smile formed a dimple across his right cheek, and his blue eyes protruded against the dark skies. I stayed fixated on his appearance, then summoned the ability to speak.

"Privet," I repeated, slightly hesitant that my pronunciation was correct. I have always been like this in foreign countries, not wanting to sound like I'm mimicking an accent while simultaneously respecting their correct pronunciation.

"*Ne naydiotsa prikurit?*"

"Sorry," I shrugged. "I. Don't. Really. Know. Russian." I said this slow and loud, knowing very well that he would not understand this any better than my regular cadence.

"Uh. Not Russian?"

"Not Russian."

"Ivan." He held out his hand. Assertive and composed, I continued to observe his appearance, then reciprocated the gesture.

"Cleo." Not much we could say from here, between two broken languages. I wasn't one to handle awkward silences too well.

"So you have no light?"

He had a heavy Russian accent, but he spoke English! He was quite articulate too, which caught me off guard. "You speak English quite well." It was a relief to have avoided the bowed-head-nice-to-meet-you inaudible greeting. "And no. Sorry, no light." I let go of his grip, now embarrassed by the length of the handshake. The eye contact too. He wouldn't look away. So, I did.

"So, Cleo. Where you come from?" He gave up on his smoke and put the cigarette back into his jacket pocket.

"London. Have you been there?"

"I haven't. I haven't really left Russia." He looked up and smiled, proud of his surroundings. As if it were something he owned. I felt his gaze so intimately return to mine. "I saw you play piano tonight. You are really, really good."

"Thank you," I replied, then paused a beat, since I now understood why he looked so familiar. "You play the violin, right?"

I caught a glimpse of his practice backstage. After exhausting my practicing hours, I used the opportunity to observe the other musicians. I remembered the trance I slipped into as he played Dvořák Romance in F minor. It was a sensation that I had not experienced before. The impulse to stay put, the permission to pause.

"True."

"Did you make it to the second round?" I automatically regretted asking. What if he didn't make it through? How inconsiderate of me

"I did."

"Oh, congratulations!" I almost sighed out of relief or laughed. Worse than that awkward silence was that awkward moment when you must console a stranger.

"You?"

"The piano and voice winners will be announced tomorrow." My car arrived before we were able to have a conversation with any form of substance.

"This is you?" He seemed impressed, pointing to the black Escalade. The driver hurried around to my door and held it open. How pretentious I must have come across.

"Well, it was a pleasure to meet you, Ivan." I took one last look and proceeded to carefully enter through the open door, still juggling my belongings.

"*Do svidaniya,* Cleo. "

I smiled back, and the door shut. I immediately tried to remember if *do svidaniya* meant "goodbye" or "see you later." For some reason, it made a difference to me. As if it were a clue to some intuitive feelings.

I settled into the back seat next to Liam, the weight of exhaustion and anticipation heavy in the air. The ride home was cloaked in silence, a reflection of the intensity that clung to us after the competition. The upcoming rounds loomed ahead, promising both triumph and challenges, but there were more battles to conquer before victory could be claimed. Conversation felt like an extravagance, our minds and bodies too drained to engage in small talk. The car enveloped us in a cocoon of stillness, the only sounds were the gentle hum of the engine and the rhythmic cadence of our breaths.

As we journeyed through the dimly lit streets, a faint smile tugged at my lips, ignited by the memory of my brief encounter with Ivan. There was an unspoken connection between us, an undercurrent of emotion that defied definition. It was as though something had transpired beyond the walls of the conservatory, something profound and elusive. And I wasn't alone in experiencing it; I could sense that Ivan, too, was grappling with a surge of feelings. It was a realization that brought a strange sense of comfort, a reminder that human connection could transcend the confines of words.

The irony of the situation wasn't lost on me. Here I was, basking in the afterglow of a triumphant performance at the Moscow Conservatory, yet the part of the night that made me smile was that, maybe, a boy liked me. How high school of me. I was turning twenty-eight the next month and was giddy that a boy had given me some attention.

What was wrong with me that I couldn't enjoy a moment shared with Ivan without feeling bad about myself? I permitted logic and reason to undermine my emotions once again. It was a question that echoed within me, a recurring theme that seemed to weave through the fabric of my thoughts. The battle between logic and emotion raged on, and once again, I allowed reason to cast a shadow over the pureness of my feelings.

To find an escape away from the turmoil within, I turned my gaze to the window. The landscape of Mother Russia presented before me, a tapestry of both beauty and history. The sights blurred together, a symphony of fleeting images that mirrored the complex tangle of emotions within my heart. As the car pressed forward, I let my mind drift, seeking solace in the enigmatic embrace of the Russian night.

2

PASSION

New York City, Present Day

I can hear the high pitched chimes echo throughout the room, filling it with a musical soundscape. Restlessness has kept me awake for well over an hour now.

The alarm is my reminder to really get up. With a deliberate stretch, I reach out to my nightstand, my fingers closing around the familiar contours of my phone. The luminous display of 6:15. The world is already astir, and so am I.

I race through the list of tasks I need to complete today. I work from home and still need every minute of my morning. My duties spread out before me, an intricate mosaic of tasks and obligations that demand my attention. Each moment is precious, every second meticulously accounted for. My mental list seems so redundant, as my days consist of two main jobs:

1) Start my novel

2) Take care of my kids

A gentle tide of melancholy washes over me at the trajectory my life has taken. I never thought I would become a writer, but life was a string of accidental events that led me to where I am today. In about a month, it will mark ten years since I bid adieu to my life as a pianist, which was also the same year I joined my father's publishing house. An unexpected divergence, a narrative twist that defied my own expectations.

They needed a copy editor, so they hired me. It was a drastic turnaround yet somehow appeared the appropriate choice.

"You always had perfect penmanship, always had a way with your words. You will be a significant asset to our team," my father hypothesized, but I saw through his transparency. Though beneath his encouragement lay a current of paternal concern. At the time, I was almost twenty-nine, single, unemployed, abandoned, and apathetic. And so, I took the job. I also put myself through university; I did it on principle. The prospect of joining a company without any credentials, no matter how appealing, was unacceptable to me since my participation would seem to be approaching nepotism.

My mother, a widely acclaimed author in her own right, happened to be represented by my father's publishing house. However, if you were to ask me, her position as the spouse of the publishing house's founder occasionally cast a shadow over her personal accomplishments in the literary world, subtly diminishing her standing in the industry. I was determined not to let such questions hang over my own achievements. Hence, I proudly graduated from Oxford University with a major in English language and literature.

I spent half my days in my studies and the other half editing, acknowledging the reality that I would be working behind other writers for the rest of my life. My lack of interest in the literary world was the irony of it all. I spent years finding my place in a particularly difficult industry, and I didn't know if I wanted to be a part of it or not.

My husband rolls over and kisses the back of my neck.

"Good morning," he whispers and gives me a slow hug as his body warms over mine, spooning me from behind. I can feel his hair tickle my neck. I can feel his heavy breathing indicate he's awake but not that conscious.

I let him stay there for a minute, and then, "Okay, I actually have to get up now," my fingers tapping his hands as a subtle cue to loosen his hold. He stirs, reluctantly releasing me from his enveloping grasp.

I'm not sure why he doesn't race out of bed quicker than I do. He must be out of the house in an hour. Such is the essence of Conor McCarthy, the embodiment of calm amidst the bustling chaos.

I know, Conor and Cleo McCarthy. The rhythm of our names, it's embarrassing. A symphony of syllables that felt almost too idyllic.

Do you know those weird deal-breakers you create, the ones that cement your decision on whether to accept a date from someone? The single almost-deal-breaker was his name. I can't give you an exact reason why it bothered me so much. Maybe our names sounded too cutesy together. The quintessential couple residing behind a white picket fence. A life that echoed convention rather than aspirations. A hardworking husband and that ideal domestic wife. Why our names would imply that lifestyle, I don't have a real rhyme or reason, but it's just where my mind went.

Submitting to suburban life was the antithesis of who I wanted to be. It wasn't my plan to live a life without drive and determination, without the appetite to achieve something greater.

While not the suburbs, a three-bedroom townhouse in the heart of Greenwich Village wasn't a world too different. I am married to a successful psychiatrist, the breadwinner of the family. All the while, I struggle to succeed as a writer and raise my three children. I am now attending PTA meetings (forcibly) and accompanying my children to their after-school activities (impatiently). My days go by simultaneously too slowly and in the blink of an eye: no more competitions, no more big arenas, no more potent charges of ecstasy.

I left my life in London, my life as a pianist. The truth is, I can't be that person anymore. I ran so far away, so I don't have to face the reminder of who I once was.

When I try to remember the exact moment I realized I had to run away from the world of classical music, the timeline seems blurry, but I still remember that feeling.

It was a love I had for classical music that eventually became unhealthy— my drive for success manifested as toxicity.

That's when everything started shifting drastically. The direction of my days. The way my mind worked. The pandemonium is slowly fading out of my life, and now my mind has room to think. To imagine, to dream. I have no more noises, just thoughts.

I can't help but ponder the past, a time when I had it all. Back when I held the reins of control. I had achieved the highest accolades in the classical music world with my tenacity and grit. I couldn't imagine a life without aim or purpose guiding me to the end of the day.

But the moment I met Conor I knew that I had to accept the reality that music was no longer in my future, and I had to find a new purpose in life. I thought perhaps settling down with a husband and starting a family would be good for me. I set aside all my apprehensions and agreed to a date. That decision marked the beginning of a new chapter in my life.

I mean, he was—is—ridiculously handsome. Not in an arrogant, pronounced kind of way, but just the right amount. He also checks off all the other hypothetical boxes I've manufactured in some subconscious part of my brain. And let me tell you, I have some high standards. He is kind, loyal, and intelligent, an accomplished psychiatrist, but at the same time, extremely easygoing—a perfect complement to my own intensity.

What's wrong with me that a silly name combination can take all that away for me?

Occasionally, but not consistently, I find myself feeling resentment toward this new life I've created in New York, and that feeling quickly transforms into guilt. I am taken care of; I have a life permeated with love. I must shake off the person I used to be and focus on who I have become.

Who have I become? Intently, I scrutinize the reflection before me. I notice the remnants of broken joints, aching backs, and calloused fingers from my past. A body, maternally sacrificed. Beneath my eyes, a purple tint clashes with a somber, sunken blueness. I lift the delicate skin with my fingers and let it fall— a silent dance with gravity. I ponder when the day might arrive for me to succumb to societal pressure and undergo some cosmetic procedure to revive my youth. Dark roots have grown inches; I make a mental note to, perhaps sometime next week, schedule an appointment at the hair salon down the street.

After brushing my teeth, Conor comes into the master bathroom, impeccably groomed and dressed, bearing a generous cup of black iced coffee— a tradition etched into our relationship since the beginning. See? Taken care of, permeated with love. I thank him and inhale the caffeinated serotonin my body craves.

I shed my black jersey pajama set for an ensemble of all-black activewear, my signature uniform. Time is a precious commodity; there's no luxury to squander on coordinating colors or patterns.

Our choreography of routine operates like clockwork. I immerse myself in an intense elliptical session, dual wielding both water and iced coffee, and Conor packs the kids' school lunches and makes sure they are fed.

The door is locked, and I treasure my few moments of isolation. You lack control over the sounds of your home when your children are around. So, I increase the volume of my headphones with what little power I have.

The eerie strains of **Edvard Grieg - In The Hall of the Mountain King** fill the room, mingling with the sound of my labored breaths as I propel myself through the punishing workout. It's as though the music itself has taken on a tangible form, its notes curling around me like tendrils of smoke, both comforting and foreboding. Amid the burn and strain, I'm not alone; an imagined symphony materializes around me, an ethereal orchestra of my own creation.

The cascading piano keys bang as they evoke memories of my past struggles, violins emerge, their high-pitched cries resonating with the tension I feel. They dance alongside the frantic pulse of my heart, like ghosts of the past that I can't quite shake. Clarinets add their mournful voices, wrapping me in a cocoon of bittersweet nostalgia, while violas hum with a muted intensity, a reflection of the emotions I've buried deep within.

As the symphony of my imagination builds, so does the intensity of my physical effort. Sweat drips down my skin like tears, and the harmony of the imaginary instruments mirrors the chaotic rhythm of my heart.

And just as the orchestra reaches a crescendo, the outside world barges in once more. A knock on the door, a jarring dissonance that disrupts the harmony I've constructed. "Mommy! I need to be on time today, and nobody is ready yet!" The intrusion is a stark reminder that my private symphony can only hold sway for so long before reality pulls me back into its grasp.

I inhale deeply, as I ready myself to face the challenges of the day. The symphony fades, but its echoes remain, a constant reminder that beneath the surface of my daily routine lies a symphony of emotions, waiting to be played out in the unpredictable score of my future.

"Mommy!"

Breathe.

That's my eight-year-old, Ciara, pronounced "Kee-ra." I know, I know. I'm well aware of another 'K' name that appears custom-crafted for our suburban sanctuary. I might have resisted this choice stubbornly, yet it pays homage to my late mother-in-law, a remarkable Irish matriarch who left an indelible mark on Conor's heart.

When we found out we were expecting a daughter, it brightened Conor's spirits.

"It's a sign!" He said, and later that sign was satisfyingly validated by how much she resembled his mother. I can still recall the day Ciara was born—Conor tenderly caressing our daughter's dark, luxurious locks as he enlightened us with the fact that "Ciara" stems from the Gaelic word ciar, meaning "dark." All I could ponder was the countless articles linking my months of heartburn to the fetus sprouting a mane inside me.

Conor, also a vision of his mother, brought down those genes. They have matching dark hair and piercing blue eyes.

I had bright blond hair as a child, now perpetually tethered to a regimen of hair dye and chemical straightening. My eyes are blue, but their eyes are blue! Structurally, our faces are different too. Although there is one similarity we share. Like me, Ciara is quite the type A personality. I often wonder, the same way our daughter's appearance reflected Conor's strong gene pool, is character something you can pass on too? Or maybe it's that nature vs. nurture conundrum. You know, since she was the oldest like me? Or can it be the influence of my anxieties that spawned a replica of another stubborn, solicitous, and hardworking human being?

The second knock.

"Mommy, where is the strawberry yogurt? Daddy can't find it anywhere!"

Breathe.

My sweet, silly, might I add blond five-year-old: Olivia, Olivia Rose. I had all the power when it came to naming her. There were no family members or ancient messages behind her name. I just simply loved the sound of "Olivia Rose."

Olivia is the antithesis of Ciara. Not just in the palette of her hair. She's the embodiment of carefree tranquility. In that aspect, Conor's genetic influence is abundantly clear, and I couldn't be more content about it.

"It's in the back of the bottom shelf of the fridge," I shout from behind the door.

"Okay, thanks, Mommy!"

My little ray of sunshine. Always with the please-and-thank-yous.

Olivia is that quiet but vibrant child who will play with her dolls for hours, and when she doesn't clean up after herself, Ciara comes in and tidies after every little mess.

My job here is done.

Or so I thought.

"Moommmy!" The last anticipated shriek. I take out my headphones; my workout is done. The shower will have to wait.

A year and a half after I gave birth to Olivia, my last (hopefully) child came to us as a surprise. I was too busy to notice my late period and took a blood test (Conor's strict orders) since I felt weak and lethargic. So, yes, I was stunned to get that heavily weighted information on my doctor's phone call.

"It seems as though you're just about eight weeks pregnant."

"Eight weeks?" I was shocked and quickly examined my belly in the mirror for any signs of "baby."

While I was in my third trimester, Conor's grandfather passed.

His name was Kai.

Now, I'm not that psychotic, and I agreed to name our boy after his late *daideo* on the condition I could give him a second name. That's fair, right?

So now I call him Sebastian. Kai Sebastian. "Kai" is easier to say, and I won't admit it out loud, but I do love that name. But would Cleo, Conor, Ciara, and Kai bother you?

Lucky Olivia.

Sebastian is another copy of Olivia. Same round face, bright blond curls, he has the sweetest demeanor like his father. However, the energy he possesses! Maintaining an accelerated pace with him was a learning curve. "Boys!" they say. Energetically challenging but emotionally rewarding. I agree with this sentiment.

Sebastian showers me with his affection. When his energy runs out and we start to wind down, Sebastian will find me, clambering onto my lap, effectively anchoring me in the moment.

I am not a religious person, but I do thank God for them from time to time. I never intended on raising three kids, but since I'm here now, I'm just grateful that they are at least manageable.

"Okay, I'm here!" I surrender my tranquil bubble. "Olivia, did you find your yogurt? Great!"

Olivia smiles as the pastel pink drips off her face onto her gray T-shirt.

I cringe.

Breathe.

"Mommy, look! No one is ready! Tell them we have to leave now!" Ciara proceeds to run the show, panting rapidly.

"Breathe." I say it out loud to Ciara. And myself.

"Sebastian, no, take those out." I grab Sebastian's backpack, turn it upside down, and empty the many cars he's shoved inside.

"Honey, I got this," Conor assures me as he enters the living room.

I know he's got it. We have this unspoken understanding that he'll take care of the kids while I am on the elliptical, but I need it done sooner, quicker.

The next half hour of mayhem continues as I make sure all three kids' bags are packed. The correct school projects and homework match the suitable bags. Hats, jackets, and gloves on the right kids.

I throw on Sebastian's puffer coat and kiss them all goodbye.

The noise stops. It is now me at home. Alone. Work commences.

* * *

I sit outside on my veranda. It must be under fifty degrees, but I am anything if not a creature of habit. Here is where I work best, so here is where I work.

I have been told that I have the luxury of working from home, but it never feels natural. The old me was unable to stay put for more than a week at a time. This is different, slow.

I have worked in the publishing industry for a decade and have already experienced all spectra of success. The rapid upward trajectory only ignited once I decided to attempt writing. The novel was an afterthought, an experiment I toyed with on the side. I imagined a realm of historical fiction: a novel charged with suspense, with passionate and conflicting romance. A fabricated world that monumentally and preferably contrasted with mine—disassociation at its finest.

The feeling of accomplishment drove me to believe that this was the right path. The hit of succeeding again brought me back to my former life, the life of a thriving pianist.

I fed off this success. I felt rejuvenated again. My days seemed brighter, and my mind was peaceful. I had finally found my purpose.

I met Ramona, a literary agent with ties to a prestigious New York City publishing house. After discovering my first novel, she became enthralled by my writing and insisted I pursue my calling. She was so confident in my potential as a writer that she offered me a double book deal.

I translated Ramona's determination and persistence as confidence and support in me. I wanted—no, needed—to surround myself with driven individuals to achieve greatness. I just couldn't predict the imbalance of authority that would play out in our partnership. I always felt like I had possessed the initiative and control in my past career. Now, it appears that Ramona has taken charge of everything. I committed my energy to this venture only to find myself in too deep. I signed the two-book contract. I even moved to New York to pursue my writing career.

I knew I could have worked from my home in London just as efficiently. I knew I didn't have to take drastic efforts to uproot my life and go to New York. Although, when Ramona mentioned her hypothetical idea of my working from

New York to match her time zone, I can't say it was her passive manipulation that provoked me. I believe that some form of my subconscious encouraged me to grasp at any excuse and opportunity to leave my old life, with the many tragic hints of my past. Leave it and don't look back.

So that is what I did. Seven months into my marriage and five months pregnant, we blindly uprooted our lives and moved to the other side of the world. I felt like I had absolutely no control over my life, which was a rude awakening.

My first book of two failed to do as well as my previous one.

Beginner's luck, I thought.

Leaving me with the question: how to now construct book two? The answer has eluded me so far. I lost it. I lost my touch. It seemed my initial triumph was but a fortunate accident, and now I was left grappling with a profound mistake.

Yet this contract binds my responsibilities, and I must produce something substantial.

I close my eyes and let in a deep inhale.

Breathe, I remind myself. Just breathe; it will come to you.

I purposefully positioned my workspace within the innards of deep-laid greenery. A bed of milkweed, violets, and asters to allure butterflies and provide a visionary escape. It was my much-needed mental break when the obligatory due dates would occur—a way to refocus my brain, a form of recharging.

It was my mother who taught me the art of cultivating a green thumb, to gain an appreciation of a garden landscape. The garden was my only sanctuary away from the piano, and it brought my mother and me closer. When I was younger, it wouldn't occur often, but when my mother was in the right headspace for gardening, I would go outside and chase the butterflies. She'd be there, hat on, gloves in place, and there was something so peaceful about seeing her down on all fours, tending to the plants.

It was in moments like these that she would lighten up, get silly. The fragility of her body chasing me, chasing butterflies.

My mother and I shared an inexplicable bond. Her love wasn't always as clear and articulate as many mothers', but she expressed emotions in a way I could understand.

Despite her disappearing moments, as we called them, I knew she loved me. I knew she wanted to be there for me.

In retrospect, I wonder if I understood my mother better because I see myself in her.

There was her need to close the door and isolate herself from all noises. Her desire not to engage with others, her need for solitude without interruption—freedom amid nothingness.

As a child, I digested her "moments" as matter-of-fact circumstance. I depended on distractions to get me through her transitions. She was there until she wasn't. My heart ached whenever she was close to me, knowing that those moments wouldn't last too long. Knowing I had to cherish our times together. Then, as anticipated, I saw her retreat into her room, and I waited for her return.

I hold on to this specific memory, one of us discovering a beautiful blue butterfly with a rip in its wing. My mother knew exactly how to nurse it back to well-being. Cradling the fragile creature, she gently affixed a sliver of tape, mending the wound. I watched her with a mix of awe and jealousy. I wanted someone to treat me with such consideration. From that day on, I made it my calling to learn everything I could about butterflies. I went from researching Bach's compositions to reading The World Encyclopedia of Butterflies.

It was my way of savoring this connection and commonality with my mother. Then, the time would come when she possessed little interest in the outside world. The gardeners would take over, and I would go back to the piano.

My sister Annie was a different sort of person. She had a more linear, verbal approach to emotion. She needed company and stimulation, and it was my father who was able to speak in Annie's language. He displayed his feelings more obviously. There was just too much work to be done in his office off Hyde Park. So close to us, yet so far away.

The London house that used to hold our dreams now stands as a distant memory, its walls echoing with the whispers of a shattered past. Annie found her own path in Manchester, entwined in a new love, while I navigate an entirely different continent. I often dream about London and think about returning. Then I wash away those thoughts and try to place my focus on today.

There are some similarities between London and New York. Living in the city is my preferred setting; I find comfort in its busy streets and share the need for isolation among crowds. It's a paradoxical haven, where connection and isolation coexist.

At first, the lack of greenery in New York was a shock. It was hard to find any form of outside garden when searching for a home, and we paid a good amount extra for this one.

It was worth it. I had to have some green space, someplace that can take me back to that point of stillness.

Our place overlooks the New York skyline, with its gloomy gray sky sending me into nostalgia. I have this incredible ability to block out the tumultuous noises of New York City. I can make the constant beeping, sporadic shouting, and other miscellaneous noises evaporate into the thin, polluted air. The stillness becomes a place where I settle in and where I thrive. Yet the continuous stimulation of notifications popping up on my screen is harder to disguise.

"Please confirm Sebastian's dental appointment." Or, "Don't forget, bake day for second grade next week." And then the most stabbing reminder: "Cleo, call me right away."

Ramona, that twat. I know I should be grateful; she played an integral role in shaping my career's path, but Ramona.

Ramona, Ramona, Ramona. She knows she has me by her strings. She says, "Do this," and if I don't, she reminds me how much I owe her. If not for her faith in me as a writer, I might still be working as a copy editor for my father's company. I would be in the background, not using my voice.

What voice? I lost my voice, and Ramona is that constant reminder.

I set Ramona to the Illuminate ring tone, her own personal sound to separate her from the others. That way, I don't accidentally miss any important messages, which would only trigger her into a scathing attack.

I look back at my phone and rub the tension from my neck. I'm not sure if the stress is what's causing this pressure or if it's sitting in my hunched position all day. Possibly both.

What to do? I can reply and keep this conversation on text—it's far less intrusive when you don't hear the tone of Ramona's roaring voice. What does she want to talk about anyway? She told me to write; as far as she knows, I'm writing right now. There doesn't need to be any updates to this process.

The chimes of Illuminate generate a shiver down my spine. I shrug it off, and before I can think what to say, I answer.

"Hi, Ramona."

"Cleo, you didn't call." Her voice is sharp and raspy with a profound New York accent.

I got her message not two minutes ago.

"This is urgent. Sophie from publishing is expediting your due date. She wants to see your complete, edited manuscript by March fifteenth now. We have been overstocked with projects this month, a lot of new and aspiring authors. Younger voices with a more progressive approach."

I roll my eyes. Creatives are taking on a new direction—with a more inclusive, more politically correct voice. My work always came from sarcasm, dark humor—a more realistic perception, I think. And apparently, society doesn't respect that these days.

"If you want to get your manuscript in, editing needs to have it by March, okay? Otherwise, your shit will get buried at the bottom of their pile. Are you following me? I'm dead serious, don't waste my time, Cleo."

"Oh. Okay."

"All right, I expect an update later this week. You better—what? Are you kidding me? What do you mean—" She's distracted by other happenings in her office. "I gotta go, bye."

That was it—I spoke merely two words in this severe and abrupt conversation.

"Shit." I fall back on my chair and laugh, the paradox reaction of what's going on inside. If I don't laugh, I will cry, and I don't have time for that right now.

I have nothing to show for my next book. My screen is blank; my mind is empty. I achieved so much success on my first attempt at a novel—I topped the bestseller lists. Times magazine named my novel one of the best fiction books of 2013.

One of my mistakes was to believe that my achievements proved my abilities, enabling me to continue to greater heights.

I worked extremely hard as a pianist but tried very little. I assumed I could bring the same work ethic to my writing. It was devastating when my second book did okay, but not good enough. I never felt so distraught before—so dismayed. I never failed at anything, and once I was in the proximity of failure, I froze. I lost my ability to continue.

My debut novel exposed the depths of desire and love. Through its characters, the readers lived vicariously, investing themselves in their love story. The reception was overwhelmingly positive.

Love serves as the universal thread binding us all. It's an emotion that transcends language, a sentiment we comprehend in myriad forms—a quintessential human experience.

It would have been easy to incorporate that sentiment into my next book, but I decided to try a new angle, a more realistic approach to love and its power. Instead, I depicted that belief in its own universe entirely.

I wasn't going to give everyone the happy ending they got in my first novel. Instead, I addressed the way love can manipulate and create a false sense of security. I explored the blurry lines that will deceive one into believing they've found their true love.

Love is what we're deceived into believing we feel when it is indeed passion, and passion is one of the most selfish emotions humans can experience. It's all about us as individuals when it comes to passion. What do we need? How do we fulfill this enormous feeling that we carry? We believe we cannot survive without this entity, experience, or person that makes us feel so passionately. Some might fight, kill, or steal when passion is so potent.

The thing about passion is: it fades. It fires the same neurotransmitters as cocaine; the information sends euphoric receptors from your brain and allows your body, mind, and soul to reach realms you never saw achievable. Then, the feelings diminish, they die down, and you are left with nothing but that void where passion once belonged.

Passion is not love. Passion actually derives from the Latin word *passio*—suffer.

In essence, these love stories are tales of suffering.

I quickly learned that people read for happy endings, not to relive their traumas and insecurities. People prefer memoirs or nonfiction for that. My second book made no profound impression, and the critics made sure I realized that.

I swallow the feelings of trepidation. Ignore. Breathe. Ignore.

The anxiety-induced performance begins.

I edge forward on the uncomfortable wicker patio chair, my gaze piercing the blank computer screen.

A metallic taste appears in my mouth, and I realize I have bitten too heavily into my lip. I dab away the blood with my sleeve.

My caffeine-riddled knee won't stop twitching.

I look around—damn writer's block.

I return to the keyboard, repeatedly typing and backspacing.

I stand up and pace around the veranda.

Time for my ultimate go-to. I hesitate, then continue to fish out my "secret stash," hidden behind a few potted plants—a pack of pre-rolled hybrid blends, a gold Zippo lighter, and a black marble ashtray.

It isn't a daily habit. At least, I try to make sure it isn't. I don't consider weed to be the mastermind of my creations, more like a chaperone escorting me to the creativity that I have already manifested somewhere in my consciousness. I have nothing against some "creative support," but I never want to become dependent on any substance for creativity. I am better than that. My potential is more than the potency of some brain-altering herb.

Today, I need it. Today, I am suffocating in quicksand. I inhale, then suddenly and slowly exhale. My medical marijuana card allows all the weed access I require. I have this weird sense of pride in how I didn't need to play up any symptoms to register for a license.

Pains? Check.

Nausea? Check.

Chronic anxiety, stress, and a touch of insomnia? Check.

I inhale again, feeling my weight sink heavier into my chair. I let my black loafer swing off my foot as I rock it back and forth, waiting for my juices to flow.

I wait for some change. I stay fixated on the butterflies hovering in front of me, begging my brain to send me to a place of inspiration. When that doesn't work, I throw on an oversized gray coat and leave my apartment.

Strolling or pacing often unshackled my creativity in the past; I'm hopeful the same holds true now. I head to Washington Square Park, slipping on my headphones, and unleash the emotional tapestry of **Mozart- Symphony No. 25.**

3

THE LIST

Moscow, Ten Years Ago

I woke up rested, not awakened by an alarm or startled by another urgent phone call at the crack of dawn. I woke up on my terms, my body simply working the way it should. Chaos was brewing on the horizon. I was confident that, after tonight's announcement, I would be among those who advanced to the next round.

So, the practice would continue until the winners were announced. These were the last hours of calm before the mayhem.

Just a few remaining moments of stillness.

The light shone through the transparent curtains, indicating that it was early, but not too early. I still had some lasting effects of jet lag but had finally succeeded in adjusting my circadian rhythm to Moscow Standard Time. I began to feel an influx of energy as the drowsiness left my body. I automatically smiled. This was the life.

From outside the stained-glass windows, I could appreciate the charming view of the bustling streets of Moscow. I can see the Fontan Vitali, the greenery, all the people commencing their days with cups of coffee in hand. At first glance, this can look like any cosmopolitan city, but the underlying significance of Russia separates it from the rest. It's both historical and futuristic. Romantic and dark. It is a smorgasbord of possibilities; you just have to know what your intentions are.

I hurried back to my bed and picked up the rotary phone off the solid mahogany nightstand. I gracefully extended my limbs over the bed as I waited for someone to pick up the line.

"Room service, please," I said with buoyancy in my voice. The sounds of jazz music filled the silence on the other end of the line. I slowly verbalized my order in my rehearsed Russian: "Uh, *dobroye utro. Odin kofe, pozhaluysta.*"

I was relentless. I knew I could speak to the hotel staff in English; they all spoke to me fluently. It was a warped way of thinking I was doing them a favor. I'm sure it was quite the opposite.

"Oh, um, *stakan vody,*" I added.

Coffee and water; that was all I needed.

I had been working on my Russian for weeks before the competition, and I was quite pleased with myself that I had managed one conversation in Russian. Yes, technically one sentence, but it was something.

I had roughly twenty minutes until my coffee would be delivered, just enough time to wake up slowly. It had been years since I was able to wake up peacefully. The past six months of training for the Moscow Classical Music Competition had consisted of six to eight hours of practice. So, for this one rare moment, I took in the calm.

The crisp wind seeped through the slightly opened windows, causing the curtains to hover above the carpeted floor, immersing my body in the cold air as I sat in the lotus position. I had one foot tucked carefully under the other, and I let my room go dark as I sat there, eyes closed, in a meditative state.

I've played piano since I was three. I have been competing since I was thirteen. The majority of my days involved warm-up exercises, rehearsals with Liam, and traveling.

As a solo musician, you get a lot of solo time—no moments left for friends or celebrations. When I wasn't rehearsing or performing, I was traveling.

You would assume that these countless hours would organically create an undeniable bond between Liam and me. It's not that I didn't feel connected with him, but our relationship had always been and would always be strictly professional. As I said: not a moment to joke, laugh, or decompress. We shared the same level of determination. We had the same perpetual blinders, our efficiency highlighted throughout our routine. How else could we accomplish everything and more in a short twelve-hour day?

There was a sharp knock at the door, which startled me right out of my meditative state.

Room service! I thought as I flew toward the door.

"Good morning." It was Liam. Tall, powerful, enchanting Liam. He smelled freshly showered, and his gray slim-fit suit was tailored perfectly to his body. He was holding a tray that held my coffee and water.

"Someone left this outside." He passed the tray over. "For you, I presume." He let himself inside, then cocked his head to the side. "Nice pajamas," he teased, and I was suddenly aware of my appearance.

My bright pink silk pajama set, my unbrushed and disheveled hair, my face bare of any makeup, the apparent juxtaposition to Liam's composed stature.

Occasionally, I had this unwarranted thought that Liam was here by force rather than by choice. But we both knew that was not the case. I would find myself very apologetic when asking him to do the work he had traveled here to do, work that was paid for by my mother.

It was my mind that generated those judgments. Those beliefs and queries.

Why events unfolded the way they did, why people said the things they said, why I felt the way I felt.

Everything needed an explanation.

I often made lists in my head to organize these thoughts. They usually consisted of contemplations and a multiplicity of questions. I could then go on to filter out such reflections when they didn't manifest as expected. Or I could eliminate them from my list when my questions were answered, and those thoughts were no longer significant.

In one of the many lists, I created a place where I would organize my inquiries about Liam:

```
LIAM
1. Liam is handsome; there is no denying it. Has this
   played a significant role in overcompensating that
   emotional distance?
```

That mystery still lingers on the top of the list.

"So, since I believe it's inevitable that you'll make it to the next round, why not get in an extra day of practice? Rehearsal officially starts at two, but I think we can use a head start?" Liam asked as though it were a question, but it had a rhetorical undertone. I just stood there, still trying to come up with something witty in response to my pajamas, but now I was just in pajamas, mute.

"Oh, okay. Let me just get dressed." I finally got into motion as I stumbled around, grabbed my already chosen outfit for the day, and headed to the bathroom.

"Um, I'll just be a minute," I shouted behind the door. Thank goodness I had already laid out my toiletries and makeup in my bathroom.

Liam was a substitute one term at the London Music Academy. When my mother observed his work and how it complemented my strengths, she requested he mentor me, manage my bookings, and train me. What Mummy wants, Mummy gets.

That was my life growing up. My mother was both unavailable and demanding—somehow, she pressured me to ace everything.

I didn't have the typical musician's introduction to music. At just three years old, I showed no inhibition in playing it. I never played the piano without a teacher attached, without any stage of improvisational familiarity on the keys.

As I dedicated hours to studying the piano, the intensity of my training increased. It wasn't the seductive mastering of classical music that drew me in, but the interest in connecting to the composers. At a very young age, I built up an encyclopedic knowledge and understanding of the composers' symphonies and stories. I spent my extra hours away from the piano at the library, thoroughly researching these melodies' backgrounds and understanding the stories that inspired these great compositions.

After my talents advanced, my mother's involvement increased. Her pride in my dedication was something I welcomed. At dinner parties, she would request I perform Liszt or Bach for her and her companions, disregarding the time of night. I enrolled in music schools of the highest caliber and then immediately withdrew so that I could study one-on-one with a private teacher.

If you can't tell by now, my mother is a prosperous woman. She came from money, married money, lived and breathed money. And she expects nothing less from her kids: Annie and me. She carefully handed us a remarkable quality of life. Constantly petting our egos, always encouraging us, always embedding the mentality of what it meant to be one of "The Wilsons." We could and would achieve anything, as long as we put in the hard work and effort.

My father was quite the opposite: soft and fastidious, an unpompous character. To the outside world, he held great stature. He was the co-founder of a distinguished publishing house in London, a frequent member of London's high society. Yet at home, he was just Daddy. He would find me at my piano and begin to play Chopsticks, or Heart and Soul—badly, which would lighten my mood. He was a constant that the piano should be a fun hobby, not a punishment.

When I wasn't at home, I became stripped of that reminder. So instead, I worked hard, pushed my potential, and succeeded at checking off all the boxes of my calculated bucket list of aspirations.

I replaced that paternal figure with Liam. Although, the relationship with Liam felt more authoritarian than with my father. My success was a direct result of our collaboration, his leadership. As a result of my confidence in his artistic, business, and life judgments, he told me what to do. And I obeyed.

```
2. This is probably why I find myself constantly
   trying to prove that perhaps, in some way, we are
   equals.
```

Like Liam, I aspired to conduct myself in a poised, gracious, and competent manner. Other times, I just froze and waited for him to lead the way.

In the bathroom, I tried to emulate how I wanted Liam to see me in the early morning.

Oh, this old thing? I would nonchalantly reply.

That never happened.

I had more confidence once I slipped on my cobalt blue coordinated set, more potent once I paired it with a simple monochrome stiletto. I took comfort in feeling complete and polished. The way I dressed made me feel bolder and brighter, literally and figuratively. I painted my signature cat-eye, red lip combo. I brushed my bright blond hair back with the tiniest bit of gel to ensure it wouldn't intervene with my performance. Only then did I revert to the main room.

Melodious sounds were coming from the piano. There was Liam, playing a piece I had never heard before.

"That was lovely," I said once the melody faded.

He looked up and shrugged. "Just something I wrote."

Oh, just something he wrote. How nonchalant and effortless.

* * *

The hall seemed different from the night before. The quiet eeriness of the room penetrated my skin; literal goose bumps appeared on my arms. It was what I assumed it would feel like to go back to a bar after a night of black-out drunkenness. That sensation of *Oh, right.* That happened here.

Liam jumped up onto the stage, where the rest of the orchestra began with each instrument's tweaking and tunings. He, too, examined the piano like a mechanic in a body shop.

Gradually the stillness of the silence shifted into disordered chaos. I found it fascinating how you could have a room of established musicians adjusting their instruments in a hermetically isolated manner. The noises they created resembled a child's shrieks or amateurs testing out an instrument: the shrill, off-key, anxiety-inducing sounds.

These sounds were the precursor to an incredible orchestra, and the disassembled chaos beforehand was vital to creating something great together.

"All set." Liam patted the bench, motioning for me to join.

I sat down next to him, overly conscious of my arms. I wanted to avoid our forearms touching. I always had an inner monologue in Liam's presence. I wondered if any of these thoughts were wrapped up in his brain, or was it just me?

"We don't need to do any Hanon exercises since we warmed up at the hotel. Okay, so, **Fantaisie-Impromptu**. I want to begin with the descending passage. Remember your wrist's movement and flexibility, okay? And after that, we can begin again from the start." He seemed focused.

My mind drifted back to the training as my weight settled onto to the bench.

"Cleo, we are all alone in this performance."

We. The word was small, but I treasured it.

"No orchestra, no conductor. Okay, whenever you're ready. Let's practice until perfection." The words flew out with singsong lightness, a way to ease the emphasis on demanding perfection. We both knew there wasn't a second option. Liam taught excellence, and I delivered excellence, nothing less.

        3. That may be why I find him so intimidating, where
           my need to please him originated.

In playing Chopin, I returned to the hypnotic state I experience when I play. I always brought the same passion to my rehearsals as I did to my performance. It never interfered, only enhanced them. The piano always has been and always would be my liberation. It was a channel for me to recognize my true motives and weakness. To escape yet draw in pure ecstasy. Then, in my joyous state of existence, I caught eyes with Ivan.

Almost unrecognizable with his untidy hair and informal white T-shirt and jeans. His arms were folded over his chest as he leaned against the wall, absorbed in concentration.

Had he been there the whole time? Or had he just entered? I reverted my eyes quickly, not wanting to disengage from my rehearsal.

Then the melody faded out, and the room went back to isolated chaos.

4

ART

New York City, Present Day

Every day is predictable; every day has an unwritten schedule that my family follows.

Wake up. Kids go to school. Conor goes to work. I work from home. I pick up the kids. We have dinner together, bedtime. Fewer details in between, but there is an organized structure to the day.

I generally end the evening fatigued. I alternate between lazy stay-at-home nights with Conor, reclined on the couch, catching up on old TV shows while I drift off with my thoughts. Or I join my neighbor, Diane Miller, on her rooftop with a freshly rolled joint and a glass of wine while we bitch about parenthood, our PTA requirements, and life as it is.

Then, the day comes back around, Conor is at work, the kids are at school, and I am faced again with the reality of relinquishing control over my future.

Every day I face the same realizations: I am stagnant, my work won't materialize, and I have to repeatedly give up.

There is an Albert Einstein quote about how repeating the same steps and expecting a different outcome is a sign of insanity.

Maybe I am insane. I am sitting on my veranda, listening to **Amilcare Ponchielli - Dance of the Hours**, staring at my screen and expecting progress.

I do this every day.

Starting from eight in the morning.

Same seat, another wonderful piece of music in my speakers.

Expecting a different result.

I'm insane.

The anxiety spurring through my brain, the constant heart palpitations, the thoughts of repetitive daily defeat are excruciating for me. I have always been a person with a plan. I plan, then I do. I know no other way. The pacing until I find some inspiration doesn't work anymore. The walks around Washington Square Park don't spark any interest or creativity. My life has become dull, and now it's reflected in my art.

Art. Ha.

It feels so conceited to say my writing is art. When I hear actors describe themselves as artists, I find it to be intolerable. They are not artists; they aren't the ones creating the art. They are merely pawns in the big game of chess that is their industry. It is their writers, producers, and directors who are the artists. They are the real craftsmen who guide their many puppets' strings, transforming them into little dance monkeys for everyone else's appreciation.

My writing, too, can hardly be described as art.

I am not composing music. I am not formulating poetry. I have this consequence of inspiration and then proceed with the necessary research to develop a detailed and recognizable story. Then I structure the narrative so that audiences can follow along. It doesn't feel like art to me. It feels like a distorted diary entry—a form of expressionism that would allure people's curiosities.

It is a place deep and dark in my brain, an afterthought of a story I have imagined.

I remember learning how there are about six plots expressed throughout movies and novels, and they formulate in hundreds of different arrangements. As a society, we can't see anywhere past the thick, drawn-out line of creativity. I am finding it difficult to get past that line.

As I said before, my life has grown repetitive; my day-to-day has become tedious. If I haven't found any inspiration in my past, I most definitely will not have anything to contribute from my present. Thus, writer's block.

So, what might be my premise of inspiration?

In the past, I had stories to share about my tolerated childhood. A child prodigy, a pianist, a genius. I was not too fond of that heavy burden, which I had to carry throughout most of my life. It created the need to prove everyone right. To live up to expectations.

Investing in something as a child leaves you little room for other interests. I had no desire to use up my brain's capacity on other subjects throughout my school years. I wanted to learn everything there was to know about classical music, and somehow, with that alone, I would get by in life.

I reminisce back to a time when I was in school. What I thought I wanted to be "when I grow up." Did I anticipate that I would succeed in the music industry, or did I ever show a glimmer of interest in any other field? Perhaps, deep within my heart, I enjoyed English and literature. Maybe that ultimately led me to where I am today?

Those questions were answered for me one day while I was packing up to move to New York. My mother presented me with a pile of old schoolwork. Why she still held on to it, stored away, is unbeknownst to me. I came across a folder from my prior years of English studies. I had a spark of curiosity to see how much I'd developed over the years.

I held a file with a stack of hole-punched papers. The first was titled "Othello," and underneath it, "Iago—the antagonist."

After that came scribbles and what I would only describe as some form of doodling. That's it. That was my capacity of interest in this subject. In any subject, really.

My report cards often came back with the same feedback:

Daydreamer.

Distracted.

Unwilling to try.

Didn't complete her lessons or school projects.

I was always a disciplinarian and never disrupted a class, but not participating was worse for teachers. My lack of interest or enthusiasm became so frustrating for them that eventually my mother pulled me out. She thought homeschooling was the most suitable option. I'd go for half the day, and the other half I dedicated to music at the conservatory.

I've always had a lingering feeling of what if.

```
WHAT IF:
What if I tried harder in school?
What if I stuck with music and hadn't refocused my
brain on a new career path?
What if I didn't move to New York?
What if I could do it all over again?
What if, what if, what if?
```

I often entertained those thoughts, and I despised them. *Despise* is a harsh word, yes, I know. And I stand behind that power of that feeling. It's simply not worth going there.

So, instead, I brush off those apprehensions and concerns and find ways to quiet my mind, so I can get through the day.

Today, I need that silencing. I am feeling increasingly sick with anxiety as a stabbing headache starts to form in the back of my head.

I look at my watch. I have an hour until pickup time. The countdown of my much-needed serenity is ticking away. I drew myself a bath because that's what people do to recharge and recover, right?

I find some bath salts I once received as a birthday present, probably now three years old. Do they have an expiration date?

Bath salts are always the go-to gift when you don't really know someone. These smell like lavender: lavender and defeat. I pour a ridiculous amount into the bath; it seems about right. I then light a few candles that I've neglected. They're still in their original boxes. It's almost as though I am acting the part of a person who regularly does these midday soothing bath rituals. The water is burning my skin to a red hue; I scoot down until my chin is just above water level and put on my headphones: **Strauss - The Blue Danube Waltz** plays on full volume.

5

IVAN

Moscow, Ten Years Ago

My thoughts kept drifting to Ivan after my rehearsal. I felt something energetic in his presence.

I now know why we analyze the level of chemistry we create. It is a natural chemical reaction that vibrates through us. It's not based on logic or intellect.

Ivan didn't come up to me or say hi. Just that lingering eye contact at rehearsal, and then poof! He retreated into the assembly of unknown faces frolicking about the hall.

```
WHAT IS IVAN THINKING?
1.  Maybe me averting my gaze sent a misconstrued
    message of disinterest.
2.  Perhaps he could sense the intensity burning out
    of me and Liam's insides. Like he had to wear
    flame-retardant fabric if he got too close.
```

These thoughts occupied my mind until the competition. Then the "maybe" scenarios gradually dissipated from my brain. Finally, I was able to perform with clarity, my subconscious leading the way.

Competitions were the measures you had to take to become a well-known pianist. A way to get your talents heard and seen across the world. You wore your wins as achievements of validation, propelling you further along the path of your musical career. I had been competing since I was thirteen. Many of these competitions had an age limit, so you were boxed into a time frame of when you could achieve these goals.

Yet competing never got more accessible or less nerve-racking. You still built up those jitters before each show, your arms felt like jelly from practicing for days on end, and then you were expected to play back-to-back concertos using endurance like an athlete.

Then, there's that moment when you finish. That millisecond of silence before the thunderous applause. It's like no other feeling I've ever experienced. Like you've completed a marathon, and your finish line led you to the Garden of Eden.

I survived my first performance, and now I was finding out my fate while I sat through the excruciating moments before the results were announced. I was confident I'd go through to the next round, but the thought of me leaving abruptly—the thought of this being where it all would end—was sickening. The process didn't take long, about ten- or fifteen-minutes total, but the anticipation was dreadful. I tried to sit patiently while I evened out my breath and waited for the presenter (Russian) then the translator (an English-speaking Russian) to announce the finalists.

"The artist who will pass to the second round are as follows."

I concentrated so hard, as though I would not know my outcome if I took my mind off the presenter's words. It was alphabetized, so I wouldn't know until the last minute.

Then, the anticipated announcement: "Cleo Wilson, United Kingdom." I finally let out an exhale—a sigh of relief. Liam patted my back in a paternal way. Then we both cowered, caught off guard, as a loud whistle sounded from the back of the hall, then a cheer ensued. A few chuckles followed as I drew my attention to the sounds.

"Yeah, Cleo!" It was Ivan, clapping and cheering.

I immediately looked up at Liam's face. He seemed unimpressed with the unnecessary disruption. A soft laugh escaped my lips. It was nice having a cheerleader. Even though I wasn't sure how genuine it might be—I'd just met the guy— I could pretend for a little while that he cared. Like he knew what winning would mean to me, so therefore he honestly wanted me to exceed. I wasn't sure I had anyone who truly cared if I won a competition or succeeded in accomplishing any of my goals.

```
WHO CARES IF I WIN:
1.  Liam cared, though I suspect he had a clutch of
    underlying selfishness. He wanted me to do well
    because it was his job.
2.  My mother wanted me to do well so that she had a
    daughter who was spectacular at something.
3.  My dad wanted me to be happy; if I was happy
    playing the piano, he was content.
4.  My younger sister possessed no interest in what I
    did musically. She was your typical, run-of-the-
    mill, London-raised lass. Into boys, parties, and
    drinking; her main goal being whatever brought her
    joy at that moment. My victories would have no
    effect on her life.
5.  So too for my friends. They had that same
    indifferent feeling toward me and my recitals.
    When I was working toward my next goal, I'd
    disappear for the next few months, but going on
    with their lives seemed unchallenging.
```

It must be extraordinary to find someone who understands what it takes to succeed, someone who shares your ambition.

As my mind came back from its continuous reflections, I quickly noticed everyone gathering their belongings and saying their final goodbyes.

"All right, I'll bring the car around." Liam stood up as he buttoned up his blazer.

"You know what?" I was uncertain how to continue after seeing Liam's astonishment at my spontaneity. "I, uh, think I will stay a bit…and schmooze," I said unconvincingly while I gestured my arms around to virtually nobody.

"Are you sure?" It was an embarrassing account of my desperation.

What did Liam think? That I thought my "colleagues" were here to hang out with me? Or did he see right through my bullocks and know I would seek that one noisy Russian who showed a glimpse of interest? Regardless, my entire being was immersed in this uncomfortable situation.

"Oh, okay." He slowly turned around, took a few steps away, then leveled back to me. "Don't forget, we will need to rehearse tomorrow morning. So try not to schmooze for too long, okay?" He placed emphasis on *schmooze*. He winked before he wandered off toward the exit. I was unsure if it was a playful, teasing kind of wink or a more patronizing, ok-sure-enjoy-your-schmooze wink.

I rolled my eyes as he left. What was my plan exactly? What if Ivan already left? The announcements concluded; he had no reason to wait around. But now Liam left, and I was alone.

It was not a thought-out plan. I was contemplating my alternatives. I had been indoors almost all day and had no idea what the weather was like outside. So, if the wind wasn't achingly brisk, I could tolerate the roughly fifteen-minute walk to my hotel. I hadn't had a chance to check out Moscow. Maybe this walk would be the opportunity I fancied.

I prepared by covering my mini pink jacquard dress with a matching coat and changing from heels to trainers, hoping that this would suffice.

Outside hit me in the face with an icy blow of reality.

Bloody hell. I felt like crying. This walk was going to be a long, excruciating fifteen minutes. Where was Liam when I needed him?

"Waiting for car again?"

I jumped. "Oh gosh!" That damn unanticipated greeting.

It was Ivan, of course.

"You've got to stop scaring me like that, Ivan." I held on to my heart as I forced it back to normal tempo.

"Do people not come to say hi to you?"

"No, not really. Not here, at least." The sad truth. "I am actually walking home tonight. I thought I might get a chance to take in a bit of Russia."

"You chose a night to walk home." He referred to the icy breeze that currently besieged us, although he did not seem to shiver in the slightest in his crisp suit and shirt, which was unbuttoned maybe one too many, while his black tie fell loosely around his collar.

"You are not staying at Marriott?" Ivan asked.

"Hotel Metropol."

"Ah, only the best!"

"I don't expect anything but the best."

"You are getting Russian royal treatment."

"So I have been told."

"Executive suite?"

"Ambassador."

He let out an impressed "Pssh." And then, "Look at you."

"Well, there was no way I could stay in a room without a piano." *Or with a roommate,* I thought. Liam made sure to take care of that small detail for me.

"Of course."

It went silent as we stood there smiling. Even with Ivan's heavy Russian accent and broken English, we could exchange conversation effortlessly.

"Can I walk? Through Teatralnaya Square, it is…ah, not, uh, shortcut, but nice walk."

"Sure." The directions failed to register with me.

He grabbed my shoes and bag from my arms and nodded his head in the right direction.

"So, Ivan. What brings you to the conservatory tonight? Your results were already announced yesterday, no?" I asked, trying not to be too presumptuous.

"Well, I wanted to see if you went to the next round." It was the answer I was hoping for but didn't expect. I felt my face heat up and reverted my gaze to the ground.

When I couldn't say anything, Ivan spoke again. "How are you enjoying the competition so far?"

"It is kind of chaotic. I wasn't expecting that."

"Kay-oh-teck?" He annunciated, as though learning a new word.

"A bit disorganized, if I'm being honest. Not what I'm used to in previous competitions."

"And you don't like this, des-organ-eized."

"Eh," I said in a high pitch, which made Ivan laugh.

"Okay, so, Cleo, tell me about yourself." A broad question. Where to start?

"Well, I'm from London. I have a younger sister, Annie. She has nothing to do with classical music. No one in my family does. But I've played the piano since I was three…" I was boring myself with the lack of enthusiasm I put into the factual list that was my life.

"Three? Wow."

"How about you? Did you also start at a young age?" Quickly, I shifted the focus back to him.

"Not three, but six, seven? I start playing the harp my mother had at her job. She is a server at a restaurant. I would go with her to work and always run toward the harp. I sit there for hours and hours. With my little fingers, making these sounds. Then, they got piano. I love to go to her work. I taught myself how to, uh, make up a few songs on the piano."

He spoke with such passion, such animation, such nostalgia.

"How did you end up with the violin?"

"I always loved strings, you know? How it sounds so effortless and peaceful." He mimicked the bow of the violin. "The harp became still for me, yeah? So, I say to my mother, 'Mama, I want to play the violin.' She said, 'Of course, Vanya,' and she made my father sell his father's watch. You know, we were poor. This was the only expensive object we have. My parents know this was something I wanted so bad. For life."

A sense of envy crept up on me. These were the stories you heard from many skilled musicians. A road of vitality and determination that brought them to their most significant potential. My success came too easily. It would be unfair for me to complain about not having struggled, about missing out on the dramatic turmoil that most musicians face. It would only come across as bratty and pretentious. My mum gave me a piano, and I excelled at playing. I started competing. I've won every competition thus far.

"Cleo, do you have any other, uh, thing you like to do for fun?" There was this thing that happened to my heart every time he said my name—a little flutter.

"Hobbies?"

Ivan nods, "*dah*, yes, hobbies."

"Um…" *Sound interesting, Cleo.* My mind remained blank.

"Art? Dancing? Going to theater?"

"Well, sure…" By not giving an honest answer, maybe I'd avoid the need to elaborate.

"Okay." He smiled. "What about music?"

He was not giving up, huh?

"Well, yeah," I laughed, somewhat perplexed. "I kind of like music."

"I know, but do you like listening to other music? Pop, rock, R&B?"

"Sure."

"You don't talk a lot, do you?"

"I do, just… Yeah, I listen to a variety of music. What kind of music do you like?" Again, deflecting.

"Okay, I have idea." Ivan stopped and turned his body toward mine. "I want to take you somewhere special."

"Okay…" I hesitated.

"It's very, very close. And after, I will walk you back to hotel."

"Okay," I repeated. "Where to?"

"No questions. *Davai*, come with me."

6

THE BIG MOVE

New York City, Present Day

I slowly inhale a gulp of water that wakes me right up. The suffocation of drowning causes a coughing fit as I spit it right out. The water is now lukewarm.

Oh no!

How long have I been in this bath? I stand up and notice my earbud has fallen into the bathtub.

Shit! I grab it and pat it with a hand towel. I throw a larger towel under my arms and grab my phone.

Shit!

It's 4:35. Pickup was at 4:00.

There are many missed calls and voice mails from the kids' school, and one from Conor.

"Arrrgh!" My throat strains as I let out a primal scream, the anguished cry filling the air. Without hesitation, I lash out at the cursed porcelain tub with an impulsive kick. As searing pain shoots through my foot, I clench my teeth, swallowing the urge to give in to it. I hop back into my room as I find the closest outfit to throw on: a wrinkled T-shirt, black leggings, and trainers. An oversized trench conceals the mess underneath, and I run out of the apartment.

Running for pleasure is biomechanically different than running with purpose. My chest aches as the icy air numbs my insides, and somehow, I am at the same time sweating. The school is merely three blocks away from where I live; nevertheless, the adrenaline pumping in my veins causes a visceral reaction.

The school grounds are bare. Is everyone else on time and well-adjusted? I make my way to the principal's office. That dreaded room, where the delinquents were to pick up their neglected children as the faculty and staff judge the lack of respect we have for their time.

"Sorry! I'm here!" I come in loud and apologetic.

"Cleo." I hear Conor's voice hiss at me.

Shit, Conor got here before me.

He seems a bit taken aback by my appearance. I probably resemble a damp and unkempt dog. My hair is knotted and wet. My clothes, now not so hidden beneath my coat, display patches of bathwater as they cling to my body. I self-consciously cover up and continue to apologize.

"I. Am. So. Sorry, Conor," I begin. "And to you, of course." I address a stern Principal Howard with my palms pressed against one another. Her frigid, icy manner always seems to frighten me. I hug my kids. "I'm sorry, you guys! I will not be late again!" I collectively reassure everyone.

"I…long story…" I'm not sure how to explain myself.

Conor gestures for me to stop. My telepathic abilities know he is screaming, *'let's discuss this at home, away from everyone.'* Conor is not one for showcasing any kind of behind-closed-doors family drama.

"Sorry again, Principal Howard. Okay, kids. Let's go home."

I walk home in silence. Conor does too. I could bless the kids and their every-detailed recount of the day for killing the silence between the adults. I know Conor is fuming inside.

He waits until the kids are quietly in bed to finally ask me:

"What the hell is going on here, Cleo!"

"I-I am not sure what happened," I stammer as I help clean off the dining room table. The kids are finally fast asleep, and I have been playing out this conversation repeatedly for hours. I seem to be more eloquent in my brain. Once the words come out, I have nothing substantial to say.

"I was taking a bath—"

"A bath?" The thought that I would take a bath alone caught Conor off guard.

"I know… I don't know, I… I needed to get work done. It—nothing was coming to me." I am stuttering and trying to make sense of it all. "I thought a bath might help. I guess I just fell asleep." I cringe at the thought of my drying earbud sitting on the towel next to the sink. I make a mental note to buy a new pair tomorrow.

"They called me at work."

"I know…"

"They said they tried you, but you wouldn't answer."

"I know."

"I was with a patient, Cleo. You know how I only answer the phone for emergencies? I was feckin' petrified by the thought of what might have happened."

"I'm am so sorry, Conor, really."

He is pissed, understandably. He demonstrates patience, but with an articulation that lets me know this was not okay. It's the downside of marrying a psychiatrist. He is so great with his words; it's annoying. Having knowledge and awareness of the human psyche gives him a leg up in all our arguments. It can almost feel a little manipulative if you ask me. Why can't he just shout and get pissed like the rest of us? Show some unexplained frustration and aggression?

"I know; I promise it won't happen again." I am more than happy to avoid the bath at all costs. That bloody thing didn't give me any sense of peaceful recovery anyway.

"Good." And that was it. That settled this conversation. No lingering passive aggressiveness or silent treatment. We'll go back to being that annoyingly happy couple.

I sit across from Conor.

We are both on our laptops.

He, finishing some work.

Me, trying to force inspiration via the sounds of **Franz Schubert - Serenade** in my ears. The bent-out-of-shape wires cause a minor panic attack, but I close my eyes and let my fingers hover over the keyboard.

I make another mental reminder that Tomorrow, I'll buy new wireless headphones.

I open my eyes again and feel a warmth form in my chest when I catch a glimpse of Conor.

My relationship with Conor has been perpetually easy from the get-go. The issue is: I don't do well with easy. It, ironically, gets me on edge, but I also find that chaos spirals me toward anxiety. There doesn't seem to be a winning situation for me.

To be fair, I have felt anxious about everything lately. The way Conor clears his throat All. The. Time. The sounds of the kids slurping their cereals, or shouting as they play on the veranda, the uproar that breaks loose at home. These are everyday noises, yet I have to block them out constantly. Each sound is nails on the chalkboard for me.

It's unfair for me to complain; I know this. My kids are well-adjusted. Conor is a gem. I feel this terrible sense of unwelcomeness when I find myself in the deep waters of depression. Like I did not earn these feelings, like I may take up space from somebody who actually deserves their depression. Conor is the reason for my happiness and the root of the guilt about my depression. Is it unfair for me to feel down when I have been so lucky in life? Was I lucky? I suppose it depends on the angle from which you look at it.

I used to think I was.

After I turned twenty-eight, I met Conor, which seemed pretty lucky.

The night we first met was quite serendipitous. Conor and I, sitting alone at opposite ends of the long granite bar. The two of us drowning our pities in syrup-heavy cocktails, as you do in response to being stood up. It was a dimly lit bar overlooking Hyde Park; it felt sumptuous and lush. I felt dizzy and pissed off. I had committed to a night out with a stranger, which I would never give the time of day, and now this?

Conor must have sensed my aggression, so, naturally, being the empathic psychiatrist, his reflex was to comfort me, the distressed lady sitting by herself.

He was charming and attentive as I released my frustration over two more sugary drinks. I could see why he was successful in his career. He had an altruistic sense of ability that allowed me to open up, which I usually resist. Maybe it was because he was a stranger and I owed him nothing. No apologies, no reason.

Maybe it was because he was incredibly handsome, seven years my senior, successful, and communicated a genuine interest in what I had to say. You could tell right away that his eyes were kind and his smile trustworthy. Those weren't character traits I encountered often.

I'd gone on countless blind dates that year—blind and forced—and never got past the second date. Friends or family members often configured these dates; anyone who felt distress about me being single in my late twenties. God forbid!

This date was different; it felt pure and delightful and, might I add, voluntary. There was no predisposed notion of who we were going to meet. We had no time to act restrained or over evaluate the conversation. It felt like we were "just going with the flow." That was something unfamiliar to me.

Conor rescued me from all my troubles and worries as soon as I confided in him. And, for the first time, I let go of my identity as a musician and was able to be myself completely.

So, I suppose my luck was confirmed when I dodged a date with a belligerent human being and found Conor instead. You would assume that I could hold on to that luck, but when I met Conor, I had to start all over again.

I am not a well-known, skilled pianist anymore; those days are behind me.

The harrowing experience of pivoting when life presented caveats has left a lasting effect.

At first, I was determined. I dedicated countless years working my way up, interning, editing, publishing essays, and getting one published book under my belt. The choice to leave my father's company and move on with Ramona in New York felt validating. Like I'd made the right decision. And then, suddenly, the decline began. I was suffocating and deteriorating at work. The pressure to force my way out of this thing I called a "funk" or "just a phase" felt like walking through molasses.

Conor reassured me that this was just part of the ups and downs of life, that the move to New York was not a mistake. He was more than okay with the change of location from the beginning. When we first met, Conor explained how it was almost a tradition for men in their twenties to leave Ireland and make a life for themselves elsewhere, which was when I knew to grab hold of him and anchor him in England.

He also explained how they would then go back to Ireland after establishing a clear life path, to live near their parents. It seemed backward to me. How do you set yourself up, commit to a life, and then transport it back to square one? It seemed illogical.

But Conor is the one who manages to balance an organized and repetitive system while adjusting to life's events at any given time. He proved this the day I got the call from Ramona and plans shifted.

"Why not just move to New York? There are so many more opportunities here."

I was intrigued by her hypothetical proposition. Finally, I found my excuse, my escape. "Really? Should I?" Could I?

The minute Ramona saw my interest, she perked up. "Oh, absolutely!" She listed the many reasons writers move to New York City. She told me she could connect me with her network to help strengthen my career.

At first, I felt reluctant to tell Conor. I knew he would agree to whatever I chose, so I decided to contemplate the idea for a week.

Eventually, I knew it was time to share the news. As expected, Conor almost immediately jumped out of his seat, grabbed my hands, and shouted, "If you think this will benefit your career, then of course you must take it! You rarely get opportunities like these."

His reaction blindsided me. Yes, there is being supportive, but this?

I can't say I would have supported the idea if Conor were on the receiving side. I questioned every possibility about this move to New York. It would be my first time living outside of London. Yes, I'd traveled to numerous countries, but never for longer than two months.

```
RESERVATIONS ABOUT MOVING TO NY:
1.  Making new friends
2.  Finding a new hairdresser
```

```
3.  Searching for new favorite cafés or dining spots
4.  Would Conor move his practice to New York?
5.  Will he be able to continue his success?
6.  The visa application alone will be torturous
```

"You have a great opportunity; everything else will follow." This sentiment was repeated to me endlessly until I made my final decision.

Ten years and three kids later, we are all still living here in New York.

So this is where I am now.

Still absent the second of a two-book contract.

The downward trajectory is painfully apparent, infuriating, and mortifying.

It is now evident; my luck has subsided.

"All right, I'm all done. You?"

I blink and see my surroundings.

A blank screen stands before me.

"Yeah." I shut my laptop. "I'm done."

7

UNPREDICTABILITY
AND MONOTONY

New York City, Present Day

The following week forces me back to predictable monotony: no baths, no late pickups, no pissed-off husband, and no development on the work front. I am like any old stay-at-home mum without a career—except I don't cook, do laundry, or clean. Instead, I pay for a housekeeper and takeout. On the weekends, Conor—good ol' perfect Conor—whips up an impressive garlic and herb-infused chicken roast or some other tasty trick he had up his sleeve. No complaints here, but it highlights my lack of purpose.

I feel burdened with this love-hate relationship between unpredictability and monotony. I thrive at maintaining the habitual livelihood I designed, but the notion of becoming dictated by your everyday routine disturbs me. I find it both boring and necessary.

It is pretty apparent that I don't have a clear understanding of my actual desires.

For almost three decades, I had just one path I needed to follow, just one goal: to be the best pianist. This meant participating in competitions or featuring at prominent halls and arenas.

As a result of reaching my goals, I would find myself stuck in the perpetual state of a dog chasing its tail. It was a tantalizing experience for me, being unable to reach the point of total satisfaction.

It is almost as if I have expected the achievement to bring me satisfaction. But I passed that finish line. I achieved my life's purpose, and then: the comedown.

Depression is real for overachievers. You set goals in hopes that they might change something inside of you monumentally. They, of course, don't. The sense of accomplishment never really happens; it only recoils.

So I gave it all up. I said goodbye to my piano, and I haven't looked back.

The only way is forward, right? I'm trying; I really am. I set a follow-up meeting with Ramona to "see where my book is progressing."

Somehow, I have to create pen-on-paper magic in a week. However, there is a slight dilemma: I will never submit work I don't absolutely love.

The sounds of my phone vibrating bring my mind back to the present. Many writers suggest keeping all distractions away to stay in that writing zone. Like most of society, I need my phone; it has become my security blanket. If it's not in reach, my concentration gets stuck on *but what if someone wants to get ahold of me? What if the one time I place my phone in the other room is the time I get that call telling me my child has somehow ended up in the hospital? That Conor has been in a car accident? That my agent needs me?*

I look at my phone; it's Diane. Calling me from upstairs in the penthouse. She lives there with her husband, Eric, a stock market investor, and their daughter, Kitty. They were our first acquaintances when we moved to New York. Diane and I got pregnant at the same time (her with Kitty, me with Olivia). Kitty and Olivia have been great friends since birth, and Diane is really the only person I get along with here. Eric, on the other hand…well, let's just say we tolerate Eric.

Conor is more adaptable than I am. He can make conversation with a hooligan if it's the polite thing to do. I need a little more alcohol to get me through the fraudulent smiles and nods of agreement while Eric goes on about his investments. You can smell the desperation oozing from his pores. He needs to talk about how much he earns and parade his fancy cars and extravagant parties. He boasts about his trophy wife (whom he drips in diamonds and head-to-toe designer) not needing to work a day in her life.

All of it seems contrived and performative.

"Hey, girl!" Diane sings through my speakerphone.

"Hey!" I try to match her tone.

"What have you been up to?" She speaks to me like we're sitting there on our couches, a few levels apart, just *chilling*.

I admire how Diane doesn't succumb to the pressure of hustle culture, and I don't say that condescendingly—I genuinely am jealous.

"Oh, you know, writing," I lie. I haven't written a word in weeks.

"Right! Your novel! How is it coming along?"

"I mean, great! It's been busy these past few weeks," I lie again.

"That's awesome; I can't wait to read it! Anyway."

Sometimes it sounds as though Diane's animated vernacular is on autopilot. Like she knows the words to say without attention or substance, and I think I am okay with that. She never asks nosy, uncomfortable questions. Diane always holds up her side of the conversation, so I don't need to. The juxtaposition of our personalities is why we get along so well.

"So I would love it if you guys can come by for dinner one night this week. We haven't hung out in ages! It would just be me, you, Eric, and Conor."

Shit! I hate these dinners. While it's nice to spend the evening with Diane, alone, it is insufferable to hear about Eric's life for the duration of the meal.

"No, we must have you here. We always go to you. Let me return the favor." Now it's my turn for respectful autopilot gibberish. I try to shut up; I do.

"Oh no, you shouldn't, really."

"Sure?" It comes out like a question.

"Oh yay! That would be so fun! That's one day of cooking I can now check off the to-do list!"

Shit! I wasn't planning on cooking, but the effort to get out the fine china and disguise takeout as my own creation is a job in itself.

"Yay!" I repeat, dying on the inside.

"Okay, so how is Thursday night for you? Eight-ish?" I can picture Diane writing this down in her Smythson daily planner.

"Eight-ish is perfect," I say as I simultaneously compose a text to Conor:

I just invited the Millers for dinner Thursday at 8:00. Sorry!

Only one tick appears next to the text, signifying Conor's busy schedule. He'll read it when he has a chance.

I say my goodbyes, with an exaggerated "Yay! I can't wait!" and throw the phone onto the bench next to me.

Okay, so now I have something to do this Thursday. The dread creeps up. It isn't exclusively the meal that stresses me out. Agreeing to host this meal means today and tomorrow are the only days I have this week to create some magic and write something, anything. I need to bring something to my meeting with Ramona. Anything.

I look back at my screen, chew my lip for a moment, then close the computer and let out a moan.

* * *

Thursday comes too quickly. No, I don't get any work done, and yes, I must dedicate a whole Thursday to prepare for this meal.

Wine fridge stocked? Check.

Appetizers from Louis Steakhouse? Check

Main meal and dessert from The Polo? Check.

Porcelain tableware trimmed with floral designs, crystal glasses, and a barely used jacquard tapestry runner? Check.

I pour myself a hefty glass of wine. A pregame if you will. Conor still isn't home from work. I look at my phone. 7:45.

Shit, Conor, where are you?

I look at my reflection in the mirror one more time. It seems silly, dressing up so fancy in my own home, but Diane does it all the time, down to the six-inch heels and over-the-top accessories. I couldn't fathom going for heels at home. I am a tall five feet seven, giving me the leeway to feel put together in flats.

Tonight I found a dress deep in the ends of my closet, still wrapped in plastic, with tags attached—a white mini wraparound with a plunging neckline that reveals my bony chest. I figured it was composed enough to match whatever fancy ensemble Diane would show up in, but minimal in a way that suggests I just threw it on last minute. I pair it with my brand new, crystal-embellished flats, still in the box, a red lipstick, and then struggle with my hair. I still haven't gotten my roots touched up, so I gel it back in a tight, low bun, hoping it won't attract attention. I play the romantic sounds of **Khachaturian - Masquerade Suite**, on our turntable. The music relieves my anticipation of tension that will yet occur.

In an anxious state, you plan ahead by default—there is always a future perspective.

A depressive mindset makes you dwell on your past.

My present self remains elusive to me. I have never felt content in the present. There is always a feeling of restlessness.

I am interrupted by the sound of the door slamming and the clattering of keys hitting the table.

"Sorry I'm so late!" Conor looks flushed, briefcase in hand, as he reaches over and kisses my cheek, barely grazing it. "Well, aren't you looking nice!" He gives me a quick once over.

"Hey, don't seem too surprised." I wink and smile back. I have the most challenging time accepting compliments, even from Conor. I always reciprocate with a witty or sarcastic remark.

"Do I have time for a shower? Do I smell?" Conor sniffs his suit jacket.

I look at the oven clock: 7:59. They said eight-ish. Does that mean eight or eight-thirty?

"It's fine, and you don't smell." I take out the grilled artichoke and risotto with crispy mushrooms from the oven. "Just maybe change out of your suit?"

"Can I get away with joggers?"

I give him a death stare.

"Okay, I would never." He holds his hands up in surrender, then reaches one arm to the tray and stuffs a roasted mushroom into his mouth.

"Hey!" I slap him, then get startled by the sound of the doorbell.

"What? They are here already?"

Shit! Apparently eight-ish means eight on the dot. It's as if they were standing outside, counting down the milliseconds. "Go get changed. I'll entertain them." I hurry to the door. "But be quick!" I shout in a whisper, hoping that he heard me and the Millers did not.

I take a big inhale, then open the door.

"Hi!" I plant my most convincing smile across my face and welcome them inside.

"Hey, babe!" Diane gives me a tight squeeze. As expected, she is dressed to the nines. An Alessandra Rich floral print minidress with a twill Chelsea collar. Her blond hair looks freshly blown out, falling just below her shoulders. Her large brown eyes and petite frame gave her a youthful appearance. Even though she's a year older than me, I resemble her older, ragged sister.

Eric then grants me a courteous kiss on the cheek. Actual lips on the cheek action, not the dramatic air kiss I would have much preferred.

I wipe my cheek with my palm as they both help themselves to the lounge area.

Eric is significantly taller than Diane as he walks in, chest first, demanding authority.

They make a beautiful couple.

He dresses in meticulous detail, keeps his beard neatly trimmed, and has almost-black, intense eyes. He may be handsome, but his knowledge of that ruins it for me.

"Conor is just getting ready. Can I get you both something to drink? Wine? Scotch?"

"Oh no, I'm going sober," Diane starts. "We want to try for baby number two." She pats her imaginary fetus and smiles up at Eric. He looks at me and says, "Scotch."

Sir, yes, sir.

I have a chance to devour another long gulp of red wine in the kitchen. Thankfully, that's when Conor decides to grace us with his presence.

"Conor!" Eric bellows, exposing his frat-boy persona. "How are you, my man?" I roll my eyes, praying he won't wake up my kids. Or that he does. Kids are always a great reason to excuse oneself.

One more gulp of my red wine, and I come back with Eric's tumbler.

The night proceeds as follows:

Eric raves about the status of his stocks, the amount of money he made just by sitting here with us at dinner, the new earrings he surprised Diane with today (interesting timing).

Diane mostly lets Eric do the talking. She says things like, "I love what you have done with this space," I have not changed anything since she was over last. She says, "You are looking so great these days; what is your trick?" Forgetting to eat and running off adrenaline.

Then they let us in on details of her preconception plans and provide intimate details I did not need to know about her and Eric's sex life.

Conor seems to be enjoying these conversations, or he's a great actor. I catch his eye, and he sends over telepathic waves of *Please shoot me.* I smile back, happy that I'm not alone in this.

I feel a foot creep up my leg, and I smile again at Conor.

Naughty, naughty. I try to telepathically flirt back, then I suddenly realize it's not Conor's foot but Eric's. *Shit, he probably thinks he got Diane's leg.*

I try not to make eye contact as I pivot my legs under my chair. I look up, and Eric is staring right at me with a cunning smirk on his face. My body goes cold.

Oh no.

Please let this gesture not be intentional.

I quickly stand up. "Is everyone done?" I grab my plate. "No rush, of course," I add, hoping they disregard that last remark. Please, rush out. I think I've hit my capacity.

"Let me help." It's Eric.

"No, no. Please, I got this!" Please, no.

"Oh, let him help!" Diane pleads "It's the least we can do!" She says this as though it's a joint effort. I stop debating and pile on the plates. Eric follows me to the kitchen with a few empty dishes.

I start to rinse the plates in the sink, hoping he'll return to the table so I can stay a little longer to get a much-needed gulp of wine from the glass I left in the kitchen.

"Here, I can take over," Eric says from behind me, way too close.

"No, no, I got this," I insist.

Eric ignores me and continues to "help" as he takes the dishes from my hands and places them into the dishwasher.

"Well, Cleo, that chicken dish was incredible. I never knew you were so good in the kitchen." Eric's eyes remain fixed on me. "It makes me wonder what other tricks you have hidden from me."

"Um, Eric, go back to the table." I try to come off friendly, but it's getting impossible. "We have more scotch there if you like." He does not need more liquid courage, but I'll do anything to shoo this sleaze away from the kitchen. There is not a world in which Eric is helping without the goal of profit. There's always an ulterior motive.

"Uh-oh. Are you trying to get rid of me, Cleo?" he asks with a slurred voice and a mischievous grin. Leaning in too close, he sways gently, dilated pupils betraying his intoxicated state. His unkempt hair falls messily over his forehead, and he brushes it back with a shaky hand.

Yes, I want to answer, but instead I just laugh.

"Okay, fine." He wipes his hands on the dish towel, then tightly squeezes my shoulders and rubs my arms.

Ew.

"Let me know if you want any more help," he whispers. A lip touches my ear.

I drop the plates in subliminal reaction.

The crashing sound gets the attention of the spouses in the next room.

"Honey, are you okay?" It's Conor.

"Shit." I notice my finger has a shard of glass in it. I pick it out, and the blood starts pouring. I guess this is the last time I'll be using the only-for-occasions china.

"I'm fine," I shout back.

Eric rips off a paper towel and holds it tight on my finger.

"Here," he says, squeezing. I jerk back; his existence alone brings on this visceral reaction.

"I got this," I reassure him.

Conor and Diane come in to see what's going on.

"Hold it tight; hold your arm over your head." Eric comes closer and pulls my arm over my head.

"I GOT THIS!" I scream—loudly, I presume, judging from the perplexed expressions staring back at me.

I finally got their attention.

"I'm good! Okay?" I compose myself. "Please, go back to the dining room, and I'll bring out dessert."

Flustered but obliged, the Millers exit.

Conor, thankfully, stays with me in the kitchen and helps clean up the glass from the sink.

"What was that all about?" he questions, attempting a whisper.

"Oh god." I know I can't possibly speak just yet, but I am itching to. "I'll tell you after."

Conor looks confused, but he knows it's best to finish dinner and see our guests out.

The moment they leave, I wait a polite five minutes and then explode.

"Oh. My. Gosh!" I shout in a mock whisper.

"What happened, Cleo?"

I recline my body across the couch like a woman in a Renaissance painting, theatrical and buoyant.

"What are the chances of us moving?" I ask, half joking.

Conor laughs, and I feel his weight drop down beside me on the couch. His closeness shows me that he is ready to talk. "Really, what happened?"

"Eric is just…" I can't find the right words to describe him. I dramatically shiver my body in disgust.

"What did he say?"

I look up at Conor, his dark hair falling into those innocent blue eyes. He wouldn't hurt a fly, let alone aggressively harass my friends.

I tell him everything. From the footsie we played under the table to the rubbing of my shoulders in the kitchen.

"It's not normal, right?" I ask. "Like, I have a right to think that's strange, no?"

Conor's face is still in disbelief. "No, absolutely!" He rubs his palm against his clean-shaven jaw. "And she was just talking about trying to get pregnant!"

"Um, hello!" I sit up and hit Conor enthusiastically in conversation. "Did you see how handsy they were all dinner long?"

"So gross," Conor agrees.

I love him for that. I'm not sure if it's the lack of physical touch I received in my youth or an obvious distinction between Americans and Europeans: they don't seem repulsed by public displays of affection, which always seemed to me like desperate acts of proving the strength of your relationship.

I finally speak. "So should I say something to Diane?"

"Uh, I don't know. It seems like a kill-the-messenger kind of situation. Do you really want to get involved?"

"I mean, I would want to know if you ever did anything like that behind my back."

"I would never." Conor smiles reassuringly with a pat on the lap.

"Sounds like you're missing out."

"I mean, I would, but you know." He weighs his hands in contemplation as he continues the charade. "Between work and home, I don't really have the time."

"Well, I heard Diane is in heat. If you're on the prowl, she's just upstairs."

Conor throws a decorative pillow at me and laughs. "You nutter."

"Yes, but I'm your nutter." I laugh and throw the pillow back.

Thank God for Conor. In my chaotic life and brain, he is the calm.

8

TWO GUITARS

Moscow, Ten Years Ago

Listening to Ivan speak was a great distraction from the wind that was penetrating my fur coat. He talked with his hands, waving them around, demanding his space. He could have been talking about metaphysics or epistemology and it would have still been entertaining. He was only two years younger than I was, but his character took off another five years. He was youthful and uncomplicated.

He went on about his childhood, and I learned we shared a common trait. He, too, made music the center of his attention, disregarding all other classes on his curriculum.

"Although, I did want to be an architect if this didn't work out," he said.

I didn't have an if-this-didn't-work-out plan. I was relying on this working out.

It was only five minutes before we got to a pedestrian zone; the deeper we proceeded, the louder the electronic bass reverberated.

There were crowds as if it were the middle of the day. At first, it seemed like anywhere in London. It could have been Oxford Street, lined with Zaras and Cartiers, bars and eateries. But there was something distinctive, something special. It was the music, the people, the lights. It was like a festival, a celebration of some sort, but something made me believe that this was a natural occurrence, just your regular Moscow Tuesday.

"Welcome to Kuznetsky Most Street." Ivan walked backward in front of me with his hands in the air. We were face-to-face. "One of the oldest streets here in Russia!"

I didn't say anything. Just stared, wide-eyed, capturing the moment like a kid's first amusement park or an adult's first high.

"The most incredible musicians come out and play here, for no other reason but to share their sounds."

How poetic.

We dined at a local bar where we indulged in a couple of Russian delicacies (*pelmeni, blini, and piroshki*), and I had my first shot of authentic Russian vodka.

Then we made our way out to experience the sounds of these musicians.

Ivan drew me into a crowd, an audience relishing an old couple performing folk music with nothing but a balalaika and a microphone.

They sang words I didn't understand, but I recognized the notes of romanticism.

"This is very romantic song," Ivan stated.

Aha! I'd guessed correctly. These musicians expressed sentiments of love by lyrical magic, by the way the audience took to the music. You don't have to define love or romance through a mutual understanding of language; that much is clear. Passion reveals itself in a multitude of ways. In art or music, in proximity, body language, or facial recognition. You are not required to verbalize how you feel with solely the use of words.

"It is called **Millions of Red Roses**." He spoke close to my ear. "About an artist who tried to win over the heart of a lady. She loved roses, so he sold his art and his home for an ocean of millions of roses."

"Wow, that's intense." People romanticized extremities into something noble and honorable. I viewed them as barbaric and useless.

"Yes, but the sad part of the song? They don't end up together, so now he is alone, with nothing but a million roses."

"Not such a romantic song, if you ask me. More of a tragedy."

"I still think it is romantic." Ivan shrugged. "However the ending might be."

The mood changed as the couple shifted to something more upbeat. Ivan gave me another courteous explanation at the start of each song.

"This song is very patriotic, also a bit romantic, about a lady whose loved one is going off to war." - **Katyusha.**

"This song is a love poem by Yevhen Hrebinka." - **Ochi Chernye, dark eyes.**

"This song is about a man, he's hungover, and two gypsies are playing music. He is hurting and telling them, *Ekh raz esho raz*—sing again and again. Music will help with these sufferings. Drinking less won't help, but music, music is like a Band-Aid." - **Dve Gitary. Two Guitars.**

I could relate to that sentiment.

I looked up at Ivan as he concluded his explanation and tensely watched the performers. He'd never left Russia, and now I could see why. He didn't need the culture of any other country in the world. It was all right here in his backyard.

There was such passion coming from his upbringing, his traditions. He was genuinely happy with the life laid out for him.

Now the crowd chimed in and sang along, Ivan included. Everyone clapped to the melody; some whistled loudly.

"*Ekh raz esho raz,*" the audience vocalized.

It was as though they were all in this musical production together. There was no focused attention on one performer, but, rather, a celebration, an integrated experience.

Ivan linked his arm into mine for a dance, and I immediately declined. He shrugged it off, so I nodded my head and clapped along, keeping seemingly preoccupied to avoid any other offers. The other audience members, however, partnered up and joined in solidarity.

This was a moment of true happiness.

We made it to my hotel room. I didn't notice how close it was to this outside party. When would I be able to return to this moment again? Finals were getting closer by the minute.

"Thanks for tonight," I started to say, in a predictable and cheesy manner.

Time stood still by my door—I lost all feeling in my fingers as I grasped my keycard.

I was wondering if it was too forward to let him in, or if it was the perfect opportunity. I could butcher this moment or allow something extraordinary to pass me by.

What was the proper Russian etiquette here?

"Of course, Cleo." He held a sheepish smile across his face, his one dimple visible on his cheek. Perfect teeth, perfect face.

Time passed by slowly as I faced the door, tapping the card to the handle.

I turned back. To say goodbye? To say come in? I wasn't sure.

A little air left my body as Ivan took one step closer. His large hands covered my cheeks, and there, in front of my room, he finally took the initiative and kissed me.

* * *

The following morning, I woke up in euphoria. How out of my character. How reckless of me. But I was proud instead of remorseful. I felt like I was trying to impress myself, and maybe Ivan as well.

Yeah, I could be both: the former child prodigy and someone who allows a stranger to stay overnight.

I peeked over to the alarm clock on the nightstand. It was 6:00 a.m.

While Ivan was sleeping, I ordered my standard coffee, plus one. I ignored what I felt was judgment when the clerk asked, "So you want two coffees?"

Then I went on with my morning ritual. Yoga, meditation, my comprehensive skincare routine. Then, with impeccable timing, Ivan woke up.

"Good morning, beautiful!"

"*Dobroye utro*," I repeated to him.

I hadn't gone for my typical matching set pajamas last night—rather, a silk blush camisole and a matching robe I once bought "just for me." Well, now it was for Ivan. Something that would make me seem mature and sophisticated.

The aroma of coffee forced its way from the other side of the door, and I went to retrieve the tray.

"Wow, what service!" Ivan sat up, took his coffee from my hand, placed it on the nightstand, and pulled me back into bed.

"Come back!" he petitioned. "It's so warm here."

"No!" I laughed and sat back up. "I need to start practicing."

"Now?" He raised his watch to his face. "It is seven in morning! You have two days before performance!"

"I still have to practice."

"But you said you have practice later on today, no?" Ivan wasn't giving up.

"I need to warm up, get familiar with my fingering."

Getting up, still in his boxers and charming bed hair, he took a deep breath and said, "How familiar can one get?"

I shrugged. For me, there was no such thing as too familiar. I could never have too much preparation.

"Play for me. Show me how Cleo practices before practice."

I shot a mocking death stare and approached the piano.

I stretched out my fingers, cleared my throat, and played my next performance choice: **Chopin - Fantaisie-Impromptu.**

I could feel the proximity of Ivan's attention. The *ah, hm,* and *da* dictated his focus on my repertoire. I sensed the shift as I captivated myself in the concerto. The way the room started to clear, and the world surrounding me became muted.

"May I?" The words interrupted my flow. I looked up in confusion.

"Cleo, you are so magical when you play, but…" I could see him choosing his words carefully. "Do you feel the emotions? This was Chopin's, uh, they call 'delicate melody,' yeah? But it gets happy at times, dramatic, romantic. It can be all these emotions. There is so much to feel there."

"I'm feeling it," I lied. I wasn't sure what he was getting at, but something told me he would continue either way.

"Why you choose this one?"

"Are you questioning my choices?"

"Just tell me this. Why?"

"Okay, well, I go for the melodies that drive me. As you said, this one can be emotional; it is an easy way to connect with the audience. And," I went on, "on a mechanical note, I think this piece is an excellent way to highlight the pianist's virtuosity." I was rambling, overcompensating. He'd questioned my abilities, and it left a bad taste in my mouth.

"Okay…" he mumbled as he paced the floor, then stopped in front of me. "Play, um…" His hand swung in the air, motioning his train of thought. **"Hungarian Dance, No. 5."**

"But it's—"

"Ah ah ah." His finger touched his lip. "I know it sounds better with a complete orchestra, but it, uh, original was a four-hand piano duet. It was so intimate, just two people with piano. Now they made it so"—he waved his hands dramatically—"emotional when you add the strings and the brass. Try to express that with just the piano, like it used to be."

He stood behind me on the bench. "Here." He found his tie hanging from a vintage baroque armchair and wrapped it over my eyes, tying it tight on the back of my head.

My body stiffened as his hands grazed against my hair. My emotions were high, and my heart was racing. I felt the warmth of his body next to mine as I sat there, blinded by the tie, all other senses heightened. Waiting for his next move.

He spoke softly, close to my ear. "Sometimes, you need to be in a dark room, without score sheets, and just play from your heart." I felt him moving further from me as his voice regained its climactic resonance. "Try it, but don't focus so much on the keys. I want you to hear the strings and the stomping of the brass; let those feelings tell your fingers how to play."

"You know you're crazy, right?" I said, as I felt around for my starting keys and played with the intentions Ivan presented.

I'll show him emotion.

I imagined myself on stage, in the center of the orchestra. I painted a clear picture of the audience—not the single one I had in my room, but a sold-out arena.

The conductor swinging the baton, the sounds of the violins…then the flutes chimed in, and one by one a new instrument was introduced: the oboe, double bass, the trombone.

The audience was clapping along as I allowed my upper body's natural sways to move my hands.

A vague thud brought me back, and then silence.

I ripped off the tie, let it fall around my neck, and followed the sound toward a confused Liam standing by the door.

"I'm sorry." He looked bewildered. "No one was answering my knocks, so I let myself in."

I suddenly became conscious of mine and Ivan's half-dressed state and felt the need to cover up quickly.

Liam continued to excuse himself. "I heard you playing, so I assumed you were just unable to hear me."

"Um. Yeah, that's okay." I tightened my robe.

"Liam, Ivan. Ivan, Liam."

Ivan stretched out a hand to Liam, who discarded it completely.

"All right, Ivan. I think Cleo and I probably should start practicing."

Ivan took the hint. "Ah, yes! The practice before the practice." Ivan chuckled at his joke. "Now, my clothes!" Our clothes were scattered around the suite. Ivan retrieved the items one by one as I sat there, watching Liam watching Ivan. Every step felt like slow motion. Slowly buttoning up his shirt, slowly kissing me goodbye, slowly grabbing his coffee, stuffing a complimentary baked good into his mouth. Then he was gone.

I felt like a teenager caught by their parents. The anxiety was making its way to my chest while my mind went over the many excuses I could tell Liam.

This is crazy. I am an adult; I don't need reasons. Why did I let myself get like this? Why this pang of guilt any time I had a little fun?

Liam's attention was back on me. My heart beat fast as my leg bounced in anticipation. Please give it to me, Liam. Tell me how irresponsible I was for having a stranger—a competitor—over for a presumably late night.

"Okay, are you ready?"

Huh? That's it? Must the show go on?

He adjusted his seat next to mine.

Oh, okay then.

"So you wanted to switch to the **Hungarian Dance**?" He smirked. He was teasing.

"Oh no, that was just for fun." I felt my face flush with embarrassment. I folded my arms over my robe, hoping it wasn't too late now to change.

"Okay, so **Fantaisie-Impromptu** it is. Let's start with the warm-up."

9

THE UNTITLED DIARY

New York City, Present Day

I do not answer Diane's calls for the rest of the week, not until I have an outline of what I will say or do.

I'm sitting on my veranda, joint in hand, **Dvořák - Serenade for Strings, Op. 22**, blaring on full volume.

I exhale a cloud of smoke over my bitten-down nails. As a pianist, I never grew out my nails or accessorized with bulging rocks. I needed my fingers to be bare and without distraction. I remember Diane's nails at dinner the other night: long, acrylic, mismatched, and bejeweled. *Can I pull that off?* I think, then go back to my screen and start typing.

Title: *The Untitled Diary.*

I laugh in mockery. This is pathetic. Months of writer's block and my dam of creativity is still tightly sealed.

I compose a new list in my brain:

```
FICTION VS. NONFICTION
1.  What if I shift gears and tackle nonfiction, write
    about my life?
2.  The question remains: What would I honestly write?
3.  Where would I start?
4.  Would people want to know what it's like to grow
    up  with  one  plan  in  mind?  The  stories  of  my
```

<pre>afflictions and tribulations caused by attempting
to conquer the classical world?</pre>

The places I traveled, the people I got to meet, the men I loved—my memories?

In the past, I wrote about a few experiences I have lived through, projected them into my novels, concealed them in fiction. What would happen if I opened up those layers, removed the fabricated elements, and told my real story?

I begin to type and then stop.

I remind myself why I never told this story before: there is no happy ending. This little girl who devoted her life to music, sacrificed her childhood and celebrations, fought her way to the top, lost people along the way, and then— nothing. The story is done. *Fin.*

I add another item to the list:

<pre>5. What if I composed my alternative ending?</pre>

What if I took control over the way my story ended? The way it was supposed to be? That way, the reader gets their happily ever after, and I can finally move on to my next endeavor.

Isn't that what everyone wants? A happily ever after? A way to satisfy your afflictions vicariously?

The bullshit we put out there to capitalize on what people crave and what they want us to bestow.

My fingers hover over the keyboard, contemplating the direction I want to take.

Authenticity, or fabrication?

The buzzing sound of my phone snaps me right out of my consciousness.

Bloody hell, I almost had it.

It's a text message from Diane:

Hi! I just signed you up to try out Spin City with me at 9:00 tomorrow morning! Don't be late!

Really? Spin class? On the bright side, we will be preoccupied—no actual chatting while we are working out. I can probably get away with not mentioning anything just yet.

I write back:

I can't wait! xx

Goddamn it. My creative juices are gone.

* * *

Diane awaits me the following morning outside the studio. Somehow, she always looks polished and put together. Her shiny blond hair is in a high pony, yet still sophisticated. Her outfit is complete with a Moncler parka and head-to-toe matching activewear. Her detailed nails are still blinding. Her makeup is minimal; her veneers, perfect.

Diane and I used to complain about all the other mums at the school. Their commitment to putting on a perfect façade, to portray life without creases or complexities.

Now I worry that I was the odd one out. I glance at my reflection in the window behind Diane. I am tall, slim, and blond: the trifecta of elements required to make a woman attractive in New York City. Yet I look worn out; I can see the bags in my reflection six feet away. My hair! Well, that's on me, but I seem to have lost interest.

"Hey, babe! Carlos is the instructor this morning. I'm telling you, his class is going to kill you, literally! I go every Sunday, and my body has completely transformed." She says this while air kissing my cheeks, then drags me behind her to the loud and low-lit studio.

I don't necessarily mind working out, I just like working out alone. I never fancied team sports or group classes. For me, working out is a time to regroup, recharge, and release all my stress. How can I possibly do this while Carlos, all smiley and condescending, is telling me, *That's it, you can do it, girl!* It all seems so fraudulent. Then you have the music choices. How can I possibly recharge with Destiny's Child preaching "I'm a survivor!" or t.A.T.u. yelling, "They're not gonna get us!"

Songs I am familiar with yet evoke a visceral response.

I am getting better at blocking out environmental noises by substituting them with the music I play in my head: my own playlist. For example, right now, I am pedaling quickly, getting up from the saddle, getting back down, pushing forward and backward, and doing whatever else Carlos instructs me to do. My subconscious somehow hears the demands, but I choose to focus on the sounds of **Flight of the Bumblebee** that is currently playing in my head.

The enchanting melody fills the air, as each instrument plays with precision and passion. Their bows dancing with an almost supernatural speed. The woodwinds add a whimsical touch, their notes fluttering like delicate butterfly wings.

This music, this masterpiece, consumes me completely. Its tempo enthralls me, urging me to move, to let go of all inhibitions, and surrender to its chaotic energy. It ignites a fire within me, a burning passion that courses through my veins, infusing every fiber of my being with a sense of purpose and determination.

I am unaware of my surroundings; my consciousness transports me to a realm where the sounds of the orchestra are my only reality. A multitude of bees swarm the studio, their numbers rapidly multiplying, occupying every nook and cranny. Their loud buzzing envelops me, and I can feel the hum pulsing through my bones. Then the musicians appear, their faces contorted with concentration, their fingers flying across their instruments. The maestro, standing tall at the podium, sways and weaves his arms in perfect synchrony with the orchestra's erratic tempo.

Suddenly, a jolt of realization snaps me back to reality. I find myself standing amidst a crowd, their curious gazes fixed upon me.

Ow! I am holding onto my forearm. I guess I said that out loud?

"Fuck!" This time I know I say it out loud—slow and loud, for emphasis.

My arm is throbbing with excruciating pain. It can only be my neglect that caused me to crack, twist, or dislocate something in that region.

Carlos and the other spinners shoot me judgmental looks.

I'm sorry, but am I an inconvenience? Was everyone just going to stand and watch? New Yorkers have this natural way of monitoring chaos without interfering.

"Here." Diane quickly gets off her bike and comes over to help me down. She unbuckles my shoes and grabs our bags, trying to avoid any further embarrassment from her spin buddies by escorting me out and hailing a cab.

* * *

Bandaging my arm takes about four hours.

"A quiet day today at the ER," mentions my too-young and right-out-of-med-school doctor. It makes me wonder what a hectic day might look like.

"All right, so I'll come back with your prescription, and Sheila will help sign you out."

I already know I will not be taking whatever meds this sweet child of a doctor prescribes for me. The pain, I can handle. The risk-reward ratio of going down the path of pharmaceuticals is not worth it.

Growing up, I rarely went near any form of medication, unless I fell extremely ill. It was a taboo subject for me, a stigma I built up. I once mistakenly shared the idea with Conor that maybe it came from seeing that my mother's only way to function was through her pills. I never knew or asked why she felt so imprisoned by these pills, why she never tried to get by without them. Conor tried to eradicate my fear with his magical words—like that would automatically change the way I felt.

I just want control over my body. I don't want these pills to dictate how I am going to get better. I am strong enough to get there on my own.

When the doctor brings my prescription, I'll smile politely and thank him.

Diane sits with me throughout the whole process. She messages Conor for me, letting him know that I'm fine, that she's got this. In this moment I felt the depths of our friendship. It isn't all surface-level outings and bitch fests.

"Thank you, Diane. You honestly didn't have to stay this whole time."

"Oh, don't be silly!" She waves me off. I guess this is a benefit of not having a job. You have the flexibility to be a good friend without the stress of wasting a day away. Would I do this for Diane? I thought about it. My guilt gets the best of me. I have to be a good friend; I have to tell her about Eric. I feel my nerves send a shiver down my spine; the spike of adrenaline causes my teeth to chatter. *Just spit it out!* No amount of preparation can equip me for this.

"Diane," I start. "I have to tell you something, and it's not easy."

"Oh no. You and Conor are breaking up?"

"What? No!"

"You're pregnant!"

"Wait, no, Diane, listen to me." I have her attention. "Something strange happened the other night…" I pause. "With Eric."

"What do you—"

"He was a bit too touchy-feely at dinner. I just thought, as a friend, that I should let you know."

She is mute, possibly digesting this information.

"In the kitchen—" I stop myself. Maybe she should talk first.

I hold her hand with my good one and wait for her to speak. She lets go.

"This. Is. So. Typical." She slowly emphasizes each word.

I nod. Maybe Eric has done this before. Poor Diane.

"Your life is going down the shitter, so naturally you have to drag me down with you."

"What? No, I—" This is not what I was expecting.

"I saw you and Conor at dinner. My brother and I have more affection for each other than you two."

I've pushed a button, and I'm not sure how to reverse it.

"No, Diane, I'm sorry." I want to take it all back, but the damage has been done. We will never go back to a place where these words are unsaid.

"I can't believe you would make this shit up, just for your own benefit." She is fuming at this point, unaware of the scene she is causing. "You know what? I feel sorry for you, Cleo. You are either a pathological liar or extremely arrogant to believe that someone like my husband would initiate anything with you." She is animated, speaking at full volume, and I just sit there and take it.

"Diane, I'm not making this up. I would never have said anything if I didn't truly believe—"

"You know those moms you ridicule at PTA? We can see right through you, Cleo. We can see that you are trying to fill an empty void. You want to be them, be me. They pity you, you know. They see how much you're struggling, how hard you try to be something you're not."

I try one last time to see if she'll listen, see that I bear no malintent. That I'm coming from a place of love—but there is no rational way to show her, is there?

"Diane." I try to put a stop to this. "Please." My voice is breaking.

"No, you know what, enough is enough. I'm out." She grabs her purse and starts walking away, then quickly turns back and points her finger at me. "Don't even think about calling me again; we are so done."

I have no idea how all this transpired. I sit there shocked and confused.

```
WHAT HAPPENED WITH DIANE?
1.  Was I making it all up in my head? Was Eric just
    acting friendly, and I created a theory that he
    was flirting and being suggestive? No one else was
    there. Not Conor, not Diane. It was all up to me
    to decide if Eric crossed the line. I did drink a
    lot that night, and I do have predisposed feelings
    about Eric.
2.  If any other man had acted that way, would I be so
    quick to judge his actions?
3.  Did I deserve this beating?
4.  Would I have reacted the same if Diane accused
    Conor?
5.  Was I out of line, or did Diane overreact?
```

I play back the night with Eric and the conversation with Diane repeatedly in my head. I question my memory. I question my right to bring it up. I regret mentioning anything.

10

IVAN GROZNY

Moscow, Ten Years Ago

The next day was my last day off before the next round, so I devoted three-quarters of my time to rehearsal and the other quarter to Ivan. We took pleasure in every shared moment. Every second symbolized a countdown to separation, so we had to embrace the time we had left.

Our evening encouraged the temptation of gluttony as we indulged in even more pierogi, caviar, and ice cream at the mall.

Ivan conducted himself as my tour guide while we walked along the Moskva River. He educated me about the history of the Krasnaya ploshchad'—the Red Square.

In his best attempt given our language barrier, Ivan explained that the land we were stepping on, this infamous, picturesque Kremlin, the symbol of Moscow, was all here thanks to Ivan the Great.

"Ivan the Great? Have you been referred to like that before?" I asked, half joking.

"No, no. My parents would call me Ivan Grozny—Ivan the Terrible. My parents, my teachers, my *babushka* and *dedushka*. They all said I was Ivan the Terrible."

I let out a laugh. "Really? Why?"

"I was just so naughty growing up, so bored. I had to keep myself busy. I think this is why my parents loved when I played the instruments. It made me sit down for a minute, stay away from trouble."

I understood that impulse; my parents were like that too. There was an underlining purpose as to why I was put by the piano for hours at a time—a means to conceal me from some form of trouble. Different, I supposed, to the troubles Ivan was referring to. Troubles I wasn't entirely aware of, something I couldn't label. I always had a vigilant eye out; I built up a cavalier attitude toward any event or person that passed me by. I was unaware of what might happen if I stopped with my plans, if I pivoted my career, or even let it all come to an end. So I stayed there, by my piano. I didn't want to deflect from this trajectory.

As time went on, I tried to ignore these fears. The concentration on my music intensified until I had no more headspace for disturbances.

The noise quieted down there in Moscow, there with Ivan. It was almost as though I had a magnetic response to Ivan. I didn't want to leave his side. Us separating meant I had to go back to the person I was before, the person without Ivan.

After the second round, I established a routine in Moscow.

Ivan and I would spend our nights together at Hotel Metropol. Mornings were filled with music and coffee in my room, followed by a small break while I went to practice.

Practice, practice.

I performed **Chopin - Waltz in C-sharp minor Op. 64, No. 2.**

Ivan performed **Tchaikovsky - Violin Concerto in D major, Op. 35.**

We celebrated our victories, and then my time with Ivan was replaced with Liam, and suddenly I was back to Cleo the pianist, hypervigilant Cleo, Cleo with the blinders on.

Practice, practice.

I performed **Liszt - Liebesträum No. 3**.

Ivan performed **Mendelssohn - Violin Concerto**.

We made it to the semifinals. It was me against two other pianists. These results determined whether I would compete in the final round and take the pianist category's first place.

Then, there was the potential for a paradigm shift. During the closing ceremony, only one winner from each category had the opportunity to take home the gold medal—the Grand Prix Award. If Ivan and I both won first place in our categories, we would compete against each other for the most significant honor of all.

* * *

I was about to retire for the night. My arms ached after my performance. My body—heavy and fatigued. My mind—light and liberated. The buzzing sound alerted me just as I was about to doze off. I could not imagine who would be contacting me. It wasn't terribly late, but, at this hour, I was under no obligation. My family wouldn't call, and Liam most certainly wouldn't disrupt my rest hours. An address showed up on my screen. Then the second text buzzed in:

This is my address. Come to me now! Love, Ivan.

I smiled and contemplated my options. I made a list.

```
IVAN:
1.  I have one more day of rehearsal before the
    semifinals. I need my sleep; I need my brain to
    work at its best capacity. I know I play best with
    at least seven to eight hours of sleep--that is my
    Achilles' heel. Going out again will mean risking
    a perfect performance.
2.  Also, I am in pajamas. I have already brushed my
    teeth.
3.  But Ivan is something I never knew was a
    possibility.
4.  When will I have another opportunity like this
    again? Tomorrow isn't an actual performance day,
    just another practice. I should be okay.
```

> 5. My days with Ivan are limited; it is either now or, if I don't make it through to the next round, probably never again.

And that prospect alone triumphed over all other alternatives. The chance of not having a night like this again, to have wasted an opportunity with Ivan, was all I needed to consider. I didn't bother changing out of my pajamas. I concealed them underneath my fur coat and left to see Ivan.

I had to ask the hotel clerk to call me a cab. It wasn't worth asking Liam for my driver's number, not worth having that conversation.

Fourteen minutes later I was standing outside Ivan's flat. It was about nine levels high, a brown brick building, modest, with an industrial feel.

The buzzer outside listed about forty or fifty tenants—and only then did I realize I didn't know his last name.

I messaged him instead.

I am outside.

Not a millisecond later, the door buzzed open.

The moment I walked into his apartment, Ivan grabbed me and embraced me with a violent kiss. He picked me up and carried me onto his couch. Here, with Ivan, I felt comfort. Yet there was an added element of intense desire. When he held me, when he drew me close, I was unable to retract. There was an indefinable force of attraction between us, and I could not rationalize it away - allow reason to trump emotion.

His home had a seventies ambiance: deep wood accents and light blue walls surrounded us. Even though he shared his flat with two other roommates, the place had Ivan's touch. We lounged by the ample windows, overlooking the other commercial-like buildings. It was comfortable and natural, us mindlessly catching up, almost as if we hadn't been together all day. The conversation continued over some wine as we went deeper into our desires, revealing a transparent pathway into our griefs and emotions.

The real passion came out once we discussed music. The key to my soul. The source of my happiness.

"So when do you practice?" I finally asked. "If you are as deep into this as I am, you must be somewhat nervous or tenacious with the competition closing soon."

"Ten-what?"

"Tenacity, fight, passion!"

"I don't like to overdo it, the practicing. What I do on stage, it's all coming from my heart, my emotion."

"But you still have to practice!"

"I do, well, I play. I play the violin, piano, guitar…" I looked around his small room, and instruments started showing up all around, like the hidden man in the pages of *Where's Wally?*

"One thing we must accept is that we may never be perfect. No matter how well you play, there will always be a greater musician, someone better."

I wasn't ready to quit striving for perfection. If we completely give up on it, how can we ever grow?

"The most important thing, I think, is to enjoy the process. Have fun with music. Don't take it so seriously."

"Okay?" I wasn't sure I was taking music too seriously. I did enjoy the process. For me, working hard didn't equal hard work. Playing was my favorite pastime; it was where I thrived the most.

"Do you ever enjoy listening to radio? Rock, R&B, ballads, pop?"

"I can't. For me, personally, that is not real music." I shrugged unapologetically. "Music on the top hits lists, it's kind of tacky, unpoetic. You can't ever compare the romance of Tchaikovsky to the rubbish you hear on the radio these days. I'm sorry."

Ivan let out a breathy, "Huh." Then he said, "Okay. *Idi syuda!* Come here!" He grabbed my hand and led me to a small digital piano compressed against the wall.

"Stand here." He lifted his arms as a cue to halt. So I stood there, in his snug room, pressed against his couch and bookshelf as I watched him sit and play with a few keys. "Listen; tell me this is not music." He closed his eyes, pressed hard on the keyboard and began to sing.

"That was beautiful." I was speechless and incredibly impressed. "Did you write that yourself?"

"What? No, Cleo, are you serious?" Ivan shook his head.

"What?" Was I missing something?

"This"—he pointed to the keyboard—"was Aerosmith! Dream on!"

"Oh?" *Whoops.*

"It, uh, how you say um, *izvestnaya pesnya*? Very well-known song? No?"

"Sorry, I'm not really familiar with that genre."

"I don't believe you." Ivan shook his head again. "Okay, you must have heard this."

He turned back to the keys as he sang a beautiful ballad.

There was a long pause. Then he said, "Nothing?"

"Am I supposed to know this?"

"Cleo, Cleo, Cleo!" Ivan shook his head for a third time.

"Wait, it does sound familiar," I protested.

"Beyoncé! Who doesn't know Beyoncé?"

"Oh, right, right, right. I knew that." I didn't.

"Isn't this what you girls listen to?"

"I wouldn't have a clue." Clearly.

He went back into his brain archive of top hits. "Okay, how about this?" He started playing again.

I furrowed my forehead, trying to make out his notes. "I don't—"

"Shh!" He put a finger to his lips as he continued singing.

I recognized the song.

"Oh no, not Britney Spears!"

"She knows Britney Spears!" He cheered. "You do know pop music!"

"Oh gosh." I buried my head in my hands. "You know you'd get an automatic disqualification if they heard you play like this."

He continued to sing and then mimicked an imaginary microphone for me to sing into, and when I didn't, he continued.

I laughed.

"Okay, okay, I get it!" I surrendered.

He continues louder.

Oh, there is more.

"Okay, is it out of your system now?"

He pulled me onto the bench beside him.

"Cleo, you have an opportunity to learn so much more about music. It doesn't stop at Lizst, Bach, Mendelssohn…."

"Look, I do listen to other genres of music, just not often. I need to feel provoked when I listen or perform; classical melodies do that to me."

"You can be moved by other feelings, not just sad but happy, love, silly, excitement…these are feelings too, no?"

"You can get those feelings through classical music—"

"Don't even try. You know it is different." He continued playing on the keys. "What is music that brings you to your childhood?"

"**Rondo Alla turca**," I replied instantaneously. This melody brought me back to a time when I would sit and play for Annie. Her baby rocker lay beside the piano, and she would sit there, eyes wide at the sounds I would create. We would stay in that position for hours at a time.

"Not Mozart." Ivan rolled his eyes. "Not anything classical. Did you not enjoy stupid music, music to just dance and be fun with friends?"

I had to think. I was sure there were times I indulged in different forms of music. I went to birthday parties where we danced to Michael Jackson's Billie Jean or Madonna's Papa Don't Preach, but those ended before I turned thirteen. I never really went to clubs when my friends did. Non-goal-oriented social events did not pique my interest or motivate me. My fun, silly, non-work-related moments consisted of playing lullabies for my sister or playing **Für Elise** with my father.

"Okay, let me give an example. Here is a song from my childhood." Ivan started to sing. "*Kaaaaalinka kalinka kakalinka moya.*" As he played, the tempo quickened. "This is a very famous Russian song." He continued, still performing, "When I was a child, I told you how I played at the restaurant when my mother worked? I would play this for all the, um, customers?"

I nodded.

"Any time I hear it now—and you be surprised how much they play this song in Russia—I think of this memory."

The keys stopped.

I was still trying to think of a memory—a memory classical music didn't play a part in.

"Have you ever go into a room, lock the door, and dance, dance so crazy?"

"Oh god, no!" I laughed, first thinking he was joking. "Look, I am not as troubled as you think I am. I love music. I immerse myself in the music I hear and play. I just have a particular type, that is all." I slowly shifted to the edge of the piano bench, wondering what Ivan was trying to get at.

"Troubled? No. A little serious." He turned his torso to me. "Cleo, I believe you can be an extraordinary pianist if you trust this more." He pointed to my stomach—my gut?

I winced as I assessed the situation, unsure if I wanted Ivan to go on or to stop.

"I hope I am not offending you, Cleo. I want the best for you; you are just so good. I never saw such a good, such a..." He raised his arms, unable to find the words.

"I get that, thanks." I figured this was the best time to stop.

"Just my opinion. You don't have to listen to me. Just think about it, okay?"

Ivan smiled, and a profound sensation permeated throughout my body. It was a feeling of belief that we were meant to be here, together, in this very moment—an undeniable force of romantic destiny. It was as if our togetherness held the promise of a brighter future.

11

THE WALTZ OF THE FLOWERS

New York City, Present Day

One flaw I can admit to is my ability to show up late at any event: school events, date nights, drinks with friends. A few years ago, Conor bought me a watch for our anniversary gift, an expensive but passive way of letting me know that something had to change.

Tonight was Olivia's first big ballet recital. Since she was three, she has been dancing, and since she was three, I have been there by her side. Every year, every holiday, Conor and I schlep the kids to the Ballerina Dance Academy, where we transform into Olivia's biggest cheerleaders.

Tonight is special. Tonight, Olivia's dance school is performing at the Broadway Musical Theater in front of a spectacular audience. It's a big deal, an incredible opportunity. I'm not about to show up late for an achievement like this.

I have a meeting with Ramona on the morning of the show. Conor's job is to bring the kids, and my job is not to be late.

I plan my whole day accordingly.

```
DAY OF OLIVIA'S RECITAL:
1.  My meetings never surpass an hour, so I'll be out
    by 2:00 (on Lexington Avenue).
```

2. Taxi to the show that starts at 3:00 (in Greenwich
    Village). Plenty of time.
3. "I will not, for the life of me, mess this up. I
    repeat: I will not, under any circumstances, mess
    this up."

My meeting goes as terribly as I'd imagined.

"Hi, Ramona."

"Oh, you broke your arm." Then, not a breath later, "So what have you got for me? Shoot!"

"Well, I was contemplating the idea, maybe…" I play with my fingers and sway my crossed leg in perpetual angst. "Writing nonfiction instead? A memoir of some sort." I do not come across as confident.

"What do you mean, maybe? Show me what you wrote, let's see." She holds her hand out, gesturing for me to pass over the manuscript.

"Well, I… I don't have anything on me." I quickly add, "Right now." As though tomorrow I may.

"Cleo."

"I know."

"Cleo." She goes a few octaves higher. "We have gone through this already. After the last book, you guaranteed me a new one."

"I know."

"Like, two months ago!" Ramona takes off her glasses and rubs her eyes. "And you have nothing? No outline? No synopsis of any kind?"

"I can get it to you soon, as soon as you need."

"Last month, please."

I hold up my arm, hoping to gain sympathy, as if this has caused my inability to work. "I'll get to it as soon as I can. I promise."

"Cleo, this is the last straw."

"Okay."

"Email me a query letter by Friday."

"Done!" *Shit! Friday?*

"You have a month to send something to Sophie. No more meetings until you have something substantial."

I nod.

"No more excuses."

No more excuses. I have to show up. I am hanging on by a thread. It surprises me that Ramona is still holding on.


```
WHY RAMONA IS STILL HOLDING ON:
1.  It was probably cheaper for Ramona to stall than
    to break our contract.
2.  Perhaps she is so busy with her other novels that
    the only reminder of my lack of work was my
    meetings?
```


None of these possibilities convince me, but I'm out. I made it out of the office at 2:00 on the dot. I'll get there by 2:30, latest. Maybe I'll even get a coffee on the way. How is that for timing?

The traffic commences as soon as I find myself restless in the back of a taxi. No more than five minutes in, I find myself nail-biting and knee-bouncing. I can't sit still as the many future conversations run through my brain.

You're late again! Typical! Conor.

Mommy, you missed my important show. Olivia.

Mommy is always late, Olivia. Ciara.

I check my watch multiple times. One minute passes. Then another. I must have been in this taxi for half an hour now.

"Um, excuse me. Is there any way out of this traffic? I am in a bit of a hurry."

"Ah, You see this! I cannot move." He starts shouting in another language; the only option I have is to give him cash and leave.

I run down Madison Avenue. My phone notes a twenty-six-minute walk to the theater. If I jog, I can probably get there in about ten, fifteen minutes.

So, I run. I run so fast. This will not be another time I let anyone down, another reason for excuses to explain why I was late. I cannot miss this for Olivia.

My chest hurts from the icy air that is penetrating my lungs. My bandaged arm aches in motion. My Prada kitten heels, the ones I wore to portray a put-together author, and later a well-dressed mum, are rubbing against my toes, creating blisters.

I *ow, ow, ow* my way down Eighth Avenue, where I finally make it to Broadway Musical Theater. I brush my hair away from my face and pull down on my black blazer. *Good enough.* I look at my watch: 3:15. *Shit!*

I run down the hall until I see the big signs exhibiting tonight's show.

The lights are already dim. The recital has already begun. I am in dire need of finding Conor; my ticket has no guidance concerning our seats' location. Eventually, after much shushing and many passive aggressive sighs, I find them: Ciara, Conor, and Sebastian. My crew.

"So sorry," I whisper.

"Where were you?" Conor whispers back. "You missed her introduction."

"There was so much traffic—"

"Shh!" An older couple shushes us from behind.

I mouth "sorry" and get comfortable in my chair.

"Will she be on soon?"

"Shh!"

"I'm sorry!" This time I don't whisper.

My eyes avert as I look behind the noisy shushers; there sits Eric and Diane.

I can feel the cold in Diane's face, and her gaze focuses on me, not wavering.

I don't even dare to catch a glimpse of Eric and hastily turn around. This will not ruin my night, Olivia's night.

The **Waltz of the Flowers** melody penetrates the hall's speakers as the little sugar plumb fairies chassé on stage. We McCarthys never attempt to stay incognito in public. We whoop and cheer as Olivia dances. She stops, smiles, and waves the moment she hears us. No old lady nor the Millers could ruin this moment.

Watching Olivia dance brings me back to when I was her age and performing. Music does that to you. It brings you back to a place or time with the sharp articulations of your thoughts, memories, and senses.

I close my eyes for just a moment, letting the sounds of flutes, harps, and trombones enchant me. I have memorized the tempo (60 bpm), the key (D major), the range (D4–E6). In the past, I had analyzed these compositions, dissected them to their core. I might forget appointments or the placement of things, but these are the memories I have carved in my brain.

With Sebastian swaying along with me as we listen to the music, I smile at the melodious sounds and laugh with abandon. I can hear Sebastian's giggles fade, along with the rhythmic clapping. And then suddenly I can just hear the music. The notes. The vibrations.

I feel a nudge. Ciara.

"Mom." She aggressively elbows me in my ribs.

"What?"

Ciara rolls her eyes and looks back to the stage.

I hear the faint sound of Diane's giggles.

I follow the laugh and see Diane rolling her eyes.

I look back at Ciara and then at Conor.

Conor reaches over Ciara and puts his hand on my knee, a sign of comfort. There's a slight look of worry or shame in his eyes.

Ciara looks annoyed.

I feel disoriented. What did I do?

The crowd cheers. Olivia bows. It is all over.

* * *

I don't speak of that moment again, but it does create a massive knot in my throat. Why did Diane think I was so hilarious at my daughter's recital? And what caused Ciara to look at me that way? Or Conor, for that matter?

I ask Conor after the recital what happened, and he leaves me with an ambiguous, "Nothing, don't worry about it."

It didn't feel like nothing. So, I push those feelings deep down, and instead I disguise my thoughts with a forced concentration on my work. At the very least, I have to develop a rough outline of this book's plot. Something to show, something to hand to Ramona. I know if I don't have this, I will be back to square one, which is not an option.

The caveat here is my broken arm. I try many positions: standing and typing, leaning to the left while typing. I try letting the mic type out the words.

Just imagine. Imagine what you would write.

Once I know where to start, the rest will come. Was it Hemingway who said, "Just sit by the typewriter and bleed?" I will get there; I just need to visualize my start.

Okay, music.

I need music.

I curate playlists according to intended purpose—sonatas that enable me to concentrate or concertos that soothe my sympathetic nervous system. As I go through my playlist, I choose a piece I feel is relevant to the current moment.

I find a playlist I have meticulously curated featuring my favorite contemporary composers: Einaudi, Richter, Pärt, to name a few. Some of whom I had the privilege of meeting and performing alongside, some I looked up to. Their music carries poignant nostalgia for me. Each note stirs a whirlwind of emotions - nostalgia turns to happiness. Which eventually turns to melancholy, a deep ache for the person I once was. A person I would never be again.

I select **Max Richter - On the Nature of Daylight** and let my creative thoughts flow freely.

Writing the beginning of my story should be the easy part. I lived it; it happened. The middle is where I get stuck, and with no middle, there is no end.

I thought of my past life, the changes, the transitions—the departure from piano keys to a computer keyboard. Such different types of skills and mindsets for these two ways of storytelling. Music is a way of telling a story using no language but sound. Now I need words, I need structure.

The beginning and the end are essential components of storytelling, but the middle…the middle is what binds it all together.

When composing music, you must choose the right keys to allow the story to flow. For instance, the note E has a finite expression. It will enable the listener to acknowledge the end of the melody. The composer will deflect until they are ready to end. With an E, they are ending their story.

I do this with writing too. You don't get to your big reveal right away; you stall with plot twists and turns until you are ready for the end.

Another similarity these forms of storytelling share: I must deal with the ramifications of carpal tunnel syndrome's excruciating pains.

And now, in addition to my aching, fractured arm.

I rub my right palm and let out an ironic laugh. I think about how the shooting pain used to be a pianist's battle scar, but now it seems to note incapacity.

I feel disabled. My arms, my hands, they took me places, and now I have nowhere to go, nothing to do but pace the veranda until something erupts. As I listen to the repetitive melody, it viscerally intensifies emotions within me. I try to untangle my headphones, hoping to be transported back to a time when these compositions surrounded me. A time when I had a purpose, direction. Back to when I moved with passion and allowed my creativity to expose itself.

I feel my book in the beginning stages of creation. It's coming to me.

I am visualizing the beginning, where I would start.

12

DOM

Moscow, Ten Years Ago

Meet me outside Teatralnaya metro station at 1:00.

I woke up to this text from Ivan. It was 6:00 a.m. What was he doing at this hour, practicing? Was this when sneaky Ivan practiced? Before dawn? I couldn't fall back asleep. Ivan knew my schedule for this weekend. No performances until Monday, and I was grateful that he was taking the lead. The following two days were set up for uninterrupted practice, practice, practice—until I could find a plausible enough reason for Liam to let me take a break with Ivan.

I lay back on my bed and watched the ceiling, going over the many reasons why I should risk swapping out practice hours for Ivan. How do I speak Liam's language?

```
EXCUSES FOR LIAM:
1.  Hours  of  break  help  reframe  my  mind  so  I  can
    concentrate more. (He knows I don't believe that.)
2.  Can  seeing  Russia  create  more  inspiration?
```

All bullocks.

Liam would see right through my lies. The thing was, I really liked Ivan, and while I wasn't sure how we could last past these next two weeks, something was pulling me toward him. No logic or reason. Just a feeling. Was it comfort? Infatuation? Fascination? I couldn't spell out these feelings just yet, but I wanted to try.

I gave up on excuses and replied.

I will be there.

I would. Now that I'd made that commitment, it would happen.

Liam showed up with my coffee on schedule. I wanted to get done with this morning's session as soon as possible.

7:45: Warm-up

8:45: Two hours of Beethoven.

"If you push hard on the keys, it's good. It's fine, okay? The momentum is great, but perhaps try a softer approach. You can really expose the tenderness and intimacy that way."

"Okay." I let out a little sigh, which Liam obviously ignored.

"And you need to loosen your wrists, let it flow a bit more. Remember: this is a dialogue between you and the orchestra."

It didn't matter how much I practiced; my wrists caused static pressure, and I did my best to shake off the tension.

"Try to use a circling motion while playing. It might help."

I had my eye on my clock.

"Cleo, come on," Liam snapped in my direction. "You're distracted."

Cue excuses.

"Um, yeah, sorry." *Words, I need the right words.* "I guess I am. Maybe I should take a break." I caught Liam's confused expression. "To regroup, is all."

"Regroup? Cleo, you usually got this. What's this about? What could possibly take your mind off of your practice?"

I contemplated the possible outcomes of continuing the lie or trying with the truth.

"It's Ivan." I surprised myself with this choice.

"Ivan?"

"Yes, well, he wanted to take me out today, see the—"

"You can't possibly think that's a clever idea, Cleo."

"Why not? What's the harm in an hour's break? It can only help, no?" I was hoping Liam would catch the bait.

He lifted his arms in defeat. Or was it disbelief? Either way, he was pissed.

"Cleo, at the end of the day, you're an adult. You make your own decisions. I'm just here to do my job and get you to your finish line. So far, it seems we can accomplish that."

I gave Liam too much control. He got me to where I wanted to go, so I continued to let him guide me there. But I am an adult. If I think I can take an hour or two for myself, I should.

"I think I am going to go," I said slowly.

"By all means." He gestured to the door and grabbed his coat. "Just do me a favor, will you? Remember that Ivan, at the end of the day, is competing against you."

"What is that supposed to mean?"

Liam stared at me with a void in his eyes.

"What do you mean by that? That he's competing, so what?"

"You're on top, Cleo! A good distraction might show in your next performance."

I was gathering my thoughts. "He's not even competing against me. He's in the violin category." I felt my blood boil. *Just let me have this.*

"And then who will get the Grand Prix Award? I hope you're not just stopping at the best pianist of the competition."

I scrunched up my brow, trying to debate his argument. "You honestly believe that Ivan would choose me to sabotage, over any other violinist in his category."

"You're on top, Cleo. Just be wary. That is all I'm going to say."

"I don't think you're right."

"I just don't want to see you get hurt."

"Get hurt or lose?"

"Both, I suppose."

"What's it to you if my feelings are hurt? Maybe I need a little heartbreak, for a solid production?"

"Cleo, I have known you for years. I care if you're hurt." He seemed sincere, but the words felt weird.

"All right. Goodbye, Liam. I'll let you know when I'm back." I was pissed. It was the first time in twenty-eight years that I desired to try something fun and spontaneous, something I could enjoy without responsibilities holding me back. Why couldn't I just have this? This little life outside of the competition, this little outlet of fantasy? Why must everything consume me? Keep me in this solo artist box?

"Goodbye, Cleo. Just, please, think about it."

I walked him out. I wanted to slam the door behind him. How dare he ruin this for me. I was going to make sure I thought about everything but his silly conspiracies.

But they were all I could think about.

Ivan greeted me with a kiss. Long and passionate. But was it real? Was he luring me into a web of lies and mistrust? He held my hand tight as he took me around the train station, giving me the usual Ivan interpretations of Russia's historical lessons. He smiled as he talked. When he wasn't holding my hand, he would be ahead of me, facing me, walking backward. He would have his hands on my shoulders, rubbing them warm from the icy breeze.

```
IS IVAN TRUSTWORTHY?
1.  Are all these gestures of romance just a big lie?
2.  Is Ivan, indeed a great actor, distracting me from
    my piano, from my possible victory?
```

We went to a restaurant called Dom, which is Russian for *home*. I was confused why we'd specifically traveled for it. The restaurant seemed charming, but we'd passed by many attractive options on the way here.

The traditional interior brought warmth, with its brown wooden walls and carpeted floors, heavy curtains, and rich colors. The aroma of fried onions filled the air.

"Vanya!" An old, bearded man greeted Ivan with a tight hug. In his flat cap, vest, and round glasses, he reminded me of a character from the early 1900s.

Their conversation was in Russian. I was not following along, but they spoke loudly, with lots of hand-talking, face-touching, hugs, and kisses.

The man finally acknowledged me and continued to say something in Russian. I smiled politely, waiting for Ivan to take the lead.

"Iliya, this is the beautiful Cleo. She is from England."

"Cleo, beautiful face, come in, come in." Iliya covered my hand with his warm, damp one and let me in.

"Uh, best seats in house."

They weren't very unusual seats at all. A little privacy was the only real difference. We had the booth closest to the kitchen: VIP status.

"Vanyishke!" A kindly old lady approached us. "Chow are you?" She got the memo to speak English.

"Good, good. Lena, this is Cleo."

"Hi." I raised my hand in an awkward wave. She took my hand and kissed it profoundly, leaving a noticeable amount of saliva on my hand. I quietly wiped it off onto my dress.

"Cleo, so beautiful." Seriously, I should come here on my off days. Having these people in my life would boost my self-confidence.

I smiled back, unaware of what else I could do. *Ivan, take the lead!*

"Okay, I bring you the most tasty food. Vanya's favorite." I was sure I saw Lena skip with joy as she went behind the kitchen doors.

"Okay, tell me, *Vanya*. Why is everyone here so obsessed with you?"

"They are like my family." I stared blankly, waiting for more. "I worked here."

"Really? How long ago?"

"Ten years I work here. I say goodbye last month."

"Last month! What? How?" It made no sense to me. How could you be at a point in your career to compete in prestigious competitions without it being your full-time job?

"I need to work. I need money."

Lena and Iliya came back with a bottle of vodka and four glasses.

"No." I waved my hands in disagreement. Not a chance.

Ignoring my refusal, they placed the bottle down and poured a generous glass for all four of us. "*Za zdorovye!*" they chanted in harmony, clinking each glass. I raised my glass but took the smallest sip.

Lena and Iliya mentioned something about the finest caviar and were off.

I turned back to Ivan, hoping he'd continue with the explanation.

"Drink," he said.

"No, thank you." The skepticism came back. "So, you were saying?"

"Cleo, I don't know how it is for you, but I am not making a lot for just playing music, you know? I need to make more to pay for my bills."

I guess this was true. I guess I was lucky that I didn't have to think about anything but my one goal.

"I come here, to um, bring food to people, and on weekends, I play." He pointed to the raised level, some form of stage. It was poorly lit and held a few instruments, a stool, and a microphone.

Ivan gulped the rest of his vodka and said, "You want to play something with me?"

I looked around. It was the middle of the day, and not too many guests were dining. "I'm okay, thank you."

"What? You leave me all alone?"

"Yeah, I think you're on your own today."

"Okay!"

Onstage, Ivan projected his voice over the mic. "*Damy i gospoda,* ah, ladies and gentlemen." There were a few claps, howls, and whistles. Ivan continued in Russian as a few laughs murmured in the crowd.

"Cleo," He now turned the attention to me. "I say…today, I bring a very special girl. So I ask them to please make me look good and maybe clap along." A smile found its way on my face. I'm trying not to enjoy myself. I'm trying to push my feelings for Ivan deep inside. Just incase…

"Cleo, you may not be the greatest Russian speaker," Ivan continued, "but this one is for you." The large accordion fit perfectly in his arms—because of course Ivan knew how to play the accordion.

"*Zingarella, Zingarella,*" Ivan began to sing. The crowd let out a collective "aw." Cheers and whistles followed as they swayed and sang along.

I wanted to experience this moment. I really did. I just couldn't shake off the questions about authenticity. What was he singing? Would those words mean anything to me either way? Instead of the feeling of joy and romance that flooded the crowd, I felt angry, almost sad. I was the outsider. I was alone. They cheered louder as Ivan's song ended. He reciprocated with a theatrical bow, but it wasn't over.

Over the mic, he declared, "Cleo, I think I need to share your beauty."

Oh god, no.

Ivan continued to his Russian speaking audience. He presented a little chef's kiss, and the crowd laughed.

What is he telling them? What is he asking of me?

His eyes were back to me. His arm reached out in my direction.

I shook my head. *No, no, no, no, no.*

"Come up, Cleo. I tell everyone how magical you are on the piano."

I concealed my face in my hands. I really couldn't go up. I had a lousy way of hiding my feelings, and I didn't need to project them onto this Vanya-loving crowd.

"Cleo! Cleo!" Ivan started chanting, and the audience chimed in.

I grasped the full glass of vodka in front of me, feeling the warmth fill my insides as I emptied it in one gulp. An unattractive expression and an automatic shudder followed. I stood up. There was nowhere else to go, so I joined Ivan on stage. He was sitting by the piano, caressing the seat for me to join.

He whispered in my ear, "**Hungarian Dance,** duet."

His breath was hot and smelled like vodka.

I nodded and thought, *Just get on with it. Let's get this over with, this charade. Then I can go back to Liam, back to where I should have stayed.*

We played the four-handed romantic melody together.

I wouldn't say I liked it. My thoughts were suffocating me. Was this just how Ivan was? Spontaneous, fun-loving Ivan. What if he was using me? I was getting in too deep, becoming too vulnerable. If this was all an act, it would be unbearable.

It was over. The audience cheered, asked for an encore, but I stubbornly declined and sat back at the dark corner table.

"We really should be going." I hastily grabbed my jacket, ready to leave.

"*Shto?* Cleo, we didn't even eat yet."

"I'm not hungry,"

"Cleo, what is it?" He took my hands into his, and, as Ivan always did, looked me straight in the eye. A calming effect washed over me; I wanted to cry.

"Nothing. It's just getting late, and I have to get back to rehearsal."

"Ah." He waved his hand. "You have the whole tomorrow. Why don't you join me for a little longer, more vodka?" Ivan poured two more glasses.

"No! No more vodka!" I exclaimed too loudly, startling poor Iliya and Lena as they appeared with a caviar tray, complete with toasted baguettes and appetizers. They took their cue to leave, setting the tray down in front of us before backing out slowly.

"Okay, no vodka. But please, join me. Ten minutes, please."

I didn't answer.

"Please," he said again as he gazed into my eyes, coaxing me back to my seat. "What is the real problem?"

"Are you using me, Ivan?" If I was giving him ten minutes, I'd better get on with it.

"What?" I couldn't tell if he was genuinely not understanding my English or questioning my thought.

"Are you trying to distract me, Ivan? Offer me drinks, take me out, show interest in me, all so I will fail?"

Now he looked hurt. "I can't believe you think like this."

The silence was deafening. I started second-guessing my theory—well, Liam's theory. *Bloody Liam!*

"Why would I? You know I am competing too, yeah? If I distract you, doesn't this mean I won't rehearse too?"

I stayed mute.

"Cleo, I'm disappointed. It makes me sad to think I do this."

The impediment built up inside of me. If I let myself feel something, the tears might flow, not out of pity, but frustration. I'd possibly destroyed a great moment by indulging in my thoughts and worries. Ivan brought me to his place. He introduced me to his old friends, invited me to be a part of a world for which he held so much love. I'd messed it up terribly.

"I'm sorry. Let's just forget this, okay?" Could I patch it back together? Could we go back to forcing vodka down my throat, back to everyone being blindsided by my beauty?

Ivan shook his head, but he didn't say no.

I waited for his validation.

He poured himself another shot—and poured one for me.

"Enjoy, try some food, and I'll take you back to practice."

I politely tasted one of everything Lena and Iliya brought out. I smiled and told them their food was delicious. Ivan stayed silent.

Once we decided that we'd had enough to show Lena and Iliya our appreciation, he grabbed his coat, hugged them goodbye, and walked out.

I silently followed him back toward the train station. This time, there was no backward walking, no handholding, no animated lesson of the stories beyond the walls.

13

THE FINAL ROUND

Moscow, Ten Years Ago

I didn't hear back from Ivan the next day.

I'm sorry if I offended you. I don't believe that you're using me.

I typed it but didn't hit send. I erased it and threw my phone on the bed beside me. The truth was, maybe Liam was right. Maybe Ivan got caught, and now, since no feelings had been involved in the first place, he was back to making his way to the top while I wondered who genuinely cared about me in the first place.

Liam never asked about Ivan. We went back to practice.

* * *

Liam scheduled a practice session backstage in the Great Hall.

As I walked toward the room, I noticed the monitors. They displayed the final round of the violinists' category. *Liam can wait*, I thought. I remained rooted in place, unable to look away as Ivan, the virtuoso, took the stage. With his violin in hand, he performed **Vivaldi - Four Seasons, L'inferno.**

I felt possessed. My eyes welled up. I was overwhelmed by the sheer intensity of the music. I held my breath, every note resonating deep within me, sending waves of emotion cascading through my very core. I felt the goose bumps, the shivers—every orifice of my body was affected. It was as if some unseen force had taken hold of me. As if Ivan's music had reached into the depths of my soul and set it ablaze with fervor and passion.

Then I could feel Liam coming toward me, his eyes burning. Was he upset? Not now, I couldn't think about that. Now I was controlled by the music. The notes, the melody, everything spoke to my soul. Whether Liam would have approved of these feelings remains insignificant."

The performance was over. Ivan bowed. My heart hurt.

* * *

Liam decided to continue practice in my hotel room, "Fewer distractions," he said.

I sat on the piano bench, restricted in my floral-print suit. Liam sat by my side, an accurate metaphor for our relationship. I knew that if I won, I would owe everything to Liam. Job duty or not, he always went that extra mile, dedicated hours to formulating plans, spending time articulating the importance of these concertos. I was the puppet; he was the puppet master. He pulled the strings, and I played responsively.

My arms were jelly from the double act I'd performed earlier that day. Being a great pianist requires the endurance of an athlete. Moving your arms to a tempo humans are not built to sustain. The injuries a pianist encounters in their career are monumental, sometimes life-lasting. Stretching or no, you can't prepare for that physical challenge. All in the name of music, right?

I sensed tension between Liam and me. Had I mistaken the pressure for something more, something different? I wasn't sure. I sat there waiting for Liam to lay out instructions.

Puppet. Puppet master.

The puppet master seemed to be pondering something. I could not translate the furrowed brow or tense palm rub against his stubbled cheek. He almost spoke, but then retracted his words. I sat there silently.

"Is this too much?" he finally said. "Am I pushing you too hard?"

Where was this coming from? A place of love and care, or was he patronizing my capabilities?

"No," I started, almost inaudibly. "No," I said louder, in case he didn't catch it the first time. "Where is this coming from?"

A lack of self-confidence washed over me. How did I go from *I'm acing this thing* to feelings of self-doubt so quickly? All from one question? The instability of my emotions at that moment scared me.

"No, I mean. Cleo…" Again pondering his words. Why was he so careful? Was he treading lightly over my feelings? Was he worried I would get hurt?

"I just worry sometimes that me and you, well, we complement each other." Then he quickly added, "In our work ethics." God forbid he perceive our relationship as anything more than teacher–student collaboration.

"You know, we are both hard workers, perfectionists sometimes. Am I working you too hard? Do you think you need a teacher who gives you moments to breathe?"

"No!" I said almost too suddenly. "I want perfection. I need it!" *I want you, need you,* is what I wanted to say. I had never had a teacher that taught me, mentored me, managed my career in such a unified manner.

"Just do me a favor, will you? Think about it. Think about taking a breather. You have achieved what you set out to achieve. Maybe think about taking a break."

A break?

I felt confused, betrayed almost. Where was this need to pamper me coming from? My feelings must have shown on my face; Liam quickly grabbed my hand in consolation.

"This has nothing to do with you," he assured me, his deep blue eyes piercing through mine. "Or your work, okay?" His palms blanketed mine, warming them in comfort. "I promise you, and I am only reflecting on my abilities as a teacher. Making sure I am taking the right measures to allow you to reach your potential."

"I mean, haven't I? We are at least on the right path, ticking off our bucket list one honor, one recognition, at a time."

I could tell he'd tapped back into reality. He pulled his hands away, back to formal position, then looked away.

"Liam? What is this really about?" He had created a contemplation so deep that I was unsure if I should continue questioning.

"Nothing, I just…" He pressed his hands over his face, rubbing his eyes in frustration. Then he looked back at me. "It's okay, Cleo. If you think it's working, it's working. You're a testament to that."

"Okay…" I said, still unsure of what was going on.

"Do anything fun last night with Ivan?" he then asked, changing the subject. Or was it all connected? I was not sensing his ulterior motives.

"Yeah, I…" I wasn't sure how much he wanted to hear, or how much I wanted to tell him. I didn't want to mention that I'd upset Ivan, or that he probably wanted nothing to do with me. It seemed redundant. "He took me to the restaurant he used to work at, performed for me. I performed there too." I smiled, picturing the crowd clapping, singing, and dancing.

"It was so eye-opening, so invigorating…"

"Did we have any fun?" He interrupted with a question in a voice that seemed hurt. "Doing this?" He pointed to the piano. What was he getting at?

"Of course!" I reassured him. "I wouldn't sell my soul for these melodies, waste my blood, sweat, and tears over all this if I didn't enjoy it!"

His leg was twitching, his jaw clenched. Utterly impossible to read.

"Liam?" Out of my element, no longer a puppet, I was assertive. I demanded access to his thoughts.

"Let's go out." His words caught me completely off guard. He was out of character, incoherent. Was he spiraling?

"What? Now?" I gestured to look at my watch. Although my wrist was bare, it must have been close to ten o'clock.

"Yes! The last hurrah, if you will. I'm sure the clubs are just opening up now."

"Clubs? Liam…" I was dumbfounded. What changed? First, he was worried about me taking a break with Ivan, now he was worrying about me needing a break?

"Liam, don't bail on me now! Not so close to the finish line!"

"Bail? No, you got this, Cleo! You will be fine, more than fine! You already achieved perfection in tonight's repertoire. There is no need to push yourself anymore. Tonight is the last chance to let go, let loose before it's too late, before life becomes static. Before you become cemented into your future! Once you win, life will demand more from you. This is your future! So yeah…" He stood up, hung his jacket from his pointer finger, and flipped it over his shoulder. "Let's take this opportunity to make some memories, indulge in some unsolicited pleasure."

Before it's too late?

He was breaking. If Liam broke, I broke. Was this how it would end?

At a crossroads, I surrendered to the influence. I couldn't tell if I was making the right decision. All I knew was to choose from the paths authority had placed in front of me, which only led me to greatness. Who was I to define what was right or wrong? It was always a gray area, the assumption that hard work was good, slacking off was bad. Do I now reduce the right option to equal happiness? A way for me to define or rationalize my choices? I was unsure of what my gut was telling me to do, so I followed, and I trusted authority.

Liam took me to a nightclub called Pravda, which means "truth" in Russian. What a fitting name. How desperately I needed the truth right now.

Why are we here, Liam?

Why don't you like Ivan, Liam?

I want to win, Liam.

Do you think I will, Liam?

There was a modern, trendy feel to the ambiance, with alternating florescent hues hovering above.

"Vodka?" Liam asked rhetorically. It was strange seeing my teacher out of his natural habitat. Like I was obligated to treat him as if he were *one of us.*

"What? No!" I protested. "We need to be up bright and early tomorrow."

"I'm not suggesting we get drunk, just live a little. When in Rome, right?" Oh gosh, what kind of idiom-stating, vodka-drinking-mayhem was Liam getting into, and, consequently, who would I become?

Liam ordered two shots of vodka that came with a mini pickle on a toothpick.

"What do they say here? *Nostrovia!*" Liam clinked our glasses and poured the vodka down in one gulp, chasing the bitterness with the pickle. I squinted and mirrored him. The burn slowly trickled down my throat.

"Quick! The pickle," Liam laughed.

He was unhinged.

My eyes watered from the heat circulating throughout my body as I placed the whole pickle into my mouth. "That was disgusting!" I shouted over the annoyingly loud house music that was echoing through the speakers.

"When was the last time you had a shot of vodka?"

"Oh god, never, I think." I made a point not to mention the shots I'd shared with Ivan.

This was not the time.

"No, that can't be true."

"Um, maybe once or twice I tried it, but clearly it's not my taste."

"Well, at least you respected the Russian traditions. You can say you had your shot of vodka in Moscow!"

This was a side of him I wasn't familiar with. He was joking, he was calm, he wasn't micromanaging his actions or words.

"So, Cleo, what's your poison?" He leaned his forearms comfortably on the bar, a smile of mischief printed on his face.

I sipped an occasional and courteous wine at public events, but I did not have a "poison." Never had I felt pressured to conform to society's expectations of adolescence. I always had blinders screwed on tight to the goal set up for me. I never felt the need to distract myself.

"I'll have what you have."

It was only with Liam that I had no control over my choices. I usually knew exactly what I wanted, who I was. But when I was with Liam, it was all about impressing him, echoing him, attempting to become some reflection of him.

"Two vodka tonics."

Sometimes you hear, "One thing led to another." For me, it was always an excuse. One thing doesn't lead to another; it is always premeditated. You see what you're doing along the way, between the bookmarks of two contradicting experiences. How is it that the points between A and Z come out of nowhere?

Such logic was lost on me that night. Maybe the "how" was alcohol.

But one thing did lead to another as I found my head bopping, sweat dripping in the heart of the dance floor, Liam echoing my movements. The vodka had me soaring. I felt placid and happy. My head fell back, I smiled. I felt free.

During dance breaks, we found a comfortable lounge area far enough from the main stage that screaming people did not surround us, but we were close enough to distract ourselves easily during uncomfortable silences.

"It's good, no?" Liam smiled as he watched me mindlessly swallow yet another bitter concoction. It was good; I almost forgot it was alcohol.

"Is this smart?" I snapped back to reality.

"Ah-ah-ah." He pointed his finger at me. "One hour, and then we go back home. One last hour to breathe."

"Okay, fine." I drew the straw toward my mouth and took another sip. I heard the slurp of an empty glass. Was I done already?

"Russia is really something." I smiled as I gazed around the room at the dancers, so effortlessly moving to sounds, seemingly without a care in the world. Maybe one day I'd accomplish some version of this balance. Maybe I could work hard on the weekdays and go harder on the weekends. Is that what I wanted? I wasn't even sure.

The DJ transitioned to a familiar Russian melody. I concentrated, waiting for the familiarity to expose itself.

"Ha!" I let out a loud laugh, then quickly covered my hand to my mouth.

"What?" Liam reciprocated a laugh in response.

"No, nothing. This song..." I paused and listened while the beats transformed the melody. "**Kalinka.** Ivan mentioned that I would be surprised to see how often they play this song in many variations. He wasn't kidding!" It was a club remix of the traditional Russian song Ivan played for me on his piano. So different, yet it held the same patriotic optimism.

Liam grabbed my hand.

"Come, let's dance." He led me to our designated spot on the dance floor. I laughed and joined in with the crowd, with the clapping and the shimmying. Words I would never think I would use to describe my dancing.

Suddenly I experienced the second result of one thing leading to another: my face was close to Liam's. His eyes were seriously penetrating mine. His paternal demeanor vanished, and a new person was standing in front of me— remarkably close to me, his hot, vodka-infused breath on my face.

I froze. Was it my intoxicated mind? Were we just dancing, as friends do? Was my lack of experience in romantic relationships twisting our stance into something more tender?

But I knew. It didn't take logic or reason. I knew what was going on, what was forthcoming. He placed his hand on my cheek. Our eyes locked. And then, it happened. Liam kissed me. It was a kiss filled with passion, longing, and a hint of uncertainty. For a moment, I allowed myself to be swept away by the intensity of it all, losing myself in the intoxicating taste of his lips against mine.

But as quickly as the moment had come, I withdrew. My mind and heart were in a turbulent state, unable to process the depth of emotions that this encounter brought forth. The sudden rush of thoughts, theories, and possibilities flooded my mind, and I was overcome with an instant wave of nausea.

In that instant, I knew I couldn't handle this right now. I needed time to sort through my emotions, to unravel the complexities of what had just transpired. With a heavy heart, I took a step back, creating a physical distance that mirrored the emotional distance I needed to create for myself.

"One moment." I retracted, gravitating toward the exit. The way I saw it, I couldn't walk back in. How? What could I do or say that would explain his behavior without addressing all my desires, hopes, and fears?

It's not fair. Why? Why now?

Liam had captivated my attention for as long as I could remember. It was only once I met Ivan, once I demanded clarity to play my life's work in less than twenty-four hours, that he did the thing I wished he would have done years ago.

Why now, Liam?

I heard a door opening and Liam shouting behind me. "Wait, Cleo!"

"It's really getting late," I reasoned. "I should be asleep by now."

He was handing me my coat. I didn't notice the cold until I retrieved it from him.

"Okay. Can I at least get you a cab? Make sure you get home safely?"

"Sure."

It was an excruciating ride home, each passing moment filled with unspoken tension and a heavy weight of emotions. I could feel Liam's mind working overtime, desperately searching for the right words to explain his actions, yet he remained silent. The silence between us was deafening, amplifying the intensity of the situation.

In that moment, everything felt at stake. Our relationship, my next performance, and even my future seemed to hinge on finding some resolution. The pressure was suffocating, the weight of it all threatening to crush me. I knew that we had to be all right, that we needed to find a way to navigate through this storm of confusion and uncertainty.

As the taxi pulled up to Hotel Metropol, the familiar exterior offered no comfort. All I yearned for was an escape, where I could forget the chaotic events of the night. With a heavy heart and a forced smile, I mustered a strained "goodnight" before hastily exiting the cab, desperate to break free from the cloud of uncertainty.

Once inside my room, I locked the door behind me. But even within the confines of the room, the thoughts continued to unravel, each one more confusing than the last. It was impossible to calm myself, the restlessness within me manifested in relentless pacing.

Back and forth I went, my footsteps echoing in the silence, as if trying to outpace the whirlwind of emotions raging within me. Every step seemed to amplify the intensity of my thoughts, the weight of the situation pressing down on me with each passing second. The room became a prison of my own making, the walls closing in on me as I grappled with the overwhelming turmoil that consumed my mind and soul.

```
WHAT HAPPENED WITH LIAM
1.  Why is he acting this way?
2.  Why did he kiss me?
3.  Does he like me, or does he dislike the thought of
    Ivan and I becoming something?
4.  Why doesn't he like Ivan?
5.  What am I actually feeling?
```

I ran to the toilet bowl, my body convulsing with the intensity of my emotions. The nausea overwhelmed me, forcing me to release the turmoil within. I hunched over, gasping for breath, tears streaming down my face as the remnants of tonight's agony spilled out of me.

For the remainder of the night, I lay in my bed, on top of the covers, eyes wide open, Floral suit still on. I played **La Campanella** in my head, moving my fingers. My next performance would mean the future of my career.

* * *

Despite the unaccustomed-to feeling of a hangover, the lack of sleep, and the lack of time and therefore effort into my appearance, I forced my perseverance into action. I'd fallen asleep in last night's outfit, so I changed into an ethereal Giambattista Valli gown. I'd carefully structured my wardrobe to imbue power and resilience. I was going to win through the complete production that I displayed today. I wasn't going to let the actions of last night's screw-up dictate tonight's outcome.

I started my final performance with **Beethoven - Concerto No. 5** and then followed with **Liszt - La Campanella**. Feelings withheld took over my body as I played. I became transfixed by my melodies, transported to the place where emotions hibernate—a place where love, fear, anger, and desire exists. I played for my life's purpose, for all the time I'd dedicated to the music, for all the time taken away from childhood, for the relationships I couldn't formulate, the relationships I avoided.

And then, as the final notes lingered in the air, there was silence. It wasn't just the absence of sound; it was a profound stillness that enveloped the room. In that moment, it felt as though I had bared my very soul to the world through my music, leaving me vulnerable yet profoundly fulfilled.

Hurrying off the stage, I navigated through the sea of photographers, fans, and fellow musicians, until I found Liam waiting, a mix of pride and apprehension etched on his face. "That was brilliant! You were brilliant!" he beamed, desperately clinging to the hope that my performance had erased the memory of last night's mistakes.

With a trembling smile barely clinging to my lips, I raised a finger to signal that I needed a moment. The corridors stretched endlessly, amplifying the sound of my hurried footsteps as I rushed past him. I beelined to the closest women's lavatory and locked myself in.

The bouquets I carried slipped from my arms, cascading like fragile dreams around my ankles on the cold, unforgiving bathroom tiles. I collapsed to the floor, the tears flowing freely, my sobs echoing through the empty space. I covered my mouth with trembling hands, desperately trying to muffle the sound of my anguish.

Why was I crying? I had no idea. The nerves, the anticipation? The buildup of emotions over this past hour? Over the past twenty-four hours? Over the past twenty years? I stopped questioning and surrendered to the torrent of emotions, my sobs blending with the distant echoes of the bustling halls.

14

THE TROPHY WIFE

New York City, Present Day

The world stands still. Time seeps through my fingers without my awareness. Time races by rapidly and stalls in a motionless image.

There are repercussions for my actions.

Conor, too, got the phone call from Principal Howard's office, letting him know I did not show up for pickup.

Conor was there as I got scolded.

Conor was there when she informed me there would be a hefty bill next time this happens.

"There won't be a next time," I promise all who were affected.

There were no lectures. Instead, there was silence.

Conor is upset, and I see that for what it is.

But I finally got work done! I want to tell him. *I managed this with one working arm!* I grow a sense of pride. I want to share my win with Conor, but I know my boundaries. I'll wait until the dust settles.

* * *

I have written the plot of my next book. It became far more interesting once I assembled the words into an engaging narrative. The outline began to take shape, and I was unable to break free until I had a complete synopsis.

The severity of my tardiness has increased considerably. I can barely hear the noise surrounding me; my mind is in a distant realm.

I often find my body leaving my presence, making its way inside another paradigm. I often feel the heat as Conor, frustrated, removes my headphones from my ears, notifying me that he's had yet another one-sided conversation.

I often deal with my kids scowling at me in distress when I don't attend to them immediately.

I find comfort in separating my mind from where my body settles. It sustains me, helps me get through my daily routines. So I stop attempting to socialize. My social scene involves a compilation of:

a) the mums of my children's friends or

b) the wives of Conor's friends.

I can manage the gossip that ensues behind my back due to the snobbery I exude or my absence at said event.

Besides, I like my own space. The noises I choose to hear: the white noise of the AC, the selected compositions over the speakers. Silence.

For almost a decade, I have been suffering from the permanent headache of not publishing anything substantial. Then I had children, one after the other. When do I get the chance to reach my full potential with a bit of leg space? How do I give myself entirely to all aspects of my life?

I know it's a universal question most mothers have, but what is the answer?

Don't be an exceptional mum?

How about a great wife? Ignore that too?

Don't work full time?

The only sources of feedback come from gurus or motivational speakers who rant about setting goals, how the power of thought holds such potential.

Those people don't have the answers.

I don't either.

I am just trying one task at a time.

```
TASKS:
Email query letter - check
```

Things will be different now. I will slowly get back on track.

Now onto task number two.

I feel my phone vibrate in my jeans pocket; it's Conor, calling me during work hours. I panic. Did I forget something again? An errand to run? A scheduled meeting, perhaps?

"Conor?"

"I got it!" His voice breaks. Is it grief? Excitement?

"Got what?"

"The AMHH award!"

The American Mental Health Honors acknowledges several distinguished mental health specialists, recognizing their lifetime contributions to psychological science, lifetime assistance, and significant research.

"Oh, Conor, I'm so proud of you!" I am. Conor is extraordinary at his job. Not only does he master his one-on-one sessions, but he also researches new studies to support a better mental hygiene system. He volunteers with nonprofit organizations that help disadvantaged groups receive mental health care.

His hard work and dedication are finally getting the recognition they deserve.

I think about the email I sent Ramona and smile.

Things are looking good for us.

* * *

Friday passes, and I still haven't heard back from Ramona. The anticipation is killing me. Possibly literally—I forget to eat. I live off black coffee and weed, then gobble down dinner with Conor and the kids.

When Conor notices my clothes hanging off me and my mind constantly elsewhere, we go through the same repetitive conversation.

"Go see someone, please." *Someone* being a therapist. Conor taking charge of my mental state was never on the table.

"I'm fine. I'm just a little stressed."

"It's okay to take something. You don't have to do it all on your own."

"I don't need it. I am managing."

"Does this have anything to do with your—"

"Don't say it." I know he wants to bring up my mother's condition.

A sleeping pill, a waking pill, a happy pill, a calming pill. Pharmaceutical artificial intelligence.

That is the extent of our conversations.

We have them all too frequently.

Like the following:

"Don't be late."

"I won't be late."

"You're always late."

"Don't assume my actions."

"Cleo, this is very important; be on time."

We have that conversation the week before Conor accepts his award at Manhattan Penthouse.

"Of course I'll be on time. I'll drop off the kids at Shannon's and go straight to you."

"Cleo, really, please."

"Conor, you're getting on my nerves now."

The conversation resurfaces three days later. Then again in another two days, and then the day of the awards.

I am growing tired of these conversations. I don't need another headache. It's been a week since I sent my synopsis, and I still haven't heard back from Ramona, that knob. Rushing me to email her, and then radio silence.

I avert my mind from Ramona. I will take a break from those worries. Tonight is about Conor. Tonight, I have a list of tasks to check off, and all in a matter of eight hours.

```
1.  Drop off the kids at Shannon's
2.  Transform into something presentable
```

Shannon, a retired psychiatrist from Conor's practice, had become our go-to babysitter, fostering a mutual affection between her and my children. They eagerly anticipated Shannon's visits, relishing the attention and pampering she showered upon them. In return, Shannon found solace in their companionship and cherished the opportunity to care for someone, especially after her husband's passing a couple of years ago and her children leaving the nest. It was a symbiotic arrangement that benefited us all.

What sweetened the deal further was Shannon's reluctance to travel late at night. We would drop off the kids at her place before heading out for our evening escapades and retrieve them the following day. This allowed Conor and me to extend our date nights in an empty house, even if we usually succumbed to exhaustion the moment we returned home. Having the option was comforting.

As I sat in the back of a cab, I grabbed a compact mirror and flipped it open. What had I been thinking? I was far from presentable. A sigh escaped my lips. My makeup required touch-ups, my outfit lacked flair, and I wasn't in the right frame of mind to play the role of the flawless companion among esteemed guests, presenting myself as a trophy wife akin to what Diane did with Eric. However, for Conor's sake, I needed to look a bit more captivating.

With an hour to spare, I devised a plan. Bloomingdale's was a mere twenty-minute walk from the event venue. I decided to make a quick pit stop there to freshen up. I estimated that I had about thirty minutes to spare, allowing me to stroll, rather than rush, and arrive just in time.

My phone buzzed with a message from Conor.

Conor: Are the kids at Shannon's yet?

Me: Yes!

Conor: Are you on the way now?

Me: Conor!

Conor: Well, are you?

Me: Yes! I'm on the way.

Conor: Okay, great!

The micromanaging is entirely unnecessary at this point. I get it; I tend to be late. Tonight, it is essential that I am on time. I am a capable woman who has been punctual plenty of times before.

```
New list for Bloomingdale's:
1.  Buy my go-to lipstick, Chanel shade 466
2.  Find an outfit
```

I add some liner from the counter too. Like second nature, I apply it the way I used to, back when makeup was a part of my daily routine.

"Need assistance finding anything?" a saleswoman asks.

"No, thanks!" I hold the eyeliner to my eye. "I'm all set."

She shoots me a disapproving look.

Excuse me, but aren't testers meant for precisely this purpose?

I hurry to the women's clothing department and spot a pricey black Coperni slip dress. It's a bit of a splurge, but I suppose it'll do the job. It should pair well with the Saint Laurent coat I'm currently wearing. Then, a rather insistent saleswoman convinces me to look at those Khaite over-the-knee boots. She's quite adamant that they'll make a bold statement, peeking out from the dress's high slit.

"Okay, add it to the list." What's one more item in the grand scheme of things?

I pay the saleslady, rip off the tags, transform myself in the dressing room, and place my worn outfit into the large Bloomingdale's bag. I am good with time, and I may even be early.

I listen to my music, letting the breeze wash over me as I stroll down Fifth Avenue. Stroll, not rush. No rushing necessary today. I will be early. Tonight, I will show up for Conor. I am even smiling now—weird.

I feel my phone buzz in my hand. It is probably Conor with another "You better not be late."

I can't wait to let him know I'll be fifteen minutes early.

It is not Conor, but Ramona. Ramona!

My surroundings come to a halt. The air drops in temperature as it seeps through my insides. I know that the feedback I receive will lead me toward my next destination.

It reads:

We need to discuss your email. I went over it yesterday. It needs help.

What? That's all I'm getting? March is two weeks away, and I need more feedback before I can develop my work any further. I quickly write back:

Can you please elaborate? I will get right on it!

The pedestrians do not like my multitasking. I stand still mid-sidewalk.

"My apologies," I say to them all. Then I quickly replace my headphones and play **Tchaikovsky - Swan Lake Op. 20** as I continue hurrying down the street.

I quicken my jogging pace, and the world starts to spin around me. My breath comes in rapid bursts, my heart pounding like a drum solo. The fluttering in my stomach multiplies and spreads to my chest. Tears threaten to spill from my eyes.

No, I can't let this happen now. It's Conor's night. I can't make it about me. I'll deal with it later.

But my body doesn't cooperate. I'm trembling, my breaths shallow and uneven. I try to calm myself by slowing my breath consciously, but it only intensifies the sensation of panic.

It will all be okay. It will all work out. It has to. I don't have any other choice, no plan B.

This was my plan B.

Manhattan Penthouse stands before me with ten minutes to spare.

The world stands still. Time seeps through my fingers without my awareness. Time races by rapidly and stalls in a motionless image.

15

THE DAM

Moscow, Ten Years Ago

I won. Claiming the coveted first place, the magnitude of this illustrious Grand Prix Award weighs heavy in my hands.

And yet, as I stood there, bathed in the spotlight's warm embrace, I felt strangely disconnected, as if I were a spectator to my own success.

I won, but I didn't feel special or different. I'd envisioned this moment repeatedly in my head. I pictured myself owning it, living on cloud nine, yet all I could think of was Ivan. Ivan and Liam.

The violin contest concluded with Ivan in second place. As expected, he was just as ecstatic as if he had placed first. Regardless of how far Ivan got, he would have still been fulfilled to the same degree. In an inspiring and foreign way, Ivan led a life filled with appreciation for where he was and what he possessed. It was a special kind of happiness.

I wanted that in my life, wanted him in my life. Was that ever a possibility? Where did this leave me with Ivan? With Liam?

```
MY ROMANTIC ALTERNATIVES:
1.  Will Ivan ever speak to me again?
2.  If he does, what are we to do now that I'll be
    leaving Russia?
3.  Will I see him again?
4.  Will I feel that intensely again?
```

<pre>
5. On the other hand, what am I doing with Liam? He's
    coming back with me, but there is so much we need
    to unpack.
</pre>

Is there, though? Maybe we can go back to where we were before this trip, before that moment of romance? Was it romance? Did it come from a moment of impulsive desire? An act of manipulation?

Neither seemed promising. That was my belief: once you crossed certain lines, there was no return to the innocence of the past. And who makes a long-distance relationship work? Especially when I had no plans of ever going back to Russia.

It was time for me to move forward. The only problem was that I had no clear destination in mind.

The winners' gala concert was anticlimactic.

A final performance, all winners of all categories. My final performance in Russia. One last moment to share.

Then the Grand Prix was awarded to me.

I held on to the statue.

Finally, I was able to take it all in.

My winnings. My future. It all looked promising.

Everything was going according to plan.

Yet, beneath the veneer of success, a deep-seated knot remained in the recesses of my chest, gnawing at me relentlessly.

Was this not the victory I dreamed about for years? Was this not enough? Did I want more?

I won. The audience cheered. I accepted the award, the attention. I spoke with the press, and I posed for the photographers. Yet my mind was elsewhere.

Ivan.

Liam.

On the plus side, I couldn't talk to either of them since I was much too busy. If I could press the pause button for just a moment longer, maybe the answers would come to me.

They didn't.

The comedown numbed me as I packed away the score sheets, gowns, and memories I'd formed over these past few weeks.

When I destroyed everything at Dom, I had sealed my fate with Ivan. My last chance for a life of stability, comfort, and uncomplicated happiness.

Then I remembered: I was leaving Russia. Did Ivan and I ever stand a chance? Could we make this more significant than what we had? A short-lived romance?

I withheld these emotions. It wasn't worth drowning in my feelings. Drowning in emotions seemed futile, powerless.

A gentle knock at the door pulled me from my reverie, making me aware of how far adrift I had become. I remained motionless, having made no progress with my packing. Minutes, maybe even hours had passed unnoticed.

Another great wave of tears was hindered by the dam I'd built. It was Ivan.

My heart stopped; my body went cold. I was mute, helpless, dizzy.

I felt the little room between us as he leaned one arm against the doorjamb, leveling with me. His blank eyes held no clues to his emotions. The look on his face was vacant.

"I just came here to say you won, so, you know, I don't have to pretend to like you anymore. Goodbye, Cleo." He turned to leave.

I stood there, desperately trying to process his words, searching for something to say that would keep him from leaving. It felt like the dam holding back my emotions was on the verge of bursting open.

Suddenly, Ivan turned back. A smile cracked wide on his face, and my heart started to beat once more. I hadn't noticed I'd been holding my breath until I properly exhaled.

"You nob!" I hit him with the blouse I was in the middle of folding.

Ivan's laughs filled my body with lightness again.

"You don't really think I can leave you like that?"

He had a calming demeanor that was contagious. Ivan allowed me the chance to appreciate my win, to feel again. Feelings of happiness to be near him once more and sadness, as it was nearing its end.

"Ivan." My tone changed to earnest. "You know I am truly, so, so sorry,"

"Cleo, do not worry."

"You're not mad?"

"I was never mad. Maybe a little confused or hurt."

"You know I don't honestly believe what I said."

"I know."

"I was confused."

"That's okay!"

"I would take it all back to get back these last few wasted days without you."

"I would too."

The words seeped into my heart as we both inhaled this moment.

"You forgive me?"

"Of course I do, Cleo. I just needed a little time."

The tears came out; the dam collapsed.

I felt the comfort of Ivan wrap around my body, and we stood like that by the door for a little while.

It was a forced engagement to pull away from Ivan. A harrowing feeling, knowing that these were our last moments for the foreseeable future.

"Come in!" I finally said, walking back to my meticulously organized piles within the large trunk, the symbol of my disappearance.

"Don't go!" Ivan grabbed my waist from behind, pulling me closer to him.

"I wish." I did. I wished I could stay, but that wasn't practical.

"When will I see you next?"

"When will you finally leave Russia?" I turned to face him.

"For you? Whenever you want!" Charming.

"For real, though, what is next for Ivan the Terrible?"

"I don't know."

I dropped the pajama set I was middle of folding as he held my hands. "Tell me to come, and I'll be on the next flight. I want to see what you will do next!"

That was a good question, and I knew Liam would have an answer on our flight home. He was great at his job, and he had all the right connections to bring my plans to fruition.

"I'll let you know the moment I find out." I went back to folding.

"And I will be there the moment you tell me."

My face remained smiling as I continued to fold.

So this was it? Would there be a long-distance plan? I certainly hoped so. I had a desire, a need to be around him. My heart was drawn to Ivan by magnetic force. We would not be swayed by logistics or practicality.

"Cleo," he whispered tenderly, his arms enveloping me in a warm, protective embrace. As he pulled me closer, I could feel the reassuring thud of his heart against my chest. His words hung in the air, heavy with sincerity. "I really, really like you. You are very special to me, you know?"

My heart skipped a beat, and I felt a rush of warmth flood my cheeks. No one had ever been so candid and direct about their feelings for me before. It was both thrilling and intimidating, leaving me momentarily speechless.

I managed to muster a shy smile, my gaze locked with his. "I want to make sure to see you again," he continued, his eyes earnestly searching mine. The world seemed to fade away as he turned me around, positioning us so that we could see each other clearly.

"We'll make it happen," I promised, the words escaping my lips with a sense of determination, even though I had no concrete plan in mind. But I knew that there was something undeniable between us, something worth pursuing.

In that moment, as I stood in his embrace, my breath was stolen once again. Ivan's lips met mine in a gentle, lingering kiss. It was his way of expressing agreement, his silent vow that we would find a way to be together again, no matter the obstacles. Yes, we would make it happen, somehow.

Another knock at the door interrupted the moment. It was Liam. It was always Liam interrupting those moments.

He looked at Ivan and back at me. I could tell his blood was boiling as he clenched his jaw but said nothing. He started with that nervous cough, a way of saying, *Everyone stop what you're doing.*

"Uh, Ivan, can I have a moment with Cleo? We have a few matters to discuss."

Was us one of them?

"Of course!" Ivan gave me a passionate kiss, a way of marking his territory. A gesture I had no problem with, but it made Liam avert his eyes.

"Goodbye, Cleo. I will see you tomorrow morning before you leave."

Every time Ivan kissed me, every time our bodies touched, I felt the vibrations run through my veins. I felt my heart beat a little faster, I felt whole.

And when he lets go, I was left broken.

Liam wiped his forehead in agitation. He never seemed to allow himself to stay calm around Ivan, begging the questions:

```
LIAM 2.0
1.  Was our kiss real?
2.  Are there some unresolved feelings? Or is it just
    Ivan?
3.  The competition is over; there is no question of
    purposeful distraction or grand schemes to mess up
    the chances for one another. Ivan wants to continue
    whatever this is with me long distance.
```

So, what is this underlining dislike toward Ivan? I may never know.

"Cleo, I have great news," Liam almost shouted the moment Ivan left. "LCR wants to organize a meeting with you, a potential record deal, and possibly a world tour. They want it all! They want it now! While you're still hot in the press."

I had dreamed of signing on with London Classical Records. "Already? I thought this kind of news would start coming up once I got home."

"I know! Isn't it great? It is everything you wanted. They are talking La Scala, Sydney Opera House, Hollywood Bowl, Carnegie Hall, even a feature at this year's Proms!"

"Wait, what?" I let out a nervous laugh. Then the tears came, that paradoxical reaction of crying when filled with joy.

This moment felt like the culmination of every dream I had ever held close to my heart—everything I had struggled for and hoped for had finally reached its long-awaited revelation. It was like witnessing a beautifully choreographed dance of destiny, a domino effect of everything falling perfectly into place.

Liam, the steadfast and silent supporter who had been there through thick and thin, pulled me into a tight hug. His embrace was comforting, a testament to the bond we shared. "I'm so proud of you,"

Liam's arms enveloped me in a tight embrace, his words of pride whispered into the crown of my head. The warmth of his tears mingled with the unspoken tension that had simmered between us for far too long. This intimacy was unfamiliar territory for us; we had rarely acknowledged our own accomplishments, as if celebrating them might somehow threaten us from continuing forward.

The night at Pravda, his affection was evident. Now he was hugging me, and I didn't want to let go. The sensation of his closeness was intoxicating, and I wanted to savor it, to etch it into my memory forever.

So, I lingered there, wrapped in his arms, trying to capture every detail of the moment. I yearned to encapsulate this feeling, to compress it into a pill-like form that I could keep for those inevitable days when I needed an extra dose of ecstasy. I was precisely where I should have been. I was finally whole.

Then, to ruin it all, I raised my face to Liam's and kissed him. He didn't reach for me; I started it. I kissed him for the hours he'd sacrificed for me, for the connections he'd created, making all my dreams come true. I kissed him because, in that moment, I felt a rush of love for him. Was it romantic love? I wasn't sure. I wasn't sure if it was passionate love or platonic sensation, but it was undeniably some variant of love.

A desire, a pull, an outpouring of incredible emotion.

He pulled me closer and reciprocated. Before I knew it, the clothes I'd spent an hour folding were on the floor. Friction wrinkled the score sheets to minor tears. The Grand Prix bounced off my bed and onto the soft carpet. My acid lime green gown was unzipped and scratching against Liam's bare chest. I couldn't see the significance of this moment, but it felt right.

16

DODGING BULLETS

New York City, Present Day

I have heard about blackouts before. I never drank to the point of blackout. Conor did, in the past. He told stories all the time—a uni student working hard for his degree, drinking harder on the weekends. The thought of drinking to that point confused me. Why would someone willingly put themselves into a position where they lose all control?

I had never experienced a blackout. Not until tonight.

I can't explain what happened. I can't fill in the blanks between standing outside of Manhattan Penthouse, when I just needed a moment of silence, and walking in an hour late. I don't know how I can explain this to Conor. I see on my phone the many worried texts he sent me. When? Am I losing my mind?

This frightens me.

I do not try to manufacture a logical understanding of my behavior, one Conor could fully comprehend. If I mention the blackout, he will treat me like one of his patients. He will send me off with a prescription for an antipsychotic or an appointment with the very best psychiatrist.

So, I say nothing. What is there to say? I know I made it to his event on time, but somehow, I missed his acceptance speech. How?

I missed the opportunity for Conor to kiss me passionately and thank me in his speech. Did he thank me, his absentee wife, in front of his colleagues?

We are home after an eerily silent Uber ride. The kids are still at Shannon's. It is the perfect opportunity for Conor to have it out with me.

In these four walls, it is just me and Conor, Conor and I, no distractions. The volume of our voices can go up a couple of notches. No need for indoor voices when the kids can't hear us.

Conor silently grabs a stemless glass and pours himself some red wine. It is not like Conor to self-soothe like this. A sign of what is yet to unfold. The room is increasingly quiet as I stare at him, waiting to see who should speak up first. I take the liberty—it's safer that way. I can set the tone.

"Conor, talk to me."

"I am just so done, Cleo." Conor takes off his glasses and rubs his eyes. "I have no energy for this anymore." His voice is sharp as the words cut through his teeth.

"For this?" I point between us. "Or just me?"

"All of it! My vitality is spent!" His voice is still calm, quiet, although I can hear the rumbles of a cry stirring.

Scream at me! I want to shout. *Get pissed. Let those bloody emotions out! Let's give it to each other so we can get past this.*

"What are you saying?" That is all that comes out. "You want to end it all? Over a little incident? What about—"

"Cleo! This wasn't a little incident! It was a life-changing event, and I was alone." There is disappointment and hurt in his words. The bitterness is devastating.

"Did you care that I wasn't there because of what people might think? Or was it—"

The explosive sound of glass crashing buries my voice.

I jump.

"Enough!" Conor has thrown his glass of wine onto the floor, the glass fragmenting recklessly about our feet. There are stains on the furniture. I know Conor is thinking about cleaning up the mess.

I'm not sure if I should be concerned or turned on. Finally, Conor is showing me his emotions—a decade of buildup. But my worries are greater. Not for his mental state—Conor is unlikely to break—but for the state of our relationship.

"You need space. I need space. I'm going on a walk," I finally say.

"That's grand! Just grand!"

Is a walk the right move? It's almost midnight. Probably not—no, definitely not. What is my plan anyway?

Am I dodging bullets because I want to keep myself safe, or get away from ramifications?

"Go." He shoos his hand after me. "As you do. Just run away from our problems before we actually get a chance to work on them."

"I am not running away!" I hurry back into the kitchen. "I am giving you time to think before you say something that you will later regret." That isn't the truth at all. I am running away, so I have time to consider this obstacle. I need to breathe, and maybe strategize. How can I get this issue ironed out?

Is it one particular issue, though?

I grab my phone and my knotted headphones and leave before my conscience forces me to stay.

I surrender to the enchanting sway of **Vittorio Monti - Czardas** as I wander through dimly lit streets. With each step, the music becomes more haunting, and I respond by hastening my stride, my heart echoing the rhythm of the melody, a silent duet.

Ivan materialized like a spectral figure from my past, running alongside me, his violin cradled beneath his chin, his bow swaying dramatically in the air, coaxing heartbreaking melodies from the strings. Together, we fled the clutches of my present-day problems. His form remained elusive, a shadowy silhouette, while his violin emitted mournful strains that seemed to mockingly echo the growing distance between us. Where I find myself now, the trajectory of my romance repeating once more. Another love slipping away, and I'm left with a sense of powerlessness.

17

THE CONFESSION

Moscow, Ten Years Ago

Yesterday was a blur.

It was not a dream, this sudden fantasy that occurred between Liam and me. I still recall the lines we crossed because of my initiation. My mind went right back to that moment when Ivan forgave me, when I could have imagined a life with Ivan outside of Russia, outside of this competition.

Yet it was as though I was under a spell. The moment Liam and I stopped, the questions built up again in my head; I formulated the list instantaneously. I tried to ignore them as we both got dressed in silence, back to teacher and student.

I tried to force up my stalled zipper as my breathing accelerated. I would not allow the list to repeat in my head. I couldn't ruminate, not now.

"Cleo."

I stopped and looked up.

"Let me help." Liam came closer and helped the zipper into a seamless closing.

The rush was over. I began to feel shy again. I felt goose bumps appear on my arms, and the heat accumulated by proximity.

I turned around; he didn't move. I automatically sensed the need to separate, to be able to think again. I stepped backward, feeling my thigh hit the bed. I was still unable to look Liam in the eye.

"Cleo," he repeated, forcing me to make eye contact. "Breathe."

"I am breathing."

"You're shaking." He smiled and held on to my forearms.

"Just a lot to take in." I wasn't sure if I meant us, or the tour, or the record deal; I was mapping out a plan for where to go from here.

Would this, Liam and me, turn into something more? I owed Ivan an explanation, but not yet. Maybe this would go nowhere, and I could pursue a long-distance affair. It seemed like my schedule would be jam-packed for the foreseeable future, so perhaps a long-distance boyfriend was all I needed.

Honestly, I didn't know.

"You are going to do great. You always have." Liam assumed I was talking about the tour, the record deal. So, I left it at that.

* * *

The following day, it was as though a switch had been flipped, and our relationship resumed its regular dynamic. Like we'd been ensconced in an alternate universe for that brief flash of time, and now we were back where we started.

We all said goodbye. Goodbye to the competition, to Russia, to Ivan.

Liam had expected Ivan would come to say goodbye. He turned away discreetly as Ivan lifted me up and kissed me passionately, holding onto me as if he never wanted to let go.

I reciprocated but I couldn't shake the sensation of Liam's watchful gaze from my periphery. As Ivan embraced me, I felt every minute of the hug, all my senses heightened. Time went by slowly as I held on to every memory that I could collect: the touch, the breath, the feelings of love and romance. I owed Ivan a proper goodbye. I just couldn't muster one up with Liam by our side.

Those were my last moments with Ivan, and the room was charged with an unspoken, heart-wrenching sadness. We held on to one another as a cloud of melancholy enveloped us, as the time arrived for us to go down the hallway and into the elevator, to follow the bellboy to my car, rolling away my gowns, score sheets, and the Grand Prix Award.

It was just the three of us: Ivan, Liam, and me—a trio filled with palpable tension.

This was it, our last chance at a proper goodbye.

Our last embrace. Our last kiss. One last kiss to make Liam squirm in rage, one last kiss to remind me of what I will be missing. One last kiss for me to hold on to fondly as I made the painful decision of which path to choose.

"You did it, Cleo," Ivan exclaimed, his eyes ablaze with genuine excitement. "You said you were going to win this competition and look at you now!"

In that moment, I wanted to tell him that winning didn't matter as much as being with him, that his presence was more special to me than any victory. I longed to fast-forward through the confusion and uncertainty and finally embrace the man who had captured my heart, whoever he might be.

But instead, I swallowed the surge of emotions welling up within me. I was afraid of what I might say, fearful that confessing my feelings would only lead to more suffering and confusion. So, I bit my trembling bottom lip and fought back tears, choosing to keep my emotions locked away for now.

Ivan cradled my face in his large hands, and in a voice trembling with emotion, he began reciting something in Russian. If he hadn't held my head, I might have turned away, overwhelmed by the intensity of his serenade, especially with Liam bearing witness. The serenade came to an end, and Ivan gently kissed my forehead. There was a glistening tear in his eye that mirrored my own sorrow.

"What does that mean?" I finally asked, my voice barely more than a whisper, wanting to keep our intimate moment private from Liam's ears.

"Oh, I am not good at making it English." He smiled and looked away. I never saw Ivan show a glimpse of timidness or reservation; he was always confident. He looked back at me, now holding my hands.

"It is a poem called…um, 'Confession,' by Alexander Pushkin. I thought about it last night when I saw you win. It made me think about how I feel about you at that moment, at this moment. I don't want to say goodbye."

I would have surrendered completely to the emotions welling up inside me, but I couldn't—not with Liam in such proximity.

"Don't say goodbye," I said quietly, "I will call you when I land. We will talk every day until you visit me. Who knows, maybe we will meet halfway? I believe it's Poland; I searched it online last night." He smiled at the idea of my investigation.

Liam interjected, "I'm sorry to interrupt, but we really must be going." He had likely tried to intervene before Ivan's passionate serenade.

My hand reached out, clinging to Ivan's until we were too far apart, and we reluctantly let go. The back seat of the car felt stiflingly warm. I longed to turn back, to share one more embrace with Ivan. Instead, I settled into the seat beside Liam and watched Ivan recede into the distance. I raised a hand in a silent farewell, silently conveying, "*Do svidaniya,* Ivan. Until next time."

An intense and somber silence filled the car during the drive to the airport. On our flight, Liam and I exchanged only a few words. It was as if last night hadn't transpired, as if I weren't grappling with the impending farewell to Ivan. Was it because we had too much to say or because there were simply no words to express the depth of our emotions?

* * *

I craved solitude the moment we stepped back into our empty home.

It felt hauntingly quiet, devoid of the familiar presence of family, friends, Ivan, or even Liam. Just me, engulfed in the silence.

This was my chance to breathe, to let my thoughts flow freely, to dream once more. The weight of my emotions and the exhaustion of the journey threatened to pull me into slumber, but I resisted. Throughout the entire flight home, one persistent thought had consumed my mind.

I turned on my computer, my fingers trembling slightly with anticipation. My first action was to search for it: "Alexander Pushkin, Confession."

I started reading as I dissected each word.

"However, I am sick with love;

Without you I am bored, I yawn…"

Did I hold the right to believe that these words, this poem was Ivan's way of projecting his emotions towards me? Was this in fact Ivan's confession?

"I have to tell you, how I love you!"

I read that last line over and over again.

It was just the beginning, but I'd read enough. As I lay back, a torrent of tears streamed from my eyes, and my heart throbbed with an overwhelming ache. I could feel the depth of my emotions surging within me, a profound confirmation of the passionate, romantic love that bound me to Ivan.

18

THE ENCHANTED FLORIN

New York City, Present Day

The next week is overshadowed by an ominous silence.

Monday starts with robotic motions as we play out our tasks. There are a few tweaks and shifts in our routine now, since the night of the awards. Conor has stepped down as my full-service barista. I understand, and, in any case, I wasn't too bothered to get up earlier. It allows me time to prepare my iced coffee and enjoy the peaceful serenity before the family wakes up.

Our paths cross, but we never linger in one place for long. There are no more aimless conversations. The only words we exchange must hold some importance.

I try to fix this, try to show Conor that I want to go back to the way we were before the event. I try to make small talk, but Conor finds a way to end the exchanges abruptly.

Once Conor and the kids go about their morning routines, I hide in the home gym and blast Bach or Grieg. With passive aggression releasing on the elliptical (one-handed), I crush through the thirty minutes of alone time.

Every morning, before I take my shower, I send Ramona a courtesy text. A quick hello: Hi? Remember me? That sort of thing; Give or take. But Ramona ignores me. One week remains before my deadline, and I have a brief write-up; I have something to send. But that doesn't matter if Ramona won't respond. So why am I even trying?

However hard I try approaching Conor or asking Ramona for help, I get pushed five steps backward.

I try to put effort into my appearance. I switch out my favorite dark hues for a rib-knitted teal minidress with dramatic cutouts. It's a tad short and maybe not age-appropriate, but it's a significant improvement from my usual matching sweats. I must have gotten this dress years ago. I'm not sure I've ever worn it, so why not today?

I anticipate some reaction. Instead, as I enter the kitchen, I face the unexpected sounds of Peppa Pig. The kids sit, pajamas on, eyes glued to the telly. Conor is on his phone. A very social family indeed.

I want to rush them out of the house; they have to leave in two minutes. Why is no one ready? *Breathe.* I know that my meddling will only perpetuate chaos.

Breathe. Conor will deal with this. Breathe.

Instead, I kiss Sebastian on his full head of hair and start with:

"Good morning, children!" *Shit, should I have said "everyone"? Did I exclude Conor unintentionally?*

"Parent-teacher conference is today at three. Don't be late." The first words Conor has recited to me in what feels like days. No "good morning," no glance at my attractive outfit.

"I know, I'll be there!"

I completely forgot. I now understand why everyone is so calm: the kids are home today. Great! There goes one wasted day of not writing. I fall back in my chair, realizing I now have nowhere to go.

"Mommy, can Kitty come over?" Olivia oh-so-innocently asks.

"Sure, let me ask her mum," I say before I can strategize.

I haven't even thought about how Kitty and Olivia's friendship may be affected by my falling out with Diane. They are only children, after all. Olivia will go through many friendships. She'll be fine without Kitty's excessive playdates.

Or maybe their bond will force Diane and I to get together, mend things. Go back to the way we were.

But for now, I'll wait a bit, then let Olivia know that "Kitty is actually very busy today. Maybe some other time." And hope to God we don't bump into her in our building.

Conor says his goodbyes, although I can't detect if the farewells are exclusively for the children or all-encompassing.

"Okay, bye, Daddy!" I say after he's already shut the door.

"All right, kids, telly off! Let's do something today, huh?"

After several hours of screen time, a walk to Washington Square Park, snack breaks, and remnants of arts and crafts covering the floor, all four of us are finally dressed, fed, and ready to go to school.

The kids play outside as Conor and I manage to fit ourselves into uncomfortable, child-sized chairs. We play the part of a happy couple querying for the reports of our little kids.

I've committed to this skimpy outfit, and now I regret it. Why did I not change back into the dull suits I usually wear? I pull at my hem as I try to sit appropriately in front of the teachers. My shifting postures become distracting, and I can feel the heat of Conor's angst.

Yet we smile, chat politely, respond with, *Oh, thank you, I know, he is such a doll at home too,* and, *What? Did she make that? That's incredible!*

"Ciara is a wonderful child."

"Oh, thank you—" I begin.

And then the unexpected.

"There is one thing I want to discuss," Mrs. Clarke says.

Completely off guard, Conor and I exchange confused looks—it almost feels like we're in unison again.

"I want you to review her decline in school performance."

That is a harsh word to describe my child's work. I almost feel the need to defend Ciara. She is a diligent eight-year-old: intellectual, studious, and wise beyond her years. What can Mrs. Clarke possibly expect from this child?

A pile of papers makes a loud thud on the table in front of us.

"As you see, this was Ciara's work from earlier this year." She points to the front paper, which displays a red A. In Ciara's neat handwriting, she's marked all the correct answers.

"She's a bright one." Mrs. Clarke smiles.

Then I watch the smile fade and take a glance back at the papers.

"I want you to look at these." She slowly flips the papers one by one to the back of the pile, showing declining grades and fewer answered questions. One page catches my eye, and I inhale in response. It looks so familiar. The little doodles around her work are shapeless and hard to identify.

"You see, I started noticing little hints of distraction, daydreaming…"

I keep quiet.

"I figure it's just a phase; maybe she's bored. Maybe it's a reaction to something happening at home?"

"Our home?" I look dumbfoundedly at Conor. "No, no—"

"We will have a talk with her," Conor assures the teacher before I unintentionally suggest any truth to our secrets. The possibility of Ciara catching on to our cold behavior toward each other. Or the repeated neglect. Can I possibly have done anything else wrong?

I sincerely hope Conor will not psychoanalyze Ciara. That's a promise I made Conor make when we got married.

Don't go using this psychiatry, analytical bullshit on me, okay? And not on our kids either! I could only imagine it doing damage.

"I'm sure it's nothing," Mrs. Clarke encourages us. "I will keep an eye on her and keep you both posted. But a talk sounds good. See what Ciara says."

* * *

As Conor showers and brushes his teeth, I slather on my nightly moisturizers. We are two individuals going about our ways. The room is quiet; the house is soundless. The kids are sleeping. The lights are out. It is the first time since the awards I can feel the space between Conor and me. Before today, we were just slipping by one another.

"We need to speak about Ciara," Conor finally says as he starts getting into his pajamas.

"It's a phase, I'm sure." Deflecting, detaching from the reality of what might be going on.

Conor sits down. "There was this weird thing that happened." There's no animosity in his tone, just the voice of a concerned father.

Regardless of the topic, it feels so good sitting next to Conor, feeling his weight on the bed, looking into his eyes.

"What?"

"Well, I once walked into her bedroom. I assumed she was studying or reading. Her back was to me, and she kind of just stood there in the middle of her room."

"And?" I am anticipating more.

"And nothing. She looked kind of hypnotized, just somewhere else…. Her arms were moving a bit, and I could have sworn she was whispering something or mouthing—"

"Oh, that's nothing." I continue to button my pajama shirt. "I spaced out all the time as a kid. She was probably just thinking about something she read or learned." I get comfortable in bed. "It's nothing," I reassure Conor again. "I'll talk with her, okay? Tomorrow, when I pick her up. Oh gosh, you scared me." I rest my head on the pillow and shut off my lamp.

"Oh, okay…goodnight."

* * *

Over the next few days, we go back to our regular programming. We slip back into passive-aggressive white noise. The only words Conor mutters to me are: "Did you have the talk with Ciara yet?"

The excuses interchangeable: *She had homework. I didn't want to disturb her. No, sorry, I was so busy today. She seemed tired; I didn't think it was the right time…*

The truth is, I don't think there is an issue. Why open up Pandora's box for no reason?

I realize that doctors may have too much information when it comes to human functions. Psychiatrists have an archive of knowledge about our psyche. A little girl's daydreams and fantasies have now become a conversation about something larger.

Sometimes I feel like I have to be the voice of reason, to tell Conor to step out of psychiatry and just be a father. Let an eight-year-old be an eight-year-old. But I seem to be pushing Conor's buttons unintentionally lately, so I choose to accept his wishes.

* * *

I'm deep into my nightly routine, unpacking the kids' school bags, preparing their baths, pouring my glass of wine—the basics—when I feel a vibration in my pocket.

Sorry. I got held up at work. Have dinner without me.

The frustration grows as I throw my phone on the table with a huge exhale. When will life go back to normal?

I don't even know what normal is at this point.

It vibrates again.

Don't forget to speak to Ciara.

I moan out loud this time.

"SHIT! Shit, shit, shit!" Breathe. "All right, kids, Daddy is busy at work. Pizza is on its way."

Once the kids are fed, bathed, and in bed, it's a ticking time bomb. I have to get this conversation in before Conor comes home.

I knock lightly on Ciara's door.

"Knock, knock," I say softly, even though I've already let myself in.

Ciara is lying in her bed, tucked in, book in hand. The night-light is reflecting down on her shiny dark hair. She looks like a miniature woman. So put together, such wisdom in her face.

"Mind if I join you for a sec?" I made sure to shower and get into my pajamas before helping myself to her bed. Ciara is particular about not allowing "outdoor day clothes" on her bed.

She nods and moves over to give me some space.

"What are you reading?"

Ciara shows me the cover.

"*To Kill a Mockingbird?*" I gasp. "Is it ever too early to teach barbaric discrimination literacy?" *Not to mention rape*, I want to add.

"It's how you look at it. I find this to be very educational. It is showing both good and evil in the world."

Seriously, a miniature woman.

"And Mrs. Clarke is having you read this?"

"No, we are always reading boring books like Pippi Longstocking or A Series of Unfortunate Events…not much you can learn from those stories."

"Um, missy, firstly, that's not true, those are great stories! And anyway, you shouldn't be reading this, especially before bed! You'll get nightmares!"

Ciara rolls her eyes.

"Um, there is something I want to talk to you about." I place her bookmark on the open page and put her book on her nightstand. I need her full attention.

"You know how Daddy and I spoke to your teachers a few days ago?"

She nods.

"Well, Mrs. Clarke seemed a bit worried that you weren't…" I pick my words carefully. "Interested in your classwork anymore. Are you bored? Do you need an extracurricular?"

"Sure," she mumbles quietly, those blue eyes gazing right into mine.

"Oh, well okay then." That was easy. "I will talk with Mrs. Clarke tomorrow. See what she can do." I make a mental note to send her an email, the efficient choice of communication for introverts. Get your message across at your own pace, expect replies at their pace—no need for that extra chatter bullshit we all put on.

I kiss her on her forehead and tuck her covers back up to her chin.

I stand by the door in hesitation. Conor will ask me if I mentioned his little "incident." Better just get it over with so he will stop with the questions, or, worse, deal with it on his own.

"Um, Ciara?"

She looks back up at me.

"Daddy did mention something else." I'm not sure how to word this exactly. I come back to her bed to show comfort.

"He came into your room one day, said you seemed like you were just standing there? Moving your arms, maybe?" I wait for a response. When nothing comes, I continue. "He said you looked like you were dreaming. Do you know what he may be talking about?"

"Sometimes I daydream," she states blatantly.

"Oh yeah? Like what kinds of things?" I stroke her face as I speak. Sometimes she does just look like a young, innocent child.

"I don't know; sometimes it's fantasy, and I make up a world in my head. Sometimes it's just about a movie I watched or a book I read."

I furrow my brow.

"Not *To Kill a Mockingbird*, don't worry."

I fake a dramatic sigh. "Well, that sounds wonderful! Are you in these magical worlds?"

She shrugs. "Yeah, sometimes."

"Tell me about them."

"Oh, it's nothing." Ciara looks down.

I wait silently.

"Just…" She looks back up. "It's usually me, with make-believe people, like fairies and princesses. I'm kind of exploring a made-up world. And…"

"Yes?"

"It's a bit embarrassing, but I kind of made up a name for this world."

"Oh, babe, that's not embarrassing, that's fascinating. Do you mind sharing the name?"

"The Enchanted Florin."

"Oh."

"You know where it's from?"

"Um, don't tell me, it sounds so familiar!" I close my eyes and obviously ponder.

"It's that place from *The Princess Bride*."

"Oh, right!"

"So sometimes, Westley or Count Rugen or even Fezzick show up in this world." The more she speaks, the more she shows conviction, passion, and excitement.

"Oh gosh! And what about Princess Buttercup? Does she show up?"

"Well, sometimes I am the princess."

"That sounds magical!"

"It is." She lies her head back down.

"Okay. Well, I'm glad you shared your wonderful creation with me." I stand up again. "I would love to hear more about it some other time." I lean over for my second kiss. "But now, it is way past your bedtime. Goodnight, my dear." I hold her cheek in my hand one last time. I look into her innocent bright blue eyes, kiss her forehead, and leave her to her fantasy.

Nothing to worry about here. Just an eight-year-old with some imagination.

Later, when Conor (finally) comes home, he does his routine:

"I hope you spoke with Ciara." No, *Hello, darling. Sorry I'm late.*

"As a matter of fact, I did."

His eyebrows raise. "And?"

"And I'm right!" I clean up the paper plates and oversized pizza box as I speak. "She is just bored at school, and therefore daydreaming. I'll send Mrs. Clarke an email just to see if she has any work she can contrive." I revert to my glass of wine. I like to nurse it throughout the night. The little carrot dangling in front of my nose to get me through.

"Did you mention the—"

"Yes." I silently thank myself for that. I'm hopefully scoring some brownie points. "I said you saw her in her room, and she, once again, said it was just daydreaming."

Conor follows me to the living room. We haven't sat beside each other in at least a week.

"It wasn't a daydream. She was almost…she was sleeping while standing. Completely out of it."

"Conor, she said she created a little fantasy world. This is what children do. They fantasize, they make up stories in their heads. What we should be worried about are the books she's been getting from the library."

I'm not sure if Conor is listening to me.

"You wouldn't guess what I caught Ciara reading tonight!" No answer. "*To Kill a Mockingbird.*"

"What?" Ah, he is listening.

"Aha!" I drain my glass of delicious deep red. "Focus more on that!" I return the glass to the sink, wash it, and put it away. Conor follows me to the kitchen.

"Oh, and I got you that Cesar salad you like from Mike's Pizza. It's in a bag in the fridge."

"Cleo, I'm not convinced yet. I have a bad feeling about Ciara; I feel like it's something she may be going through."

"You're thinking too deeply. You have a lifetime of other people's experiences and problems that you are now projecting onto Ciara. Listen, if it gets any worse, I promise, you can then, and only then, step in. Okay?"

Empty promises.

19

I SEE YOU, MY DEAR, IN DREAMS

London, Ten Years Ago

My phone was ringing.

It was Liam.

Despite my intentions to avoid his phone calls, there was always the possibility that it would be about work, a new project, or the future. I was nervously anticipating which Liam I might get: caring and spontaneous Liam, or the teacher I placed on a pedestal, my authority figure?

A stern voice greeted me. "Hello, Cleo!" he said.

"Liam."

There was a pause, almost as if to say, *It's about work.*

"So I have great news." I could hear enthusiasm in his voice. "LCR wants to schedule a meeting to discuss their vision of this record deal." Another pause. "Can I schedule you for one?"

"Today?" That got me out of bed. I hadn't slept so deeply in quite a while. It was 9:15; I never slept that late. Once again, it was back to work, back to reality.

"Okay, yeah, great. Sounds good."

After a collection of polite goodbyes, we hung up.

The meeting went better than expected. We discussed "my greatest hits" (who knew I had them?), as well as some compositions of my own. Liam dressed the part of coach/manager: a clean-cut, crisp navy-blue suit, hair perfectly set, reeking of power and authority. He was the one initiating these meetings, keeping up with the business. As for me, I was the pretty face, the performer. I wore my bright-colored dresses, polished my features, and only exposed my voice once the piano was out to play.

The business side was equally important, but not my point of strength. I dragged my feet through the motions and sucked it up, waiting for the moment the curtain would rise—that is when I would revive.

Unfortunately, these meetings and plans and form-filling-out and handshaking could sometimes take up a whole day, for days at a time.

It was now day two and I was six hours deep. I was famished and spent. I either looked it, or Liam was a mind reader. He asked me to join him for a bite.

His whole demeanor changed once we sat down. Sitting across from Liam when he wasn't so serious was enjoyable. It was quiet as we sat there, sipping our water, not saying much.

"Today hasn't been all that enjoyable," he remarked with a knowing smirk, casting a meaningful gaze into my eyes. "But I feel like we accomplished quite a lot, eh?"

In response, I scoffed lightly, taking a sip of water, biding my time as we waited for our food to arrive.

Liam carried on, his demeanor exuding a sense of calm that extended beyond just his body language. Even his tone of voice had shifted, making me feel at ease, as though I was here with a friend rather than someone I held in high regard, my mentor.

I couldn't help but smile, gathering my thoughts before speaking. I wasn't sure where to start, but I knew I owed Liam a heartfelt thanks for guiding me to this point.

Finally, the words left my lips. "I wanted to say thank you, Liam."

He arched an eyebrow inquisitively. "For what?"

"For today, for everything. These past few months have been quite the journey, and I can see that you've gone above and beyond."

Liam nodded, a faint smile tugging at his lips, and I couldn't help but notice how his presence felt like a reassuring embrace, even during our professional relationship.

"Ah, but I love it, you see." He seemed genuine. "Honestly, Cleo. It's my pleasure." His expression shifted, a serious intensity taking hold as he visibly wrestled with his words. "I have something for you," he finally managed to say.

Thoughts raced through my mind. What other documents remained to be signed? My curiosity grew as he retrieved an item from his briefcase, but it wasn't the expected folder or paperwork; instead, it was a small gray jewelry box, delicately tied with a white ribbon.

He placed it gently on the table before me, and I found myself at a loss for words, utterly baffled by this unexpected gesture.

Encouraged by my silence, he grinned crookedly and urged, "Well, go on, then. Open it."

I couldn't hide the depth of my confusion. "What is this?" This gift held profound importance—it was the very first gift Liam had given me, distinct from all his physical labor and hard work throughout our journey.

The realization hit me like a wave. Liam had carried this box with him all day in his briefcase, and I had been completely unaware.

"Happy birthday, Cleo," he said softly, his voice filled with warmth and sincerity.

I sat there, unable to move at first. Then, an overpowering curiosity surged within me, compelling me to untie the ribbon and reveal the contents -a gold necklace strung with a red pendant surrounded by a halo of sparkling diamonds.

Liam broke the silence, his voice tender. "I know you're not fond of rings or bracelets, so I hoped this would be something you could wear."

Tears welled up in my eyes as I struggled to find my voice, touched beyond measure by this unexpected gift.

"The lady in the store said it's a carnelian stone. Apparently, it is protective. She mentioned something about keeping you safe, keeping you motivated, and getting rid of negativity. I don't know." He wasn't able to look at me as he spoke. "I don't personally believe in this shite, but it made me think of you."

"I love it!" The words found my mouth. "I love it so much. It is too generous, Liam."

"Nonsense."

"Thank you, again."

The cold metal imprinted into my skin as I held on to it tight. I wanted to wear it. I wanted to keep it locked away in a safe. My gaze kept lingering on it, hypnotized by the diamonds.

"Cleo, I can't stop thinking about…you know. That night in Moscow?"

It was only a matter of time before this discussion would occur.

I returned to my silence.

"Can we discuss what that meant?"

What did it mean? I didn't have the answer. I had to deflect. "Can you first explain what happened the night before the last performance, at Pravda?"

He let out a scoff this time. "I don't know," he started. "It was an instinctive reaction, what I was feeling in the moment."

"But you never just go with your instinct; you plan everything. I know this because I do too; we have both always been that type of person."

It was Liam's turn to be silent now.

"Does it have anything to do with Ivan?" I asked cautiously.

He hesitated, sensing my confusion and the potential hurt behind my question. "No. Yes, I suppose it might have. But not because I was worried that he was a distraction to you. I'll admit, that was a feeble excuse."

"Why then?" I pressed further.

"In the past, it seemed like dating wasn't a priority for you. You often rejected lads, prioritizing your music above all else. Then, Ivan entered the picture, and everything changed. I realized I might be missing an opportunity to explore if we could have something more."

"Wait a moment," I interjected, trying to process the information. "What do you mean, 'rejected lads'? What lads?"

"No matter where we go, you always have men trying their luck with you."

"Really?" I was genuinely surprised. I couldn't recall a single instance where this had happened. Had I been completely oblivious to it all? If I had known, would I have been more open to dating? Perhaps it was a subconscious decision I had made without even realizing it.

"Cleo, I know it seems weird. I have known you since you were young. I have seen you grow up into this brilliant human. And I know you probably think of me as your dryshite coach."

I laughed at this. If he only knew.

If only Liam knew the all-consuming feelings I had for him. A love that had silently and relentlessly blossomed since that very first encounter. The awe and adoration I held deep within, how he consumed my thoughts day and night. It was more than admiration; it was a burning, all-encompassing desire, a connection that transcended the boundaries of teacher and student. My heart was fueled by an insatiable hunger for his presence. If only I could find the words, the courage to convey what he truly meant to me.

The idea of expressing my deep affection was both exciting and frightening.

And now, at the most inconvenient moment, he chooses to disclose his reciprocated feelings for me. This is when he decides to say what I've longed to hear, what I've dreamt about for years.

"I just…I have these deep feelings for you, Cleo. And I've always known that if I made a move, it could potentially jeopardize our professional relationship. I couldn't bear the thought of causing you any harm, of taking that risk."

I was in shock. Hearing those words spill from Liam's lips, directed at me, felt surreal. I had to pinch myself mentally to ensure I wasn't lost in a dream. I clung to his every word, hanging on to each syllable with unwavering intensity.

"Then Ivan came along. He quickly captured your attention, and even though he lives in another country, I saw my chances fading."

"I…I don't know what to say. I had no idea."

"Well, I didn't give you many clues. Until I did and made a hames of it."

"You didn't. It has just been a confusing couple of weeks."

"So?"

"So?"

"So are you going to now explain to me what happened the other night?"

"Well, I guess it was an instinctive reaction."

Liam smiled at this answer.

"Listen, I'm confused. It's confusing. You were not even an option until you suddenly became one."

"Can we at least try? See where it takes us?"

The waiter came with our food, allowing my brain to contemplate for a little bit longer.

"What if it doesn't work out? Would we part ways?"

"No. We have a good thing going here. We make a great team. I'll just go back to being your arsehole coach, and you'll go on and date whomever you like."

I smiled at this idea. I wasn't sure if after this I could see Liam in the same light as I did before our time in Russia. How could I possibly forget the imprint of his kiss, the warmth of his embrace? Those memories would forever be etched in my heart, cherished and unforgettable.

"Cleo, please?"

A feeling emerged and hit me like a ton of bricks. Ivan.

My communications with Ivan never stopped. He never left my world. I received his birthday wishes today, along with a poem I had not yet translated into English. Every night, after a day of meetings, I would engage in lengthy conversations with Ivan. He was what I woke up to, the calm to my storm.

Our relationship wasn't anything but long-distance, and Liam was right here. He was perfect for me. Perfect in general. He was intelligent, loyal, aspiring. I could count on Liam to provide me with everything I needed. With Liam, everything made sense.

"Okay," I finally said.

"Okay?" A smile crept onto Liam's face.

"Let's give this a try."

* * *

Later that night, I translated the poem Ivan sent me.

"I See You, My Dear, In Dreams" by Aleksey Apukhtin

I see you, my dear, in dreams every night, In crowds of wonderful beings,

You smile at me, and to your heavenly sight, I sob on my knees at my

feelings…

20

SURRENDER

New York City, Present Day

Butterflies. Not just an insect, but a multifaceted meaning. Eric would bring up butterflies all the time. I would pretend to understand what he meant. I even had a few moments when I piped up. I thought that maybe we had a common denominator, something we could discuss that wasn't money related. He laughed at me, that nob. He explained how, in finances, the term "butterfly" is a strategy for taking on a short-term investment risk. The whys and hows of it all bored me to death, and I honestly can't recall the rest of the conversation.

The "butterfly feeling" is one I know too well. I have a clear memory of feeling nervous, and Lottie, my piano teacher, telling me it was just butterflies. I was comforted by that thought. A bunch of butterflies in me, coming with me onto the stage, making sure I do well through my performance.

Then there's the chaos theory called the butterfly effect. How one small move in existence can have a significant effect on the future. This term reflects a meteorologist's belief that a tornado could occur from the influence of a butterfly flapping its wings weeks earlier.

That sticks with me. That is the epiphany I hold on to. Every little move I make can somehow be the outline for my future. The steps I have taken somehow brought me up and will shut it all down. What are those minute details I am missing that have caused such a ripple effect?

Once I've taken care of the Ciara situation, Conor goes back to the silent treatment. How is this helpful? How can I determine our direction? Are we heading in the right one? In addition, I got a text from Ramona this morning stating, in true Ramona fashion: *I'm balls deep in work, I will get back to you later.* So vague, no direction. I would rather rip off the Band-Aid. The uncertainty is killing me. So I have that extra headache to worry about.

One step forward, five steps back.

I am surprised by Conor's first sit-down, eye-to-eye sentence.

"Hey." He sits across from me at our dinner table. The kids are sleeping, and I have my computer in front of me. I am pretending to work while online shopping.

"Is something wrong?" I look up and shut my computer.

"I think we need to talk."

I wait. *Yes, I agree.* There is a lot to discuss, but what? Where to start? I'll let him lead the way.

"I think the only way we can move on from this, from these feelings…" He is hesitant, speaking slowly and carefully. "Is to go to counseling."

That dreaded word. Conor knows how much I despise the idea of any form of therapy. Ironic, I know, that I married a psychiatrist, but I couldn't seem to bring myself to see one.

I wait. Maybe he'll give me another option. Therapy or?

"Now, I know you are not so fond of this idea."

I grunt a quiet laugh and let him continue.

"But I don't see any option."

I sit there in silence.

"Cleo, speak."

"I honestly don't know what to say. I…" I stop and gather my thoughts. "Is this really the only way? Can't we just talk it through without that intrusion and analytical bullshit?"

Now it is his turn to stay quiet.

"Is this an ultimatum? Is it this, or we are over?"

"Yeah, maybe."

I am shocked by those words. It is not the answer I expected.

"Really?" I'm hurt. Is our string so thin it is about to snap? Why am I unaware of how bad our relationship has gotten?

"Is this all because I missed your AM—"

"No! Cleo!" He breaks into a hysterical scream. In my desperation, I poked the bear once again, unintentionally.

"Are you really that blind? Do you honestly think we are in a good place right now?"

"Before the event, yes, I honestly did."

"You're delusional!"

"You tell me, wise doctor! You should know! Am I? Am I delusional, Conor?"

He stands up and paces, not wanting to say things he'll regret. When he returns, he speaks like he's taken a few big inhales and gathered his words.

"We are not where I want us to be. You are never present, so it is hard to be in any form of relationship. It seems like you don't even want to be here anymore, like you just want to be somewhere else. I don't know where, but it's apparent that it's not here. It feels like you checked out a long time ago. You and those bloody headphones."

Wow. Anything else, dear husband?

I finally speak. "I do want to be here, with you and the kids. I am just—" I don't know how to finish the sentence. "Struggling."

"I know you're struggling! So get help!" It is uncharacteristic of Conor to be so direct and blunt. His usual benevolent demeanor does not enter this conversation. Gloves are off, battle armor is on.

"I don't need help!" I match his loud tone. "I can manage this on my own!"

"Why?"

At this point, we aren't even trying to stay quiet for the kids. If they wake up and hear our screaming, so be it.

"Why do you need to do this on your own? Don't you see how it is affecting us? Your husband, your kids! Why put us all through it? It doesn't have to be so unstable! You see Ciara going through something, and you're ignoring that too!

You're trying to get me to ignore her struggles! Trying to play it off like an active imagination—bullshit. Ciara needs you, Cleo! Or she needs me to take over. You need to get off your fucking high horse and start realizing what is going on around you!"

"My fucking high horse? Wow! I am not ignoring what is going around me out of arrogance! I am fucking aware of my surroundings! I am just experiencing life! And you should know, Mr. Psychiatrist, that life is not always easy. So give me a fucking break!" I sit down, not wanting to cry, too tired to cry. I'm so completely over all of this. "And are you even going to pretend to sympathize with me? Or is that not what you're doing here anymore? You think—"

"I have been sympathizing with you!" Conor shouts over me. His arms are shaking with pent-up frustration. He seems over it too, but we have to go on. "I have played the silent husband, allowing you to do things your way, keeping my therapist notes far away from you. I have been patting your back, telling you that you'll be okay, that I'll be here for you, that I will do anything you want me to do." His anger simmers, threatening to boil over. "But eventually, Cleo, enough is enough. Call this an intervention if you want. This is me telling you that there will be no more right and respectful words. No more treating you with such fragility. Because, eventually, it takes a toll on me. I am crumbling. I am trying to hold up all four walls of this home to ensure the kids are okay. I can't go to work and talk through everyone else's problems when I can't get my fucking shit together! How can I properly give them my all when I am breaking?"

Conor is done. I hear it in his voice.

"Okay," I surrender. "I will go to therapy."

* * *

Like all dreaded events, a little countdown runs through my head from the moment I wake up.

Five days till couples counseling. Commence daily rituals.

Four days till couples counseling. Commence daily rituals.

Then, eventually, the day arrives. I wake up earlier than I usually do. I look at my phone; 4:29. I lie on my back and stare at the dark ceiling. It feels nice that, through all our issues, we still share a bed. A comforting way to feel like we can get through this. Or maybe Conor's way of showing the kids that everything is okay, nothing is changing.

The lies we tell our kids. I wonder how much they know. I analyze their actions, trying to detect if they can sense it. They say, even subconsciously, kids pick up on things. It is what ultimately shapes them.

Lottie once gave me the analogy of a tree when it's first planted. It needs to be held up by ropes so it can form a strong foundation and grow in a straight position. Once the trunk stabilizes, you can remove the ropes. The tree can now hold itself up.

This was her way of letting me know that one day, I wouldn't need her assistance as much. It was Lottie who practically raised me. When I was struggling in school, when I was trying to maintain a social life, when my parents were absent, she was there for me. It was Lottie who laid the foundation and established my roots—just until I was able to take off my supporting ropes and grow independently. Up until I was ready to leave for the academy, and then for Liam.

I now wonder if Lottie released the ropes too soon. Maybe I'm not fully developed and, therefore, all wonky.

I also wonder if I loosened my kids' strings accidentally—or are they too tight? As their parent, I have everything to do with their foundation. It's a scary thought. One I cannot handle before dawn.

So I get up and go for a run. The one-handed elliptical got too messy, so I opt for a run around Washington Square Park instead, a track I could aimlessly and mindlessly follow until I am ready to go back home.

My cast is coming off tomorrow. Maybe this damaged look will play in favor of me in counseling. The poor battered, struggling wife. Would the therapist then treat me with more conviction? Or will Conor get the upper hand since they are both a part of the counseling hierarchy? They can talk in another language, use terminology I don't understand.

Will our therapist write us a script for date night and call it a day?

I am just going to have to suck it up and get through it.

* * *

The appointment is getting closer. Conor emptied his afternoon just for this. It is something I can force myself to do—for the sake of our marriage.

My body is unable to move.

I am listening to **Ludovico Einaudi - Experience.**

Those bloody headphones. Conor's words ring in my head.

But these sounds, these melodies, are the only oxygen pumping into my heart. Letting me know I am indeed alive.

As I sit on my veranda, I gaze at the butterflies dancing through the warm, golden rays of sunlight, as I beg them to enchant me. The weight of my body feels almost unbearable as I close my eyes, exhale, and sink deeper into the chair. I keep repeating the mantra in my head, "I will get through this. I will." It's a simple formula: stand up, place one foot in front of the other, and navigate through the tumultuous sea of this day.

But, despite my best intentions, I remain rooted in place, as if an invisible force holds me captive.

21

THE JUGGLING ACT

London, Ten Years Ago

The arrangement was seamless. I had mastered a world where everything played its part flawlessly. Liam and I would spend our days together as professionals (work meetings, recording, rehearsing, event planning), and then we would transform into Liam and Cleo, your run-of-the-mill couple frolicking about London. Coffee breaks at boutique cafés and dinners at exclusive restaurants. Then I started visiting him in the evenings. Evenings turned into nightcaps, and nightcaps turned into sleepovers.

His lonely one-person home was way too big for a single man. Despite the interior's opulence, the house had a French country feel to it, with toile fabrics, elegant lighting, tapestries, and floral prints—as if a woman had influenced it at some point.

Every day with him felt like a journey of a thousand steps in the right direction. Each moment we shared became another memory etched deep into my heart. The day he entrusted me with the keys to his home, the moment he proudly introduced me as his girlfriend, and the way he brought a sense of lightness even in our intense working hours—all these milestones were building blocks of our connection.

Our afternoons were a beautiful blend of intimacy and passion, whether we were wrapped up in each other's arms in bed or lost in the hypnotic melodies of the piano in his office. We seemed to exist in a realm of our own, consumed by our profound infatuation.

It all just felt so undeniably right, like we were two souls entwined in a love story written in the stars.

Ivan was still there but hidden. I didn't want to discuss him with Liam. Not until I knew how to find the words. I didn't think I was being unfaithful. Was it cheating if there was never anything past friendship? I mean, our conversations were beyond friendship, but the physical distance implied no future. Still, I wasn't ready to get rid of Ivan. I wanted Ivan in my life, needed him. I needed the calm.

Was that so awful?

I would take out my phone as soon as Liam fell asleep and hide beneath the covers to conceal the bright light.

When the conversations between Ivan and me were a bit broken, Google Translate came in handy. I even downloaded a Russian keyboard to my phone and attempted to spell out the little Russian I understood.

He would tell me about his long days and small "gigs." He mentioned how he went back to working at Dom, and he sent regards from Iliya and Lena. I would read his texts in his voice. The animation shone through his words. He would recite Pushkin and Lermontov, and I would copy and paste the poems to translate. My heart would hurt as I read them, almost as if Ivan himself had composed them.

I knew it was wrong. Liam was right beside me, and I told myself would fix this mess before it got messier, but it was the medicine I needed for now. It was my life finally paying me back in the happiness I deserved. I sacrificed a great deal to live my dream, and now I was dedicating my efforts to myself, with my priorities set high.

The next few months flew by in the best way possible. Liam and I were forming a deep, emotional connection. If you'd asked me, I would have said I assumed this is what marriage felt like. We were practically living together—well, not technically. I stayed at his home all the time, and I had my shelf and some closet space for my belongings. My toothbrush and toiletries had their corner on his vanity. We would often go to sleep together, wake up together, have morning tea on the patio, go to recordings, and end the day together. The kicker was: I wasn't sick of him. I missed him terribly when we were separated, and we got deep into conversation once we were reunited. The work side of things was almost nonexistent in my head. It became just another chore we did together, Liam and me.

And, yes, months into my relationship, and I was still in touch with Ivan. I kept him posted on my next endeavors, told him about the process of recording for a label. Sometimes when Liam was out late, working on the business side of things, I video-called Ivan. It was so refreshing to see his face again. His bright blue eyes, his icy blond hair! I knew, deep down, that this connection was both a comfort and a temptation, a dance with danger that only served to intensify our desire. I hadn't mapped out a plan yet, but I knew it would all work its way out. It has to.

I told him about my first big break. I was throwing myself into the deep end. I would be performing alongside the BBC Symphony Orchestra at the Proms, the world's greatest classical music festival right here in London, at Albert Hall. Adverts were plastered over the newspapers, bus stops, and TV screens: UK's Moscow Classical Music Competition winner, Cleo Wilson—debut performance. I told him how I winced every time I saw the graphic of me on the piano displayed next to such renowned musicians. As determined as I may have been, there was always an underlying feeling of imposter syndrome, like I didn't belong.

And then Ivan, my unwavering source of strength, would put my reservations to rest as he reminded me of my brilliance, of the magic I possessed within. And though the path to perfection demanded grueling practice, I welcomed the challenge, knowing that it would forge me into an artist worthy of the stage.

Maybe my life was going too well. Maybe I expected a ticking time bomb to go off. Or maybe life would settle the way it does, and it would all fall into place.

Ivan promised to catch my performance live, whatever time it happened to be in Russia, and I believed him. He was my support system from the start.

22

NEW DIANE

New York City, Present Day

I messed up. Bad.

I never made it to therapy.

For years, I struggled with exhausting nights so that I could perfect my repertoire. Throughout my career, I traveled countries back-to-back and performed immaculately. My mindset has always been to seek challenging, uncomfortable tasks. I have always been comfortable with the uncomfortable.

But today I just can't face my challenge.

I can't leave the veranda.

Conor does not talk to me when he gets home. He packs his bag and declares he needs time to think. We tell the kids it's a business trip, and then Conor is off.

We plan to alternate our days with the kids. The days he brings the kids home, I will be at some random "meeting." They don't ask questions or seem too weirded out by this. I am relying on their oblivion to get us through this rough patch.

Once Conor has successfully settled the kids into bed, I slip through the front door, discovering him sound asleep on the couch. With careful steps, I make my way to our bedroom without disturbing him. The hushed silence of the night prevails as we both fall asleep.

However, the next morning presents an unexpected twist to our unusual routine. The children wake up before we do, leaving Conor no time to gather his things and seamlessly descend the stairs, pretending he'd spent the night right there with us.

"Why did you sleep on the couch, Daddy?" Olivia laughs.

"Oh, I— I fell asleep here, watching telly. Silly me."

"So why is your pillow and blanket on the couch?" Ciara outsmarts Conor. She always does, with her observant eye.

"That's probably why I fell asleep. I made myself too comfy. All right, let's have breakfast."

And that's that.

Our stupid, nonsensical method.

No real direction. No real plan of action.

Are we separated? Are there rules to separation? A plan for how long we need to separate? What constitutes a separation?

Is it that middle ground you hover over until your relationship's final outcome is decided?

Rekindle or divorce?

If it were up to me, I would choose to rekindle.

Every time, I would choose to go back to Conor. Make things right with him. Be the person he deserves. Every fiber of my being aches for reconciliation, for a chance to rewrite the narrative of our love story. I long to mend the broken pieces, to be the partner he truly deserves, to rekindle the fire that once blazed brightly between us. The thought of losing him terrifies me beyond words.

Conor, as far as I can tell, has emotionally withdrawn completely. In his eyes, our relationship is beyond salvation, irreparably broken. I feel a profound sense of failure. I've pushed him to the brink, testing the boundaries of our love, and now he's taking measures to protect himself and shield our children from further turmoil; from me.

I struggle with a heavy feeling of self-doubt. Are my children better off without me? I've always prided myself on being a loving and dedicated parent, but what good am I when I'm not "mentally there"? What can I offer them if

I'm struggling with my own inner demons? The question gnaws at me, leaving me feeling lost, uncertain.

Until we figure that out, we continue to drift past each other, avoiding the painful truths that have brought us to this place. We search for ways to evade, to ignore, to distance ourselves, all in the hope that one day we'll uncover a path that leads us out of this emotional abyss, and perhaps, maybe, back to each other.

*　*　*

Today is a "me day." Conor drops the kids off at school and plans to pick them up. It is my time to be incognito or, as the kids were told, "at a late book appointment." Whatever that could mean.

My book.

Ramona.

Somehow Ramona manages to remain in my consciousness, even in all her secrecy. There have been no updates. There are no rushed calls, not a hint as to how my synopsis will transpire, where my career might be heading.

I have to ignore these concerns. I'll go on with my "me day." My attempt at health.

I am in no rush to get home. Home is my reality check. Home is where I can witness all the fragmented pieces of my life falling apart.

This separation has brought an unexpected upside. When I am alone, there seems to be less clutter in my mind, fewer worries, and for fleeting moments, I can pretend to be single again, not a mother or a wife.

Those thoughts strike an aching stab of guilt in my chest. I shouldn't entertain such thoughts. I should develop a plan to get Conor to trust me again, not weigh my pros and cons. But my brain can't go there; this is my way of protection. The hurt and harm it would cause me to stop and look at my life's events. So, I shrug it off and go on with my "me day." I finally have the perfect occasion to get my hair dyed. Maybe I'll throw in a manicure. Hell, why not a pedicure as well. Writers must live to form inspiration for something substantial, so that is what I'll do. I'll live, and hope that something will click.

Oh gosh, is this me living? A spa day?

Instead of going to the nearby hairdresser, I take a subway to the Upper West Side, to check out a salon the mums' circle is always gushing about. They call it an "impeccable salon with a hefty price tag." I can emulate those other mums. Maybe if I pretend hard enough, I'll eventually turn into one of them. I won't have to work. I'll go to spin class, I'll bake, and maybe I'll finally be present at my kids' playdates. Who knows? Maybe I'll enjoy this kind of lifestyle. Perhaps it will help free me from all disappointment I'm handling.

I don't honestly believe this, of course, but I try.

The salon smells like cedarwood and white musk. It resembles an art installation at the MoMA. The chairs and washing stations are abstract, and the hairdressers are clichés, all with their colored hair and asymmetrical layers.

They offer me champagne, so we are off to a good start.

"Hi, hon. Do you want me to touch up the roots and maybe a little trim?" my hairdresser, Indigo, asks as she fluffs up my hair from behind.

"Oh, okay." I suddenly notice my dead ends. I guess a trim is way overdue.

"You know what." I look a bit longer at my reflection. "Can we go a few shades lighter?"

Once upon a time, I used to meticulously ponder my appearance, always primed for the public eye. However, as I transitioned from a performer in the spotlight to a recluse behind screens, my motivation to maintain my looks waned. It all felt like a futile endeavor. Yet, today, I feel a flicker of that old self returning. Perhaps that's the version of me Conor fell in love with—the polished, put-together wife with freshly painted lips and platinum, slicked-back hair. And maybe, just maybe, if I embody this persona, it will rekindle his memories of the woman I once was, and the woman I aspire to be once more.

Two champagne flutes, hours of bleaching, and a mani-pedi later, I feel reborn; I look alive again. It's fascinating how shallowness affects one's depth. It might sound trite, but there's undeniable truth in dressing for the person you want to become, not just the person you currently are, and, in this moment, I am convinced.

I catch myself smiling as I walk down West Seventy-Second Street. I never smile without reason. I even make the spontaneous decision to stop at Magnolia

Bakery and indulge in one of their banana pudding bowls. No phone, no computer.

During those few minutes, I enjoy the smell of the banana pudding, the overlapping sounds of chatter and beeping, and—I stop eating. I have this weird feeling of déjà vu.

The funny thing about memories is they automatically respond to sensory experiences. Like some archived data you hold on to that you didn't know existed.

Almost half a kilometer away lies Lincoln Center. It feels like centuries ago I was in their Great Performers Series. Can I just...go? Walk there and revisit those sacred halls?

I know if I want to live, if I want to have something to write about, the answer has to be yes. I'll go to the theater, buy a ticket to whatever show is playing, and breathe the same air I did another lifetime ago.

Walking back into these halls sends a chill down my spine. It is all too familiar, yet I feel so removed from this world. The next performance is only twenty minutes away, so I buy a ticket to The School of Ballet performing Tchaikovsky's *Romeo and Juliet.*

How fitting.

The carpeted steps down the aisle, the mission to locate my seat, the smell of old wood, and feeling the damp air settle—all so very familiar. It is like trying to reassemble a dream. You know bits and pieces and objects, yet it doesn't feel complete. Something is missing.

I look around as the theater starts to fill up.

After an apprehensive battle to quiet the trials in my head, the show finally commences. My stiff shoulders relax. The show is the distraction I need to escape from reality for just one more moment.

It becomes challenging to concentrate. I find myself having a contradictory reaction to performances from the audience's point of view. My mind is lost in another world, bewitched by the melodies, yet, simultaneously, my brain is running at rapid speed. There is no quieting the catastrophizing. The more energy I use to block out these thoughts, the more I concentrate on not thinking, the more power I give to those thoughts. The more I become imprisoned by my beliefs.

The Dance of the Knights projects loudly as Romeo encounters Juliet at the Capulets' masquerade ball.

I think about my relationship, where Conor and I will end up. Will he move on with ease, leaving me to drown in a sea of sorrow? Will he be granted full custody, tearing our children away from me? Would the kids prefer that?

The world around me transforms into a nightmarish scenery. The empty spaces that surround me become filled with haunting images of couples, their grip on each other suffocatingly tight.

The walls start to feel closer; my breath gets louder. I try to slow it down, but that only quickens the pace. My palms grow clammy, and a dizzying wave washes over me, threatening to pull me under. The performers' faces contort, their once serene expressions twisted into grotesque masks of hostility. Their heads turn in unison, and suddenly, every gaze is fixated upon me. The orchestra, the conductor, even the audience—they all bear down upon me with a malevolent intensity.

Romeo's face transforms into Conor's, and I am thrust into a realm where reality and nightmare intertwine. I know deep down that this cannot be real, that it is an illusion born from my tortured mind. But his gaze is a piercing beeline to my eyes, into my soul. His face looks angry; Juliet dances opposite him. Their faces are now ugly, devilish. Their angry, demonic dance unfolds. Features melt into a monstrous blur as the double bass crescendos, amplifying the chilling nightmare.

Overwhelmed and terrified, I instinctively cover my face, desperately trying to shield myself from this grotesque nightmare. "This is not real," I repeat, hoping to find peace in the mere sound of my own voice. But the heat of the theater crawls over my body, suffocating me with a sense of impending doom. If I cannot partake in the twisted love that Romeo and Juliet embody, if I cannot merge with the audience's collective adoration, then I am an outcast in this twisted realm.

I know I can't stay much longer before I pass out. I clutch my jacket and bag without concern, bump against those sitting between me and the aisle, and stumble out of the theater.

The dizzy spells increase; my knees start to shake. I make it outside, and while the air feels medicinal, it can't hold me up.

I presume I fell to the ground, because that is where I wake up. I am not sure how long I was out, and I feel a fury, wet sensation brush against my cheek.

"Oh, stop it, Henry." The bells of a dog's collar ring in my ear.

I open my eyes and in front of me is a lady. Elderly, with short white hair, beige glasses, and a slight red tint to her lips. She wears a thick knit sweater and a thicker coat on top.

"Oh, thank goodness, you're awake!" She speaks in a gentle manner. I feel a sense of calm wash over me.

She holds out her knitted gloved hand and helps me up. I raise one hand to my head in confusion as I notice the many others viewing the spectacle.

"How long was I out for?"

"Not too long. You know, I saw you coming out; I knew something was wrong, and by the time I came over, you'd fainted."

"Oh."

"Must have been three, maybe four minutes total."

"Okay." I feel a lot better. I still feel disoriented and a bit dizzy, but my heart rate has decreased. The atmosphere feels wider again. I can gather my thoughts and breathe.

"Well, thank you so much." I'm not sure what the correct protocol is here.

Just then, a young boy, maybe fourteen, comes over and passes me a small plastic water bottle.

"Good job, Nathan!" The lady smiles at the young boy, then looks back at me and says, "Drink."

"Thank you." I open the bottle and gulp it down as they awkwardly watch in silence. "Thanks again." I raise the bottle at them.

"You should sit down here." She points to the famous Revson Fountain outside the theater. The one I walked past so many times in my previous life.

"Oh, okay."

She follows me there.

"Nathan, take Henry for a walk, will you?" She hands the leash over to the boy, and, just like that, I'm sitting next to a perfectly kind stranger who knows at this moment, I need help.

"I'm Cleo." I extend my hand in her direction.

"Diane." Of course, she's a Diane. I lost a Diane. Maybe I'll gain one too. Perhaps this is the substitute who shows up when I need a Diane the most. I almost laugh, but I know it would startle her and seem mocking, especially after her kind gestures.

"How are you feeling now?" She cares. So kind and considerate.

"Much better, thank you."

"Where is that accent from?"

"London." I smile and take another sip of the lukewarm water.

"I have been to London. A lifetime ago, it feels like."

"Yeah, I know what you mean."

"If you want," New Diane starts, "you can share with me what happened. I'm just a stranger, and it won't go further than here." She points to herself and then to me. "It might feel good to release something."

"Where to start?" My elbows rest on my knees, and I bed face in my hands. "Where to start. Well, I may be heading for a divorce. I figured a ballet might be the ideal distraction, but star-crossed lovers made it quite hard for me to ignore this new reality," I display my program, and New Diane can't help but chuckle at the delicious irony of it all.

"I am always late to pick up my kids, never present with them. He is much better at the juggling act—Conor, my husband. So, I'm certain he'll be getting the kids in the divorce. I also lost my best friend; her name is Diane as well."

New Diane finds humor in this too.

"I used to be so functioning, so successful, and now my job, my life, motherhood…everything is falling apart."

I keep going, and New Diane just listens. She listens until Henry and Nathan show up, seemingly bored.

New Diane stands up, and I mirror her.

She holds my hands in her knitted, blanketed palms and says, "Cleo, everything will be all right. I feel that for you."

"You are too kind." I reciprocate a genuine smile.

She lets go of my hands and faces her crew.

"Um, Diane?" I call out before she walks away.

She turns around, still smiling.

"Would you like to get a tea or something?" I feel like I am asking her out on a date, which I suppose to some degree I am.

"Oh dear, I would love to."

I sigh. Here comes the "but."

"But I am here with my grandchild tonight. Special grandma bonding time." She smiles back at the boy, who doesn't seem too impressed.

"Oh, that's okay. Thanks again."

"You know, dear, I know it is not my place to say, but when my husband died, a therapist did wonders for me. It might help with that load you are carrying around."

"Yeah, okay." I don't debate her, and there isn't time to discuss my lack of interest in therapy when she's already given me a lot of her grandma bonding time.

"Thanks," I add, and just like that, I lose my second Diane.

I stay seated by the fountain under the moon's glow and observe the passing figures as the world unfolds into darkness.

My knotted headphones are in my ears, and I listen to the sounds of **Rachmaninoff - Concerto No. 2** until I find myself regaining my serenity.

23

TICK TICK TICK

London, Ten Years Ago

That time bomb. That anticipated ticking time bomb.

It didn't take long for it to explode, for it to bring me back to reality, for me to lose sight of all I'd accomplished.

It all started on the night of the Proms.

The night started off exhilarating. I was nervous, but they were the good kind of nerves. I'd heard how nerves and excitement read the same to your brain waves. Your body reacts the same to both. Yet nerves are what pushed me, what ultimately drove me to my next destination.

I was floating through rehearsals. I was high on cloud nine, Liam by my side, escorting me through all my dreams and aspirations. I was living this! I was living out my dreams! All of them, and with someone I loved by my side. My heart beat for Liam; it pulsed with the raw, powerful emotion. Love was more than a word; it was a feeling of respect, a yearning, those intoxicating spells that captivate your soul when he speaks.

This had to be love.

I didn't confess my love to Liam. I didn't want to admit how deeply I was falling for him, not until I felt my feelings were reciprocated. His actions showed me the potential. He possibly did love me. I just needed to hear those words. Cement our relationship and make it official. Only then could I swim freely in these emotions.

The night fell upon us. I was ready to perform.

The wait backstage heightened my anxiety. The anticipation that would build before the real me emerged. It was only when the spotlight beamed down on me, when the audience cheered, that I could take it all in. Recognize how far I'd come.

It was the first time since Russia that I would be performing in front of a live audience. I never seemed to see the gap between shows. My life existed during performances; the in-between moments went unnoticed.

But this break was different. This time, I'd found a way to mold into my own. I made a life for myself, a relationship; I experienced love in many dimensions.

This concert would be my metamorphosis. I would transform into an even bolder, more powerful vision—the person who showed up on stage and demanded attention.

There were 5,272 seats at the Royal Albert Hall, a capacity of about 5,900 with a standing audience. There would be over three and a half million viewers watching it live, broadcasted to more than two million listeners.

It was my moment of triumph.

Everyone would remember my name after tonight—my voluminous, ruffled bright orange Valentino gown with a plunging neckline. My platinum hair, gelled in my signature slicked-back look, My cat-eye and meticulously painted red lip. People would remember me.

I felt a tug. It was Liam. He molded himself to my back, enfolding me in a tight embrace. His voice, a breathless whisper against my ear, sent shivers down my spine, "You're going to do amazing, my love."

My knees threatened to buckle at those words. It wasn't the three elusive words I longed to hear, but being his "love" in that moment felt like an intoxicating affirmation. My heart raced in response.

Liam's lips found the curve of my neck, and my breath hitched. "Liam, not now," I protested weakly, trying to resist the pull of his touch. I smacked his hands off my waist but turned to smile to let him know I didn't hate it.

He ignored me, grabbed my hands, and pulled me in again.

"You look like a masterpiece." When his piercing gaze met mine, it caused a visceral reaction within me. "You are going to do so well tonight; you always do."

I kissed him because I couldn't handle the compliments. I tried to rub the red tint off Liam's lips as he smiled nonchalantly.

"You really are something special," he said.

"Oh, stop it, you." I waved my hand and walked back to the vanity to reapply my lipstick.

"No, really, Cleo. I don't, I can't—"

I put my lipstick down, looking at his reflection behind me. He had a serious tone, and it demanded my attention.

"I don't remember a time when I was this happy, this fulfilled. You do that for me. You make me feel so…"

I turned to face him now and walked toward him.

To avoid another smudging of the lipstick, I hugged him. The embrace felt more intimate, conveying the depth of my emotions far better than words ever could.

Liam's response was warm and welcoming as he held me close, his hands cradling the back of my head and the small of my back.

And then, the words I had been yearning to hear finally came, hanging in the air like a cherished melody. "I love you, Cleo," Liam confessed.

It was the declaration I had longed for, the missing piece that made me feel whole. I had known love in many forms throughout my life—love for my family, for my sister, for Lottie, for the piano. Yet this love, this romantic, intuitive, and adoring love, was the most potent elixir of the human experience.

With a heartfelt smile, I whispered in response, "I love you too."

We heard a knock on the door, the stagehand telling me it was time.

"How do I look?" I tried to regroup, but this all seemed so unimportant. I just wanted to go home—to Liam's home—and revel in this moment.

"Perfect." He placed his hand on my face. I didn't want to move away from his gaze, but the knock sounded again.

"Coming!" I took one last glance in the mirror, then ran to the door.

Tick tick tick.

The bomb exploded.

It was Ivan.

"Ivan." I was in shock.

"Ivan?" Liam repeated. He approached us from behind. The tone of his voice was accusing and hostile.

"Wow." Ivan rested a hand on his chest and took a small inhale.

"Cleo, you…" He was as speechless as I was.

Shit shit shit.

"Ivan. Hi!" I tried to conceal the ghostly silence. I embraced him—a friendly embrace in front of the man to whom I just confessed my love. The one who had no idea I'd kept in touch with the man I was hugging.

Oh, but it felt so good to be in Ivan's arms. So profound, so nostalgic.

"Wow, what are you doing here?" It was hard not to feel Liam's eyes piercing holes through the back of my head.

Act like friends, friends from the past, not like we've spoken every day and night of these past few months.

"I told you I will see you live."

Shit. Ivan gave it away; poured out my deep, dark secret. Now Liam knows that we've spoken about this, and he will end it. The longest relationship and the quickest breakup.

"You did." I managed a nervous, unconvincing laugh.

"You did, eh?" That was Liam.

"Cleo, you look so unbelievable." That was Ivan.

What to do? What to say?

"Cleo, we need you out here." That was Alfred, the event coordinator. Thank God for Alfred.

"Oh, okay, coming. I can't wait to speak to you later, Ivan," I muttered quietly. Too friendly?

"Bye, Cleo." He grabbed my hand and kissed it.

I quickly looked at Liam, then back at Ivan.

Liam followed me toward the stage.

"We'll talk after," he hissed in my ear.

I stayed silent. Shake it off, Cleo. I couldn't have prepared for caveats like my Russian paramour surprising me only minutes after my boyfriend confessed his love.

Time for my triumph.

* * *

"Cleo, how could you?"

"I can explain."

We were back at Liam's home.

I'd delivered an outstanding performance. I'd compartmentalized my feelings and transported myself to my world of escape. For the next 17 minutes, I played all three movements of **Moonlight Sonata.**

Still, the performance was melancholy and hopeless, emanating from a place of captivation, lust, and appetite.

I'd let my mind wander as I played the notes, but the melody had helped me feel lighter once again. That high was back. I fed off the audience. It was invigorating.

Then the melody ended. The crowd cheered, and the moment they stopped, reality hit me; I remembered what I had to deal with.

Now, in Liam's home, I was facing my consequences.

Leaving without lingering to talk with Ivan, the man who'd traveled the globe to watch me perform, who'd come from a country he'd never left, was brutal. I'd promised him coffee the next morning amid all the excuses about why I had to go.

I couldn't explain my conversations with Ivan to Liam. How could I? He would never forgive me; he would leave me, not only as a boyfriend, but maybe even as a coach.

"Explain, please."

"I-I…I speak with Ivan sometimes. It's no big deal."

"It is to me."

"He's a friend."

"Oh, I believe you were more than just friends, Cleo. I was there the whole time, don't you remember? Those darling kisses I had to watch right after you'd kissed me, those long moments where I got shooed away so you two could spend more time frolicking around instead of rehearsing."

"Liam, please. I'm with you now."

I desperately needed help getting out of my gown; it was suffocating me, but I decided it was not the time to ask.

"Are you, though? You can't be with me if you're there too."

"I-I couldn't ignore him just because I am in a relationship." It was true—if I hadn't been holding on to those profound feelings, that is.

"Do you love him?"

"What? You're crazy. I just met him."

"Do you?"

"No, Liam. No!"

I lied. But how could I tell Liam the truth when I'd just told him it was him I loved?

Liam was panting now. He sat down and hid his face in his hands. I felt guilty. I was guilty. I knew I was in the wrong, but I would never admit it. Admitting it meant giving up Liam. I'd figure out one thing at a time. I just knew I couldn't lose Liam now.

"Do you honestly think I have nothing to worry about?"

"I know you have nothing to worry about." I felt sick. "I love you." I kneeled down and rested my hands on Liam's lap.

"Show me." He lifted his head and pointed to my phone.

"Show you what?" I leaned away.

"I don't know, a text. Some proof that I'm overreacting."

"Don't you think my word should be proof enough?" Another pain in my heart. I hated myself in this moment. I stood up and walked toward the gold antique mirror, attempting to undress. "Come on, let's get some rest. We had a long day; tomorrow will be another long day."

Liam saw my trembling hands as I struggled with the stubborn zipper and approached me with a gentle, pained expression. I sighed. In that moment, all I wished for was to turn back the clock, to return to the way things were just twenty hours ago when life felt simpler and love was less complicated.

Yet I didn't want Ivan to leave. The conflicting emotions swirled within me, a relentless storm of hurt, passion, and longing.

"I'm sorry, Liam. I don't want to hurt you." He didn't know how much I meant that.

I held his hands and looked him in his eyes.

"I love you," I reminded him.

"I love you too," he affirmed, his voice quivering with the profound hurt and longing that mirrored my own.

24

THE ULTIMATUM

London, Ten Years Ago

The following day, I got out of Liam's house as quickly as possible. I decided to go with the truth. A way to feel better about myself, I suppose—nevertheless, the right choice. I explained to Liam that I would just thank Ivan for coming all this way. We would catch up, as friends do, and I would tell him that I was with Liam, so there wouldn't be any mixed messages.

Only one of those wasn't a lie. I would be thanking Ivan for flying all this way, but it wasn't like friends catching up.

I didn't mention Liam, and there were many mixed messages.

First, the hug put me in a hypnotic state. I was immediately transfixed. I wanted to jump into his arms the way I used to, kiss him like it was our last days together. I wanted to stay wrapped in his body and allow that magnetic force to conquer.

But I don't.

Maybe I felt this way when I was with Ivan because it transported me to a time of my life that brought on such ecstasy.

Yeah, that could be it, a genuine friendship and nothing more—just like I told Liam.

It wasn't. The more I spoke with Ivan, the more I fell back into those feelings. Was it possible to feel so strongly about two people? Was I lucky to have found such love, or was I being punished? It was hard to concentrate on Ivan's words, when in my head I was planning out life decisions.

I had to tell him I was with Liam. It was the right thing to do.

But telling Ivan meant saying goodbye. If I didn't say anything, I would have to say goodbye to Liam. Neither possibility proved more devastating than the other, so I didn't mention anything; I couldn't. I could wait one more day and weigh my options some more.

Coffee turned into lunch; lunch turned into a stroll around Hyde Park. I couldn't say goodbye. I knew Liam would be waiting for me, but Ivan had come all this way, and I physically couldn't distance myself from him. It wasn't until Liam sent a text about work that I forced myself to leave. I promised Ivan that I would be back, planted a platonic kiss on his cheek, ignored his confused expression when I did so, and hurried back home.

* * *

Liam was sitting alone in his bedroom when I got there. Seated on his bed, elbows resting on his knees, he presented a severe demeanor that obscured any indication of its source.

"Hello, love." I decided to ignore his mood and hope it would fizzle out. "I was wondering where you were."

"Give me your phone." His tone was sharp, unforgiving.

"What?"

"Give me your phone."

"Wh-why do you need my phone?"

"Ivan called last night when you were in the shower."

"What? What did he say?" *What did he say?*

"He wanted to make plans. Also, it happened to come up that you guys have spoken since Russia."

How long did they talk?

How did it just come up in conversation?

In that moment, I thought, *How stupid that I believed I could honestly have it all.*

Passion. Lust. Comfort. Both Ivan and Liam.

"I had a gut feeling, Cleo. I knew."

"I—"

"Why did you lie to me?"

"I didn't—"

"Cleo! Just tell me what you want from me!"

I froze. His tone of voice brought me back to our teacher-student relationship: him in his superior position, and me upsetting him.

"I want you! I want this! Us! What we have!" I whispered urgently and lowered myself to the ground, sinking to my knees, meeting Liam eye to eye. So he can witness my sincerity, the love behind my eyes. My regret. I didn't know if I had any regrets. I didn't know if I was excited to have Ivan here, to have Ivan in my life. Ivan always tainted my potential with Liam. Yet I wouldn't change anything.

I tried to hide my tears. I still wanted to be his equal, not his inferior. I wanted so badly for him to look at me with awe and adoration, not the way he was now, his eyebrows furrowed, his lips stiff. He looked at me with anger and disappointment.

"But you thought Ivan on the side was perfectly rational?"

"I-I…I don't know. It's hard to explain."

"Try."

When I didn't respond, Liam stood up and got off the bed. I lost my balance and watched him as he walked out. Quickly, I got up and followed.

"I didn't think Ivan was going to come here. I didn't think it was going to get this complicated!"

"Not an excuse, Cleo!"

I followed him closely down the stairs, Liam's heavy steps indicating his frustration.

"I can't just ignore him! I can't—"

"Why not?" He stopped in place. I halted behind him.

That was a good question.

One which I simply couldn't answer. When you form such agile and powerful feelings for someone, how are you supposed to say goodbye? Do you give up on one love if another coexists?

"Why not, Cleo?" Liam repeated.

"I…I don't have an answer." I took a step backward, feeling shame and defeat.

"Well, I'll make it easy for you. If you truly want to move forward with me, Ivan is out."

"What?"

"You heard me." He grabbed his coat and started walking toward the door.

"But he came all this way…he came to visit me. I can't do this now!"

"Me or him, Cleo!" And he was off.

* * *

My hands trembled uncontrollably, mirroring the chaos within my heart. I attempted to stifle the quivering, but the unease ran deeper than I could fathom. With Ivan's impending arrival, the weight of an excruciating decision bore down on me. It was a choice that would require me to sacrifice a piece of my very soul, no matter which path I chose.

Should I opt for Liam, I would return to a life that made logical sense, a world of familiarity and contentment. But in doing so, I knew I would leave behind the intoxicating allure of Ivan—a love that promised freedom and an incomprehensible depth, something unique and impossible to replicate.

Conversely, embracing Ivan meant forfeiting the comforting simplicity of my life with Liam, bidding farewell to a love that had been a guiding light in my world. The intricacies of Ivan's love held me in a mesmerizing grip, but they were accompanied by uncertainty, a nagging doubt about the life I was about to enter.

Two loves, each with its own enchanting and heartbreaking qualities, pulled me in opposite directions. My heart ached with the weight of my decision, for either way, I knew I would leave behind a part of myself—a part I might never fully recover.

"*Lyubimaya moya,* my sweetheart!" I felt the genuine expression in his words. It was never fabricated with Ivan.

"Ivan!" He took me in his arms—the warmth wrapped around my body both figuratively and physically.

"I just had the best morning! And yesterday I went on the metro? Tube? The tube, yeah? I went to the big..." He circled his arms wide. "Um, how you say..."

"The London Eye? The Ferris wheel?"

"*Da,* yes! So beautiful! I see why you love it here."

We were at the small restaurant where I'd generally spent my mornings for the past ten years. Introducing Ivan to my everyday surroundings had been my way of sharing a bit of my life with him. It was no Dom, but it was my version of that—if you just switched out the blinis for crumpets and the Russian folk music for bossa nova. I liked this place because no one I knew ate here. It was my little escape in the morning, before the storm.

"What do you want to do today? Do you have time? Can you show me what you do when you're not competing?"

Today was empty. Not a regular occurrence. All I had on schedule was to plan my whole life around this very challenging choice.

I allowed Ivan to continue speaking, relishing the sound of his voice. It also gave me time to think. I wanted this day to drag out. I wanted to inject this day into my blood. I didn't want it to end. The day ending meant I had to decide; I wanted to be in this world for a bit longer.

London was my home, the haven in which I was born and grew up. I truly believed that I would live, marry, and die there. No other city or country I've been to has lived up to the panoramic, sarcastic, and moodiness that is London, my London.

Yet I never got to truly live, breathe, and walk the streets of London the way I was right now. I was usually on the road, half here, half there, floating through life. Ivan's presence forced me to stop and appreciate what was right in my backyard, literally.

We began with the museums: the Wallace Collection, the British Museum. We window-shopped at Covent Garden and then finished off at Regent's Park.

The day went by too quickly. The banter was so seamless; catching up felt so natural. We were able to pick right up from where we'd said goodbye at Hotel Metropol. Disconnecting from my busy solo pianist life was only possible in Ivan's presence.

"Cleo, I have a surprise." We sat in the vibrant greenery of Regent's Park. It was a hot summer day. Flowers were blooming all around us, a private paradise.

"Yesterday, I spoke with a music agency here in London. They want me to come in for a meeting. I can stay here for a little while, get a working visa, travel Europe, stay close with you." He covered my hands in a tight grip. His bright blue, innocent eyes, excited as a puppy's, gazed into mine. He did this? Had he planned to make this monumental change? For me? I knew it was a sign. I had to finally decide and do what I was trying to avoid until now. I had to choose: Liam or Ivan.

The gravity of this decision weighed heavily on my shoulders, a moment of reckoning that would shape the trajectory of my life, inevitably altering its course. There would be no retracing my steps, no rewriting history. Once I made my choice, its echoes would reverberate through the tapestry of my future.

I couldn't fathom that my choice, no matter the path, might ultimately prove to be the wrong one.

25

CRESCENDO

New York City, Present Day

It has been a month since I've spoken to Ramona and her publishing team. I will not be the first to call. I know what her silence means, and neither my assumption nor my circumstantial evidence indicates good news. In the end, money is everybody's main priority, and if you're not able to contribute, you'll continue to slide down the priority list.

After a month and a day, Ramona finally calls.

She invites me to her office to discuss the future of my novel.

Suddenly I feel hopeful. Maybe this is a good sign? I am sure that someone of her character would be more than happy to let me off over the phone. Perhaps a discussion is necessary—a reason for my presence.

I am wrong.

"Let's cut through the crap and get to today's issue."

Ramona seems busy and disinterested as I sit across from her at the conference table. Her next words hold so much power over my future.

The fact that I've become so dependent on Ramona infuriates me.

Just say it! Blurt it out! Tell me what the future holds for me!

"I brought you here because I believe you should be here in person when I tell you: I'm sorry, Cleo. We can no longer work together."

The shock paralyzes me. I had a feeling this may happen, but now I have no words.

This outcome was something I'd considered in the past, but I never actually imagined it would be the case. When I hear those words come out of Ramona's mouth, it doesn't feel real.

Surely I misheard? My vision begins to fog up; my legs start to shake as the adrenaline kicks in.

It is my body's way of telling me, *Run, leave. Let yourself go before you fall any further.*

But I can't leave. My legs stop working. I just watch Ramona talk, but her words are inaudible. My mind is elsewhere.

Where is the loyalty I experienced during my successful run?

We will help you every step of the way, Ramona once said. Bullshit!

The first moment I begin to falter, they write me off. Ramona doesn't want to spend her time and effort on a project that feels like a waste of her time.

I could retaliate. I could cause a scene and demand what Ramona owes me from the contract.

Yet I have no more strength in me to fight. I am numb.

Eventually, I pack up my metaphorical cardboard box and leave the building.

I am done with this partnership, done with my chance at publishing my next novel. It is all over—another failure.

I can't cry or reflect on what just happened. It is my day to pick up the children, and God knows I do not need another late pickup.

During my robotic duties, I stay in an ambiguous headspace. The walk home is silent. While I am aware that the kids are speaking, I am not listening. Nor am I thinking. I am not functioning.

One brick at a time, the walls of my life are slowly crumbling. I tried a second chance at a career. I tried to mend my relationship with Conor. Am I even a good parent at this point?

Honestly, I am not sure anymore.

I need a moment to think, to digest.

We finally arrive home, and I crave some space, some quiet.

"All right guys, Mummy has work to do now."

I drop my keys on the ground in a state of detachment, dump my coat and shoes on top, and head to my room.

"Ciara, go do your homework, Sebastian, Olivia—ten minutes of screen time, okay? When I come out, it's going to be dinner, bath, bed." I hear the words come out of my mouth, but I feel nothing. I don't wait for the kids' answers and close the door behind me.

I just stand there.

What am I going to do? I have no job, no publisher, no purpose, not even a hobby.

What will Conor say? Will he be sympathetic or frustrated?

What will my family think, my mother?

In times of crisis, you often hear about the body's instinctive responses. The brain detects danger, signaling the adrenals to flood the system with cortisol, priming the body for the fight-or-flight response. But there's a lesser-discussed reaction: the freeze response.

That is what is happening to me right now. I remain in my room, as if time itself has stopped. I am stuck, stagnant, encased in cement. I squeeze my eyes shut, my phone just out of reach, and, unable to move, I resort to playing music in my head as my last attempt to escape the chilling grip of paralysis.

I shut my eyes shut until I can picture myself playing **Moonlight Sonata, (1st Movement)**.

The sounds became visual, the images audible. I am not sure if my body is moving through the emotions as aggressively as I play the keys, maintaining my posture: light hands, allowing gravity to pull my fingers down onto the keys.

I don't cry. I don't need that release.

Tears would offer a more conventional outlet for these overwhelming emotions. They would release the pent-up frustration, the raw pain, the searing humiliation. But I resist, focusing solely on the sonata. The music surges through me with fierce and resolute vibrations, igniting a symphony of sensations. I can visualize the black piano in front of me, smell the ivory keys, see my voluminous Valentino gown, feel the audience before me, hear the—

I startle from my hypnotic state when Ciara runs into my room.

"Mom! The kids are gone!"

What? I am still unable to speak. What is she even saying?

"Come quick." Rousing me from my trance-like state.

When I enter the living room, the veranda door is open. *Ohmygosh, ohmygosh, ohmygosh.*

I run outside onto the veranda. The kids aren't there. I look over the balcony. Just the busy streets of New York. No neglected kids.

"Sebastian? Olivia?" My voice echoes through the silent house.

My heart lurches in my chest, threatening to stop altogether. The front door stands wide open, a chilling draft creeping in, and their jackets are nowhere to be seen.

Without a moment to think, I grab Ciara, and we both run out of the house.

I continue to shout their names, my voice carrying through the street.

"Olivia! Sebastian!" The world around me seems strangely indifferent—cars honking, sirens wailing, and passersby unfazed.

"Olivia!" I cry, desperation gripping me. "Sebastian!"

I'm trapped in the throes of my worst nightmare, oblivious to the cold air biting at my skin or the dampness seeping into my socks. Beside me, Ciara shivers, her fear mirroring my own, her confusion palpable.

What mess did I drag my kids into?

Where are my kids?

I continue to chase the invisible children, not knowing if I am heading closer or further away.

"Olivia! Sebastian!" I cry again. Tears are rushing down my face.

Olivia! Sebastian! Help!

The tears start to freeze upon my cheeks. The broad streets begin to close up around me. I am not going to allow my kids to suffer from my affliction. It isn't fair. They are much too young, too innocent, to have their lives ruined by the one person who is supposed to protect them.

Mothers are supposed to have superhero strength, gain animal instincts, produce so much adrenaline they can pick up a car to save their children. Where is mine? Why do I feel so overpowered, so defeated?

I feel the bile forming inside me; my legs start to give way. I want to fall to the ground, crying, screaming, surrendering. I have no more in me. Nothing would better this situation.

"Mom, there they are!" Ciara shouts.

"Oh my gosh, oh my gosh." I tremble as I cry. My knees are buckling, but I manage to run across busy Fifth Avenue toward Washington Square Park. Cars beep, Ciara follows me, our hands grasped.

I see my two innocent kids. Happy, laughing, watching the fountain.

Their matching bright blond curls, their rosy cheeks. So unaware of my neglect.

Then everything goes black.

PART TWO

26

CLARICE

New York City, Present Day

How do I start this? Dear diary? No, that sounds too cliché, something I would have written in my preteens. Dear Cleo? No, that's strange. Greetings and salutations? Hello, you? Dear you, Dear me?

Oh, I don't know.

Why don't I just start with why I am writing.

Start with last week's events and work our way forward from there.

I almost threw my life away in that moment. In retrospect, I wonder if it was a defining event that sparked me into action and eventually helped me break the cycle.

I guess it's all in the way I view it.

It took a while to escape the haze that imprisoned me--an entrapment where nothing could shake the feelings but time. Gradually, the fog started to disintegrate; my breathing began to slow down. However, my body was still unable to move. Unable to grasp the severity of what had happened.

The situation had reached the point where it couldn't possibly get any worse--the point where I lost control over everything.

The many possible scenarios circulate in my brain. I was so close to losing my kids, my husband, my life, and my world.

But somehow, I didn't lose it all--not yet. My kids are safe. In their blissful simplicity, they didn't realize what was going on. Only Mummy's fainting startled them, and they recovered rapidly.

Conor is with me at home. The kids spent the night at Shannon's.

It was fortunate that Mrs. Laurence, a teacher at the kids' school, was walking past and noticed a commotion. Apparently, Olivia and Sebastian dropped their ball over the veranda and left the house to retrieve it.

She knew to call Conor straight away. I'm still not sure about the timing of it all. How long was I out for? At what moment did the kids see me? What was Ciara doing while I was out?

Ciara. That poor girl is taking on so much because of me. Is it inevitable that as parents we damage our children? Do we have any option for them to come out free of harm? I'm still a product of my parents' wrongdoings.

The ambulance was already there by the time Conor arrived. I guess they checked my vitals, checked my blood pressure, determined a possible panic attack, and helped me home. My awareness of those actions was limited. Even though I awoke at the park, the first time I felt like I truly opened my eyes was at home.

I couldn't stand; I couldn't hold my weight. I sat on the bench on my veranda and let my mind draw a blank. A warmth enveloped my body and caused me to snap into my surroundings. Conor had placed a blanket on top of me. I didn't know if I was cold or not. I still felt numb.

Was I in shock? Is that what I was feeling--or lack thereof?

I detected pity in his face. Or was it disappointment? I expected him to leave then, to not have the ability to face me. Instead, he kneeled beside me, handed me a mug of tea, and rested his hand in my lap.

"I'm sorry." Those were the only words I could come up with at that moment. I saw my future; there is no way Conor won't leave me now. I have failed as a wife, as a mother.

Not only will Conor leave me, but he now has an excellent case for full custody. I am an unfit mother. I have proven my abilities today, and they are terrifying.

"I'm sorry," I repeated, and the tears started to flood. The feelings began to arrive--all at full blast.

"I'm sorry, I'm sorry, I'm sorry." I couldn't stop. I was wailing now. My kids! I started to shake.

Conor came over and sat beside me on the bench.

He held me.

"I know." I think he was crying too. From anger? Frustration? Hate? Relief?

"Shh." He held me tighter as I continued to tremble into his torso.

"I'm sorry!"

"I know." He was comforting me. He was embracing me.

I looked him right in the eyes. I couldn't tell what he felt unless I studied his face.

It was close to mine. I could see up close how his eyes looked worn out, tired. I was the reason for those worries. But those eyes were still clear blue. So innocent. So loving. I missed him so much. I missed his love, his comfort.

He looked straight back into my eyes. I hoped they were as easy to read as his.

He moved my wet hair out of my face and leaned his forehead against mine.

"I'm sorry," I whispered again.

"I know."

"Conor, something is very wrong."

"I know."

"I need help." It was my first time realizing this, my first time admitting it.

"I know."

Which leads me to today. My first entry. My first attempt at getting my life organized, ironing out the creases, undoing the damage.

If that is even possible.

I met with a psychiatrist who has advanced training in psychoanalysis. She is a colleague of Conor's. Someone who comes highly recommended. Her name is Clarice.

Clarice. Immediately, I thought of Clarice Starling from The Silence Of The Lambs. Which would make me Hannibal Lecter or Buffalo Bill--the monsters. The inhumane creatures that Clarice tried to figure out.

I sat across from Clarice; weirdly, she resembled my mum. She, too, was a proper Englishwoman with a thick, posh accent. She was bony and pointy, just like my mother, and wore her straight hair in a short bob. They even smelled the same: Chanel No. 5. A classic but very noticeable scent.

The only difference was Clarice wore thick black glasses, and, despite her pointy appearance, she spoke softly and calmly.

"So why are you here?"

"That's quite the generic question, is it not?"

"I would like you to verbalize why you think you're here."

"On my husband's strict orders." I laughed. It wasn't funny.

Clarice responded with a smile. A sad smile. A worried one.

"I am here because I am stuck." I tried again. "I have officially hit rock bottom, lost control over my life, and all the other cliches you can come up with."

"Define 'rock bottom.'"

I had a feeling that this was how therapy would be. I could say, 'I ate a burger,' and the therapist would respond with, 'Now, why do you think you ate that burger? What does it represent?' But I decided to humor her and continue.

"Well, where to start? First, I ruined any chances at life as a pianist. Then I failed at two more jobs after that. I lost my contract with my agency, my husband hates me, my best friend hates me, my mother and sister don't seem too fond of me either--oh yeah, and I almost lost my kids the other day."

She sat there silently.

"You think you can fix that for me?"

"Well, if you're open to it, I am willing to help you through the 'ramifications.'" She used air quotes.

"So why not begin from the start? You mentioned a pianist. What age were you when you started?"

"Well, I suppose I was three."

This shocked her, as it does many. When I tell people I started playing at the age of three, they succumb to the notion that I played the ABCs or was just figuring out the sounds of the piano. But no. My piano came with Lottie. While we did mess around a bit here and there, I immediately picked up the sounds and the notes simultaneously. I was understanding the compositions by the time I was five, and I'd really elevated my repertoire by seven.

I started performing at concertos and recitals at the age of thirteen, had my first record at twenty, sold out my first tour before I was thirty. And that is where it ends.

"Why do you suppose it ended so abruptly?"

"Well, I don't know." I really didn't know. My automatic thoughts were, I just stopped loving it. So I stopped. But how to word that in a way that someone might understand? I had fallen in love with the piano, had accomplished so much, was headed in the right direction. How can I convince someone that, all of a sudden, I stopped loving it? So much so that I quit while on top? I didn't fail miserably and then think, Well, okay, now is probably the time to leave. No. I had sold out an arena. I was performing at the Proms. I featured at Carnegie Hall, the Sydney Opera House. Then I decided it wasn't for me.

Clarice didn't speak. I knew this tactic from when I worked with journalists in the past; they used this trick. The interviewer would stay quiet until the interviewee would be so uncomfortable, they had to speak and reveal more.

It worked. I hated the quiet, so I had to continue.

"I guess I just fell in love with the classical world, the only thing I ever knew, much too fast and too deep. When you love something quickly, it's only natural to fall out just as quick, no?"

"You tell me."

I thought I just did.

"Cleo, what is your fondest memory from three to thirty?"

"Music-related?"

"It doesn't have to be."

"It probably would be."

I thought for a while.

"I can't pick one. It's performing, though. I never was able to match the high I got from performing. Every performance felt like an Olympic event. If I missed one note, I messed up everything, I accidentally told a different story. The rush is what drove me."

"And still, you gave it all up. There must be a reason."

Was that a challenge, finding my reason for ending it all? I knew she wouldn't understand. No one really does.

So no real memory came to mind.

I was silent.

"Okay, let's think about it from another perspective. When you met your husband, did you feel as though you'd filled a void previously satiated by your career?"

I thought about it.

"It's different."

"Different how?"

"Different, like I felt it was necessary, the right steps to take."

"But I assume there was love involved."

"Yes. Yes, there was."

"So do you think this love may have substituted for the piano?"

What was she getting at? I thought about it.

"No, it's different," I repeated, not knowing how to articulate my answer.

"Different how?" she asked again.

"I felt safe. Maybe I needed to feel safe more than I needed that rush."

"Did you meet your husband while you were still playing?" It was weird that she kept calling Conor "your husband," like she didn't want to blur the lines of her connection to him.

"No. It was the same year but months after I stopped. Maybe seven, eight?"

She took in this information, pondered a bit. "Let's move on."

Oh thank god.

"What caused you to believe that your husband now hates you?"

"Well, he mentioned that I'm a miserable human being, he asked to separate, and then I went and lost his children. So." I raised my hands, as to say, That's all folks!

"Can I ask you to go deeper?"

The rest of our conversation stayed here. The reasons why my husband hates me. How fun. I relived all the moments in which Conor would say I'm not present. I told her about not showing up for his award, about not showing up to counseling. I didn't mention my blackouts. Why not keep that little gem for another day? Before Clarice could dig any deeper, she said, "All right, that's it for today."

Just like that, she closed a metaphoric chapter of my life. And just like that, I survived my first appointment.

I don't feel healed by any means. I'm not sure what to journal here. I just figure I'll talk about my days, and maybe the pieces will fall into place.

Clarice ended our session by giving me this homework assignment.

"Too many blank spaces," she said. "Maybe writing will help clear up some of those memories."

So this is precisely what I am doing--writing until the story makes sense.

These journal entries are not for Clarice, she made that clear. Maybe I can write knowing no one will ever read this. Maybe I will "metaphorically" burn it once Clarice heals me. Maybe I'll never turn back to these thoughts or memories.

I'm not sure how to end my diary entries, so I leave it at that. I close my computer and take a nap. I never nap. Even when my kids were newborns. *Nap when the baby naps*, they say. Such rubbish. Those alone moments were gold. I couldn't waste them on rest. Yet today, I nap. My body needs it. I've traveled through hell and back—well, not back, but here's to hoping.

27

THE FLASHES

New York City, Present Day

The flashes.

They started two days ago.

I call them flashes because that is what they are. A flash. A picture running away so fast that I can barely grasp it. I can't freeze the image and analyze the pixels.

Upon Clarice's request, I put time aside to focus on my memories. I took out my laptop and started a new document. Having to accompany my work with music, I looked through my vinyl collection and came across a piece that took me back to Russia. Moments that led to my romance with Ivan.

Chopin's Fantaisie-Impromptu. This melody brought me to that second day of the competition, practicing for my subsequent performance. The same joy, the same liberation, permeated my being. I had Liam by my side, paving the way for greatness. Then, the abrupt moment where I glanced up and locked eyes with Ivan. How powerful that felt.

Yet these memories weren't materializing in my brain. I grasped the facts and timelines, but the feelings escaped me. I closed my eyes, tried to reel them in; that didn't work. I blasted the music louder. Maybe the acoustics weren't the same?

I stood up and paced. The pacing always worked for my writing. Maybe it would spark a memory.

That's when my first flash occurred.

I saw a vision of myself vividly; I was playing Chopin. Liam was by my side. The halls looked different than I remembered them. It wasn't the Great Hall. Instead, we were in Liam's home, in his office. No audience watching me, no Ivan.

The pixels faded, and I was lost again. More lost than when I began. Why was that memory showing up? Why couldn't I focus on the memory of me and Liam? When Ivan watched me practice? No explanations, just more confusion.

I tried to get to that place again, to prolong this memory, but I couldn't.

Today I experience another flash. This time, it is unintentional.

In my attempt at a better quality of life, I decide to go for a complete purge. To get rid of all the excess. A way to start over. It seems like the right move; it feels healthy.

My closet is full of useless items. The colorful party dresses I used to give attention to. Lipsticks, many of which have expired. I hope to eliminate any remnants of the person I once was. Or do I wish to save them, exchange them for the dark and moody palette I've adopted?

Then I find it, in the depths of my closet. An old jewelry box. It's dark wood on the outside with cushioned blue interiors. I feel gravitated nostalgia and an overpowering sense of trepidation.

I feel my hands quiver as I reveal the gold chain, the red pendant. The carnelian stone. The second flash reveals itself.

A hasty image of me holding on to it, hiding it. Burying it in my pocket.

The memory leaves a taste of vague discomfort in my mouth. When was that, and why did I hide it? From whom?

I plan to elaborate with Clarice. First, I'll tell her about my clear memories, which I often have, and then the new, unidentifiable ones. The ones that feel distant, the ones I don't know if I truly own.

28

HOMEWORK

New York City, Present Day

The therapy appears to be working. I am more diligent and present now. I mean, it has only been a week, so we'll see how long I can last.

Another step in the right direction has been my return to writing.

This time there will be no Ramona and no publishing company. From now on, I will solely depend on myself.

My desire to recount my memories compels me to write them down. There might be an interesting story in there that people would like to read.

These stories will recount my breakthrough as a musician and my runaway. They will narrate my thoughts before I disappeared from the world of classical music—they will look at my successes and the romance that brought me to the brink of destruction.

In my previous novels, I knew the beginning, the middle, and the end before I started to write. Now, I do not know what will come of this story. What will I discover on this exploration?

Nostalgic memories with Liam let me reflect on our time together as we rose to the top. I feel so different from the person I was then, the person I was with Liam. And yet, in some ways, my past always followed me.

Every day, I immerse myself in the symphonies of Tchaikovsky, Rachmaninoff, and many others. At this moment, I'm tuned in to **Mozart's Symphony No. 40.** This music enhances my concentration.

When I go for my walks, I listen to music. When I relax, when I need to think, music always follows me.

The only way I can reach my emotions is through music. Despite its qualities of serenity, safety, and security, it has, in some ways, undermined my personal efficiency.

It gets me in trouble.

It is hard for me to immerse myself in the melodies without getting lost, both metaphorically and literally.

While listening to music, I often lose my sense of time and space. I wake up suddenly and wonder, *Where am I?*

Music keeps me from attending most meetings or events on time. It is preventing me from interacting with others. It is holding me back from excelling. Yet I can't let it go.

I never gave up on my love for music; it's what has gotten me through since I was three. But once I left Liam and that world, the piano left me. I could never touch a piano again. Whenever I was close to one, it would wound me.

Conor asked for a piano, my children asked for a piano. But I refused. I have been married ten years now, and Conor has never seen me play. I doubt he ever will.

I mention all of this to Clarice in our session.

"Why do you think that is?"

"It is too painful."

"Painful, how?"

"The visuals, the smell, the touch…it brings on memories that are too explicit."

"And what is wrong with that? You talk so highly of your past, yet you don't seem to enjoy reliving it. Why do you think going back will be painful?"

"I'm not sure. Maybe because I won't ever be that person again? Almost like it's a tease."

"Why do you think you won't ever be that person again? You *are* that person. A person who also grew up and moved on with her life. They are not two separate worlds."

"They are, though, and I am not going to be that person again because I tried to be that person, and it proved detrimental."

"Ah, let's get into that."

I roll my eyes any time Clarice says anything like a psychiatrist. It brings me right back to our dynamic.

"Why would you say that life was detrimental?"

"I…" I start to answer, and then stop. I'm not sure. I never really gave myself an answer. "I don't know."

"What memories come up when you think about those times?"

"Fond memories. Happy memories, I suppose." A smile appears on my face. "It was a time in my life where this drive inside me had such an intense force; I felt alive, I felt energized. I was pushing myself to my limits, and that feeling when you succeed after sacrificing so much…there is nothing like it." I think I'm making sense.

"Yet nothing substantial comes to mind? Nothing that tells you it was detrimental? Maybe memories of ending it all?"

My mind goes blank.

"Why did you give it all up, Cleo?"

Blank.

"I'm about to ask you something far-fetched, but I want you to think about it. Don't answer right away." She leans in closer, establishing comfort and support. "Is there any chance of trauma linked to you playing the piano?"

"No—"

Clarice shushes me with nothing but a look, reminding me to think, then speak.

I squint. The vagueness of my memories leaves me impatient.

"I don't know," I answer. "I don't think so, but I don't know." Truth be told, how could I know if I had a blank space of memory? At this point, I know as much as Clarice.

"Psychologists tend to diagnose certain symptoms using bubble diagnoses and then recommend medication as treatment. I do not believe this is necessary for you."

She has my attention.

"I like to approach each of my patients individually. I focus on their personalized treatments. I try to tailor it to where the symptoms originated."

I find it hard to let go of my skepticism, my expectations. There is a desire to prove to people that I can do things on my own. However, I want this to end—all of it.

I want to feel better again. *Need* to feel better.

Clarice needs my cooperation and trust for her to help me. I want to feel vibrant and alive again, and I need to be there for my husband and kids. I am listening.

"You mention selective memories—some of which you choose to remember. The fond memories, the happier times. It appears you set yourself in these places as a coping mechanism."

"Coping mechanism?"

"Wouldn't you agree? To a certain extent?"

I think about it. "No?" It comes out like a question. The truth is, I'm not sure if what I am doing is coping.

"I don't want to assume anything, but you say you take yourself back to these times when trouble arises, when things get hard."

"Okay." I suppose there is some truth to that. "And that's bad?"

"If the thoughts are getting in your way, it's probably best to try and keep them under control."

Under control. Like I am some manic disaster who needed taming.

"I have some homework for you."

Another eye roll. Clarice ignores it.

"I'm sure you know this, Cleo, but music holds so much power. The way music impacts the brain is unique. There are certain regions of the brain that become activated when needed. For example, when you are reading or writing, you use a designated part of your brain. But when listening to music..." She leans in closer; I do too. "With music, those areas are scattered all across your brain. Music activates your visual, motor, and memory responses. So, I am sure you are tapping into different times of your life involuntarily as you listen."

I nod. I think about the moments when I drift off. How every melody brings me to a moment of my past. How every sound causes an intuitive reaction deep within.

"In many ways, music seems to be beneficial for you, a way of dissociating and coping. However, at the same time, it may trigger you into an altered state, which takes you far away from your present reality."

"So I should stop listening to music?" My breath quickens; the skepticism comes back.

"No, absolutely not."

I let out a big sigh. I'm not ready to give it up entirely.

"It is not possible to completely rid anxiety or stress from your life, but it is important to learn how to deal with it. Imagine a life without stress? That's just not reality. So, instead, we want to learn how to confront those feelings head-on."

In the past, stress ignited a fire in me, made me feel invigorated. I loved experiencing anxiety, almost as a rush, or a high. But now, I am unable to cope with it.

What happened to me? How did I get so weak?

Clarice goes on, "I think music is something you need in your life. I also believe that listening to it will help you get a clearer picture of what really went on in your past. So we will have to find a way to keep it in your life without it taking you away from the present. But one thing at a time, okay?" She gets her clipboard ready. "There is a technique called exposure therapy. I would like to try it with you, if you are willing."

I nod. Clarice has gained my trust.

"I believe music can help us clear up some of those memories, but I want to work on, once it feels safe, of course, eradicating your resistance toward the piano. Once you get back to that piano bench, I expect you'll find a lot of answers."

Answers? How, exactly? My skepticism must be evident, because Clarice continues.

"Exposure therapy involves exposing the person to what they fear, but safely." She ignores my puzzled expression. "Changing the pattern of fear and avoidance can help the patient develop a new relationship with it. We change the original behavior and introduce a calming, relaxing element."

"So, the homework?" I ask.

"Right, your homework. Once you are ready, I would like you to explore your memories thoroughly. Find a way to bring them to the surface and confront them."

I'm not sure I am ready. I am simultaneously exhilarated and terrified to go there. It is an opportunity to confront fears I didn't know I had.

"I want you to think of something that brings you to a place of calm, such as a smell, a touch, a sound, an environment. Fear and relaxation cannot coexist. Our aim is to rewire your brain to associate the piano with a more pleasant memory. Your piano seems to be a relic, a tool for bringing up memories. If you decide to return to it, you might be able to piece together what happened and perhaps find closure. However, I do not wish to force you, especially not immediately."

Clarice explains a systematic plan that will align the piano with a calming focus. She gives the example of a child who is petrified of dogs after being attacked by one. Hearing a dog bark or the ringing of a collar puts this child in a state of fear, because the only association they have is the deep scar of memory. The method involves reinforcing safety around the animal. To accomplish this, they slowly introduce the dog back into the child's life while simultaneously implementing a pleasurable sensation. Say, ice cream.

During the process, the child is shown a photo or video of a dog, or they sound dog's collar chimes, while they are eating ice cream. In each moment, the child will show fear, but their brain emits dopamine and serotonin from the pleasure of eating sugary cream. The memories of dogs will gradually be replaced with the joys of ice cream. In the end, the child will be serene and content next time he hears a bark.

HOMEWORK: Try to find something that will calm me, something that will restore my connection to the piano.

It seems simple enough. Too simple.

"It will take a while. It's not a quick fix." Clarice makes sure I understand that.

Shit.

I will start by finding a tranquil state while I envision the piano. I'll watch a video of me playing piano, I'll stand close to one, so I can eventually build myself up to sit on the bench and play once again.

And that, Clarice hopes, will be the key to restoring the memories I have intentionally erased.

I know that it's this or pills. So I agree.

Later that night, I ponder my options.

What is something not music-related that brings me pleasure?

29

THE SLEEPING BEAUTY

New York City, Present Day

"Butterflies?" Clarice asks, nonjudgmental yet surprised.

"I have always had a fascination toward them. No, actually, that's a lie. My mother began it. I just mimicked her interest to connect with her. It was the only time I spent with her away from the piano." I can feel Clarice note "Mummy issues" on her why-Cleo-is-like-this list.

"But it became something I held on to. I grew a little garden on my patio at home. That's also a lie. I didn't grow it; I have some gardeners who grow it for me. I enjoy the activity of gardening, yet I am never able to give my plants enough attention. But these plants bring the butterflies, and I would often sit and go to another land while watching them."

The next day, Clarice writes me a prescription: a visit to the American Museum of Natural History. They have a butterfly conservatory there, and I have strict orders to take a day off and visit them.

Since I have nothing planned, not the next day, or at all, I take a yellow cab uptown.

Picture yourself playing the piano, really picture it, using all your senses. Imagine the touch, the smell, the sound. All of it.

Then, just wait. Don't force anything. Sit still and see what may come. Even if nothing happens, it is the first step.

I sit on the bench. I watch people as they observe the butterflies. There are five hundred of them, the brochures tell me. They encourage you to feed the butterflies, touch and hold the butterflies, but I am here with another mission.

"Bring your music with," she said.

I never go anywhere without my music.

"Play something that brings happy memories." I play **Tchaikovsky - Sleeping Beauty Op. 66.**

I'm having trouble concentrating, so I close my eyes.

Sleeping Beauty evokes innocent, romantic, and loving memories. It feels strange to visualize them, not as a flash but as a continuous image. With my eyes closed, I undergo an out-of-body experience. I can visualize myself there, at the museum. I see the melody as I sway to the rhythm. A moment of pure ecstasy. A moment of pure innocence.

As the butterflies draw nearer, the surrounding people gradually fade into obscurity. I reach out to touch the butterflies, and each contact births a radiant, animated sparkle. The contagion spreads, infusing the room with fresh colors and intensified brightness.

I stand up now, and my gray monochrome outfit turns a holy white.

The music doesn't stir any memories, old or new, but it awakens a feeling I had once upon a time.

It was a time before I understood true love or encountered the world's darkness. It was a life of innocence and unadulterated happiness, where I could simply close my eyes and let the music shape my soul. This memory isn't clear but is a revival of a cherished emotion from a lifetime ago—a time when I hadn't yet faced love or the world's harshness. Clarice told me that even if nothing else happens, it is still the first step.

30

ACROSS THE UNIVERSE

New York City, Present Day

I feel as though I'm progressing.

Conor promises to put couples counseling aside for now. He knows not to push his luck. One issue at a time—that is all I can offer right now. The good news is, Conor is now settled at home. We are no longer creating elaborate plans to distance ourselves, to avoid each other. At least he is home.

Tonight I want to express my appreciation. I order takeout from his favorite Thai restaurant. I put on a pink midi ribbed dress I haven't worn in a decade. My nails are still painted, my makeup is fresh; I feel polished again. I really hope my efforts will be apparent to Conor.

I drop the kids off at Shannon's. The house is empty; the wine is aerating. I put on **Shostakovich - Waltz No. 2.** I finally feel at peace.

It is the first time in a while I feel euphoric. It is a feeling of optimism, a feeling of having been so low it can only go up from here. I sip the smooth, rich red wine; I sway to the oboes, saxophones, and bassoons.

I hear the key turn in the door and Conor's voice over the music. "Hello? Cleo?"

"Hey!" I say, feeling a bit tipsy. I'm not sure if it's due to the wine or the joy coursing through my veins.

"Hey." A laugh leaves Conor's mouth. "What are you so giddy about? Where are the kids?"

"Well…the kids are at Shannon's." I help Conor out of his sports coat. "And the house is ours," I reply through kisses. There is a chance I am overwhelming Conor. I'm not sure if he has properly forgiven me or is just being nice. Doing what a supportive husband should do in moments like these. When the wife loses control, the husband sticks by her side, in sickness and in health, till death do them part.

"I like the music; what is this?"

"It's Shostakovich." I pour Conor a glass and top off my own. "It really brings me back to when I was in Russia."

This seems to hit a nerve; Conor's face suddenly shifts. It's almost as though Conor doesn't like when I speak of Russia. Like it is unacceptable to have had a life before him, to have had relationships before him. But he speaks freely of his exes—fondly of some. Some are funny stories I tease him with. Why does he have a reaction toward my memories?

He accepts his glass, lowers the music, and then proceeds with, "I was thinking, it may be good for us to take a trip to London. Visit your family. Maybe we can visit Dad too while we are there."

I wait for him to finish.

"I think it would be good for you. You can use a little more support, maybe not just from me."

Conor has probably hit his limit in trying to support me; he needs to share the burden. It must be hard standing by your wife while you're constantly tested.

"What about therapy? Would I put it on hold?"

"There are always online sessions; I do them all the time. And this might be good for you. To go back home, clear your head a little."

"And the kids? They'll miss so much school. Ciara is already behind; I don't think now is the best time to pick up and leave."

"They're kids; they'll be fine. We'll take some schoolwork with us if needed. Come on, it's been a while. I think we are way overdue. I don't think my dad or your parents has even met Sebastian."

That's not true.

Oh my gosh, it is. We've been so busy with our regular routine I haven't been back home in five years. They see him in pictures, and over video calls, yes. But Conor is right.

"Okay, I guess we can book tickets."

There is no smile on Conor's face. He is much too serious to smile. However, he is content.

So, I guess we are going to London. I have to face my family. Show them what a mess I have become. What I moved 5,567 kilometers across the globe for. Honestly, I don't care. I am so over it at this point. Reality hits me so hard I can't even fake it. There is no energy in me for that.

31

SIX HOURS AND
FIFTY MINUTES

London, Present Day

I have six hours and fifty minutes before I face my past. Until then, I have to sit on this plane and deal with altitude sickness while balancing the needs of my three little children and my worried husband.

Yet, somehow, they all seemed to find a way to fall asleep.

I have not.

How could I? I have six hours and fifty minutes to muster up a plan of action. How do I explain to my parents what happened? How I lost my job, my kids. How Conor almost left me. What exactly am I going to say?

Do I blame it on exhaustion? Everyday stress that resulted in a downward spiral?

I'm not sure how to word this to my father, who is too sensitive, or my mother, who is too pragmatic.

I don't want their assurance or their help. I want this trip to stay focused on my children getting reacquainted with their grandparents so I can take a moment to breathe in the air of where it all started. I want to be brought back to those memories, to make sense of it all, experience closure, and close that chapter in my life so I can move on.

I need to sleep, but the panic prevents that from happening.

I try all the cognitive-behavioral techniques Clarice has taught me.

The breathing exercises: breathe in, hold for six seconds, breathe out. When that doesn't work, I try plan B.

The five senses technique. Name five objects you see, four things you can feel, three you can hear, two you can smell, and one you can taste.

Okay, five things I can see. Five things. I look around.

Screens.

Scrunchie.

Water bottle.

Glasses.

Barrette.

I feel a tight squeeze disrupt my mindfulness.

It's Ciara's hand. She woke up amid the turbulence. She seems incapable of moving until the plane settles down. Her worried eyes are glued to the seat in front of her. Her grip is tightening on my hand.

"It's okay, darling," I try to reassure her.

Takeoff consisted of entertaining Olivia and Sebastian while Conor explained to Ciara the statistics of plane crashes and the safety precautions taken to ensure a safe flight.

He had a wealth of knowledge and could calm a patient out of a panic attack, which wasn't in my wheelhouse.

How should I respond? As she stares ahead, her eyes widen, and her face is filled with fear. Ciara has traveled before, but she was never old enough to consider the logistics, until now.

She tightens her grip as the plane shakes some more.

Conor is fast asleep with Sebastian on the opposite aisle. It is up to me to support her.

"Hun, let's try to sleep now." I pat her lap, but Ciara doesn't respond.

A few minutes go by, and Ciara's eyes are still wide.

"What's wrong, dear?" I try to keep my voice calm. I don't want to project my impatience.

"I can't sleep. I can't calm down when the plane is shaking like that."

"But it's all over now. See? Let's try to sleep now. You will be exhausted in the morning if you don't rest."

One minute later, and still no progression.

"Want to try a movie?" The world's best babysitter.

She shakes her head.

"Did you bring any books?"

"Yes." She quickly grabs her knapsack and takes out *Matilda*.

"Can you read it to me?"

"Sure, lay your head on my lap." It is my only hope.

I quietly read aloud as Ciara's breathing became heavier, and her body relaxes.

I read until I am confident she is asleep.

Cognitive behavioral therapy has failed, so I turn on my music to calm me into slumber.

The headphones slide into place, cocooning me in the world of **Beethoven - Piano Sonata No. 17**, the volume cranked up to an excessive level. My eyelids are heavy as I surrender to the music's embrace.

The memory is like a movie in my head.

I am somewhere…not sure where, but I am playing on the piano.

I look young.

My hair is bright blond and perfectly combed into a silk tie.

My dress is floral and ethereal.

I watch myself play as my body sways with the melody.

I am in a state of ecstasy. It is visible.

My lips turn up to a subliminal smile.

I know this feeling.

Suddenly, darkness descended upon the piano, I felt an unnerving force propel my hands, urging them to move faster, faster than my own will. The once-joyful smile had vanished, replaced by a grim mask of unwavering determination. I couldn't stop the music; instead, I pressed the keys with a relentless force, my wrists stiffening as I emphasized each note.

The piano keys themselves seemed to bleed, the red staining my fingers as they slowly transformed into bony digits. The notes reverberated, a discordant symphony that gripped me in its unsettling embrace.

Then, in an instant, a deafening, jarring bang shattered the stillness, erupting from the piano. The music suddenly halted, and I found myself face-to-face with a chilling sight—a large, imposing hand pressed firmly against the piano keys. His presence was unmistakable, his scent familiar, his sleeves rolled up to reveal powerful forearms adorned with protruding veins. He stood there, a formidable and haunting figure.

My breath quickened, anxiety coursing through my veins like a torrent. Beads of sweat broke out on my forehead, leaving me trembling and deeply unsettled in the wake of this haunting memory.

"Are you all right?"

I look up at the stewardess standing in front of me.

I pull out my headphones.

"Sorry, what?"

"Are you all right? Would you fancy some water?"

"Oh, yes." I reposition myself. "Thank you." I slow my breath, and the stewardess is off.

When she returns, I close my eyes and feel the cool water trickle down my throat.

Who was that shadow? Who is that man? He is unidentifiable and at the same time eerily familiar.

I can almost feel the intermittent breathing patterns of Ciara, Olivia, Conor, and Sebastian. They are all sound asleep.

I sit back in my seat as I listen to the white noise of the engine.

I need to go back to that memory. Yet I know I've had enough. I want to hold all the answers, but at the same time, I don't want to revisit those feelings.

So I put my headphones back in and examine the scenery.

Screens.

Scrunchie.

Water bottle.

Glasses.

Barrette.

32

THIRTY YEARS AGO

London, Thirty Years Ago

Where is everyone? I don't hear anyone!

I am guessing Daddy is at work. Daddy is always at work, and I think Annie is with Hélène. Annie is always with Hélène.

Why is it so quiet?

Hélène and Annie are usually downstairs in the play area, and Mummy likes to spend time outside in the garden. That is where they must be.

I look over at my clock. I never really liked trying to tell the time, so I made Mummy buy me a digital clock for my room. Mummy doesn't like this clock because she says it doesn't suit the rest of the home. So I keep a small alarm clock inside my nightstand.

It's 8:16.

I am usually at school by 7:45.

I am now in year two! I can't be late!

But maybe it's the queen's birthday or some other holiday that closes all the stores and schools.

I decide I will get up and try to see where everyone is.

When I look out my window, I don't see Daddy's car in the driveway, so he must be at work.

Downstairs I can't see Hélène or Annie. Maybe they went for a walk to Hyde Park?

I take a banana, find some already made porridge in the fridge, and sit outside. Sometimes, Mummy spends her morning in her garden.

She isn't there.

I sit there anyway.

I watch all the butterflies that surrounded Mummy's plants.

They are so colorful, not like the other insects I find in the garden.

They look magical. They look make-believe.

I sit there for some time as I finish off my breakfast. It's been hours, and I still don't hear anyone inside.

Perhaps Mummy joined Hélène and Annie.

I decide to practice the fingering techniques Lottie taught me. Lottie is my favorite person. Besides Mummy and Daddy and Annie and Hélène, Lottie is probably the person I spend most of my time with.

She teaches me how to play **Rondo Alla Turca**, a very hard sonata. But she always teaches me how to do challenging tasks. It starts as difficult, then it becomes fun, easy, and then too easy, and then she teaches me something challenging again.

I go to the room with the piano.

It has these two big doors that I always close because it can get very noisy when I'm playing. Sometimes Mummy tells me to leave the doors open when I practice. I guess she likes the sounds I make.

I decide to leave them open today. That way, when Mummy, Hélène, or Annie comes home, they will know where to find me.

I practice **Rondo Alla Turca**, or what we call the "Turkish March." Lottie will be so proud of how well I am doing. My fingers work without me thinking.

B A G sharp A C D C B C E F E D sharp E.

I don't even use a score sheet. I am just doing this from my memory.

It's quite a long song, but I play it repeatedly. My hands don't even feel tired, and I am almost doing it with no mistakes. With no score sheets and no mistakes.

"ENOUGH!"

I jump at this loud voice. It is the first voice I've heard all day.

It's Mummy. She does not look happy.

"I am trying to sleep! Why is this door open?"

"Sorry, Mummy, I couldn't find you anywhere!"

"Cleo! This fucking noise! You are giving me a headache!"

"Sorry, Mummy." I don't like it when Mummy uses bad words. Daddy doesn't like it either; he says I will learn these swear words if she keeps saying them in front of me. But I always hear adults use these words. It's nothing unusual.

"Can you please just give me some peace and quiet! Where is Hélène? Where is everyone? I need some bloody quiet—and why are you not at school?"

I feel like I am in trouble. I thought Mummy would know why I'm not at school.

"Is it the queen's birthday?"

"No!" I see Mummy close her eyes and her lips disappear. She looks angry, but I don't know if she is mad at me.

"Cleo." Mummy's voice gets quieter. "Can you take a break from your music for once and go find Hélène?"

I nod even though I don't know where to find Hélène.

"Go get ice cream or something, but for God's sake, don't play that bullocks today! NO MORE MUSIC, OKAY? My head is pounding from those…" Mummy walks away, and I can't hear what she is saying anymore.

All I know is that Mummy warned me to stay away from the piano.

Why? What else would I do today? I already went outside, and the piano would be the only other fun activity.

I find the little porcelain bowl that has coins in it. Mummy leaves those coins for when Hélène takes us to Hyde Park to catch the ice cream van. Maybe that is where Hélène and Annie went.

I take the coins and go to the park.

33

RACHMANINOFF

London, Present Day

"Mommy."

My eyes slowly open. Did I actually doze off? How long was I out for?

"Mooom." It's Olivia.

Okay, I am up.

"I'm hungry!"

"Where is Daddy?" I ask, repositioning myself as I look around. The lights inside the plane are bright and everyone seems to be enjoying their breakfasts.

"Daddy took Sebastian to the bathroom," Olivia whines. "Where are the snacks?"

I look at the time.

One and a half hours left.

Wow. I guess I slept for a while.

"Mommy! Please, the snacks!"

I find half a bag of crisps, most of which are crushed into tiny pieces, and an apple. I'd call that a decent breakfast.

As the kids watch their Disney and munch on my attempt at breakfast, I sit back in silence.

It's not long until we touch down at London Heathrow airport. I am only moments from the path that led me to where I am today.

* * *

The home I grew up in has not been affected by time.

It's an impressive Georgian home built in 1818 on a quiet street next to Holland Park. A detached house wasn't typical in London, but Mummy needed her space, and Daddy needed to be close to work.

It feels all too familiar as I stand facing that house—the brick walls, multi-pane windows, the pilasters at the entryway.

I take a much-needed deep inhale as Conor pays the driver and empties the cab of our luggage.

I guess there is no turning back now.

The children run past me and knock furiously at the door.

The door opens to Hélène, the elderly Polish woman who was my housemaid since birth.

"My Cleo!" She places her soft hands over her cheeks, then quickly gets distracted by the little ones rummaging around her waistline. "Oh my, they have grown so big! Come in, come in!"

I walk in, taking in all the nostalgia: the smell, the feel, the high ceilings, the antique mirrors and paintings, the spiral staircase off the main hall.

"Mummy isn't home yet; she went to get treats for the little ones. Come, follow me to your room."

Without saying a word, I follow Hélène up the stairs. Conor and the kids follow too.

"I hope you don't mind. I set up for you and Mr. McCarthy to sleep in your room, and the kids will sleep in Annie's and the spare room."

My room looks as if I still lived in it. Everything is in its correct place. My four-poster bed is now big enough for both Conor and me. Before, I used to drown in it alone.

The wallpaper is a beautiful pattern of olive trees and pastel flowers. It coordinates with my bed cushion, the Victorian chair, and the draperies that cover the large windows.

I look over at the window, where the branches of an old bird cherry tree stand erect. Still hanging in there, I think, after all these years. I would face that tree every morning as I gazed over the large garden out back.

"That should be the last of it." Conor slams the heavy trunk onto the carpeted floor, and I regain consciousness.

"What? Oh, thank you."

"The kids are busy with the toys your mum bought them. I'm just going to take a shower and freshen up a bit. Are you okay?"

I still feel far away. I try to refocus my brain. Perhaps it is the jet lag, or is it the undeniable feeling of my memories streaming in all at once?

Even though I have been back home since moving to New York, the newborn sensitivity, the cerebral approach to taking in my life experiences, has opened my eyes to too much too fast.

I nod, and Conor continues to the bathroom.

I take this opportunity to go outside, back to the haven of my past.

My mother's garden.

The place where I would sit alone for many hours, no friends, no company. Just me, alone, trying to force my way out of the piano room, trying to distance myself from the urge to play. A place where I would sit and watch the butterflies, the botanical charm that served as my support. I would sit and wait for my mother to come outside and show me how much water each plant needed, ensure the violets were getting direct sunlight, and that I was using the pruning shears carefully.

It was all gone. My sanctuary ruined to bits, spoiled into a rotten, overgrown landscape, transposed to soil and weeds.

What happened?

A little air left my body.

Why?

"Well, hello, dear." A high, posh voice pulls me back into reality.

My mother.

"Mummy!" I embrace her bony frame. She smells the same: Chanel No. 5, fags, and a touch of brandy.

"Oh, it's so good to see you, Cleo."

"Mum, what happened here?"

"What? The garden? Well, I am much too busy to stay on top of it, I'm afraid."

With what? I want to ask, but I hold back.

"Let's go inside and talk over tea, or would you like something stronger?" she says with a wink. "I know I would."

She wears oversized tortoiseshell sunglasses and a floral silk kimono wrapped around her petite body. She always appears so elegant.

"You couldn't hire someone to maintain it?"

"What? Oh, are you still going on about the garden? Drop it, Cleo. It's over."

I know it's over. It just feels so final now.

The kids enjoy playing with their new toys as my mother showers them with more presents, hot Ribena, and chocolate digestives. Memories of my past.

Conor is locked in my room, working with a patient. It reminds me that my session with Clarice is tomorrow evening. I need some kind of memory that she can help me unravel.

I need to fill in the blank space.

I sit across from Mummy on a needlepoint armchair in the reception room. We are watching the kids play, trying our luck at small talk. I don't want to plunge right into the past few months' events; it would be better to ease her into my problems.

"How are the kids doing at school?"

"Great!" I say too quickly, avoiding the reality of Ciara's struggles.

"And Conor? It seems like his work is occupying him."

I explain how he was honored with the AMHH award. I leave out that I wasn't at the ceremony.

Then, finally, the loaded question:

"And how are you, dear?"

"Good." I sip from the bone china teacup.

My mother puts down her cup and shifts her body toward mine. Her forehead creases in a concerning display of affection, and her eyes expose her worry.

"Really, Mum. I'm fine!" I force a laugh and try to change the subject. "Where's Dad?"

"Daddy will be home soon. Work has been very busy, you know. I barely see him these days."

I take another sip.

"So, tell me, are you still working?"

This is a trick question. Technically, I am unemployed. When I don't answer, she goes on.

"And what about the piano?" A mention of the piano causes me to catch my breath. "Are you sure you don't want to try again? Hélène has been cleaning the piano in the drawing room, but no one plays anymore. You want to play around with it since you're here?"

"No, Mum. I think I'm okay, thanks."

It's not a pleasant topic, but since we are here and I have Clarice tomorrow, I decide to throw myself into the deep end and try to discover what really went on in my past.

"Mum," I start, contemplating how to construct my thoughts into a question. "I…" I stop. What to ask? Where to start? "I was wondering, do you know how I might get in touch with Liam?" The question shocks me too. Start from the source, I guess.

"Liam?"

"Liam, Mum! My coach."

"Oh right, yes, *Liam*." She emphasizes his name in a tone I can't identify. "I believe he still has the same number. I don't see why he wouldn't. Remind me later, and I'll get it from my address book. Is there a specific reason you want to talk to Liam?" She uses air quotes around his name. Is this her way of teasing my past relationship?

"Well, Mum." I consider mentioning Clarice or the blank moments from my past, but I stop myself. It would just lead me down a rabbit hole I'm not ready for yet. I don't finish my sentence all while my mother nods in a slow agreement. She understands. "I thought it might be helpful to revisit those days, kind of revisit what led me to…" I stop myself again. "Where I am today."

"Well, Liam would be a great place to start." My mother says reassuringly. "What is it that you want to revisit?"

"Well, all of my past, really. I kind of feel lost. I mean, I know I loved playing the piano. It was my life, my whole life. It was all I knew growing up. It's hard to shake that off, you know? The past, I guess."

She again nods in slow agreement.

"I often remind myself of those days, the hard work, the busy schedules. I miss that."

"Do you have fond memories from those days?"

I nod as a smile creeps up on my face.

"Well, that's lovely, darling." She pats my knee.

Just then, my father arrives.

"Cleo, my sweetheart!" He holds his arms out wide and hugs me with the warmest embrace. There is nothing like a hug from my father. It is an embrace I've relished ever since I was a little girl, wrapped in his strong body. It feels the same even now, when I am level with him, eye to eye.

"Oh, how I missed you so much."

Just like that, I feel at home again.

* * *

Later that night, before I fall asleep, I experience my first elongated flash. So I guess it isn't a flash at all—just an extremely vivid memory.

I looked youthful. I must have been sixteen, considering I was seated in the London Music Conservatory. My natural, collagen-plumped face, my long blond hair brushed into an updo. My eyes seemed so innocent and vibrant. I couldn't have anticipated what would happen next, how I was mere minutes away from what would forever alter the course of my life.

I sat amid students arranged in a semicircle in front of Liam. He couldn't have been thirty yet—he looked so composed and so young.

His dark blue eyes held such authority, yet they still charmed me.

His presence was distracting. I needed to stay efficient with my time.

"Hi, I'm Mr. Martin," he began. "Mr. Lewis will be out for the next few months, so I will be taking his place this term."

A girl tried to hold in her laugh, and her friend slapped her leg.

Liam ignored her.

I rolled my eyes. I would have much preferred to practice alone with Lottie rather than in a group setting. I would have gotten a lot more done that way.

When Liam asked me to play in front of the class, I felt my breath quicken and my hands get shaky. I'd played in front of audiences far more prominent than this. Why was I feeling so nervous?

I brushed away the nerves and followed instructions.

Rachmaninoff - Liebesleid was my given performance. Also known as "Loves Sorrow."

I couldn't help but feel his presence as I started to play. His eyes fixed on me, dissecting every note that escapes from my fingers. It's as if he's silently challenging me, daring me to prove my worth, to reach for the highest peaks of my potential.

I channel my nerves into raw determination, my fear into unwavering focus. With each passing moment, the tension grows, the stakes escalating. This is my moment to shine, to prove that I am worthy of his attention.

As the last note hangs in the air, the room falls into silence. The weight of his judgement feels almost suffocating, the seconds stretching on like an eternity. I hold my breath, waiting for his reaction, praying for a flicker of recognition, a spark of approval.

And then, finally, his lips curl into a slight smile. It's a subtle gesture, but in that moment, it feels like a victory.

"Very well." His fingers cupped his chin as he thought. "Very emotional, which is great." He paused for another beat. "Rachmaninoff is very romantic. It is crucial to emphasize every note in a romantic repertoire, but don't overdo it. It will be hard to switch through tempos if you do. Try to avoid jabbing at the keys. Instead, keep the control in your wrists."

"Okay," I said almost inaudibly.

"And not too much pedaling; you will feel the ease of the transitions. Try again."

I played again. I thought about the melody. I emphasized every note, didn't overdo it, held control in my wrists, and didn't do too much pedaling. The final chord reverberates, the room erupts in applause. Liam's voice cuts through the noise, his words carrying a sense of pride and admiration. "And that is how it is done! Bravo!" It was my first real moment of euphoria, of belonging, of community.

It was the first time since Lottie that someone was able to properly articulate clear instructions. Finally, someone who understood me. It was he who would take me places—he held the key to my greatness.

from then on, Liam had me captivated.

34

DREAMS

London, Present Day

The following day, there's a note placed through the crack of my door. The message scribbled:

Liam:

Underneath, there's an address, email address, and phone number.

My breath quickens. Am I actually going to contact him? Hear his voice again? Possibly visit his home?

The thought of seeing Liam after a decade of not communicating frightens me.

What is the worst that can happen? I ask myself. Yes, it may be a bit strange. Lost lovers, so much to catch up on.

But now I have a husband and kids. I am so ordinary compared to who I once was. I am no longer the same person.

"Good morning." It is Conor, lying comfortably on my four-poster bed. His hair falls over his eyes, his sweet, innocent baby blues.

Seeing Conor strive to repair our fractured relationship brings me a profound sense of relief. I hold dear his serene and endearing demeanor, his remarkable capacity for forgiveness, and his ability to love unconditionally.

I return his smile and discreetly crumple the small piece of paper into my palm.

"You're up early," Conor remarks, taking note of the time. It's 9:00 a.m., but 4:00 am New York time.

"I couldn't bring myself to sleep in," I admit, my restless night filled with various imagined scenarios for my impending meeting with Liam.

```
HOW WILL IT PLAY OUT:
1.  I ask to meet up, and he declines.
2.  He agrees but is hostile with me.
3.  He agrees, and old feelings arise, making my life
    way more complicated than it has to be.
4.  And suppose I fall under his spell again? Is it
    okay to test myself with challenges I couldn't
    overcome in the past? Is there any strength left
    in me that will prevent me from going back to the
    man I fell in love with once before?
```

"Come back to bed," Conor protests. "The kids aren't even awake!"

"Okay, fine." I happily join him and rest my head in the crook of his neck.

I still have hours before my session with Clarice. I'll allow myself to lie here, in Conor's arms, until we must get up.

I smile to myself. This, lying here with Conor, feels so right.

I look at him. His eyes are closed; he seems at peace.

How can I possibly consider Liam when I have such a supportive, loving, and close-to-perfect husband by my side?

Conor never left me.

Granted, he was close. But he didn't leave me.

He was patient, supportive, caring.

I get excited for my appointment with Clarice. I look forward to sharing my progress with Conor the way teenage girls share updates on their crush. We went from barely talking to snuggling in bed.

Then a pit forms in my stomach.

Am I ignorant to think visiting Liam won't ruin this? Will it bring the closure I need, or set back my progress?

I don't have those answers. I won't share my plans with Conor, not yet. Maybe it's the wrong decision, and he'll prevent it from happening. Or maybe it's the right thing to do, and he will push me to go.

I need a clear head.

Those first moments with Liam are still vivid in my mind. I was so young and innocent, so pure and eager to excel, eager to prove myself to him, my mother, myself.

I still remember the first lesson I had with Liam. And the first time I started caring about my appearance. I hated myself for this, since it was clear I was a child in Liam's eyes.

I remember a particular day vividly. I was preparing for our next session, anxiously awaiting his arrival. I found a Matthew Williamson floral dress in my mother's closet. My mother had been absent for two days, and sometimes her disappearances extended to weeks on end. I knew she wouldn't notice that I took it. The dress draped slightly loose on my frame, a tad too mature for my age, but I wanted to appear adult and sophisticated. My hair flowed freely, I added a little blush and a tint of pink lipstick that accentuated my look. I examined my reflection in the mirror, proud of my accomplishments.

In that precise moment, the sound of Liam's car pulling into our driveway sent my heart into a frantic rhythm. I moved closer to the window, concealed in the shadows.

It made my heart race to watch Liam get out of his car, button up his sports coat, and lean into the window of the front seat. For a moment, I couldn't tell what was happening. Then I realized a beautiful girl was sitting in the driver's seat, and he planted a lengthy kiss on her lips.

How that made my stomach turn.

Stupid Cleo, I thought as I rubbed off my lipstick. I was trying so hard to impress Liam when I was just another one of his amateur students.

I felt that way from the age of sixteen until the age of twenty-eight, when we spent almost every waking moment together. Before his eyes, I grew from a teenager into an adult. He watched me mature from an aspiring pianist to an established soloist.

I created a name for myself. Everyone knew Cleo Wilson.

Finally, he was able to see me for who I was.

He was able to see me in a new light.

An equal.

A girlfriend.

A future.

I try to remind myself of those moments.

Where did it go wrong? Why did I let go of what I'd built up? Escape from the world Liam and I created? Why did I run away from something I wanted so badly? And how is it possible that I didn't want it anymore? I had everything! I had it all!

I lay wide awake in bed, pondering. I'm slipping in and out of consciousness when another flash appears.

I was playing **Beethoven - Rage Over a Lost Penny.**

I played and played and played. The music wouldn't stop. I could hear the metronome clicking at regular intervals, driving me to the brink of exhaustion. My fingers, now blistered and raw, my upper back began to tense up.

For a quick beat, I retracted my fingers from the keys.

A powerful French voice rang out. "*Désolé, mais c'est ridicule*! No stopping!" I proceeded to play. "Da, de, da, de, yes, da, da, de, da! That's it!" The voice sang out the notes, each one a sharp demand for perfection. "Again!"

I played, my fingers racing across the keys in a distorted melody. The notes clashed and collided, and the pain in my wrists intensified with every strike of the keys.

"Again."

I jolted, my heart quickening, and continued the relentless pursuit against time. As sweat streamed down my forehead, and tears welled up in my eyes, I couldn't stop. I wasn't allowed to. I played on, every note a struggle against the mounting tension.

"Again."

The oppressive atmosphere grew heavier by the second. My wrist throbbed with pain, and an unseen force pushed me to my limits. With no other choice, I withdrew my hands and clutched my aching wrist in my lap.

"Again!" A loud thud onto the piano keys rang at high volume.

"Mommy!"

This wakes me right up.

Reality.

* * *

Conor once explained how in Freudian psychoanalysis, the patient lies down, doctor by their head. A way for the patient and therapist to avoid eye contact, so the patient can provide whatever comes to mind, without too much trepidation.

Clarice is looking straight into my face through a screen. The eye shows too much. Facial cues are too easy to identify. My truths are more articulated through my face than I could ever express with words.

We waste no time and dive right in.

"The closer I get to these memories, the more confused I become." I try to explain the flashes I have been experiencing more often these days.

These recollections play out in lucid daydreams or are triggered by real-life events. I get excited to get into bed and focus on these memories, but then I have trouble sleeping.

I had two new flashes in the past few days.

The first flash happened in the cab from the airport. I heard it, vaguely coming from the speakers: **Peter and the Wolf.**

My mind caught on before my eyes did. I felt all the senses of fight-or-flight. My eyes and throat felt dry, my palms clamed up, my heart beat faster, and then, instantaneously, I was transported in time. A picture presented itself to me, one of me wearing that red pendant around my neck, the one Liam gave me. I was clutching it, nails digging into my palms. I was in my room and looked delirious.

That was it. That was the only picture I could see.

Conor snapped me back to reality.

"Are you all right?"

"Yeah, I'm fine. Just jet-lagged. I'm good." I steadied my breath quietly.

The second flash: right before my appointment, I went for a walk to Mount Street Gardens, a place I often visited when I was living in London.

I sat on the bench, played **Tchaikovsky - Piano Concerto No. 1**, and waited.

At first, nothing. It's hard to force memories out. I usually have them on the tip of my tongue—so close, yet so out of reach.

I waited some more, and then the second flash appeared.

I saw myself standing on top of some building, wearing the red Ulyana Sergeenko dress I wore the first night of the competition. I felt like I was about to throw up, and, as a reflex, I threw off the headphones in a loud yelp.

It is time to stop trying.

I tell these stories to Clarice as she listens.

"Are there memories you don't have to force yourself to recall?"

"Yeah."

"And when do you think about those memories?"

"All the time," I state as a matter of fact.

"All the time?"

"Yes,"

"Give me an example."

"It's strange, because they come so naturally. I listen to music throughout my day, so the memories just come pouring in."

"Isn't it lovely how music is so ubiquitous? We all have some form of music playing throughout our days. And, luckily for you, listening to music is unique in the way it can tap into your brain, your memories, and emotions. As I said, this can really work in your favor."

I agree as I reflect on the vivid imagery, sensations, the smells that come back as I listen to the notes of the melodies.

"Did you know that music is often used as a treatment in nursing homes? It helps Alzheimer's patients access their memories. It can also help calm dementia patients."

Finally, someone is speaking my language. Music is medicinal.

"So I want you to take advantage of the places these melodies take you."

I nod once more.

"Let's explore this in more detail."

"Details of the memories?"

"Details of when you get the memories."

"Oh, well. Like I said, any time I hear music, so I guess you can say almost all the time. Music transports me to the time of my life that it represents."

"Do you find yourself getting lost in time? Do you find it interfering with your daily rituals? Maybe these memories are quite vivid, almost like watching a movie?"

The accuracy catches me off guard.

"Well, yes. I do get lost in time. I find myself late to many appointments. I mentioned how I missed Conor's award ceremony. I'm always late to pick up my kids. Yes, I guess it does interfere." I stop and recollect. "And they are definitely vivid. Very realistic. As you said, it's like watching a movie play out in front of me."

Clarice ponders this for a moment. "Have you heard the term 'maladaptive daydreaming'?"

"What?"

"Maladaptive daydreaming. It is a relatively new term; not too many people have heard of it. And, judging by your face, I can say that yours is the same as most people's reaction after hearing this diagnosis."

"You're saying that is what I'm doing? Daydreaming?"

"Well, let's get into this briefly, shall we?"

I am losing my patience. "How is that a diagnosis? Isn't that what everyone does? They daydream." My mind flashes to Ciara.

I have a bad feeling about this, Cleo. Conor's words ring in my head.

"Yes, everyone does daydream. It can sometimes take up to forty-six percent of one's day. We do this to get on with life in a more enjoyable manner. When one is in school, at work, doing the dishes, going for a walk, it is a way to pass the time."

"Exactly, so—"

"But, when it becomes maladaptive, we have to dive a bit deeper. Now, I am not saying this is what is happening to you, but let's dissect it, shall we?"

I take a deep inhale. I'll humor her; I'll play along.

"When do you think you started daydreaming?"

"I always have. Since I was a kid, I presume. Like you said, in school, in lectures I wasn't too fond of."

"Okay." Silence. "And when do you suppose it started getting out of hand?"

"I didn't say it did."

"You missed your husband's speech. You're late to pickups."

"Okay, fair enough. I guess a couple of years ago?" Was it five? Ten? The truth is: I had no clear conception of when this all originated. Most of the time, I don't even catch myself in my daydreams. Usually Conor or the kids force me back to reality.

"What do you think happened around then?"

"It could be that my life became too boring, or I wasn't doing so well at work. I guess I would reminisce about a time in my life when I was more successful, a time that brought me more joy."

I feel instant remorse implying my life as a pianist brought more joy than motherhood or a life shared with Conor.

But Clarice shows no inkling of judgment, so I don't backtrack.

"When you relive these memories in your mind, what time of your life are you focusing on?"

I think about this for a moment. I collect my memories, my thoughts, my daydreams.

"When I competed in Russia," I quickly add. "I think. It was a time when I had everything."

"Everything?"

"I won the competition, I was approached for a world tour, I signed a record deal. Fell in love."

"When you competed in Russia." She sounds almost skeptical. "What is the first moment you reminisce about?"

"I guess it must be my first performance."

"Describe it to me. What do you see?"

I close my eyes and my imagination fills with the details of the hall. I recall how the audience cheered for me, the red gown, and **Tchaikovsky - Piano Concerto No. 1.** I mention it all.

"Go on. Tell me what happened after you performed."

"Well, that's when I met Ivan."

"Ivan?"

"He was a Russian competitor, and we fell in love quickly. We just had this unexplainable magnetic force from the start." I explain the dates we went on, the places Ivan took me, the food we ate, the songs I discovered. Down to every detail.

"And you said you won?"

"I went home with the Grand Prix Award." A proud smile presents itself on my face.

"How amazing that you were able to enjoy life and still win." She says this like it was so easy. "What do you suppose happened between you and Ivan? Was the distance what broke you two up?"

I think about the day we broke up.

Was it the distance? Was it Liam? Did we have a falling out?

"No." I feel the lump appear in my throat. It's not the tragic end of our relationship that has brought on this distress. It's the fact that I can't recall it at all.

My time with Liam and Ivan is vague and equivocal in my memory.

She pauses, as if to give me room to speak. When I don't, she goes on.

"I have my next patient soon, but why don't you continue to write down these memories as they come to you. You're welcome to share them with me during our next appointment, or you can keep them to yourself. If you find the music is helping, continue with the exposure therapy. It might help."

Following our session, I ponder the significance of the information Clarice shared with me.

Maladaptive daydreaming.

All the symptoms seem familiar. Now what?

Do I have the willpower to overcome the pull-away from the present now that it has a name? How soon will my life return to normal?

Will it ever go back to normal?

35

THREE ICE CREAMS AND
FANTASIA ON GREENSLEEVES

London, Present Day

I have to put my plan into action quickly; tomorrow, Conor will be taking the kids to visit his father in Ireland. I will be alone for five days. I have to come up with some answers right away. I feel like I'm drowning, except it's because I tied rocks to my ankles.

I take out my phone and save Liam's number.

I dwell in my thoughts before I dial. I don't think I can handle the sound of Liam's voice right now. I can't muster up a sentence without my breath getting in the way.

So instead, I send a text message.

My fingers shake as I force myself to press send.

Hi Liam, It's Cleo Wilson. I am in town and wondering if we can have a little chat. All the best.

I send, then quickly reread my message, now feeling a spout of nausea rush through my body.

It's so formal. So unlike our natural banter. A chat? What am I thinking?

Then, I hear my phone ring. My breath quickens. A cloud of icy air rushes to my brain and slowly permeates my body. I feel numb. I won't answer. I can't.

I let the tone play until it stops.

I let out an exhale and fall onto my bed.

This is a mistake.

My phone now dings, and I quickly grab my phone.

Hi Cleo. So good to hear from you. I would love to speak, how about tomorrow? Does my place, 6:00 p.m. sound good? I will see you then.

My place. Another whiff of nausea. I will be going back to Liam's. A place I haven't been in a decade. I try to slow down my breath with the cognitive behavioral exercise.

Five things I can see:

Olive trees

Flowers

Dressing table

Lamp

Mirror

Four things I can feel:

The soft covers I'm sitting on

The cold metal of my phone

The breeze coming through my window

My wedding ring

I continue with the list. When that doesn't work, I resort to my own way of calming the storm: **Fantasia on Greensleeves by Ralph Vaughan Williams.**

Being home, lying on the same bed I did as a child in this naturally lit room, touching the hand-carved staircase railing, the large antique paintings that cover the walls… It is hard to separate myself from the girl I used to be. The girl who shaped me into the woman I am today.

The soothing sounds of the flute and harp penetrate my ears, bringing me to a state of subconsciousness. Bringing me back to that day when Mummy was upset at my piano. When Hélène and Annie were nowhere to be found while Daddy was busy running a company.

I took the coins out of the porcelain bowl and headed toward Hyde Park, where Mr. Cream's ice cream van waited every day. I was only Ciara's age, and it must have been over a fifteen-minute walk.

I wasn't sure how long I waited before I heard Fantasia on Greensleeves over the speakers, which let children know the ice cream van was here. I smiled. Not for the ice cream, but for the idea that Mummy didn't want me to play the piano, but she couldn't separate me from music. I closed my eyes and took in the melody. I blocked out the sounds of children pushing one another to get in line and the parents' protests. I blocked out the sounds of the cars and the dogs in the park.

I just focused on the harp, the strings. It was all better now.

"What would you like, my love?"

My eyes opened. There was a kind man behind the window of the van. He had a large mustache but small, beady eyes.

"Oh." I realized the kids had left the line, all giddy with their ice cream melting down their hands.

"What can I get with this?" I placed the handful of coins on the counter.

"You can get about four oy screams wiv 'at," he snickered. His voice sounded different than mine. Like he came from a different town in England.

"I will take one, please." I waited for him to count the coins and return my change.

I took my soft-serve ice cream and found an empty bench near the van, where I could hear the melody on repeat.

After a while, the kind man who served me the ice cream closed the window.

"Wait, where are you going?" I quickly jumped out of my seat.

"I 'ave avah stops."

"Where are the other stops?"

"All around. Outside Kensington Palace, then Royal Albert Haw, and then I just circle the park from there."

I brushed off the grass from my dress and started walking.

I walked to Kensington Palace.

I felt flushed. My face was warm. But I managed to catch the van.

"Oy, it's you again!" He must have been in some state of confusion; nonetheless, he presented me with my second soft serve ice cream. Then I sat beside the truck, unable to really taste the sugary cream melting in my mouth. My mind was focused on the melodies.

I watched as he packed up his truck and headed toward the next stop.

I followed and continued the routine.

"Are you sure you want anavah one?" The man went from confused to worried. "Where is your mum? Is she around?"

"Yes," I lied, and he didn't know what else to do but give me my third ice cream.

My stomach started to hurt. My toes were getting blisters from my patent leather Mary Janes. But when the truck left, I followed.

Fantasia on Greensleeves gradually faded.

Then the truck disappeared.

Where was the next stop? Did I miss it?

I wasn't sure where I was, which direction to go. So I took off my Mary Janes and ran—I wasn't sure where to, but I ran.

I panted, and my stomach felt like it was ripping into shreds, the nausea of the three ice creams and the feeling of being alone started to creep up. My head started to spin. What was Mummy going to think? Would Hélène be worried when she got home and I wasn't there to play with her? What if I got home later than Daddy?

I stopped at the tall, dark statue of Achilles. I know this statue because once I came here with Hélène, and she taught me about the Greek hero from the Trojan War.

I knew this meant I was far from home. I had walked in the opposite direction, and now I was farther from where I started.

I began to cry. I cried because my tummy hurt, my feet hurt. I cried because I thought I wasn't going to see my family again. I wouldn't have my piano. I wouldn't have Lottie.

"Excuse me, miss, are you lost?" An old lady with her two children found me wailing by the statue.

It took a couple of minutes for me to stop crying and tell the lady I lived close to Holland Park. I knew from Holland Park I could find my way back home.

It was Hélène who opened the door. She seemed shocked to see me.

"I thought you were at school," her words sat heavily in my heart.

Mummy didn't even know I went missing. She was still in her bed when I came back.

Hélène thought I was at school, and Daddy was still in his office.

I wasn't missed. No one even knew I was gone.

I ran to the bathroom and threw up my three ice creams into the toilet bowl.

I would just have to wait for Lottie to come by tomorrow. I would close the door, and I would be able to listen to the magic of the compositions once again. I just had to wait it out.

36

OLIVIA'S BALLET RECITAL

London, Present Day

I hear the faint sounds of my kids playing in the back garden, soaking in the sun. I've found myself in that rare moment of enjoying their shrieks, their banter. I catch a view of them from my window as Conor and I pack a bag for their trip to Ireland.

At first, we pack in silence, both of us in our own personal headspace.

I have my headphones in, listening to the calming melody of **Chopin - Étude Op. 25, No. 12**. Conor surprised me with new AirPods.

Finally, I can get rid of the tangled mess.

And for a moment I think, *Maybe this is Conor's way of letting me know it's okay to listen to my music. To separate myself from my environment.*

I stop my mind from wandering and watch Conor. I appreciate this moment for what it is: normal, in a good way.

It is just the two of us, no drama or arguments. Just us being a plain ol' couple.

He must have sensed my eyes burning in his direction, and he looks up.

"What?" he says, smiling as he continues to fold his clothes into his bag.

"Nothing." My gaze stayed fixed on his.

"What?" he says again. "Do I have something on my face?" He whisks at his face, wiping off imaginary fluff.

"No, nothing." I fold the kids' clothes. "It's just…I'm really happy you're here."

"Well, I'm about to leave soon."

"I mean *here*, here. You didn't leave me."

"Oh, honey." He drops the clothes and looks me in the eye.

The tears emerge. I didn't plan on crying. It just sort of happened. I guess they are happy tears. Tears of relief. I wipe them away and continue to fold.

Conor comes over. "Cleo."

"Hm?" I avert my eyes, focusing on folding now. I am embarrassed by my little outburst.

"Cleo." He holds my hands, forcing me to look up at him. "You don't have to worry about that now. I am here. Here with you."

"But what if I mess up again?" This comes out like a whisper. I don't trust my voice not to break again.

"You will." I shoot him a surprised look. "And I will too! That's life, unfortunately. We are human, and we are going to make mistakes; that part is inevitable."

"But I almost drove you away. What if I do it again?"

"Cleo, I am so, so sorry that I wasn't there for you when you needed me. You almost drove me away because I kept ignoring your cries for help. I mean, shit, this is my wheelhouse. I should have noticed the signs. Instead, I pushed you away."

"What? Conor, you're absurd. Don't apologize."

"I keep thinking about conversations we had or situations I should have intervened in, but I never did. Maybe I purposely blinded myself. If I looked at you like a patient, I don't know, maybe it would be too real. Am I making sense?"

I nod. He does make sense. In the past, I had ignored signs too. From my mum, from Annie, from me.

"And this whole thing with Ciara under so much stress, I should take some action—"

"What do you mean? You do. I always catch you two doing breathing exercises or having long talks."

"I help her in the moment, but she needs to speak to someone. Not her father, but a real therapist. Someone to get her the help she needs."

"You know, I always feel guilty about that night you asked me to speak with her. You gave me the responsibility, and I made it out to be nothing. I don't know. Like you said, maybe I thought if I ignored what was truly going on, it wouldn't exist."

We both nod in unison.

"Clarice mentioned something to me," I say. "Maladaptive daydreaming. Have you heard of it?"

"Vaguely."

"I think she is proposing that diagnosis. Probably among a cocktail of other mental disorders."

I laugh to lighten the mood, but we both look at nothing. We are deep in our thoughts.

"Do you suppose that is what Ciara might be experiencing? She mentioned movement, which made me think of that time you caught Ciara in her room."

"Huh." Conor seemed to be putting the pieces together. "It's very possible."

"Do I…" I start. "Um, have you noticed me, ever, you know?" I emulate Conor's movements when he showed me how he saw Ciara.

"Um." His lips purse as he thinks through the archives. "You know what, come to think of it…"

It is bizarre how excited I become, but having a name for it is a step in the right direction. It represents a solution.

"Maybe?" He seems unsure.

"Well, which is it? Do I or don't I?"

"There was, well…" He's fumbling his words, trying to articulate himself to the best of his ability. "For example, that time at Olivia's ballet recital. You did seem to get a bit lost in the music. Your arms seemed to play piano or conduct music. I'm not sure exactly what, but…you did seem…out of it. Like you were in another realm. Almost as though the music took you somewhere else."

I quickly recall that day: Diane, two rows behind me, laughing. The humiliation boils inside of me.

"So I guess you could say it was similar to how I saw Ciara." I look at Conor in confusion. What is he even saying?

"Diane also mentioned…" Diane? My eyes widen in horror. "That day you hurt your arm. When I asked her what happened, she said one moment you were riding, the next you were out of it. Not hearing her speak…transfixed is how she described it. She thought that may have been how you injured yourself."

I suddenly feel like an outsider to my own existence.

I am the only one unaware when something is happening.

"It can all be related, or not, but I think there were moments…" There is more? "I catch glimpses of you, I guess, kind of fiddling with your phone. I think it happens when you listen to your music, almost like you are playing the keys with your fingers."

How have I not realized I do this? Suddenly, my embarrassment turns to anger.

"Why didn't you tell me? Why am I just hearing about this now?"

"I-I don't know, I didn't think it was anything. It's only now that you mentioned it I am thinking—"

I interrupt him. "But you must have known something was odd? How…how long has this been going on for? I'm going to be sick."

Now I understand what he meant. Despite knowing something was wrong, he ignored the warning signs. The fact that he's a psychiatrist made it easy for him to understand the nature of my situation. Yet he still failed to share what he knew with me. He left me in the dark.

"Cleo, I know. As I said before, I am sorry. I didn't mean to disregard what was happening. I just—"

"So what? I am just going around waving my arms in the air like a loony person, and you let me? Then you blame me for my blackouts and my—"

"Blackouts? What do you mean?"

"I black out, another fun trick. I lose track of time, and when I open my eyes, a whole day has passed. That's why I never made it to your speech, why I am always late."

"Why didn't you tell me? Cleo, that's serious."

"Why didn't you tell me I'm going fucking crazy?"

"Don't be daft; I'm asking you seriously."

"I am serious!"

"You're not crazy. You just need help."

"I KNOW!" I shout.

"Shh! Your family will hear."

"GOOD! LET THEM!"

"Cleo, stop, please," Conor says quietly. He's back to his calm, benevolent attitude.

"No, Conor, this really disturbs me!"

"I'm sorry, what else can I say? I promise not to ignore it next time."

"Next time?" Excuse me?

Conor's eyebrows lift, his eyes open wide.

"N-no, I mean, come on," he stutters. "Just, can we drop it? Please?"

My tone lowers, but sternness seeps through my words. "Conor, I am bloody pissed." My heart is still racing, blood still boiling. "I am embarrassed, I am mortified, but I am also angry that I was taking all the blame when you clearly saw something unusual. Here I was, feeling like utter crap, while you were the hero—"

"It's not like that! I wasn't blaming you; I just didn't really want to understand why or what was going on. I was too afraid to step in. You don't appreciate treatment. So, instead, I turned my back to your troubles until I became blind by it all. I know, I know, it's wasn't right. I know it didn't make anything better."

I don't speak. I can't. I just think of the many moments I was in this other world and Conor was peeking in, just like he did with Ciara.

Why am I last to know what's going on?

"There is one more thing," Conor states. "While we're clearing the air."

I feel bile rise in my throat. What other psychotic visuals am I painting for the world?

"You mention Russia."

"Okay?"

"The story." He stops.

"Well, what?"

"Are you sure you remember…what happened there? When you competed? Why you…" He stops himself once more.

"Why are you asking me this?" Heat is rising again.

"I just, it— I don't know. Your stories, they…I guess it almost seems like you missed a few moments…" He is trying to word it correctly, but nothing is making sense.

"Clarice is helping me with my blank spaces." I sound defensive. "You know that! I told you about our sessions."

"Okay, I…it's nothing, don't worry about it. If Clarice is helping you, you're—"

"Conor! Are you f—" I take a deep breath; I don't have much patience left. "You just told me you wouldn't do this! You pull me in, deflect, then…then. I can't! I just…" I take in another couple of breaths.

"Why are you trying to find ways to be mad at me? I'm not mad at you Cleo, I just want to move on from this. I understand that in channeling your anger toward me, you're deflecting. You're trying to take the blame off yourself, but you don't need to. Because I don't blame you!"

"Oh, so now you're Mr. Therapist, are you?"

Conor throws up his hands in frustration. "I'm damned if I do, damned if I don't."

"Whatever, I'm done, I'm done!" I toss the last item into the luggage and head toward the door. "I'll get the kids."

* * *

Tonight is the first night in years that I am alone.

Conor and the children are in Ireland.

I will see Liam tomorrow.

I lie down in my four-poster bed.

The house is too quiet.

I am alone with my thoughts.

The way I left things with Conor wasn't great. I want to patch things up. Sweep that silly little argument under the rug and start fresh when he gets back. I know that I hold Conor to a higher standard when it comes to dealing with my troubles. I don't know if that's fair or not, but I see how he talks through the kids' troubles when they're upset. How he communicates with his friends when they ask for professional advice. That is Conor, ironing out everyone's predicaments, getting recognized for his dedication to his work. Yet when it comes to his wife, how did he become so blind? So unequipped. It doesn't make sense.

I take out my phone a compose a text:

Sorry about today. I love you so much.

I reread the message and erase it.

Why? Why can't I send it?

Liam. I will face my old love tomorrow.

I think about how we were together.

I was different then. Less damaged. Can I compare the two loves when I was so completely different? It's been ten years, and I have morphed into an entirely different person.

I am going to see Liam tomorrow. I remind myself again. My fingers fidget on my lap and my eyes burn holes into the ceiling.

I close my them tight, reminding myself of the moments we shared.

My heart broke.

Why is it that the buildup of romance is always so exceptional? Why are humans conditioned to feel best when things are fresh and exciting? And then, when the relationship is so desperately a part of your DNA, you get comfortable in its norms. It becomes routine, a figment of its course.

I love Conor. There is no question about it. I love him so much, yet…

Yet.

The adrenaline forces me out of bed. I pace the room before hurrying to the turntable in the corner.

I select the same vinyl that I used to fall asleep to as a child.

Music will help me get my mind off of the anxieties of tomorrow.

I'm not sure whether being back in this home has distracted or exacerbated my disassociations.

Every moment becomes another trigger for my memories.

Any song I listen to leads me to my utopia.

I slowly shut my eyes and listen to the sounds of **Dvořák - Symphony No.9** playing from the turntable.

37

THE CHOICE

London, Ten Years Ago

Ivan just informed me that he intends to remain in London, which ultimately dictated my decision.

When we decided to give our relationship a go, Liam promised that he wouldn't leave me as a coach if we broke up.

We have a good thing going here, professionally, he said.

The situation should have been a win-win for me: I'd choose Ivan and keep him in my life. And as long as Liam continued to coach me, we would remain close.

Yet I knew a life with Ivan would eventually lead to the loss of Liam.

I didn't think Liam had Ivan in mind when I asked what would happen if things didn't work out. I knew Liam would leave me if I ultimately chose Ivan.

So should I say goodbye to Ivan now and continue my life with Liam, a man I had admired for over a decade? Or did I stay with Ivan and finally live a life of equilibrium?

Either way looked promising.

Either way looked miserable.

"Isn't it just perfect?" My attention was drawn back to the sound of Ivan's voice. "We can finally live in the same country! I can watch you perform. I don't have to count down the hours to call you on the phone anymore. We—"

"Ivan, please," my voice trembled as I found the courage to speak.

His once vibrant light blue eyes now held a deep concern.

"I'm with Liam," I said, my words sharp and pointed.

His expression shifted dramatically, a somber and tortured look taking over his features.

"Since Russia, or shortly after," I continued, my voice cracking ever so slightly.

"When we spoke?"

"Yes." I clung to my cool demeanor as if it were armor, shielding me from the overwhelming emotions that threatened to consume me.

"Why? Why didn't you tell me this? Why bring me here?" Ivan's words were filled with hurt and betrayal.

"I didn't bring you here, Ivan. You surprised me," I retorted, my tone bitter and defensive, a feeble attempt to keep my emotions in check.

"Because you made me believe that you wanted me to be here, that we had…" He struggled to find the right words. "That we had love."

Love. The word hung in the air, a painful reminder of what we once shared.

The love I had for Ivan was unlike anything else, incomparable to what I felt for Liam.

```
A LIFE WITH IVAN: CAN IT WORK?
1.  Will the passion and desire eventually die down?
2.  If I choose Ivan, will I regret it and run back to
    Liam?
3.  Will I be able to maintain a life of piano without
    Liam?
4.  Is that life sustainable?
5.  What kind of love is this? A love centered around
    passion that, in the end, leaves me with nothing?
```

I had to make my decision using rational thinking, not my emotions.

I had to determine my risk/reward outcome.

My logic ultimately won out. I chose to live a life that made sense, one that was practical and sensible. Life with Ivan was heartwarming and healing.

And yet…

He was only twenty-six.

He had no concrete career.

He lived with three other roommates, didn't own a car.

I was the antithesis of his quest for spontaneity and adventure. I saw a brighter future ahead. I was in the process of signing a record deal and planning a world tour. I was heading in the right direction, and Liam had to be the right choice.

"I'm sorry, Ivan," my voice wavered as I finally spoke, my heart heavy with sorrow.

He turned away, his once bright eyes now glistening with restrained tears. It was a side of him I had never seen before, broken and vulnerable.

This overwhelming guilt consumed me. I had torn his happiness to shreds, promising him a future we could never share. I had lured him in with false hopes, only to shatter them into pieces.

The weight of my actions bore down on me. I was the one responsible for his pain, and I was still unsure if I had made the right decision.

Yet, despite the emotional toll it exacted, I clung to these words as a cold, heartless necessity, a calculated move to propel me to the top.

My heart raced, and my mouth grew dry. The unbearable weight of the moment pressed down on me, and I longed to escape. But there was nowhere else to go.

Under his breath, Ivan whispered, "I should go."

"No," I pleaded desperately. My last moments with Ivan were slipping away. "No, don't go," I implored, gripping his arm. "Please."

Regret flooded in, and I felt an overwhelming sense of remorse.

Ivan stood there, his jaw clenched, his gaze averted. I could feel his pulse quicken, matching the rhythm of my own racing heart.

He began to move away, and I followed, each step quickening.

"Ivan, wait," I called after him.

"There's nothing left to say, Cleo," he replied, avoiding my gaze.

"Ivan."

He pulled away, and I continued to follow.

As his pace increased, so did mine. "Ivan, wait," I pleaded, my voice choked with tears. "Please," I added more softly.

Ivan finally turned around, his eyes heavy and red. His usual smile had been replaced by a mask of sorrow.

"Cleo, do yourself a favor," he said softly. "Go to Liam. Otherwise, you'll lose him too."

"Wait, please," my heart raced, and my mind was in turmoil. I knew what I should do. Ivan knew it, and Liam knew it too. I should go to Liam.

So why was it so agonizing to say goodbye? What was this magnetic pull that kept me here, despite everything? How much was I willing to sacrifice for the promise of a future with Liam?

"Goodbye, Cleo. I wish you all the best."

"No!"

"No?" Ivan raised an eyebrow.

"You don't have to say goodbye," the words tumbled from my lips, a desperate plea.

A faint, unconvincing smile crossed Ivan's face as he saluted goodbye and turned away.

The image of Ivan gradually faded as I stood there, frozen. The life I was leaving behind slipped through my fingers, and I felt a sinking sense of hopelessness.

It was time to remove the armor.

Later that night, I broke down in tears. My sobs wracked my body until my eyes were dry and my throat was sore. Only when I had exhausted all my emotions did I return to Liam's the next day.

As soon as he learned that I had said goodbye to Ivan, he came running to greet me. Liam's arms wrapped around me, and he buried his face in my neck.

"I've missed you," he murmured, though it had only been a day. But I understood what he meant. He missed all of me—my attention, my love, my commitment.

I vowed to myself that I would dedicate my entire life to Liam. He would be my sole focus, and I would eliminate any distractions, any possibilities with Ivan.

"I choose you," my voice quivered with an intensity, my eyes never wavering from Liam's, "I choose a life wholly, irrevocably devoted to you. Every fiber of my being—it all belongs to you, and it always will."

That night, an eerie sense of impending darkness loomed, hinting at the possibility of the wrong choice I might have made.

38

THE SECRET OF HAPPINESS

London, Present Day

Despite my best efforts, I couldn't fall asleep—the nerves of seeing Liam, going back to that time, elicited thoughts of what might transpire.

Sunlight filters through the cracks in my curtains, bright enough to wake me up. After drawing them back, I look out the window to the landscape outside. An intuitive sadness overcomes me. What caused my mother to neglect the garden? This was a place I eagerly anticipated returning to. I was looking forward to its hypnotic effects.

It all looks so dull right now.

It makes me sad to think this doesn't bother my mother. Does it reflect her true feelings?

Giving in to sadness and pity has worn out my heart.

I quickly get dressed and leave home.

In a cab, I make my way to the nursery, a place my mother frequently took me to as a child.

I race into the shops as soon as they open. I inspect the selection and buy milkweed, French marigolds, hibiscus, and zinnia flowers. I purchase a container of monarch caterpillars already in chrysalis from the pet shop next door. I know it will take up to two weeks for them to emerge as butterflies, but some chrysalides seemed darker, not moving much. Maybe I would be present to witness the metamorphosis.

Upon returning home, I head straight for the garden. I pull weeds, refresh the soil, dig each plant its own hole.

"What on earth are you doing?" My mother comes outside in her long silk robe, holding her china teacup, the light shining on her pale skin. Her almost white-blond hair falls loosely about her face.

"Surprise!" A little *ta-da!* hand gesture follows.

"Cleo, come out from there! Look how dirty you're getting. I mean, honestly, if you wanted to revive the garden, you should have just asked. I can get Maxime to work on it."

"But I wanted to do it, Mummy." I now feel foolish for thinking I was capable of doing it alone. "I wanted to give you this. Just…I don't know. Maybe a reminder of the good old days."

A sigh escapes my mother's lips. As if to say, *This won't bring back those days.* It symbolizes the past, but nothing can bring the past to the present.

"Well, thank you, Cleo. Really. You, come on and bugger off. I'll call Maxime to finish the rest."

I shower until the soil is completely washed away.

Six hours until I must leave for Liam's.

The course of my life can change in six hours.

The terrycloth robe clings to me as I lie on my bed. My headspace is too crowded to handle any human interaction at this moment, and the thought of being around people makes me apprehensive. I don't want to leave my room.

I can't imagine eating right now despite my hunger.

I know if I ruminate on hypothetical outcomes, it will only lead me down a spiral of anxiety.

So I lie there, allowing my body to fade into the distance and my eyes to drift out of focus. I close them and breathe in the smells of my childhood home. The wind blows in from the open window beside my bed. The melody of **Ilya Shatrov - On the Hills of Manchuria**, plays on my phone's speaker.

I toy with the gold chain around my neck, a gift from Liam from a lifetime ago. I'm not sure what compelled me to wear it again—perhaps a desperate plea to my mind to somehow return me to the past. It's like slipping back into old shoes.

'That's a pretty necklace,' Conor remarked as we packed for this trip.

I spun white lies and evasions, concealing the true source of the necklace.

Conor. I exhale a heavy sigh.

I look at my phone's screen and click on my photos, scrolling through the many family pictures.

Sebastian in the bath with a bubble beard and a wide grin.

Conor and the kids before Olivia's recital.

The kids when we took them for a tea party at The Plaza's elegant Palm Court.

One catches my eye.

Sebastian's birthday party. We invited a few friends, nothing big. I am bent over next to Sebastian, holding the extravagant PAW Patrol cake. I see Diane and Kitty behind me in the distance. Kitty is beelining for the cake, and Diane's eyes seem to be looking at Sebastian. She seems to be worried sick—or pissed. Or perhaps both? I can see Eric on the other side of the living room, standing next to Jillian, one of Sebastian's friend's mother. She's perhaps ten years my junior and possesses the beauty of a young Sophia Loren. Eric seems too close to Jillian, and neither of them appears to be bothered by their proximity. Except for Diane? Is that what's on her face? Disgust? Hatred? Jealousy? Exhaustion?

I think about the night we had them over, how Eric was too close to me, too touchy-feely. Perhaps I was right, and Diane didn't want the reminder? Or didn't want her secret shared with close friends?

This picture now makes me feel sad. Sad for Diane. Sad for her relationship. Sad about how we left things, sad that we haven't spoken since. I almost swipe to the next picture, and then something catches my eye.

Conor.

He is standing behind Sebastian, and he's smiling. But he's not looking at Sebastian or the cake. He is looking at me.

He is looking at me in the way that lovers do in romance films—an exaggerated look of love delivering itself from the expression alone.

It seems like I am always missing these moments. Letting them slip on by. Every wonderful moment, every wonderful memory.

What causes me to miss them? To ignore them?

I place my phone on the bed and let my mind wander to the good times. The last nice moment was when I attempted to create a quiet, romantic dinner for Conor, hoping to impress him by portraying myself as the devoted and attentive wife. I wanted to re-create the family we were before I let my dissociations take over.

And then I remember how that dinner ended. When I played the soothing sounds of Shostakovich, how he became so bothered by the mention of Russia.

Why was Russia such a sore subject for Conor?

```
POSSIBLE REASONS:
1.  Could there be any reason for him to avoid asking
    me about the events of my life?
2.  But then he would go on and ask me to play
    something. Why?
3.  Why does he only show intermittent interest in my
    years of influence and power?
4.  What makes him recoil at the happier memories?
5.  Is it that he can see right through my
    subconscious? Does he worry that I hold these
    memories too fondly, like it may overpower the
    place where I am today?
```

Is he wrong?

As I consider the answers, I fear he might be entitled to worry.

What if I never arrive at a life of fulfillment and happiness? If a loving husband and three healthy, lovely children won't get me to a place of pride and satisfaction, what will?

As a matter of principle, I pick up my phone again and call Conor.

He answers on the first ring. "Hello?"

"Hey." I wait a few seconds. What is the purpose of my call? Am I apologizing for how we left things, or am I just checking on him?

"Hello? Are you there?"

I waited too long. "Yes, yeah, I am here. How, um, how are the kids?" It doesn't feel right. Almost as though I am talking to a stranger. Small talk between polite acquaintances.

"Yeah, they're great. They're just outside with my dad."

"Oh, nice."

More silence.

"Um, would you want to speak with them? I have a patient in about fifteen minutes though—"

"No, no, it's okay." I suddenly feel lonely. "Tell them I say hi?"

"Yeah, sure."

More silence.

"Thanks."

"Is everything all right? Are you enjoying your alone time?"

"Yep, everything is great. We'll speak tomorrow?"

"Yeah, sure. Or I can call after the appointment?"

"No, that's fine. I…I might be out."

"Okay, sure."

"Okay. Um. Bye?" Why am I so nervous? Why do I feel like I have to hold back tears?

"Oh, uh, Cleo?"

"Hm?"

"I love you."

I wipe a tear that escaped down my cheek.

"Yep, okay, love you too," I say too quickly, so he doesn't hear my voice break.

I end the call and inhale a deep breath to force the tears back in.

Right here, right now, is my need for escape and distraction.

If I think about my worries, about what is to come, I'll dig myself into a hole too deep to climb out of.

So, instead, my attention shifts back to Shostakovich.

Russia.

I smile.

Those were simpler times. Back when Liam was just my coach and my relationship with Ivan was just crossing the threshold into something serious.

Ivan's small apartment appears in my mind's eye. The night he lectured me on my attitude toward music, how I should celebrate its diversity.

I lay next to Ivan, warm beneath the covers. He lightly stroked my hand as we continued to discuss our pasts, our desires, music.

Despite my disagreement then, Ivan was right. To be perfectly honest, I wanted to appreciate all genres of music. There were times I'd been forced by circumstance to listen to the irritating sounds of radio's top hits. There were rare social occasions when the DJ would play some ear-shredding house music.

It forced me to disassociate from the present moment.

It wasn't coming from a place of pretension or perversity; I just had an immense sensitivity toward noises.

If I liked it, I'd become fixated, and if I didn't, it felt torturous.

As I lay beside Ivan, I found myself studying his vibrant, animated face. His eyes sparkled with joy, his expressive eyebrows dancing in conversation, and his hands gestured emphatically as he spoke.

"Ivan." I interrupted his monologue. "Why are you always so happy? What is the secret?"

"The secret of happiness? Hmm." His shifted his position to face me now. "The secret of happiness. I just think, well, we have this saying: *Vso khorosho v svoyo vremya.* Like, everything is good in its time. Just enjoy this moment, right now. Don't rush this moment, no? Don't go back and think, *Oh, I want to get away from now.* Now is good. Now is happy. If you run away, you will find something to be sad about. In the future, in the past."

My forehead wrinkled in confusion.

"Okay, I told you, I grew up poor. I could be sad that I didn't have the bike my friends had or fancy new clothes; I always wore my brother's old clothes. I think a moment, I can be upset, I can cry, but what? What will happen if I cry? It won't be magic and new clothes appear. I won't make money if I am busy crying. Yes, I can be sad, for a little while, cry a little, and then shake it off. So instead, I find ways to make me laugh, make me smile. Playing on my mama's piano made me smile, running around outside with my brothers made me smile. This competition makes me smile; you make me smile. Find yourself with happy things that stop you needing to feel sad and cry."

"Easier said than done," I snorted.

"Cleo." Ivan held my hands firmly. "Try it. You will be happier this way."

I raised my eyebrow and then looked down.

Inspiration can provide motivation, but it will not transform you. It is the act of manipulating your brain into believing these principles that is most challenging.

"You're not happy?" His voice turned somber.

"No, I am. I just think you have something different. It's not happiness, it's—" I had to think what word best described Ivan. "You're content."

"Content?"

"You are okay with anything life presents to you. If you don't win, you'll be okay. If I don't, it will destroy me. I won't be able to handle the failure."

The list of what would happen had lingered in my head from the moment I auditioned for the competition.

```
If I win:
I would continue to search for my subsequent victory.
I would be able to attain such high accolades.
I would treasure such prestige.
It will finally prove my worth.
If I don't win:
It's over.
```

And over means surrendering to the darkness, succumbing to mediocrity, letting go of the one thing that defines me. I can't accept that. I won't accept that. Losing? That's not an option in my world. I'll fight, bleed, and sacrifice until victory is the only reality. It's over? No, no. That's just not an option.

"Why must you win this competition, my Cleo? You know there are many, many others. You can find another competition and try again." Ivan's voice drew me irresistibly closer. My eyes locked onto his.

"It's not that I want to win, it's that I need to," I confessed, my voice quivering with passion. "It's a very important step of my carefully laid-out plan. Each step needs to go as planned. If I mess up," I think of how to finish that sentence, "Winning means reaching the grand stages like the Opera House and Carnegie Hall. And from there, it's the Proms. Do you see? Each achievement paves the way for the next. If I falter at any point, I jeopardize my chances of progressing further."

"Ah, that's not true," he dismissed with a casual wave of his hand. "Nothing is, how do we say, certain? *Dah*, nothing is certain." He held my hands, his warmth coursed through me, comforting and reassuring. "Cleo, you will be okay if you don't win. You will be just fine, you know why?" He looked into my eyes with full conviction. "Because you played at the Moscow Classical Music Competition; you made it to Russia. You had a great time here. You met a handsome young man." Ivan smiled, and it prompted one to spread across my face. "If you don't win, you will move on to the next big thing, because you are an amazing pianist. Just remind yourself that you will be okay with either outcome."

I made a concerted effort to expel my catastrophic thoughts and, instead, cling to that sentiment. I desperately yearned to believe it.

You will be okay with either outcome.

"Cleo, Hélène is headed to Bond Street to pick up some food. Would you like to make an order?"

Suddenly, I am back in my bedroom, lying on my bed in the terrycloth robe.

I look at my phone.

5:15.

"Shit!"

"Cleo? Are you in there?"

"Yeah, Mum, I'm fine. I'm about to head out."

"Oh? So nothing then? Maybe she'll get some of those scones you like, and that stir-fry dish for later?" she shouted from behind the closed door.

"Sure, Mum. Thank you."

"Um, when do you suppose you'll be back?"

"I shouldn't be too long."

Will this take long?

Will this reunion turn into a celebration? Could I possibly join Liam for dinner, or perhaps late-night drinks?

Why are these even options? No. I will pay him a visit and come right back home. No distractions!

My damp hair has settled into a peculiar shape. My eyes are puffy. I have to find a way to present myself the way Liam used to know me. He expects to see the me from ten years ago. What will he think when a disheveled older woman shows up? A ragged mother with a gaunt face, sunken eyes, and a lanky body?

In my closet, I find a floral-printed Georgette dress, one of the many I abandoned in London. I complete my outfit by pairing black loafers with a gold horse-bit detail. I gel my hair and apply my makeup just as I did in the past. Despite ten years of damage, I now resemble the old Cleo.

I have transformed into the Cleo Liam knew.

39

MR. MARTIN

London, Present Day

I approach Liam's house, a relic of the past, a place we once shared, and it appears frozen in time, just as I remember it.

The sharp buzzing of the doorbell jolts me, a familiar, haunting sound that has echoed through my ears countless times before. It used to signal my eagerness, my anticipation, almost a daily ritual, as I waited for Liam to arrive. Those were the moments when he'd sweep me into his arms, showering me with kisses, as if we hadn't seen each other just moments ago.

My heart races with each echoing footstep that grows nearer, and I struggle to steady my breath. This is the moment, the moment when I will come face-to-face with Liam, after all these years. The same old anticipation surges within me, but I must remind myself that this time, it will be different.

Liam will open the door, but I will not impulsively leap into his arms. No, I must restrain myself, must remember who I am now. A married woman. A mother. I am no longer Liam's.

My breath catches as the door handle creaks, and the door slowly swings open.

An elderly lady greets me with an expression devoid of interest or emotion, casting a shadow of uncertainty over the moment.

"Sorry to bother you; is Liam home? He is expecting me."

She just stands there.

"Oh, I'm Cleo." I stretch out my hand.

"Come along, dear," she says in a sigh. She leads the way.

It is Liam's office that she points to. I know it too well. The many hours of practice we spent in thére. All those late nights before events, and then, as we began dating, we would play more leisurely. Spend hours distracting ourselves from work. Enjoying each other's company instead. Reading books on his couch, listening to music, playing music together, falling deeply in love.

"Please do wait right here. Mr. Martin will be with you momentarily."

Mr. Martin. It has been a while since I thought of Liam as "Mr. Martin." I recall the time he told me to call him Liam, not Mr. Martin. I never called him that again.

I observe the room. The antique gramophone is playing **Fantasia on British Sea Songs**. Its eerie crackles fill the air like ghostly whispers. In Liam's office, music was always playing. It was either us or his gramophone.

The floral wallpaper, the dark mahogany furniture. It feels like yesterday when I was here, engaging in unspeakable acts with Liam.

My fingers trace the spines of his extensive collection of leather-bound books. As I randomly select one and peruse its contents briefly before returning it to the shelf, a powerful sense of déjà vu washes over me.

It's a strange sensation, almost like muscle memory guiding my every move. My hands seem to instinctively know where to gravitate, and my body follows suit. I release another book. I hesitate before taking this one down. A feeling of unease creeps up on me. Like I know I am touching something forbidden. Like I am committing a sin. The motions are slow, but I hold on to the book with intention. One of six volumes. Titled: *The Book of Russian Poetry*. A flash of this book makes an appearance, then leaves me just as suddenly. I don't look inside and quickly place it back with the rest of the collection.

The bookshelf now projects a heat, as to plea, *Stay far away*. I walk backward and feel the coolness of the piano against my back. Another flash, only this one stays. It is me, much younger, maybe sixteen. The first year I met Liam. The first year I came to this office. I was playing something; I can't hear what, but the sounds of piccolos, flutes, oboes, and English horns are amplified through the gramophone. My ghostly present moves with unsettling speed. Blood stains the ivory keys, but my face remains stoic.

The natural disposition of my past.

My hand clutches my chest, but it only exacerbates the frantic rhythm of my heart. The room unfolds before my eyes like a series of eerie flashes. I remember the leather seats. I remember the bar in the corner, set with crystal glasses and a canister that I know contains Lagavulin 16. its smoky aroma invading my senses as I draw closer.

My eyes then notice the beechwood muddler inside the mixing glass. Everything seems to form into a faint, incomplete memory.

Then I see it. A gold-framed picture, ginkgo leaves enclosing a picture of a couple. Both look to be in their late fifties. The woman's face is covered by her dirty blond fringe and large black sunglasses. Her hair is messy, yet chic.

But it's the man who seizes my attention—a shock of thick gray hair, deep-set bags beneath piercing blue eyes, and thin lips curled into a vague, enigmatic smile.

It's him.

"Hello, Cleo."

I drop the frame and the glass shatters by my ankles.

"Liam."

My memories do not match the Liam I see now.

He is no longer the man I remember. It is not that he had aged; rather, that he is someone else entirely.

It is the stillness of contemplation that firmly roots me. I'm worried about the consequences of breaking the glass, the alarm that crawls up on me as my memories try to piece themselves together.

"Are you okay, Cleo? It looks like you have seen a ghost." A subtle French accent accompanies Liam's voice.

Snap out of it, Cleo!

I muster up the courage to contort a sentence. "Sorry about that."

It's a start. My eyes are still unable to look away from Liam. Who I presume to be Liam.

"Oh, don't worry about it. Margarette will clean it up."

Our gazes intertwine, and his eyes emit an eerie aura, yet there's an inexplicable familiarity about him.

"So, Cleo, what brings me the honor?" He leans against his desk, arms crossed over his chest. He stands tall opposite me, positioning me as inferior. "Are you going to speak, or are we just going to look quietly at each other?"

I blink away the fear, trying to allow my body to retort.

"I, uh…" I try, stuttering over my words. "I-I was in town. I wanted, needed…to have a chat about something." That is my lame attempt at a sentence.

"A chat?" Liam seems amused. "What is it you wish to discuss?"

He needs a response. *Respond, Cleo!*

"I…I guess I have a lot of unanswered questions about my past."

"Go on." Our eyes are once again engulfed in an intense gaze.

"Well, I guess I am curious about Russia."

"Russia?"

"Yes, well…I kind of don't have a great memory…of anything, really, but it's a real blank space as to what happened there."

"Well, what do you think happened?" His words were slow and clear.

"I, uh. I won? I came back here with the Grand Prix Award." Then we started dating, I think. I want to confirm this but can't—not yet anyway. I still have to come to terms with the fact that I remembered Liam so differently. It's almost like a different person stands in front of me.

"So why do you question what happened? You clearly know what took place. You won!" He smiles, suggesting a more relaxed Liam as he moves to his desk chair and reclines. "I hope you went on and did big things in your career, Cleo."

"Well, no, actually—" I want to say *I am a writer*, but that feels fraudulent. "I…I don't play anymore."

"No?"

"No, not since—" I stop. He knows. He was there. Even if I don't remember what happened, he does. "Well, you know. That was my last performance."

Silence. He is taking it all in.

Then he abruptly stands up and walks toward his piano.

"Play something, huh?" he casually requested as he settled onto the white piano bench, his fingers idly dancing across a few keys. Then, with a haunting grace, the **Moonlight Sonata, Third Movement** began to flow from the instrument.

A suffocating fear seized me, a visceral dread I'd never experienced before. The urgency to distance myself from that piano was overwhelming. My fingers grew cold, and I felt light-headed, the room spinning around me.

"No. No, thank you," I stammered, my voice trembling as I resisted the urge to flee.

"Come on, for old times' sake, ah?" he urged, his knee bouncing fervently on the pedal, his arms too. Each note graduating getting louder, taking over any sound I can hear, any thought I might have, any last breath left in me.

"No, I—" I am choking on my words. "I better go." but my words were lost beneath the overwhelming power of Liam's playing.

I feared I might faint right there in his office. I tried to plead with him, to beg him to stop, but I wasn't even sure if any sounds escaped my lips. Taking a few unsteady steps back, I stammered, "Stop," but the words felt feeble and insignificant.

I take a few steps back. "Thank you, Liam. Than-th- thanks for." My words falter, failing to find their way out. Adrenaline surges through my veins, yanking me away. I have to get out of the office, out of Liam's home. Now!

I am pulled into a quick walk, then a run.

An unrelenting itchiness surrounded me, a sensation of crawling dread that refused to subside. The woman, presumably named Margarette, attempted to guide me toward the exit, but there was no time for pleasantries. It was a matter of urgent necessity. I needed to get out, or I feared I might never breathe again.

The cool air splashes over me. I start to catch my breath again. I am liberated.

40

BROKEN NARRATIVES

London, Present Day

Tonight my father is attending a publishing industry event. He thought it would be a good idea for me to join him—a little inspiration to help me move on to my next endeavor.

The last time I attended one of these events, I met Ramona. Maybe this time, I will find a different path, a more suitable, equal partnership.

We arrive at the location, a magnificent house on Bedford Gardens.

It is unlike anything I have seen before. A spiral staircase leads up three levels, with open floors on all sides and art deco on every surface. Bright hues and bold geometry dominate the living area. There's a ladder-mounted bookshelf, multiple pendant lights hanging from the ceiling, and a large tree in the center of the living room.

It has been a while since I found myself at an adult social event. Recently it's been PTA meetings or another children's performance.

I enjoyed this alone time. I relished not having to chat about my children or carry a large bag filled with my kids' necessities.

My attire for tonight is a red leather A-line midi dress. My lips are freshly painted. I am drinking a glass of wine, which was handed to me as soon as I entered.

Tonight, I will make it about me.

From the moment we arrive, my father is enticed in many directions. Our arms stay linked into one another's as he introduced me to his colleagues with pride.

"This is my daughter, Cleo. She lives in New York City now! She has written many books; maybe you've heard of them...."

He stretches the truth and exaggerates my credentials, but I don't correct him. I like the version of me that he's portraying.

Eventually, we have to unlink our arms, and I have to shake off the panic as my father promises to come and find me.

I have traveled alone for so many years. I've come to events alone and never felt the need for support. Why do I feel like a lost child now? Like I need the assistance? It is as though I have no idea how to develop the confidence to introduce myself to people, to put myself out there.

Oh no. A rapid pulse begins to beat in my chest. I've been doing so well! I thought Clarice was helping me manage my anxiety. Suddenly it feels as though a cool blast of icy air penetrates my skin as the dizzy spells begin.

No, no, no, no! I will not allow this to happen!

Nausea swelled within me, threatening to consume me whole.

Get your shit together, Cleo!

The walls cave in. I feel everyone's eyes burning in my direction.

I will not have another attack, not here, not now.

There are so many reasons why I can't be weak. I need to be strong, show these people I can handle anything! How will it look if I pass out? What would my father think?

I remove myself from the crowded room so I can catch my breath. I try to regroup, to force myself back to a place of calm. It's just a moment that I need, and everything will be all right.

I find a quiet room near the stairs.

I hide behind the door and sink to my knees. My hands encase my face.

Just breathe.

As I inhale more deeply, my heartbeat accelerates.

Breathe, goddammit! I don't allow myself to cry.

I am immersed in shame that I am still dealing with these attacks. Maybe this will just be my life, something that will always be a part of me.

I shut my eyes.

Breathe.

I am starting to be able to detect the moment my mind leaves my body. When my eyes are closed, the chatter fades away, and the sounds of **Mendelssohn - Violin Concerto** fill my head.

My mind wanders back to Russia.

The lingering melody that Ivan performed during the fourth round—its power and emotion—captivated me completely.

A perpetual smile graced my lips as I observed his performance from a distance.

The sounds of those strings set off a visceral reaction within me. There was nothing monotonous about this melody, about this moment. I could watch Ivan play over and over again.

I felt content.

There was a tapping on my arm.

"I think we should probably get to the hotel now," whispered Liam from behind me.

"Just a moment?" I whispered back, eyes fixated on Ivan.

"I think we should get as much practice time as we can." His voice is not so quiet anymore.

"He is almost done."

"NOW!" His voice escalated abruptly, jolting me from my trance. I turned back, confronted not by the Liam I had always envisioned but the Liam I had encountered just yesterday.

"Do you want to win? Do you want to go on and achieve great things? Come, NOW!"

The music came to an abrupt halt, and every eye in the room turned toward me. Ivan was looking at me.

My mind went blank.

No, that is not how it went. The memory restarted.

I watched Ivan play the Violin Concerto.

I felt the vibrations run through my veins, a spontaneous smile on my face.

This is the same night I went to Ivan's apartment for the first time.

This was hours before I received the text to go meet up with him.

Liam tapped me on the arm. I turned to face him. I smiled; my eyes lit up. He looked like I remembered him—young, charming Liam.

"We should probably head out to the hotel now," he whispered.

"Oh, okay." I took one more glance at Ivan, lost in his melody.

I could have sworn I caught his eye, but I knew that wasn't true. We were hundreds of meters apart, and I knew from experience that when you're playing, you don't notice what is going on around you.

Liam's hand lightly pulled me in his direction.

It was a quiet ride to Hotel Metropol.

We didn't utter a word when we got there. We just hung our coats carefully on the antique brass coat stand, and then I approached the piano.

Without direction, I started playing **Beethoven - Concerto No. 5.**

Liam watched me from the corner of the room. The intensity of his gaze begged for my attention, but I ignored it.

It was a moment of melancholy wrapped up in melodies.

I felt the heat of proximity as our bodies grew closer. I tried to neglect the sensation as I continued to play.

I was usually good at blocking out distractions.

I stopped.

"No," Liam said, almost inaudible. "That was perfection."

The blood rushed to my head, and I hoped I didn't turn a noticeable red.

I smiled, looked at him, and then back at the piano.

I started again from the beginning. Liam sat down next to me, and I made my best effort to ignore him. I continued playing the sonata.

He crossed his arms over his chest, then he interrupted the melody.

"Okay, here." He bent over and pointed at the score sheet.

I stopped, and Liam began with his directions.

"Here is where you can emphasize the notes a bit more. I think you are static. Let your body move with your hands so you'll get more range, less forced motion."

I glanced up to Liam, then back at the piano. His face was too close to mine.

"Okay." I took a deep breath and started again.

"Yes! Amazing!" he shouted over the music. "Just like that!"

I finished the melody.

A roar came from Liam. "Again!"

It wasn't the Liam I had known, the one I cherished. This was the different Liam—that haunting, unfamiliar presence that I had encountered just hours ago.

"There you are!"

Dad? I open my eyes and jolt up.

"Dad!" I then realize where I am.

My first instinct is to check my watch. It must have been about thirty, forty minutes that I was in here.

"I was looking all over for you."

I look into his eyes. "I, I needed…" I start to justify as I help myself up.

"Don't worry, dear. It can be quite intimidating, throwing yourself back into this world."

"Yeah, I agree." I force a smile onto my face.

"You…want to go home? I am happy to have Henry bring the car around."

"No, no, don't worry about it. You go. I'll come find you in a moment."

"To hell, I will." My father mimics a stern demeanor.

I laugh. "No, really, Dad. I'm okay."

"Come here." He sits on the upholstered bench, and I sit down beside him. "Do you think I am rushing back in there to speak with Marcus from Adam and Adam Publishing House? Or get bombarded with synopses from some hungry author?"

"Hungry authors like me?" I ask.

He looks at me and winks. "Nobody is like you, Cleo. You, my dear, are something special, you know that?"

I don't answer. There was a time once before when I knew this. I thought I had it all, and now I feel inadequate.

"Oh, darling." My father wipes away a tear that has escaped my eye. I didn't even realize I'd started crying.

"My Cleo." He holds my hand tightly in his.

"Daddy, I don't know if I can go out there again. I don't have anything to offer these people. What am I selling? What can I possibly promise these editors or agents?"

"If you don't feel ready, don't force it. You think I had all the answers, all the confidence to build my company?"

"Yes," I say, and laugh through my tears.

"Oh, feck no! I had to bullshit my way through most of it in the beginning. I took many beatings at first, but there is only one thing to do in those moments: pick yourself up and try again."

"It seems so easy when you say that, but—"

"I know, darling, and it wasn't easy. But you have the same horsepower I do. You are determined and unbeatable. You have proven it before, and you can do it again."

I shrug. It's all nice to hear, but to believe it is quite another matter.

"Listen." His hands are still gripping mine. "It's human instinct to halt when life gets turbulent, but you didn't do that. You left your career and found something new. You were proactive. You are doing what you can to gain some control over an out-of-control occurrence."

"But what if this isn't the right path? Some days I second-guess myself. Maybe I ran to the closest opportunity rather than the right one."

My father lets out a hefty sigh. "You have control over your narrative, even if you don't feel like you do. Life gets tough, but challenging outcomes don't always result from poor decisions. Or maybe they do, who knows." He takes a beat and then continues. "I remember someone telling me this when I first started out. Imagine those monitors in hospitals, the ones the patients are attached to, you know? The ones that go *beep, beep, beep*."

I nod.

"It constantly goes up and down, up and down. The moment it flatlines, well, that means you are in some trouble."

I understand his analogy.

"It's okay to have your ups and downs. That's how we know we're alive! How we learn life skills. That's how I learned, what ultimately gave me the tools to build this empire."

I nod again.

I want to let this lesson sink in. I really do. However, it is so easy to utter words of motivation and inspiration without allowing the catastrophizing to take over.

"Cleo, darling. Are you okay?"

The question that everyone wants to know the answer to.

"Daddy, I don't want to deflect, but is Mum okay?"

He takes a deep inhale and looks into my eyes.

"I mean," I continue, "was she ever really okay? I'm only asking because…" I stop. I've never fully comprehended what struggles my mother has gone through.

"Cleo, your mother is doing just fine. She has moments of isolation when she needs some alone time. But only when she feels imbalanced. Sometimes the SSRIs work, and sometimes we need to reevaluate. You know, that's just how life is, right?"

It makes me wonder if this is my future. My distress must be evident, because my father continues to reassure me.

"You don't have to worry about it, Cleo. Your mother will be okay. She *is* okay. And you are not your mother. We all have neurological signals in our brains, and just because your mother has a more challenging time balancing hers doesn't mean it's your destiny."

I replay my father's words later that night.

He ended up taking me home, and I did not connect with any agents. Next time, my father said—next time.

So here I am. A grown woman. Unable to summon the courage to go out into the real world. Afraid to leap at new opportunities, overcome the challenges that will lead me to the next stage of my life.

Instead, I am back in my pajamas, lying on the bed I slept in growing up at 9:00 p.m. Listening to my comfort music—**Schubert - Trout Quintet 3rd movement.**

I miss my kids, I miss Conor. I want to go to Ireland. Hug them. Let them know how much I appreciate them. How much I love them. How much I miss them.

And, to prove our telepathic abilities, my phone dings beside me.

Sorry I haven't had a chance to call you yet. Me and the kids are all missing you. Love you.

It breaks my heart. I have never felt such a strong urge to *not* be alone.

Where do these emotions go when life goes on? How am I able to ignore such an intense sensation? What is wrong with me that I can only appreciate their noises when I am presented with silence?

My throat develops a grapefruit-sized lump, and butterflies begin to flutter inside my chest.

I need to get my mind off reality and disengage from my emotions, from my reality. These are the moments when I listen to music to bring my mind to a simpler time, when life was easy. Then, with the help of the uplifting sounds of Schubert, I am calm, and I feel my body drift off to sleep.

41

YA LYUBLYU TEBYA

London, Present Day

The sounds of Schubert's quintet send my mind to a world where Liam looked like the Liam I wanted to remember: tall, with piercing blue eyes, smooth dark hair, and five o'clock shadow covering his chiseled jaw.

It was almost two months after we started dating. A month before the Proms.

I was lying in bed, in a white linen nightdress, the gold chain around my neck.

Liam was already dressed in his suit. He stood over me and kissed me profusely in the early morning light.

"Get up, get up, get up!" he said through his kisses. "We have a nine o'clock meeting with LCR and a lunch with the event coordinator after."

A smile spread across my face as I slowly stretched. "Okay, okay, I'm up!" I looked at Liam in adoration.

I was very fortunate, so well taken care of.

My life operated according to my needs, and I followed the necessary motions. It all felt so seamless.

"I'll be in my office. I have an international call, but it should only take about, hm…" He looked at his watch. "Let's say an hour? I'll come up to make sure you're ready to go."

"I'll be ready!" I reassured him.

"I have some breakfast waiting for you in the kitchen, and I left the tea out."

"Go! I'll be fine!"

Liam hurried out of the room.

I inhaled and took in this moment of happiness. All the smiling caused my cheeks to hurt.

Liam reentered the room unexpectedly.

"Have you forgotten something?"

He kissed my face, my neck.

"Okay, now I'm ready." He smiled and left the room again.

A little laugh escaped me, and I fell back into my bed, lighter than ever before.

Suddenly, my euphoria was shattered by a buzzing sound coming from the nightstand.

Ivan.

I held the phone close to my chest and watched the open door.

Silence.

Liam was already in his office.

I took a deep breath and held the phone up to my ear. "Hey," I said quietly.

"*Dobroye utro krasavitsa.* How is my beauty?"

I closed my eyes; my heart sank.

When would this confusion be over? How could I possibly end it? Would I be with Ivan? With Liam? It didn't matter how happy I was with Liam; I could not abandon my relationship with Ivan.

What if Liam proposed to me? Would that be the push I needed?

What was I thinking? Propose!? We'd only been together for a little over a month. What was going on in my brain that I was thinking out proposals?

"Cleo?"

My thoughts must have kept me quiet for too long.

"Hi, yes, I am here. I have a meeting in thirty minutes," I said almost immediately. "I'm going to speak to my agent at the record label, and then after I will be meeting up with some people about the Proms for lunch." I tried not to boast, but I wanted to take Ivan along every step of the way. It brought me an immense amount of joy, and he genuinely reciprocated the excitement.

He asked all the questions; he allowed the moment to be all about me. He waved off my questions and followed with, "Forget about me. I want to hear more about this. Tell me, what you play at the Proms?"

The phone call had to end; by now Liam must have been finishing up his call. If I hadn't been pressed for time, the conversation would have been much longer.

"*Ya lyublyu tebya.*" He always ended his calls with this proclamation.

I love you.

"*Ya lyublyu tebya,*" I repeated back to him.

I quickly changed into a slightly loose, pastel pink suit, paired it with white strappy heels, and tied my hair into a low, loose bun.

I looked at my reflection, and once I was satisfied with my appearance, I headed downstairs. My primary focus shifted back to Liam.

With a cup of tea, I made my way to Liam's office.

The door was ajar, and I could hear Liam on the phone. He was reclining in his office chair and speaking energetically. I was about to turn away when I heard the clicking of his fingers. Liam gestured for me to come in and held up a finger to let me know he was almost done.

To keep myself occupied while Liam finished his phone call, I explored the office in all its dimensions.

I browsed his extensive collection of books. Afterward, I perused the vinyl collection beside his bookshelf. It was there that I noticed the frames above the mantel. It was right there: the golden ginkgo frame showcasing a photo of Mr. Martin and his wife.

Those icy blue eyes. The white hair, prominent bags, the curled lip smiling back at me mockingly.

My hands lost their grip, and the frame fell to the floor. Glass shattered about my ankles. I hastily glanced to where Liam was sitting. He was gone.

I felt a chill creep through me when I heard the door slamming then locking.

I wake up.

Panting.

Confused.

42

FÜR ELISE

London, Present Day

It is like an avalanche, my brain drowning in memories. Increasingly chaotic and confusing.

These stories are intertwined with fiction.

I have to strain to distinguish between what is real and what isn't.

We have six days left until we go back home. Back to reality. I don't feel ready.

I am inspecting my habitat. I notice the butterflies erupt from their chrysalides.

I follow the steps I observed my mother doing when I was a child. First, I place a piece of orange in their habitat. Then I wait until the butterflies' wings have sufficiently strengthened before I release them.

I hold the habitat close to my stomach and bring it with me into the piano room.

Today is the day.

Today I will play the piano.

I take a deep inhale.

I can do this. It is just a piano. It can't harm me. It won't.

The piano has been catching my attention ever since I've been home. I stand there, peering through the doorway, shy of its existence.

I feel like a child inside a grown, adult body. Every day I have told myself, *I can do it*. And then, every day, I abandon the plan.

Today, I will actually follow through with my plan. I slowly enter the room, where I encounter the grand piano, still in its impeccable shape. My fingers trace the maple wood gently, feeling its smoothness and warmth.

I place the habitat gently beside the piano.

Butterflies, do your thing, and bring me to a place of serenity. Allow my mind to get past this obstruction. Find a way for my fingers to rest on the keys and let the music escape.

Every day of the past week, I would sit here and close my eyes, blocking out the surrounding environment. Blindly, I would put my headphones in my ears and listen to a song from the past as I allowed my body to lose consciousness.

But today, I will play. Today, I am ready for the next step. I am going to play.

I sit on the piano bench.

I take a deep breath.

I close my eyes and try to force my hands to rest on the keys, but my arms feel as heavy as stones encased in concrete.

The large French doors creak, forcing my eyes open once again.

It's my sister, Annie.

"You're here!" I say.

"I heard you were in town; thought I'd stop by."

I shift my body to face Annie's. My lips tremble as I say, "I've missed you."

Standing there, she smiles. Yet her eyes reflect an entirely different feeling: sadness.

"You know, I would have come earlier, but…" She trails off. She doesn't need to finish her sentence. We have a mutual understanding when it comes to our relationship.

We have purposefully distanced ourselves from one another. Even with the immense love and affection sisters unconditionally feel, it wasn't easy being together, seeing eye to eye.

Our love was never in question. The love between sisters is unlike any other.

We just don't have the right words to converse—the proper understanding of each other's psyche. Instead, we choose to distance ourselves physically and metaphorically, knowing that strategy works best.

"So," she says, pointing at the piano. "Do you play at home?"

I shake my head. "I haven't played since about ten years ago."

"What? How is that possible?"

"I don't know. Once I was done with it all, I guess there was no way I could be near a piano again. It just felt too invasive, too sad."

She nods. She understands.

"Has Conor never seen you play? The kids?"

"Nope."

"Wow." After taking this information in, she shakes her head in disbelief. "I remember how attached you were to the piano as a child. Nothing could separate you from it."

"I remember playing for you as a baby." A smile forces its way onto my face as I think about those precious moments I shared with Annie.

"Yeah," Annie laughs. "Mummy would always tell you to stop because I would cry the second you played."

"What? Are you sure? I remember so clearly; you were so soothed by the music. I would play for hours. It used to shut you right up."

"I don't know. Mum told me otherwise. She said you never got bothered by my cries and would continue playing."

"Huh." I wonder if that is true. Why do I remember it so differently? Why does everything I remember seem so wrong?

Annie laughs again. "Do you remember, when we were a bit older…I must have already been ten, eleven years old? You were practicing for some big performance; everyone was giving you attention. It was all *Cleo needs space to practice*, and *Cleo needs quiet.* I was so angry and frustrated that I slammed the piano shut on your fingers. I got in so much trouble for that. Mummy, Daddy, you…everyone got so mad at me. You wouldn't speak to me for about a week. I remember hearing Mr. Martin screaming in this room while I was sitting on the stairs outside, waiting for my punishment."

The visuals come back to me. "Oh gosh, I remember that."

This memory plays so vividly in my mind. My fingers were wrapped in bandages after they sent me to the hospital to check for fractures.

"The doctors said you couldn't play for a week after that, and somehow you still succeeded in convincing Mum and Dad that you were fine to play for the— what was it?"

"The Windsor Competition," I recall.

"Ha! right. You were psychotic, I tell you. But somehow you managed to play through the pain. And then you won, didn't you?"

"Yeah," I say faintly.

An image appears of me in Liam's office. I was sobbing at the bandage that encircled my fingers. According to the doctors, I was not allowed to play, and the competition was that night. Liam was soothing me, providing me with options.

"It's your choice," Liam offered. It was Liam—my Liam.

As my tears subsided, I considered my options while sipping a glass of water.

My choice? I remember thinking. I would never turn down this opportunity. In order to continue on my upward trajectory, I had to take this step. I needed to prove my abilities to the Windsor Competition jury, to Liam.

"Right?" My mind found Annie's voice.

"What?"

"I was just saying, you were extremely stubborn when it came to the piano, to Mr. Martin. I was kind of jealous growing up. I wish I had something I was that enthusiastic about."

"I was crazy." I say this as though I've only just discovered it. "No boundaries."

"But surely being away from it has been good for you, right?" She sits beside me. I feel her hand rest on mine.

"Yeah," I answer. My gaze stays fixed in the peripheral. I am trying to bring on the rest of that memory. How did I manage to perform that day? I remember taking some pain medication, and somehow that was all I needed.

"Cleo." Annie looks worried. "Are you okay?"

"Yeah." My eyes are still not looking anywhere.

"I mean, are you *really* okay? Not now, but…" She takes in a deep breath in. "In general?"

I then turn to face her.

My voice is barely audible. "No."

I am not okay. I haven't been in quite some time. My life is a series of motions, deflecting and ignoring signs.

I can't see the signs of my marriage failing, my mental health deteriorating, my daughter following in my footsteps.

A tear starts to escape my eye. I can't hold it back.

"Oh, Cleo. I'm so sorry."

"It's okay." I wipe away the tear and force a smile. "I'll be okay."

"No, I'm sorry for not being there for you. I knew you were dealing with some shit when we were younger, but I chose to ignore it. It was easier for me not to get involved."

"You were too young to do anything. And you're right. My mind was so focused I couldn't even notice my surroundings. I most likely would have ignored you."

We hold hands, and I squeeze hers tight.

"I have always carried a pang of guilt, between you and Mummy, with all your problems. I was aware of what was going on, and then I chose to leave. It seemed to be the only way to make a life for myself."

I nod. I am trying to imagine how things were at home. My mind then wanders to Conor's response. My attitude toward Ciara. How much easier it is to tell ourselves everything is fine. Can we really expect problems to resolve themselves?

"You shouldn't feel guilty. You didn't know how; you didn't have any resources to solve our problems," I reassure Annie.

"I know, I just feel like I should have made a little more of an effort. I was old enough to understand what was going on, I just chose not to interfere."

"What was it like from your perspective, home life? I honestly don't remember much."

Annie stares into my eyes as hers widen in worry. "Well, you know Daddy. He was always in his office, from the wee hours till late. Then there were Mummy's *episodes*. She was for sure dealing with some form of depression or bipolar disorder, but it was never talked about. You remember what it was like, not knowing which version of Mummy we would get. One day she was so loving and caring, and then she would lock herself in her bedroom and yell at us if we weren't silent."

I nod. This I remember.

"And then there was you and Mr. Martin, always playing on the piano. Every door in the house was closed shut. I had Hélène until I didn't need anyone taking care of me anymore. I guess that's why I always spent time at my friends' homes. It was a lot busier, a lot more happening."

"Sorry, I had no idea. I…I guess I didn't know what went on beyond that door."

She smiles. "We all could have done better. The problem was, we couldn't figure out how. No one is to blame here. We thought what we did, or didn't do, was necessary."

Our silence is unified as we sit still.

"One more thing." I try to think how to ask the question without alarming Annie. "Liam. Um, Mr. Martin."

"Yeah?"

"What was my relationship like with him?"

"Oh, I don't know. He was always very intense, but I guess so were you. A match made in heaven."

That brings a smile to my face and a sensation to my stomach. We were a match made in heaven—how I missed us.

"It was always about the piano," Annie continued. "You were either in this room playing or in his office. You seemed very infatuated by him. He seemed to cast a spell over you."

I need more clarity before I ask Annie about my dating relationship with Liam. I am not yet ready to admit to my mental blockages, but my recent encounter with Liam has convinced me that I must deal with them now. The time I spent with him seems so surreal. That concept seems very distant now that I have a new view of him.

"Was there anything questionable, I guess, about our relationship?"

Annie thinks about it. "Like what?" she finally asks.

"I guess…I went over there the other day. Everything looked so familiar to me: his office, his home, the wallpaper, everything. He just…I guess I remember him differently."

"Hm." Annie creases her brow. "Maybe it was seeing him for the first time, not as a teacher, but just for who he is?"

"Maybe." I can't make sense of it. Any justification doesn't seem adequate. I know I'll have to pay him a second visit to get the answers I need.

"Do you remember Russia? When I went with Li—uh, Mr. Martin?"

Annie nods solemnly.

"I…did I win? Did I…"

Her eyes say it all. Suddenly, I am unable to speak. My memories are always so vivid. Yet Liam looks so different. But I remember winning!

She finally shakes her head no and my body feels frozen. I'm unable to move, unable to gather the thoughts that are racing through my mind at top speed. This is not something you misremember. My win got me to the Proms, Sydney Opera House, and Carnegie Hall. This can't be another warped interpretation. The logic doesn't add up; she is mistaken.

I don't think I can handle this piece of the puzzle.

I finally cough out a lame attempt at an excuse. "Oh, yeah, wasn't sure. I mean, I didn't think so, just…unclear, whatever. Never mind, just forget it." I try to lighten the mood with a small, forced laugh.

"You want to hear something crazy?" Annie changes the subject. "When you left, I kind of missed the music. I liked the music more than the loneliness of silence. So, when you would leave home like every other week on your trips, I would teach myself how to play."

"What? Annie! I had no idea!"

"I mean, I use the term 'play' loosely. Now, what was it?"

She starts to play **Für Elise.**

I hold my breath at first, unprepared for the music erupting from the piano. And then, suddenly, everything feels so right.

I let out a breath.

I watch Annie as she plays, and a smile forms on my face.

Then, the music stops.

Annie rests her head on my shoulder, and just like that, we finally take the first step to open the door into each other's psyche. Maybe we won't go inside just yet—not now. But one day, we might understand one another's language.

* * *

The conversation I had with Annie was eye-opening, but it simultaneously pulled me back into the dark. So many unanswered questions, ones I didn't know I had to begin with. To keep my thoughts from becoming anxieties, I need to stay incredulous.

Like how I had never really associated Mummy's behavior with a mental disorder, just her personality.

And the more disturbing accusation. A question so scary I do not want it answered: What makes Annie think I didn't win?

I know I won. I clearly remember it. I remember that day. I remember being wrapped up in Liam's arms. When I finally made the first move and kissed him. I remember Ivan's return. If I didn't win, those details wouldn't have happened. I wouldn't have played at the Proms or signed a record deal with LCR.

Annie must have mistaken my question, or maybe she remembers it differently.

I will have to clear it up with Liam.

Annie must have mistaken it, the same way my mother mistook Annie hating my playing.

Everyone has their way of interpreting the past. Their own version of what happened.

Then the images resurface from the day of the Windsor Competition.

I remember that pain. I remember the doctors telling me not to play. Yet I ignored their wishes, and my fingers were magically okay. I even won. I remember Liam being so proud that I succeeded.

I remember his eyes, his expression. How he breathed a new sense of life into me.

That feeling is what I brought to any challenge I faced.

It was all worth it.

All the hardships, all the late nights, the stiff wrists, the muscle spasms.

Just to feel that sense of accomplishment again.

That sense of worth. Of power.

Yet again I revert to the Liam from my memories. Not the Liam I saw the day before. It's a weird trick my mind is playing on me.

The Liam I saw the other day was a foreigner, and the Liam from my memories is the Liam that feels familiar, the one I hold dear to my heart. It is important that I try to imagine the real Liam, the one I met.

For me to move on, I need reality.

43

FREE

London, Present Day

Finally, the butterflies will be released. They will feed on the newly planted milkweed, and eventually, the garden will return to its former state.

I firmly grasp the large habitat as I study the butterflies—reborn and transformed into something beautiful and brighter.

When I step outside, I see sight that overwhelms my attention.

My breath catches; I fight back tears.

On all fours, with her sun hat and gloves, my mother tends to the plants.

She looks up once she feels my presence.

"Oh, hello, Cleo,"

"Hi Mummy." I can't help but smile. "I see you found some time to focus on the plants." I make sure to come across as humorous and not malicious.

"Well, you know, they're here now. I may as well work on them before Maxime gets here. What have you there?"

"Oh, the butterflies." I hold up the habitat.

"How exciting. Well, the milkweed is ready for them."

I ignore the soil staining my trousers as I sit with my mother.

"All right, are you ready, guys?" I speak to the butterflies, feeling silly and maternal.

I open the gate delicately as I watch the butterflies escape.

We sit there silently, my mother and I.

I will make considerable effort to create new memories instead of lingering in those fragmented by distortion. My heart feels light and content right now, and that is a memory I want to hold on to.

"How have you been, Cleo?"

It seems as though I am making my rounds on this pity tour. I am somehow letting everyone know that I am not okay, getting everyone up to date on my mental state.

It feels medicinal, but, at the same time, I wouldn't say I enjoy giving this energy any attention. I would rather ignore my problems, because then, in that moment, I can feel better. When I think about what is going on, painful feelings overwhelm me like a dark cloud of melancholy, a reality check I don't want.

"Mum, I haven't been so well. I actually have been seeing someone for quite some time."

"You're cheating on Conor?"

"No! Mum, I mean I have been seeing a therapist, okay? Clarice. She is helping me through…" I try to think of the word. "Some struggles. Helping me think with a 'clear head' and live 'in the now.'" I say this ironically; the woo-woo expressions sound almost comical out of my mouth. Still, there is an element of belief in these words.

"She says I'm disassociating by daydreaming, and sometimes I get stuck in my dreams for hours. Except, for some reason, they seem to always revolve around my past. Like I am trying to re-create my years as a pianist and relive all my successes or something."

"Well, that kind of sounds lovely." My mother says this with a dismissive tone, and suddenly I hear myself in these words, speaking to Ciara, glamorizing her impressive imagination.

"Honestly, it is. I don't want to stop,"

"So what's wrong?"

"It's taking over my life. I spend hours stuck in my past instead of focusing on what's actually going on. I want to be in my old life more than my reality sometimes, which is quite depressing if you think about it."

"Darling." My mother places her soft hand on my knee. "I hope you're okay. I'm sorry I never—"

"Yes. Mum, I'm okay, you don't have to—"

She stops me with a finger. "No. I need to say this," she says sternly.

I position myself more comfortably now, staring my mother right in her eyes, wondering where this conversation is going.

"I knew you needed me more as a child. I guess there were times when I just didn't feel capable. I didn't want you to see me..." I can see her trying to find the words. "When I wasn't feeling well. I just thought you were happiest by the piano, so I made sure the piano distracted you. I thought it might be best to wait it out when..." Her voice trails off.

I think about my mother locking her door and *waiting it out*, and how I do the same. It seems safer, sometimes, to conceal myself from others. I thought if I continued to surround myself with people, the stress would ultimately cause me to break down. The best thing for me to do, for my children and for Conor, was to hide until I became the person they deserved. A patient and pleasant person.

"Mummy." I match her stern tone. "What was going on with you? Please spell it out. I need to know." Maybe it will clarify the way my brain works.

"I was sad. Depressed." She lights a cigarette and takes a big inhale. "I was angry that I was depressed. I had so much emotion that I needed to release, or it would get worse. I...I couldn't explain this to you. You were just a child."

I want to ask her, *Why were you sad? Was Daddy not enough? Was I not enough?* But then I remember that I too feel this way, and it in no way reflects on my life, on my kids, on Conor. Our brains just need some tweaking occasionally.

Suddenly, I realize that my mother wasn't taking her collection of pills because she was lazy. She wasn't opting for the easy road. She was trying to put everything together, fill the cracks, mend her well-being.

"I left you with Lottie," my mother continues, "and then with Mr. Martin. I let them take over raising so you could be happy while Daddy and I were busy. But I am doing better now. Cleo, you'll learn how to manage this along the way. You really will."

I smile. It is nice to hear my mother so optimistic. I want to believe her, but I can't help feeling skeptical. Will my kids also be in their thirties by the time I get my shit together?

Then, I hear what she said: *Mr. Martin.* Liam.

I think about my confusions, the revelations of my past. I need another perspective. I know this is the moment to ask.

"Mum, I saw Liam the other day; I didn't recognize him. I remember him to be so, so different. Then again, I seem to have erased so many memories. Maybe I just picture him a bit differently. But is there anything, *anything*, that you can tell me that might help me make sense of all this?"

My mother is hesitant. She shifts her position, gathering her words. "Well, I don't know what to say. Your relationship was intense."

Intense. The same word Annie used.

"Intense how?"

I remember the intensity we brought to our relationship, the magnetic love and desire. I remember the intensity in our achievements, working late, perfecting my repertoire.

"Well, you both worked very hard. And then you would leave for his office and practice for a whole day. Sometimes it would be two or three days before I saw you again."

That was when I was dating him. It must have been. I would stay by Liam's for days on end. I don't know how to confirm this without seeming delusional. "Was this when I was older, when I was gone for days?"

"Yes, I suppose so."

Okay, I remember. I remember living with Liam. That makes sense. I suddenly feel calmer. I am not stretching my imagination. I remember correctly. Annie had me questioning my sanity, but all the while I really did win the competition. She was mistaken.

Annie must be mistaken.

But what if she isn't?

I am no longer calm.

If there were something I needed to know, my mother would inform me, I reassure myself. I am certain.

"And then what? Anything else?" I dig for more answers.

"You always seemed tired and worn out, but if I asked you to take a break, you insisted that you couldn't. You said you wanted to go on. You were always so focused on the next challenge, on the next competition." She goes silent for a moment, like she has to tread lightly. "You seemed so happy, so I just left it at that. I should have forced you to stop at times; it wasn't healthy. I could see you drowning in your clothes, hear you awake in the early hours of the morning. I should have—"

"Really, Mum, it's okay."

I can see her trying to hold back tears.

The happiness she speaks of is still etched in my mind—the stubbornness. To stop playing wasn't an option for me. There was no stopping me.

"I don't blame you for anything, you know that, right? You did what you thought was best. I wouldn't have taken a break if you told me to."

She doesn't respond, but she holds my hand.

It makes me wonder what having a more attentive mother might be like—having someone more stable to watch over me. Then again, it may have hindered my success. Perhaps she needed to be ignorant of my well-being so I could have room to push myself harder.

"You know, I feel like I am doing the same. Ciara is struggling with something. I don't know what, but I see her repeating my mistakes and I still choose to ignore it. I don't think I can handle what's really going on with her, internally."

My mother nods, not wanting to talk in case her tears fall.

"You know something strange," I say to avoid the quiet. "Clarice, she reminds me of you."

"Oh yeah?" A little laugh escapes my mother's lips.

"Yeah, she looks like you, talks exactly like you. It's this weird therapeutic feeling, like she is saying the words I wish you would have said."

A weird noise comes out of my mother's mouth. Like she's trying to conceal her crying.

"Oh no, Mummy, it's okay. I was joking."

"No, you weren't. I am glad you have Clarice. It sounds like she is really helping."

"She is." I smile. It's funny to think how much I ran away from therapy, from helping myself. Like I knew Clarice would try to take away my dreams. It was almost as though I was dependent on the rush I got from my depression and anxiety, and I wasn't ready to let it go.

"You know, dear." My mother's voice reverts to a soft, sober tone. "It's not too late for Ciara. I should have attended to your troubles earlier. I saw you struggle, and I thought a piano would fix all your problems. Annie was always running away to her friends' houses, trying to get out of ours, and I thought, *Let her; it is probably for the best*. I can't change what I did wrong. I can appreciate how well you girls are doing for yourselves. I am so grateful for that, but I know I could have done more. It's not too late for Ciara. If you think she is struggling, help her. She will be just fine."

I nod. Now it's my turn to hold back tears.

44

ZOOMING OUT

London, Present Day

It is time to go back to Liam's. I don't call or tell anyone—I just go. Is he going to be there? This doesn't necessarily matter. It is imperative that I am there, that I go back to that house and take in what I can comprehend.

I stand in front of the stone exterior, looking at the large white wooden door of the grand French country-style home. It is a brutal struggle to get myself to ring the bell, but I succeed.

I don't know who will answer, what I will potentially say or do, but I know these are the inevitable steps I have to take.

"Ah, Cleo. You're back," Liam says with a sense of annoyance.

"Can I come in?"

He doesn't say anything, but gestures for me to follow him. He leads me to his office, and I follow.

There I am, across from Liam. He doesn't offer me a seat. It is clear he doesn't want me to stay.

"To what do I owe this pleasure—again?" When I hear him speak, the French accent feels familiar, yet for some reason, I formulated Liam in my memories with an Irish brogue.

How is this Liam? The same Liam I spent endless hours with? The Liam I once danced with at Pravda, the Liam I chose over Ivan? The Liam I lived with?

I studied his physique, trying to place this Liam in those memories.

"I…I apologize for the way I left last time. I think it was just a lot to take in."

"No apologies needed."

We stay there for another moment, not saying a word. I continue to reconstruct my memories. Why did I distort his face into someone younger? Someone more conventionally charming? I mean, this Liam standing before me is attractive. He is oozing prestige and stature. His button-down fits his muscular torso immaculately. His cheekbones are prominent, his eyes an icy blue. So why? What was the point in all the perversion?

Liam claps his hands together. "So will that be it? I have a very busy day today. Lots and lots of meetings."

"Well." I stay still. "I really must speak with you. For just a moment." I look him deep in his eyes. "Please."

He impatiently looks at his watch. "Okay, go, just please hurry."

The pressure is brewing inside me. Where to start? I can't possibly hurry with all my confusion and displacement.

"Okay, well, um. I'm just making sure…"

His eyebrows raise, urging me to get on with it.

"You were my coach from when I was sixteen, correct?"

"Yes."

Okay, we have a solid foundation—all true.

"You were with me in Russia?"

"Cleo, I mean, come on—"

"Liam!"

"What?"

"Yes?"

"Yes." His chest rises rapidly. He wants to go, but this time I refuse to leave without answers.

"Do you have any clue as to what went on in Russia?"

"You told me already, you remember—"

"I didn't win, did I?" I blurt this out, hoping he will correct me.

"You really don't remember anything?" Liam asks, almost amused.

"No. I-I don't know." I hesitate. "I am not sure if you're trying to protect my feelings or brush me off, but I have to know what happened. Did I win?"

"Well, you disappeared on the first night."

"Disappeared?" My brain can't catch up; I have forgotten how to breathe. What is he saying?

"You were backstage, all set to perform. Then they called your name, and you didn't show up. That was it."

"So where was I? Wait." I pause, suddenly realizing with a sharp pain in my heart. "So that means…" I say each word slowly as I comprehend what I am about to ask. "You're saying I didn't compete at all? I never won?"

"No, you didn't win." His response sounds more annoyed than comforting. "That was your first round. You never made it. You left Russia after that night."

My pulse begins to race as I vaguely recall the night. It plays out in my mind. At first, everything seems blurry. I can't focus on the images that are attacking me. The memories remain on the tip of my tongue; I am so close to identifying them. It feels like I am watching a movie in a foreign language. Some of the visuals make sense, and some are incoherent.

Then it hits me.

My past, my memories, my euphoria, my place of escape—gone.

"Ivan?" Suddenly, I make a heartbreaking discovery.

Please, tell me this holds an element of truth.

An expression of confusion adorns Liam's face.

I repeat, "Ivan. I never met Ivan?"

"I don't know. What are you saying? Who are you talking about?"

"But I remember him so clearly. He does exist!" I beg. Out of everything, I need this to be true.

Liam lets out a big huff, and a hand covers his face. "Listen, Cleo. I am not sure I know what you are talking about, and I don't think I am the one to help you here."

I ignore his frustration as I allow my mind to slowly process what I am hearing.

"I never stayed in Russia?" I repeat my question. "I never stayed in Russia!" My head is spinning. I am having a hard time staying upright.

"No," Liam finalized.

"I-I…I'm sorry. I need a moment." I have to stay here, with Liam, in his office. I promised myself I wouldn't leave without answers this time. Yet I can't be in Liam's presence right now. Not like this. Not while I am breaking inside.

I rush to the bathroom immediately without waiting for a reply.

My hands tremble as I manage to lock the door behind me. I pace the bathroom, shaking my hands, trying to absorb further revelations. I begin to shiver, and suddenly, my knees buckle, pulling me down to the cold porcelain tiles.

I stay there on the ground, unable to pick myself up. My hands tremble as I reach for my phone and headphones in my bag. My mind has to access these memories quickly, and music is the only thing that can bring me to a stable, tranquil state.

When **Dvořák - Symphony No. 9**, 4th Movement fills my ears, I close my eyes. I try to take myself back to the first moment I saw Ivan.

Backstage, in his quiet corner, practicing **Romance in F minor.**

He was real, I know it.

I feel those moments. I can identify those emotions.

He was real.

I thought about the moment outside the Moscow Conservatory.

Privet, I remember him saying.

I picture his blue eyes, his icy blond hair, his dimple. Oh, his dimple. Then the image becomes pixelated.

I was abandoned outside the conservatory. Alone.

Ivan was not there.

Come back! I need these memories! Don't fade away!

I imagine our walk to Kuznetsky Most Street, the visit to Ivan's industrial building, Dom. But he is fading from these images.

He was never there.

The visuals evaporate one by one, and I am unable to discern what I was seeing clearly. I start to hyperventilate. I cover my mouth with my hand as I heavily pant.

Come on, brain! Catch on! Don't bail on me!

I see myself in my blush silk camisole and matching robe. I play the **Hungarian Dance** with Ivan's tie wrapped around my eyes. I can hear his encouraging voice cheering me on while my illusions create a complete symphony right inside of Hotel Metropol.

And then the thud of the door when Liam catches us in the moment. The symphony disappears; so does the tie around my neck, and then so does Ivan. He dissolves into thin air.

I was alone. Alone with Liam. The real Liam. Mr. Martin.

"*Merde*, Cleo!" His harsh French filled the room as I stayed put on the piano chair.

Tears were streaming down my face. I could feel the warm saltiness cover my cheeks. My eyes were red and dry.

Suddenly, I am roused from my memories by a knock. I hold my breath.

"Cleo?"

I pull out one headphone.

I can feel the tears on my cheeks. Am I crying? Did he hear me?

I hurriedly get up and check my reflection.

I see a worn-out and unfamiliar reflection looking back at me. Eyes dried out and red. Face flushed.

"Cleo? Do I need to break in? Are you in there?"

I ignore him as I turn up the volume.

My fingernails imprint the palms of my hands. I am trying so hard to stay focused on what is real.

Then it hits me.

Ivan existed, but only for a moment.

It was backstage, before I performed, that I encountered him.

It happened.

My gaze strayed into his practice room.

My memories of those feelings are vivid. I was drawn to Ivan by an overwhelming sense of gravity. I didn't know how to separate myself from him. I could feel the sounds of Dvořák infiltrate my heart.

As Ivan looked up from his violin, he stopped playing. There was a brief moment of eye contact. I could not hide my presence now that he'd noticed me lurking. In that millisecond, I felt as if time had stood still, and I was floating through the air. I quickly regained my composure and walked away.

That was it. After that, I never saw Ivan again.

I never heard his backstory, I never listened to him play. I never learned about Russian music or Russian poetry.

I fantasized about a life with Ivan, and for what? Where did it get me? Why am I holding on to this one moment shared with a stranger, and why did I exaggerate it into a lifelong fantasy?

Suddenly, I am on top of a building, looking down at a commotion. There are a multitude of pedestrians looking up at me, Liam included. I can hear the sirens.

My heart begins to palpitate, and I rip out my headphones.

Liam almost falls when I open the door. I am surprised he's still there, leaning against the door.

"Ah, you're alive." He says this with annoyance. He then begins walking to the front door. I want him to stop, so I shout after him.

"Okay, I know Ivan never existed."

He turns around and approaches me with heavy steps.

"I don't know an Ivan!" I can hear him trying to keep his cool. It isn't working. With each word, his voice grows louder.

"I know, I know. But—"

"Cleo, I have a meeting in ten minutes. Can't this wait?"

"No!" I cry. "I need to know. I won't leave until I understand everything."

"You won't leave?"

"I can't," I plead. "Liam, I need to know."

He rubs his eyes in frustration. "Ten minutes." He gives in. "What do you need to know?"

I have to speak up, fast.

"What happened in Russia? Why did I run away?"

"I don't know, Cleo, you tell me. I didn't hear from you after that first night of the competition."

"The first night," I repeat, hoping again that he will correct me. I have to make sure I understand this.

"Yes! The first night! You had, I don't know, some psychotic break. You went crazy. And then..." He whistles and waves his hand into thin air. "You left. You were gone. I haven't heard from you ever since." He starts walking to his office, and I follow.

"Why? That doesn't sound like me. I needed that competition. Everything we worked so—"

"I don't think I have the answers you are looking for, Cleo."

I feel defeated. I know I am so close, yet now I feel farther from the truth than ever before.

"But..."

Liam walks into his office and grabs his briefcase. "Cleo, I must be leaving."

"I-I can't leave." I walk over to his desk, standing across from him now.

His arm is extended toward the door when he says, "You have to go, because I have to go."

My body remains motionless. "I can't, Liam," I say in desperation, barely finding my voice.

His face turns a few shades pinker. "Okay! Stay! I'll be back within the hour." He mumbles some French under his breath and shuts the door behind him.

When the door shuts, my body flinches. It isn't the loud bang that startles me, but the impression that feels so familiar. Like I've heard that specific door shut.

And lock, come to think of it.

I hurry toward the door and lightly rest my fingers on the gold keyhole underneath the handle. As my breath quickens, I instinctively turn the handle to see if it's locked. It isn't. Breathing becomes easier again.

Why did I think he would lock me in?

My examination of his office continues. Liam certainly didn't think through leaving me here, in this room full of his belongings. Did he know I would examine his possessions? Find more clues? He might have been too distracted to consider that possibility.

Muscle memory guides my fingers across the spines of the books.

I find the book I was so hesitant to look through on my last visit. I mentally prepare myself to open it.

The Book of Russian Poetry.

I grab it before my brain tells me not to.

I flick through the pages. Several corners are folded.

The first one reads: Mikhail Lermontov, "I Thank You."

My fingers skim across the words. I could recite them; they have become so familiar to me.

"Oh, let your gaze show coldness to me,

Let it kill hopes and dreams"

I read the poem out loud.

Ivan sent me this poem, I remember.

I continue through to the next folded page: "The Dream" by Alexander Pushkin. Another one of Ivan's poems.

Again, I read it aloud.

I flip through more pages.

All the folded pages are poems from Ivan.

"The Other One" by Nikolay Gumilev.

"I See You, My Dear, In Dreams" by Aleksey Apukhtin.

"Confession" by Alexander Pushkin.

I freeze. My mind returns to the fact that Ivan doesn't exist.

What is this? Some construed way of holding on to a romance?

I feel sick.

I am sick.

Why did I create this relationship? What did I lack that led me to conceive such a connection?

If it wasn't Ivan, who sent me these poems? Who folded the pages? Was it Liam?

I stop and put the book back.

Liam won't reveal any insight to me, so I keep looking for meaning.

Then I see it.

An elegant white Steinway & Sons piano in the corner. The one I couldn't bear to look at, couldn't touch the last visit.

Just go, I tell myself. *Try to feel the piano, touch the piano, go back to the place where you spent so much of your life. Back to the essence of who you once were.*

I walk slowly, taking each individual step with great force.

There I stand, facing the majestic instrument.

Slowly, my hand caresses the keys.

I force my way onto the bench and press the arch of my foot onto the peddle.

My eyes shut. I cannot not fully absorb everything at once. When my eyes open again, I start to play.

My fingers slowly make out the melody of **Lizst, La Campanella**. The vibrations spread through my veins. An all-encompassing, overwhelming feeling rushes through me. I start playing and can't stop. I am revisiting a high, injecting it into my veins, ingesting ecstasy.

I feel a rush of emotions. They all come pouring in, too quickly to release in tears, too suddenly to react. I just feel.

My mind escapes me, and I am in my old body, the one I inhabited a decade ago.

I somehow feel numb while simultaneously sensing everything.

I am living in the sphere I have occupied for two consecutive decades.

Upon leaving my body, my mind recalls actual events from behind closed doors—the precursor to the traumatic moments of my life. If I wasn't making an effort to find the memories I'd lost, I probably wouldn't revisit them at all.

That vision reappears in my mind.

From on top of a building, I am fixated by the people surrounding me below.

This memory is too overwhelming—I stop playing.

Breathe.

I close my eyes and try again.

Now I remember this room, Liam's office.

The way the door slammed, following with the lock. Sometimes Liam was with me, sometimes he was not. The expectation was for me to stay inside and play.

Play and play and play.

At times, I found perfection within a few hours. Other times, it took me days.

A memory of playing **Beethoven's Appassionata** comes back to me.

"Again!" he shouted.

"Again!" he shouted until I broke.

Tears slowly streamed out of my eyes as I rubbed my wrist.

I remember now. It wasn't my writs I was rubbing; it was my fingers, my knuckles. It was the day Annie slammed the piano shut. I came home from the hospital, and Liam was furious with me. I had a competition the next day, and somehow the bandages were my fault.

He rubbed his eyes in frustration, and then his tone of voice settled again.

"One moment."

He went to the corner of his office.

"Here." He handed me a tall glass of water and some pills.

The water looked misty. I hesitated, and Liam gestured for me to take the glass.

"Drink up. This will help ease the pain."

Liam's presence intoxicated me; I was incapable of objecting. How could I question his methods when they were a testament to his success? I would do as he said. It was easier.

I placed the pills on my tongue and downed the liquid quickly, on command. It would help, and that was all that mattered now. I needed to win tomorrow.

"Play," Liam demanded. "See if your fingers are working. It's your choice to play tomorrow. But at least you'll know you tried."

My choice.

I believed I had a choice, that it was all up to me.

I played the sonata. I played it again and again, until my fingers were numb.

The drink was proving to be helpful.

I am immediately hit with another memory, a day I was practicing my repertoire with Liam by my side.

I was playing trills with my right hand, and my left played a melody. I was tired, and my technique wasn't up to par. Without saying a word, Liam stood up and started making his concoction. I peered over to the corner of his office. His back was facing me, and I tried to make out his actions. It seemed as though he was using his muddler to crush something into the glass before filling it up with filtered water. He poured himself a glass of Lagavulin and returned to me. I quickly reverted my gaze to the piano, so he didn't catch me distracted.

At first, the drinks relieved my pain. They helped with my headaches. My attention was heightened; I was alert. If Liam saw I couldn't keep up with his stamina, if I grew tired or my fingers began to stiffen, he made another concoction.

He called them remedies, and remedies were medicinal. They must have been safe to drink.

It's like it's happening in front of me right now. All I can see is Liam in the corner of his office, and…that muddler! Its ominous presence caught my attention last visit, and I couldn't figure out why it left me feeling uneasy—until now.

I shake my head, trying to rid the vivid imagery from my mind. I stand up from the piano and walk hesitantly over to the corner of his office. There, like in years prior, was Liam's bar. The glasses, the bottles, the shaker, the muddler. Everything in its right place.

Where would I find those remedies? Were they some kind of medication? Were they narcotics? How far did Liam take this?

Just then, the sound of the door swinging open catches me off guard.

I let out a yelp.

45

GOODBYE FOREVER

London, Present Day

"Cleo, you're still here."

"Mr. Martin." I whispered.

"Oh, so now we are back to formalities? How polite." There was a hint of sarcasm in his voice, sarcasm, and ridicule.

"Mr. Martin," I repeat, as though I just learned his name. "I never called you Liam, did I?"

"Not until the last visit, no."

"I never dated you either."

Mr. Martin lets out a loud, hefty laugh. It is insulting how loud and sincere it is. "No, Cleo. We never dated." As if I'd told him the sky wasn't blue.

I was slow to connect the dots, but now I can see clearly. How was it possible we dated when I left Russia after day one of the competition?

My time in Russia doesn't exist.

My time in Russia is a realm that I created, not one participated in.

"Please, humor me. I told you I lost most of my memories."

"And from what you've gathered, you believe we dated."

I remain silent. I'm embarrassed now, and I don't know how to respond.

But watching Mr. Martin chuckle at the idea of dating me makes my blood boil.

320

I need answers. If Ivan never existed, if I never dated Mr. Martin, what were these memories?

"Well, what about the poems? Why do I remember these?" I head for the bookshelf. I grab *The Book of Russian Poetry* and open it, exposing its folded corners. "Why do I remember these poems? Poems you own, poems you folded?"

"I did not fold them, Cleo. You did." His voice is composed, calm.

"I…"

"Some days, I would come to the office expecting you to be practicing, and I would catch you going through my books instead."

I'm starting to remember—the horror of getting caught in the act. His anger at finding me by his books.

His roaring voice echoes in my head: "Get your head out of those fucking books and go back to the piano! Do you think you will become anything if you allow yourself distraction?"

"But my hands hurt," I cried.

"But my hands hurt." He mimicked my weak disposition. "You think I let that get in my way? Do you think any great musician succumbs to the pain? *Non!* Great musicians fight! They persevere! And they succeed!" Our faces were close enough that I could smell his cologne. I could feel the heat from his fire burning within. Feel the vibrations of his anger. And then I heard him whisper the words I dreaded: "Well, maybe, Cleo, it is not the right time for you to work with me."

"So I…" I furrow my brow, finding my words. "I folded them? Not you, not anyone?"

"Yes, Cleo," his voice drips with anger once more. "I don't know how many times I can stress. I. Don't. Have. Time. For. This."

Mr. Martin locked me in. There were moments I couldn't play anymore. My fingers were swollen and throbbing, my upper back knotted with muscle spasms, and my eyes were red and twitched involuntarily. I would walk around his office, entertaining myself with his collection of books. This one in particular. Love poems from famous Russian poets.

That was how I felt toward Ivan, Liam. Mr. Martin.

Each poem contained a meaning I hoped Mr. Martin would decipher. I wanted him to make sense of the messages I was sending him.

Words of devotion and passion.

Messages that exposed my hopes and desires.

It was an act of love to fight for Mr. Martin's affection. I wanted his love to be as great as mine was for him.

Through these poems, I hoped he would see me in a different perspective. To open his eyes, so he could see why I was important to him. That he wanted me in his life just as much as I needed him.

Mr. Martin's influence dominated my life. The man possessed determination and talent.

I don't know if what I experienced then was love. It was admiration. It was awe. It was jealousy.

To me, emulating him, becoming just like him, accomplishing as much as he had was paramount.

Were these feelings reciprocated at any time? My mind had tricked me into believing they were.

Now, I have no idea.

"What about the necklace?' I blurt out.

"Necklace?" I am losing him. His patience is barely there. "What necklace?"

"This necklace!" I clutch the gold chain, red pendant. *The* necklace! I haven't been able to take it off. It was like a lifeline to a fading memory, tethered to me in ways I can't explain. "The carnelian stone! You bought it, didn't you?"

"Yes."

My heart stops. There is one thing I remember correctly. Can this be an indication of something, that my memories aren't all lies?

"That was a gift for my wife. I did not give it to you. In fact, I am not really sure how you got it."

"Your wife?" I ask this like a question, but it is more of a statement. "Your wife," I repeat. I remember his wife. That short, gaunt, incredibly chic Frenchwoman in the gold frame.

"Yes, my wife. Vivian." Mr. Martin inhales a deep breath, showing the control of his temper.

The image of me hiding the necklace comes to life in my head. Now I know why. He never gave it to me.

My mind rewinds to the day I found the white bag on Mr. Martin's desk.

Inside was a box wrapped in a gray ribbon. Mr. Martin wouldn't be back for another two hours. I removed the box from the bag and opened it to see what was inside. In awe, I examined the gold chain, the red pendant, the sparkling diamond halo. I then tucked it into my pocket.

Why?

Why did I need it? I could never wear it around Mr. Martin, and I was always around him. Why did I keep this necklace for myself? Was it an act of rebellion? Of passion? Of desire?

"Cleo." Mr. Martin snaps his fingers close to my face, the way he always did when I zoned out. I blink back to reality.

"Look, I am a busy man. Will you please let yourself out?" He sits behind his desk and starts looking over documents.

I don't let myself out. I stay there, ready to say anything to get him to point me in the right direction.

"The muddler!" I croak.

"Come ON, CLEO!" His patience is gone. The loud thud of his fist on his desk, the tone of his voice, it is all so familiar. "You are really testing my patience," he growls.

"The muddler, Mr. Martin. I remember that." My chest is pounding. My voice is breaking.

Another deep breath escapes his lips as he buries his face in his hands. I am his relentlessly needy child who won't go away, won't leave him to his work.

"I remember those remedies you used to make. What were they?"

"Cleo." His voice is strict and quiet. While he leans over his desk, his fingers grip its surface. "You come to MY HOUSE!" He is shouting. "And accuse me of dating you, and what? DRUGGING YOU? I don't have time for this!"

The volume of his voice freezes my insides, but I have to commit. It is imperative that I seize this last opportunity.

"What were in the drinks, Mr. Martin?" I try to match his stern tone, but it comes out shaky, and I am not sure I succeed.

"All you have to know is that they were safe and natural. Vivian is a homeopathic doctor. She makes them for me. She knew what she was providing. It's like a tea, or a supplement."

"What was it?" I repeat. "Did it make me go crazy? Is that why I blanked out and ran away in Russia?"

"*Tu te moques de moi?*" He has had it with me. French always accompanied his temper. "It had nothing to do with you leaving. I didn't even give you the supplements for about a year before Russia. Do you think I gave you something to make you go crazy? Cleo, do you know who I am? I am the top teacher in all of Europe. I managed musicians at levels you could only dream of. You may have asked for our partnership, but ultimately it was my choice to work with you."

He steps out from behind his desk, moves closer, and towers over me in a display of power. "Do you know how many clients I had to give up for you, and do you know what happened when I made all your dreams come true? What did you do? You escaped! You ran to the top of the conservatory instead of competing. And you think it was me who was responsible for all that? You pretentious, spoiled bitch!"

"I'm sorry" is my automatic reply. Yet I know deep in my gut that, yes. Liam, Mr. Martin, was indeed the reason I ran away. The reason I couldn't compete. He was the reason I gave up my dreams and never played again.

"You were never a substitute teacher, were you?"

"Don't insult me, Cleo." Mr. Martin looks disgusted.

I recognize this now. The memories flood in while he yells at me.

The first time I laid eyes on Mr. Martin was at the London Music Conservatory. He came as a guest speaker, not a substitute teacher.

When I was brought up in front of the class to play Rachmaninoff, I felt an instinctive infatuation. His instructions were clear and concise, telling me exactly what I needed to know to improve my technique. It was the first time I tasted real satisfaction, and it was all because of Mr. Martin.

We had our first proper introduction at my house several months later. My mother informed me that Mr. Martin would attend an event at our home, and she wanted to introduce us.

I was ecstatic. In my room, I overanalyzed every item of clothing I would wear. I paid attention to every detail. My hair, my makeup, what I was going to say when I got a chance to speak with him.

My mother called me downstairs to perform for the guests, for Mr. Martin. It didn't take long for him to recognize my potential, and he took me on as a client right there.

Because of his connections, I had the privilege of playing at prestigious events. I was entered into top competitions. It was Mr. Martin who built me up. His efforts shaped me into the musician I once was.

I had distorted it all. My life became an amalgam of recollections and fictions.

What caused all this confusion?

"Just tell me what was in the drink," I say after the yelling subsides, "and then I promise I will leave." I stay there, stoic.

"Oh, for fuck's sake!" He hurries to his kitchen, and I follow.

Margarette stands there, trying to look busy, unsure of what else to do.

He pulls a box containing several small amber tincture bottles from the shelf above the sink and shoves it toward me. "Here, look."

"What? Which ones?"

"I don't know, maybe this one." He reads a label and hands it to me. "This. I think."

You think? I struggle to read the bottles while juggling the box.

I look at one.

"Tianeptine?" And another: "DMAE?" I turn the bottle to read the nutrition label. "What are these?"

"They. Are. Supplements." He emphasizes each word with anger. "They help with attention, with performance. I wouldn't give you anything that would interfere with your performance. Use your brain."

Tianeptine, DMAE, I repeat in my head. I can remember those names. Are there other bottles he's just too impatient to show me?

Perhaps the drinks weren't the direct cause of what transpired in Russia, but they had to have at least some influence on me running away. I had to believe this. I am not someone who is willing to leave everything behind.

"Just these two?"

"Now go. You've stayed here long enough." He ignores my question and walks me to the front door. The handle looks close to breaking as he opens it.

"One more thing," I say as I turn around.

He huffs out a laugh.

"When you found me that night of the competition, you said I was on the roof of the conservatory?"

He takes a calming breath and relaxes his tone. Maybe he thinks I am finally done with my accusations. "Yes."

The knot in my stomach grows. I am not sure I can hold myself up.

"How?" Slowly, I begin to recall the events of that night.

I remember the moment I opened my eyes—that feeling of being terrified, confused as to how I got there. I remember looking down; it felt like I was hundreds of meters high." The people were shouting nonsense at me.

"There was a small balcony on the top floor. It looked like you got up from there."

"Yes, but why? How? It just doesn't make sense that I would do that!"

He shrugs, as if I asked what he wanted for dinner, like it has no real impact on his life.

"I just don't understand why I would run away like that."

"I don't know. As I said, I never saw you since. You went back home shortly after and quit. Now, if you don't mind." He gestures his arm toward his front door.

I have to get my last words out. "You know what you did was wrong."

"What I did? What did I do?" He belittles my feelings with his condescending tone, but I continue. It's my last chance.

"You pushed me. You forced me to the edge until I had to jump off, leave. You locked me in that room. Sometimes I didn't eat. I didn't sleep. You would 'remedy' me to a place of perfection. And the worst part is, you think it's all okay."

His tone matches mine: cool and heartless. "You are just upset you couldn't make it. You need to find someone else to blame for your failures. Do you think I pushed you off the edge? You were just as determined as I was, Cleo. You were passionate, and you fought for your wins, so you can't come now and complain that I pushed you too hard. Passion is passion. And we both had it."

In the chilling grip of his persuasive words, I found him convincing, in some twisted way, he is right. Yet here I stood, alone in the shadow of this formidable, enigmatic figure, as his relentless pursuit of my success had morphed into a nightmarish obsession. My well-being was an afterthought in the pursuit of his ambition.

His singular goal was my triumph, and he spared no cruelty to push me to succeed. Days bled into nights, and he became my tormentor, my personal demon, forcing me to dance to his macabre symphony of dominance. He saw red, and even though I did too, I was the one who suffered.

I knew our narratives would forever remain in a perpetual clash of perspectives. He would never acknowledge himself as the villain.

Gathering the remnants of my strength, I summoned the courage to voice my truth and rid my soul of the demons that had tormented me. I looked back one last time to confront the man who had plagued my dreams for so long.

"Goodbye, Mr. Martin," I declared with unwavering resolve, a tremor of sadness and liberation in my voice. It was a farewell, a farewell that echoed with the weight of eternity.

Goodbye, forever.

46

A CHARMING DREAM

London, Present Day

That night, as I lie in bed, earbuds in, I stare at the ceiling. It's time to go back to the beginning.

I close my eyes.

I can hear **Tchaikovsky - Concerto No. 1** playing in my ears. Now I see my memories from a distance rather than up close. They appear as illusions, movies projected over me.

I imagine myself in a room backstage at the Moscow Conservatory.

I was applying my red lipstick in my red Ulyana Sergeenko gown. I could see what was going on outside the dressing room: audience members finding their seats, fanning off the heat with their programs. I saw the orchestra on stage, tweaking their instruments. The event coordinator making his last-minute orders.

Then I see me. My eyes were wide open, my pupils dilated. My mind was elsewhere, hypnotized, or possibly sedated, like I was dreaming yet conscious. My gaze was set beyond my reflection in the mirror.

There were no murky concoctions in sight. No pills or supplements. No proof as to why I was in this hypnotic trance.

I watch myself rise and walk out of the room in this soporific state. I expect to see myself walking through the double mahogany doors that lead me to the stage, but I don't. I am heading in the opposite direction, out of the room and up the stairs.

I continue toward the staircase, going up a level, and then another and another. An empty room beckons me, and I find an open window that leads me to the roof.

I'm not wearing my coat. I'm not even wearing my heels. I don't seem cold. I don't seem to feel anything.

I peer back at what is going inside the building.

"Cleo Wilson, United Kingdom." The announcement is broadcast over the mic. Applause erupts.

When I don't come out, he tries again.

"Cleo Wilson."

I now see Liam, Mr. Martin. Ruthless, nostrils flared, sweating from anger. He runs to the room backstage and notices I have gone. He is screaming.

My whereabouts have ostracized him, and he ventures outside of the hall to sniff them out.

Outside, there's a loud commotion, and he knows instantly what has caused the uproar.

I am on the roof of the Moscow Conservatory. I am not scared. I am smiling. I am conducting an invisible symphony—only I can hear it to be Tchaikovsky. No matter who orders me to get down—the urgent calls to 112 or the curses Mr. Martin is hurling at me—I cannot hear them.

Gradually, in the distance, I hear the sirens. As they get louder, my eyelids begin to open.

I can identify my surroundings. I am in a white room. My red gown has been switched for hospital attire.

I open my eyes and quickly remove my headphones. I'm sweating heavily and panting rapidly.

I can't fall back asleep.

I pace the room, trying to reassemble my past.

The pieces are finally coming together.

My first encounter with Mr. Martin was when I was sixteen. He took me on as a client.

It was the imbalance of power, intensity, and chaos that fueled our relationship. I willingly obeyed Mr. Martin's commands. He held the secrets to my success, so I trusted him. I trusted that he would get me to the top. Therefore, I followed.

Until I reached an impasse.

For a while, this system worked for us. We dreamed big and surpassed our goals. I manifested competing at the Moscow Classical Competition, and Mr. Martin got me there.

This system, however, was short-lived. By the time I arrived in Russia, I was depleted and exhausted. The joy of classical music had been ripped from me, and I was left with nothing but a shell of the person I once was.

I recall the day before the competition.

It was my first time allowing Mr. Martin to see my vulnerabilities.

"I can't do this." I fought back tears.

I was practicing my concerto in my room at the Hotel Metropol. We were approaching the third hour. My fingers had started cramping, and my mind turned hazy. My body was weak, slowly deteriorating, making it increasingly difficult to perform with such ferocity.

"That was horrible." I had a rare moment of premature defeat. As if I already knew I wasn't capable.

To even consider taking part in such a grand competition, one must be an exceptionally accomplished musician with outstanding ability and proficiency. When you are competing with hundreds of supremely qualified competitors, you must already be elite.

I took all the correct steps, made all the right choices. I had to devote extra practice hours, compete in multiple competitions, and sacrifice my youth.

I managed to get this far, only to find myself too weak to go any further.

Mr. Martin didn't say anything. He was holding back from letting the words escape his lips. We both knew this competition required grit and determination. Weakness had no place here, so Mr. Martin ignored my blatant display of vulnerability.

Our plan was to forget this minor hiccup of self-destruction and proceed with sovereign dominance tomorrow. We assumed it was an unfortunate, preemptive jitter.

On the day of the first round, I sat backstage, hollow and weak. I was unable to move my cramped fingers. My arms were sore; everything ached.

I remember wanting Mr. Martin to concoct a remedy for me. I looked over to him, wide eyed, and he simply shook his head no.

Liam.

Mr. Martin.

My vision. My world.

The man I thought I had loved. The man I had romanticized. The man of my dreams.

I think of Pushkin's "The Dream."

I have read it so often that it has become part of my mental archive, and seeing it yesterday was a stabbing realization to the heart.

"Not long ago, in a charming dream I saw myself..."

I close my eyes and recite the words out loud as I put all my pieces together. How truly this played into my reality. The accuracy of the words. The way they manifested.

"I was in love with you, it seemed, and heart was beating with a pleasure."

Tears start to emerge from my eyes as I continue.

"...Why, dreams, you didn't prolong my happiness forever?"

I choked out the last sentence, "I only lost the kingdom of my dreams."

When I dreamed of my past, I adapted it into a story more likable, more enjoyable.

I relived my memories with alternative endings.

The question still lingers: what would have happened if I'd stayed in Moscow?

Would I have played my first round as rehearsed? Would I have waited outside the hall to meet the Russian violinist?

I could have had my first-round victory, followed by winner-take-all dominance. It could have been seamless.

Did casting Mr. Martin as the charming young teacher make the story more realistic? Someone who could reciprocate my love? Someone who could eventually see me as an equal?

A teacher like Mr. Martin would have never fallen for a girl like me, given his status, his accomplishments—not to mention his marriage. There was no world in which he could view me as an equal because I was not his equal.

My privilege was to be in his presence, to learn from a teacher of such radiance and virtuosity. He was gifted, and I felt honored to have the opportunity to be under his wing, to be mentored by him.

I have lived this version of my story on repeat for the past ten years. I have blurred the lines and lost sight of reality.

I grab a pillow and scream into it.

I can't cry. I can't feel bad for myself. I just feel deceived, broken. I feel lost.

How much of my past have I verbalized? What have I told people? And why did no one stop me, tell me what actually went on? Why didn't Annie, Conor, or my parents ever provide me with information regarding my past?

Come to think of it, how much does Conor really know?

My mind is spinning with these questions.

I look over my journals from the past few weeks.

Lies. Lies. Lies.

I flick through them hastily as the heat permeates my body.

What is this? I study the words I've arranged on paper.

He told me the song was called **Millions of Red Roses**. It was about an artist who tried to win the heart of a lady who loved roses. He sold his art and his home for an ocean of them. Then Ivan went on to tell me they don't end up together, so now the artist is alone with nothing but millions of roses.

I thought it was a tragedy, but Ivan shrugged and said he thought it was romantic.

Lies.

I look at another journal entry.

Liam looked serious. He was telling me how he knew it may seem weird because he's known me since I was young. He pleaded and asked if we could at least try. See where it takes us. I said yes, despite Ivan.

Lies!

I grasp both ends of the journal, but I resist the urge to tear it to shreds.

My panting grows louder. My chest heaves.

I look around the room and grab my phone to dial Clarice.

"Pick up, pick up, pick up!" I pant as I pace the room.

She picks up. "Hello?"

"Clarice! I need you!" I beg. "I need to speak with you!"

"Are you in trouble?"

"It's all a lie! Everything I've told you about my past is a lie." My voice is shaking.

"What do you mean?" I can picture her getting out of bed.

"Ivan. The competition. I never made it! I never had a relationship with Liam." My tears come pouring out.

"Okay, slow down. I'm listening. What did you find out?"

"I went over to Liam's. I remember! I remember everything!"

47

SIDE EFFECTS

London, Present Day

I tell Clarice about my breakthrough. I compare the Liam from my dreams to the Liam I spoke to yesterday. I tell her about the necklace, the poems. These elements, warped inside my head, muddled together to create a different story. I have been an unreliable narrator of my own past. I became so immersed in the edit that I actually believed it.

Clarice encourages me to write everything down, separate from my existing journal entries, so that we can compare, analyze, and hopefully put all of this behind us.

I agree. Instead of trying to sleep that night, I whip out my notebook and start jotting down a timeline.

My daydreams begin with that first round in Russia, and they end with me picking Liam over Ivan.

And then I start all over again. I always return to that day in Russia.

It's as if I can't come up with a satisfying ending, so I restart, hoping it will eventually come to me.

I write down:

Backstage, red gown, red lipstick, eyes dilated.

Seeing everyone below me from the roof of the conservatory.

The next thing I can remember is waking up in a hospital.

According to the doctors, this incident was the result of exhaustion.

334

When I awoke, I was alone. Mr. Martin didn't accompany me. He never checked to see if I was okay. He never followed up afterward. Mr. Martin was out of my life just as quickly as he entered it.

Real memories.

I have flashbacks while listening to music, without music, during the middle of my day, without any prior preparation. The frequency with which my mind became absorbed in these narratives increased.

Flashes of my past fill my mind with the memories I had forgotten.

I had lifted the veil, revealing the truth behind each fabrication.

My vivid recollections continue:

I'm playing **Beethoven - Piano Sonata No. 27** on Mr. Martin's piano. My hair is tied into a plait that falls just above my waist. My petite body sways to the melody, and a smile appears on my face. This is where I belong.

But I can also clearly see my blistered fingers and my cramped right heel as I press the pedal.

I can see myself throwing up bile before shows, the feeling of nausea that followed, the overwhelming desire to perfect the sonatas. If I erroneously hit one key, my progress is broken.

I see myself standing in empty arenas before performances. The overwhelming sense of loneliness is palpable.

My reality.

These are the authentic narratives that allow me to recognize Mr. Martin for who he really was: a controlling teacher and a manipulative coach. He locked me in his office for days at a time, and yet I was infatuated with him, his talent, his power. I wanted to be like Mr. Martin, and I wanted so badly for him to see me as an assertive, influential pianist.

I viewed us as an undefeated power couple. I imagined a world where we utilized my abilities and his perception of my strengths perfectly.

The toxic nature of our relationship is suddenly apparent. The mutual power of our determination and strength provided fuel for each other. Our perseverance and hard work allowed us to get places.

Delusions. I'd folded the pages of those poems hoping he would delve deeper into their meaning. Hoping he would read into what I was trying to convey—love, hope, and desire.

The necklace I'd stolen from his desk was a little piece of my fantasy. Inside the box, a paper read: The carnelian stone invigorates strength and willpower. It brings calm, builds ambition, and removes negativity, silence, and fears.

I'd grabbed that necklace because I wanted to live in a world where Mr. Martin would buy me such a present.

I never wore it. I hid it. I took it off Mr. Martin's desk, and that same day I hid it in my room.

No logical explanation underlined these actions.

It was a consequence of passion.

Passion and fantasy.

Now I understand why I can't touch the piano anymore. In the end, it is what forced me to undergo this metamorphosis. Over the last decade, I'd built up a new, eventless life while articulating a reimagined story of my past.

I never met Ivan. I never won the first round or strolled Kuznetsky Most Street. I never danced with Liam. He never gave me the red pendant. I never played at the Proms.

If all that had transpired, I would not have met Conor. We met eight months after that night in Russia.

I was sitting alone at a lavish bar, not touring the world, contemplating life with Ivan or Liam.

Was this my best version of a happy ending?

The stories I crafted in my subconscious were all based on passion and love.

Passion for success, for belonging, for contentment.

Where would I be if…

I've wasted my whole life trying to design the perfect past, one that could only be realized through fantasy.

In reality, I got stood up on a date. A serendipitous meeting led me to the person I married.

Somehow I did not find that satisfactory.

I still wondered what if?

I grab my computer. What exactly was in these "harmless" drinks that kept me awake, that forced my concentration?

I type into the search bar: DMAE.

I quickly scan through the first page of results.

DMAE. Found in fish…used to be prescribed…helps with attention deficit disorder.

Seems harmless, just like Mr. Martin said. His wife was, after all, a homeopathic doctor. And Mr. Martin was on my side. We both wanted to win.

I am overreacting.

I keep scrolling.

"…DMAE is considered nontoxic and safe for short-term or intermittent use…"

I scroll back up to the bold font.

"Caution: Do not use long term. Most people taking DMAE do not experience side effects. However, there is a chance of: constipation, headache, drowsiness, insomnia, overstimulation, lucid dreams, confusion, depression, blood pressure elevation, hypomania, and schizophrenia symptoms…

…some patients with mental illness have been shown to experience more severe symptoms…"

I reread this paragraph. I am noting each possible side effect.

Vivid dreams. Overstimulation. Insomnia. Confusion. Depression. Hypomania. Schizophrenia symptoms. Worsening mental illness?

"Take DMAE a few times a week, but not every day."

Not every day!

What happens when taken every day? Or more than once a day?

Okay, this doesn't mean anything. It's the internet. They have to list the side effects—for legal reasons.

But my mind remains fixed on these words. Mania. Lucid dreams. Depression.

Is this what brought it all to an end? Is this the answer I was hoping for? The one that would satisfy my confusion?

I look up the other supplement, making sure to type the name correctly: tianeptine.

"Tianeptine is a nootropic commonly used as an antidepressant." *That's strange. Why was Mr. Martin giving me antidepressants?*

My eyes quickly scan the article. "Ah, treats anxiety."

A lengthy list of precautions followed.

"The effects of tianeptine in high doses include stimulation, sedation, motivation, and euphoria. Tianeptine can cause a dependency or tolerance, similar to opioid addiction." *Opioids?*

"When long-term use or frequent high doses occur, going cold turkey may be ineffective. Instead, seek medical help to detoxify…"

Shit. This is what I was taking daily? And I must have eventually gone cold turkey.

Did I go cold turkey that day in Russia?

It doesn't add up. I don't recall a withdrawal.

Then I remember.

Something Mr. Martin mentioned yesterday.

It had nothing to do with you leaving. I didn't even give you the supplements for about a year before Russia.

It was true. I hadn't had these drinks for a while by the time I stopped playing the piano.

An image vividly resurfaces in my mind.

I see myself. I'm skeletal, with heavy bags under my eyes. Yet I am still wearing bright lipstick; I have my hair meticulously brushed back. My once fitted rose-print dress by Rodarte now hangs loosely on my body. I am delicately playing **Chopin - Nocturne Op. 9 No. 2.**

I am in Mr. Martin's office. Mr. Martin is there.

He is feeling the energy as he conducts his hand to the music.

He screams a "Yes!" or "That's it!" every now and then.

Then I stop.

"No, no, no, don't stop! You had it!" He hurries closer to me.

I look up at Mr. Martin. "I need…" I don't finish my sentence. My voice sounds weak, tired.

"No," he says right away, understanding exactly what I mean. "You have this, you don't need anything."

"Please." I see now that I am sweating. I am shaking.

"No!" He roared. "Enough! Go again." His arm shoots up in the air.

I try to slow my breath as I return to my position at the piano and place my fingers over the keys.

"Please!" I try again.

"*Suffisant*! Play!"

"Mr. Martin, I can't, I can't play! I need that drink!" I beg.

"Cleo! I won't hear of it! Practice! Now!"

I bring my hands to the piano, and they shake vigorously.

I can't play.

"*Pathétique*," he says loudly enough for me to hear. "I will be back. You! Play!"

The door slams, and the key turns in the lock.

I stare blankly at my computer screen.

That was presumably around the time he quit serving me drinks.

Surely he saw how they backfired.

In the end, what once stimulated me, what once brought me hours of practice, became my downfall.

Mr. Martin realized how incapable I was without the concoctions, how unrecognizable I became. Once my constant nausea, dizziness, and anxiety began to interfere, the drinks disappeared.

I close the computer.

A sharp pain arises my chest. I feel my temperature rise, and my knees begin to tremble.

My greatest pain is the realization that I will never have all the answers to my many questions. Mr. Martin's dose of these "supplements" will always remain a mystery. I won't honestly know how they affected me. *If* they affected me. Perhaps they played no role in my downfall. Maybe I am so desperately looking for a reason, an excuse. There were surely lasting effects from the withdrawal process. What were they?

I stop my mind from creating a list of what-ifs.

There were multiple paths I could have followed.

Instead, I let go. It was my only option.

I left Mr. Martin's house knowing I would never return. I'd said all I could, and another visit wouldn't get me anywhere.

The reality is that Mr. Martin will not take responsibility for his actions, and speaking to him again will only reinforce the idea that I was there all along, allowing this to happen.

My negligence played a part. I never raised any objections. Do I share some of the blame?

Going back to Mr. Martin won't teach me anything new about what happened. No evidence exists that can prove what actually took place, and the outcome will always remain the same.

I have no choice but to move on.

I wasn't able to before. I brought my past with me while I dreamed about those days with an alternate 'Liam', a hypothetical Ivan—a romanticized version of my history.

* * *

"Why? Why did I do this to myself? It doesn't make sense. Why did I create a world while I was dying in my own reality?" I ask Clarice.

"From what you have been telling me so far, it seems to me that you had a lot of pressure and expectations in your life. You needed a place where you felt safe, where you were in control. You rewrote the story."

"Why did I believe it?"

"It is essential for us to dive deeper into your beliefs and desires in order to understand your behavior," Clarice states. "But for now, I can only give you likelihoods."

I wait.

"Ten years is a long time, Cleo. It became rational for you to trust the images you saw." Clarice waits a moment and then continues, "What justifies our memories to be trustworthy? I mean, we are all masters of deception, after all. The lies we tell ourselves make us such good liars, we start to believe them ourselves."

"Or?" I ask. "You said you would give me likelihoods. What else is likely?" I am waiting for Clarice to label me: schizophrenic, bipolar, manic.

Would a diagnosis feel reassuring? An answer to all my confusion?

"Stress can distort and confuse our thinking. But I want you to know that your brain is kind. To feel safe and happy, your brain gets used to filtering. We call it a memory error. It is fascinating that the brain recalls information best in the exact location it happened, which is why you were able to retrieve the truth at Liam's."

When I have nothing to add, Clarice continues.

"Just so you know, no one has a perfect memory. To store memories and retrieve them later takes both biological and psychological processes. So, a lot can happen in that decoding stage. A lot depends on how we perceive, interpret, and feel events."

Alas, no further answers. In my brain, these likelihoods appear plausible, but I have no idea why. And again, does it really matter?

Will the daydreams continue if I don't get to the bottom of them?

"Memories always come back—it just takes time. They are not something you lose forever; you will not always have to question their authenticity. Just remind yourself that you are doing so well, Cleo. Honestly. I'm sure this has not been easy to comprehend, but you are handling these realities head-on. You are allowing yourself to move forward. It is a tremendous step."

I don't feel too tremendous at this point.

Every corner seems to hold a new discovery. I have been reintroduced to a part of myself I had forgotten.

I glance at the time in the right corner of my computer. Conor will be in London in forty minutes, and I still have twenty minutes left of this session.

I am at the end of my rope, but I am grabbing any information that will help me get through.

"Tell me more about maladaptive daydreaming. Does everyone dream about their past life? Think about happier days?"

"Every experience is unique. Some people stifle their imaginations by creating fantasies of a utopian world. Many people picture themselves as heroes, billionaires, or the spouses of celebrities. In patients who experience lucid daydreams, the only similarity I see is the intensity of the images. It feels like you are watching a film that can consume your entire day."

"If I had chosen something to daydream about that wasn't so related to my reality, would I have avoided this confusion?"

"I think it's quite telling. You are not chasing a new experience but recapturing an old one, holding on to nostalgia."

I nod. There are truths to that. To all of it.

My mind was trapped in that world I missed so much, and, at the same time, I was terrified to reenter it.

I am neither here nor there but floating in a perfected version of it all.

"I don't want to leave the dreams. Even now. Even knowing it's not genuine. I want to go back. Back to my fantasy in London, deciding between Ivan and Liam. It's like waking up from a good dream and wanting to go back to sleep. I want to see what will happen next."

"And that's perfectly normal, Cleo. This narrative has become your haven of peace. And we can all use a little fantasy to get us through. This disassociation is a gift you gave yourself so you could be happy and survive. You were distancing yourself from your bad memories. Escapism allowed you to cope with the pain."

"So it's a good thing that I escape?" Choosing to indulge in my fantasies over time with my family doesn't feel like a good thing.

"When controlled, it can be beneficial. But we need to create an environment where you can grow. To function properly, one's brain cannot be separated from the world."

"Is it really so bad? Being separated from the world?" I know the answer, I just need to hear another perspective.

"You know, when we started studying maladaptive daydreaming, we were able to see with a simple brain scan how the brain looks in these trances. It responds the same way alcoholics' brains respond to a martini. So I can imagine it sometimes feels like an addiction, a rush that seems harmless. But you know that's not the case."

"I just think about Giuseppe Tartini, a renowned composer, and his 'Devil's Trill Sonata', which was inspired by a vivid dream he had. In this dream, a devil was playing the violin. Tartini was captivated by the sonata, and the moment he awoke from his dream he wrote it down. It is one of Tartini's best violin sonatas. It makes me think: what have I accomplished in ten years of dreaming? Nothing. I slept through my life."

"You survived, and daydreaming was your means to do so. You are not broken. You are reacting to trauma. It's great that you're a writer, Cleo. Daydreamers are great creative writers, according to Sigmund Freud. They create fantasies that no one else could even imagine. We must figure out how to survive. Use these hardships to your advantage. Use them in your writing. Write about that."

48

LOVE DREAM

London, Present Day

The purge has finally ignited, an inferno of emotions unburdened. It's time to unveil my litany of questions, the reservoir of expectations I've nurtured over the years. Some I've managed to answer, some remain elusive, and others may forever dwell in the shadows of uncertainty. The more I confront this truth, the closer I inch towards acceptance.

I have to be okay. The hollowness I experience at this very moment, it's a curious, bittersweet sensation. With this newfound liberation, I've found the courage to bid adieu to that part of myself. It happened—exhilarating yes, but also toxic. Yet, through it all, I survived.

Now, I stand before that room with the piano, a place that bears witness to my journey. "I am okay," I whisper to reassure myself. "I can do this."

But why, I wonder, are these nerves haunting me? I've conquered Mr. Martin's piano. I've pushed myself beyond limits. Yet the trepidation creeps in, unbidden and unwelcome. Will it plague me like this every time? Will it take this much for me to sit in front of a piano?

Clarice said it: it is still a part of who I am.

I don't have to relinquish my entire past; Mr. Martin can't rob me of everything. This is the last bit of control I maintain over my history, over Mr. Martin.

My shoulders tense involuntarily, but I command them to relax. My eyes flutter closed, then reopen when readiness courses through me.

Seated on the piano bench, my arms parallel to the keys, I make no sound, merely letting my fingers lovingly graze the ivory. "Hello, old friend," I murmur softly.

I can do this.

My fingers quiver with nervous energy, but I shake it off. I will do this.

I close my eyes once more, allowing muscle memory to guide me. And then, with profound determination, I unleash the climactic melody of **Franz Liszt-Love Dream**

It's different this time around.

Mr. Martin's office, his piano. The memories are filled with misery and pain, the hardships that led to failure.

At this moment, I am immersed in a completely new experience.

This time, I feel the emotions.

Tears form and I bite my bottom lip, holding it all in.

Just for a moment.

So I can complete this nocturne.

Suddenly it hits me. A sensation I'd almost forgotten—happiness.

I'm struggling to contain tears of pleasure and profound satisfaction, holding back the release of that pent-up tension, savoring the exquisite ecstasy of letting go.

A warmth presses against my shoulder, which brings me to the present. I stop and look up at the body standing next to me.

It is Conor.

"No. Go on," he encourages.

I continue a while longer, and when the melody fades out, I let out one long exhale.

Overcome with emotion, I cover my face with my trembling hands, unable to meet Conor's gaze.

Insecurities envelop me—my first audience in ten years.

Then, I'm reminded of the painful, unresolved feelings from our last encounter before Conor left, and finally, the tears pour out. I tremble as my cathartic purge reaches its conclusion.

At first, Conor allows me to cry. Then, as I start to settle down, he joins me on the bench.

"Hi. Oh my gosh! I'm such a mess," I say between laughs and sobs.

"Hi, you." Conor smiles and caresses my forearm. He isn't angry. He isn't frustrated. He's content. Genuinely delighted to see me.

I want to tell Conor about my discoveries. About seeing Mr. Martin, about what actually happened in Russia. I want to apologize for the way we left things. I want to pour out my love and desire for him. Yet I can't collect my words.

Instead, I blurt out the first thought that comes to me.

"You were right."

"About what?" He continues to caress my arm.

"About everything, about me deflecting. I wasn't mad at you, I…" I try to articulate. "I was scared, embarrassed. I was angry with myself for not knowing what was going on with me, what might be going on with Ciara."

"I know." I can tell that Conor wants to elaborate. He wants to say I shouldn't feel bad about Ciara and I shouldn't be embarrassed, but he knows that silence is all I need now.

In this silence, I find the space to collect my thoughts and immerse myself in the moment, alone with Conor. I can reflect on everything I've learned about my past, about Mr. Martin, Liam, Ivan, and my decision to leave it all behind.

And then, at last, I find my voice. "Why does life have to be so challenging? Why is love such a struggle?"

"Well," he hesitates, taken aback by the unexpected inquiry. "It's unparalleled in its power. It's a fundamental need, an unrelenting force, almost like an addiction. The pursuit of being desired is a perpetual endeavor, much like the ongoing effort to remain desirable."

"It feels like a disease. It consumes you."

"And isn't that a wonderful thing?"

It's true.

"It's just…" I try to find my words. "It's just a bit mad really. Love. I mean, it's always been this sort of undercurrent that just pushes me forward. My love for Lottie, for the piano, for the melodies—it's what kept me focused." I want to add my love for Mr. Martin, but I choose to keep that conversation for another day. "Well, then this love sort of gravitated toward you, didn't they?"

Conor smiled, his fingers firmly intertwined with mine.

"Suddenly, I am knee-deep in questions. Was this love just a response to my loneliness, was it filling the void of needing acceptance? Was it the kind of performance I was expected to give? The challenge of seduction?"

"Why do you feel so strongly about rationalizing these emotions? Why does love have to make sense to you? Why not just feel?"

I am starting to feel like a patient next to Conor, but I am okay with that. I hear his words.

"I don't know."

I always viewed love from a scientific perspective. I always thought about the neurotransmitters, the hormones. I am driven by logic and understanding. I wrote about love the way my audience wanted me to, which brought satisfaction to my readers.

Only once I tried to understand love, to dissect it for myself, did people turn away from me.

Was it really just about accepting love for what it is?

To be content with loving and being loved?

I look back into Conor's eyes. He's waiting for me patiently.

Is that it? Do I need to stop dissecting what makes us feel the way we feel?

Let life play out without having to understand it all?

"I'm sorry, Conor. About how we left—"

He waves me off. "Don't apologize. Quite frankly, I deserved that. You were right. I should have paid more attention." He stops talking. His eyes crease into a compassionate smile, and then comes the fateful question: "How are you?"

"Good! Good." I wipe away my tears, attempting to bring myself to contentment.

"That was really something." He points to the piano. "I wish I could hear more of that."

"Maybe soon." I smile back. It feels so good. Playing after all these years. Like a light has finally switched on. Like it's okay to hold on to a tiny part of the old me.

"Conor," I say. I want to tell him everything, but I have more important things to say right now. "I love you." I look him straight in his eyes. "I love you so much, and I am so, so sorry about everything—"

"Cleo, it's okay."

"No, but—"

"I love you too."

Conor's eyes catch my attention once more. Those eyes that told me so much. Then, he leans in, and when his lips touch mine a feeling of love, hope, and contentment washes over me.

In this moment, I finally give up on my analysis of love. I give up on trying to understand it all.

And finally, I feel ready to give up on my past.

49

RELIABLE NARRATOR

Moscow, Ten Years Ago

It was my first night in Moscow.

Awake, I lay in bed. Incapable of falling asleep again.

I hadn't slept in about three days. I'd dozed off, but never felt the true sensation of sleeping.

I wanted to cry, but my insides were numb.

What was I feeling? I should have been ecstatic.

I, Cleo Wilson, would be performing in front of a jury at the Moscow Classical Music Competition.

After an intensive, systematic plan, hard work, and determination, my dreams were becoming a reality.

What was the reason behind this feeling of emptiness? Like this, suddenly, didn't matter?

My body felt like it wanted to stay in bed rather than go to practice.

Imagine the consequences if I failed to show up.

Mr. Martin would drop me. Right then and there. There were no second chances.

In not showing up, I would demonstrate my incapacity. Incompetent musicians did not work with Mr. Martin. The musicians he worked with were extraordinary, rare, one of a kind.

Tomorrow morning, I would be there.

Despite how much I wished I could stay here and hide from everything.

I would never leave.

All I had to do was obtain the energy to put on a gown, place that theatrical smile across my face, and give my life's worth to the next performance.

I got up and went to breakfast, where I drank coffee alone.

Afterward, the musicians found their spaces backstage as the hall filled up.

I patiently waited for this cloud of uncertainty to pass.

When I looked at my fingers, I saw that they were shaking.

Time will pass, it will heal. It will all be okay.

It was then that I first noticed the sounds of **Dvořák - Romance in F minor** coming from the crack in the door.

The strings penetrated the core of my being, right into my soul.

I was cast into a trance, overpowered to stay and listen.

It forced me to contemplate whether all of this was worthwhile.

Why was this my life's purpose? When playing no longer fulfilled me, what would be left?

Nothing.

The abrupt silence washed over me when the violinist paused, and I became deeply immersed in his gaze.

I couldn't look away.

Don't stop playing, I wanted to say. *Go on. Keep me in this moment for a bit longer.*

He had such kind eyes. His face radiated warmth and gentle charisma. His smile was contagious, lighting up his entire expression. His white-blond hair seemed to glow under the soft light. I felt an overwhelming urge to stay.

It was a wrenching struggle to force myself to leave. Each step away felt like a betrayal of my own soul, an emotional and physical strain that left me feeling weak and hollow. The music, his presence, was the energy I craved, a balm for my weariness. Yet, with every step, I had to summon every ounce of my willpower to walk away, my heart aching with the weight of my decision.

I had made the choice to go to Mr. Martin, to perform like the dance monkey I was expected to be. To do as I was told, to conform to the demands placed upon me.

My hasty retreat to my room and the change into my gown took up all my remaining energy.

It was a repetitive and forced routine: getting dressed, putting on my makeup, and preparing for my performance. But at that point, my soul had slowly departed from my body. And it was then that I knew I would soon escape.

My mind was already elsewhere; now I just needed my body to follow.

I had five minutes until I had to head to the stage. My conductor would be waiting for me. Mr. Martin would be waiting.

I stood up, and I left.

I went upstairs with no real plan—just a goal to escape.

I hear Tchaikovsky's symphony, the only force of energy allowing me to move.

I continued to walk, but I didn't see anything. I didn't feel anything.

I needed to start feeling. I need to start living.

I found a large window and let myself out. I inhaled the icy air as it blew a new sense of life into my lungs.

I smiled.

I'd made my decision.

I was choosing myself. I would not choose this life dictated by Mr. Martin.

Even if it meant leaving this world of success. Of brilliance. Of music.

50

THE FIG TREE

New York City, Present Day

I lay awake. Unable to fall back asleep.

It is my first night back at home.

In a weird way, it feels so normal. Like this was all one big mistake. Just another extravagant dream I composed. Yet I know it all happened.

My life slowly slipping through my fingers, my inability to properly grasp it. Losing the children. Going to Clarice. Traveling to London. Seeing Mr. Martin after all these years.

It all happened.

Yet here we are again.

Back at home.

Back to the mundane rhythm of our daily lives. Lying beside Conor, his peaceful slumber a stark contrast to the whirlwind of emotions within me.

I study his features in the soft moonlight—those long lashes, those subtle freckles, his unruly hair veiling his closed eyes. This is the same Conor who stood steadfastly by my side, the man who raised our children with unwavering devotion, who uprooted his life for me.

He placed me at the pinnacle of his priorities, a choice he made willingly. He didn't have to, especially considering the challenges I posed, the demands I made, often giving little in return. I ran away from my problems, shutting doors just as my mother did. Yet Conor remained resolute, a constant presence.

Though he may seem conventional at times, a touch predictable, I've come to realize that I need this sense of normalcy, of stability. My life was once a whirlwind of chaos, and I was swept along with it. I was erratic, unpredictable.

I need Conor to be that anchor, to tether me to the present moment. To gently remind me that my eyes must remain open to see what's right in front of me—my children, our relationship.

I can now see my past for what it was.

Chaos.

Yet it was exciting, vigorous, enchanting, magical, harmful.

My past was a compilation of it all.

I put on my headphones, hoping **Chopin - Nocturne No. 20** will help me sleep.

The music's melancholic notes embrace me, easing the restlessness in my mind. I sink into the pillow, though unsettled feelings persist. I move with practiced silence, a shadow in the night, as I slip out of my bedroom, my steps measured and deliberate.

In the dimly lit room, I open my laptop, the blue light momentarily blinding me as my fingers swiftly type on the keyboard. The narratives I had woven now seem like mere fantasies, a reflection of my own desires rather than reality. But there's a curiosity, ignited by Clarice's words, urging me to dig deeper.

I want to unravel the intricacies that guided these narratives, decipher their underlying motives, or perhaps, accept them as they are and move forward. It's crucial to approach this with a fresh perspective, to zoom out and examine the broader canvas.

Liam and Ivan embodied contrasting life paths and choices.

Liam symbolized my journey if I had stayed within the world of classical music, a path filled with achievements and triumphant success. A life filled with struggle, unwavering power, and fervent passion.

In stark contrast, Ivan represented an alternate life, a utopian existence where I was capable of gracefully abandoning my past. Ivan offered an alluring escape, a romanticized departure from the demands of my world. All I needed was Ivan's love and proximity, and suddenly, everything felt okay. It wasn't a systematic world I would be living in but a world of dreams and seductive possibilities.

In reality, I did escape from Mr. Martin, but I never truly broke free. My actual circumstances were unfolding differently than in my daydreams. So, in my fabricated scenarios, Liam was the path I ventured down. I selected him repeatedly, yet with each choice, I harbored the knowledge that it was an error. My daydreams spiraled into a relentless cycle, endlessly circling back to that initial night in Moscow, concluding identically each time. It was a suffocating sense of entrapment.

At thirty-eight, I face the harsh truth—I can never rewind the clock to rectify my past losses. I've outgrown the realm of competing, that stage where I once thrived, now a distant echo of my past.

Did living through these alternative lives help me gain a new perspective? To be perfectly honest, probably not. Nevertheless, life has relentlessly instilled one undeniable lesson in me—it demands evolution.

Sylvia Plath's *The Bell Jar* keeps running through my mind.

An all-too-familiar metaphor about a fig tree—those luscious, tempting figs that dangle from the branches of life. Each fig a choice, each choice a destiny. On one branch, the succulent fig of a husband, a blissful home, and the laughter of children. On another, the poetic fig, a world of words and verses, a seductive realm that beckons me like an alluring siren. Yet, there's the fig of the brilliant professor and countless others, each bearing its unique allure, each whispering promises of fulfillment.

Esther, a character in Plath's tale, sat beneath the fig tree, tormented. She was besieged by the shadows of indecision, torn between the fruits that dangled before her. She could not commit, for fear of missing out on the ripe sweetness of the others. As she hesitated, those figs withered, growing black and wrinkled, one by one.

And here I am, Cleo, trapped in a similar dance of indecision. I've plucked my own figs: the roles of a mother, a wife, a writer. Yet, in my delusion, I allow them to fester alongside the rotting figs of doubt and uncertainty.

The dark specter of my own yearning looms, threatening to turn all my figs to dust. My only choice, stark and undeniable, is to savor the fruits I've already chosen, to revel in their complexities and delights. A stable home, a loving husband, children who make me proud—these figs are mine to cherish, but the ominous weight of uncertainty taints even their sweetness.

I am now, here in my New York City home.

My sleeping family upstairs.

This is where I belong.

This brings me contentment. Clarity.

Closure.

I stop writing.

The word count is seventy thousand—a manuscript almost complete. Yet, what have I channeled onto these pages? My dreams, my daydreams, my tapestry of an imagined life.

EPILOGUE

Hello again.

I finally had a moment to breathe, so here I am:
unpacking, reflecting.

Enjoying the silence.

Today, I have my silence.

Yet, in the sanctuary of this stillness, there often
emerges a maelstrom of thoughts that refuse to be
quietened.

The unresolved echoes of what transpired with Diane
linger like a persistent melody. Since the hospital,
our words have remained unspoken, apologies held back,
and forgiveness left teetering on the precipice.

Rumors have swirled around Eric, painting a chaotic
canvas of infidelity and deception. Yet, against the
odds, they seem to still be together, bound by threads
unknown. But I hold onto hope that it isn't their
final chapter, that there's more to be written in the
story of Diane and Eric.

Diane and me.

Our paths cross sporadically, like ships passing in
the night--school, ballet practice, chance encounters

that leave me yearning to bridge the chasm between us. I want to reach out, to know how she truly is, to understand if her life is veering in a new direction, whether it's away from Eric.

Yesterday, a fleeting acknowledgment smile passed between us as I exited a building. It's a small start, but it's something.

Then there's Conor and me--our love, messy and infuriatingly perfect. The idea of seeing a couples counselor still stands, a potential lifeline for us. We navigate the treacherous waters of disagreements, misunderstandings, and the cacophony of daily life. Some days, I find myself drifting into the labyrinth of my past.

Yet, this is us, adapting to life's rollercoaster ride. Morning bickering often gives way to nighttime serenity.

Ciara, too, grapples with moments of daydreaming. We're working through it, with the help of a children's therapist. Clarice once told me, "You're fixated on bettering your past, on the belief that it's beyond improvement. Here lies your chance to shape Ciara's future, a realm where you wield some control."

Her words became the catalyst for change, leading us to seek help for our daughter's fantasies. Ciara eventually agreed, opening a new chapter in her young life--an existence brimming with possibilities.

And now I am alone, my thoughts are fleeting on by.

No tasks to complete, no errands to run, no plans to attend to.

Just silence.

Conor offered to pick up the kids on his way home from work, leaving me with no responsibilities.

Well, just one:

Write.

Finish my story. Embrace that fictional glimpse into my hopes and dreams, an array of what-ifs and possibilities.

In the past few weeks, I have begun to compile narratives of my past. Those stories I'd filtered through rose-tinted lenses, the romanticized depictions of my happily ever after.

These journals, which I wrote exclusively for myself, are now fragmented into excerpts that provide me with the beginning and the middle of my story.

This fiction is the escape I hope to offer readers. I want them to fantasize and feel optimistic about what's yet to come.

The readers don't need to know whether I can match this optimism in my own life, but I do hope to achieve it soon.

The title remains: The Untitled Diary.

That is what it is--an avant-garde, distorted diary. I chose fiction over sharing true stories from my past. Who wants to read about a girl who worked so hard, only to fall short of her goals? Readers want to believe in love, humanity, and something more profound. So, I created a world for my protagonist, Vanessa, during a classical music competition. A world where she meets Alexei, a Russian competitor, and discovers the true meaning of happiness and love.

Everything changes when Sean, her brilliant teacher, steps in.

These stories are entirely fictional, but the emotions they convey are real and heartfelt. Now, all that remains is to craft Vanessa's conclusion--a conclusion that I hope will leave readers satisfied.

In my daydreams, I grapple with finding a fulfilling ending. The narrative I have now is bittersweet yet hopeful, but it doesn't satisfy. There must be another path for these characters.

I contemplate alternative endings for Vanessa, seeking a more promising outcome. Was Sean the right choice all along? Maybe Alexei and Vanessa couldn't sustain their long-distance connection, despite the authenticity, depth, and meaning of their love.

As I immerse myself in this narrative, I realize I must start again from the beginning, exploring different conclusions. I needed a more satisfying conclusion, an ending that would inevitably determine the outcome of difficult choices--blending grief and pleasure.

What if Vanessa stayed in London with Sean in his luxurious French Country house? They could continue their journey together, achieving their dreams side by side. Perhaps they'd even start a family, teaching their children about music - Tchaikovsky, Bach, Beethoven. Vanessa could remain committed to her goal of achieving greatness, reaching higher and higher.

And Alexei? He would linger in Vanessa's memories as the boy she once knew from Russia.

But that ending, as I put it into words, lacked satisfaction. There had to be an alternative.

I closed my computer, knowing that the ending hadn't revealed itself.

It will come. Just not yet.

As I recline on my wicker bench, extending the seat horizontally, I nestle deeper into its comforting embrace. My eyes closed, I draw in a deep, rejuvenating breath, surrendering willingly to the harmonious sounds of the world around me—the gentle caress of the whispering breeze, the rhythmic cadence of passing cars, and the indistinct chatter of pedestrians meandering by. In that moment, I become one with this living, breathing tapestry of existence.

Then one by one, the once distinct sounds, start to dissolve. Their echoes fade into the universe as silence envelops me, inviting contemplation.

How much control do we have over our narratives?

Will Mr. Martin face the consequences he deserves, or will he continue to live without a blemish on his reputation? Am I ever going to rediscover the world of classical music, or am I stuck in the pursuit of success as a writer? Will my relationships continue their gradual decline, or can they flourish, nurtured by the invaluable lessons I've learned along the way?

My companion, my adversary, that forbidding shadow of the unknown draws nearer. I can feel the familiar chill creeping up my spine, the palpitations of an accelerated heartbeat growing more pronounced. This is a companion I'll be eternally tethered to; like a moth to a flame. This unwavering presence looming above will forever bear witness to my inner struggles.

With deliberate precision, my hand finds my phone, my fingers moving across the screen in a well-rehearsed choreography.

I press the play button; the room is bathed in the resounding strains of **Tchaikovsky's Concerto No. 1.** The music unfurls, its fervent melodies sweeping through the air with the force of a tempestuous storm, reigniting the flames within me. Each note becomes a vivid spark of inspiration and passion, casting a fiery glow around me.

I close my eyes and allow the music to envelop me. The very atmosphere undergoes a transformation. Moscow materializes before my eyes, a snow-covered landscape with flakes falling gently from the sky. The trees, the roads, every surface is blanketed in pristine white. My dress undergoes a metamorphosis, shifting from its original tulle form into an exquisite, red gown.

The music surrounds me, wrapping its intoxicating embrace around me once more. The solo piano reverberates within my chest, stirring up passion from deep within. The rhythmic beat of the timpani syncs with my racing heart, and the oboes, clarinets, and bassoons blend into a mesmerizing crescendo that blurs the lines of reality.

Ivan emerges, his bow passionately embracing the violin. Ethereal notes dance through his icy blonde strands. His everlasting smile, dimple, and earned laugh lines—all just as vivid in my memory. Liam stands in the distance, resolute amidst a flurry of swirling scoresheets, his deep blue eyes radiating unwavering support—a living pillar of support from times past.

Musical notes flutter around me like ethereal butterflies, their melodies and harmonies intertwining, creating a symphony of vibrant colors and sounds that engulf the entire space.

I am at the center of this breathtaking spectacle, a conductor of my own symphony. At this moment, the laws of quantum physics cease to exist, and we all become one—a singular, pulsating being in the throes of artistic ecstasy.

I am transported to a realm beyond reality, where creativity is unshackled and boundless. Here, within the intoxicating embrace of this symphonic masterpiece, I am set free to explore a universe of infinite imagination and endless possibilities.

AFTERWORD

For many of us, daydreaming is a natural and harmless escape, a chance to explore endless possibilities within the confines of our minds. However, for some individuals, daydreaming can become maladaptive, consuming excessive amounts of time and interfering with daily life.

Maladaptive daydreaming is a condition where individuals escape into elaborate fantasy worlds for hours at a time, often to the detriment of real-world responsibilities and relationships. If you or someone you know struggles with maladaptive daydreaming, I encourage you to seek support and resources to help navigate this experience.

For further information on maladaptive daydreaming and how to find support, please visit: https://daydreamresearch.wixsite.com/md-research

ACKNOWLEDGMENTS

To my extraordinary support system,

I've always been a dreamer, occasionally hindered by my practicality. However, you all have seen beyond these limitations, elevating my aspirations to soaring heights. With your love, generosity, and encouragement, you've fueled my journey every step of the way.

Above all, I want to extend my deepest gratitude to my parents. Their unwavering belief in me from the very beginning propelled me forward on this new career path. I love you both immensely.

To my dear friends (you know who you are), your support has been a beacon of light. Despite delving into raw, unedited versions of this manuscript and printing your own copies at local printers, your notes and insightful feedback have been invaluable in shaping the final product.

To my family—my siblings, in-laws, cousins, and especially my Babushka—your cheers and support have been a constant source of strength and inspiration. To Zaidy and Dedushka, your influence resonates through the pages of my stories.

And to my husband and our three wonderful children, your belief in me has been my guiding force. Your faith in my potential has given me the courage to pursue the dream of publishing this novel. While writing this novel, I was surrounded by the most supportive, loving team. I feel incredibly blessed and thankful for each one of you.

I want to express special thanks to my editors for their meticulous refinement of my writing, and to the virtuoso pianists who brought Cleo's story to life.

Each of you has left an indelible mark on my heart, and I am profoundly grateful for your love, support, and unwavering belief in me. From the depths of my heart, thank you.